Crimson Rain

Tex Leiko

Whimsical Publications, LLC

Florida

To purchase the authorized electronic edition of *Crimson Rain*, visit
www.whimsicalpublications.com

Cover art provided by Tex Leiko
Editing by Brieanna Robertson

ISBN-13: 978-1-940707-48-8

Published by
Whimsical Publications, LLC
Florida

He was hungry, but he didn't care about food. He had an impulse raging in his brain stronger than any legitimate physical need. *Feed me.* It seemed to repeat in his brain. *I don't want to!* Max kept fighting back as he trembled and sweated, his body craving the toxic bite of a boost.

He spotted a pharmaceutical locker on the far end of the lab and decided to investigate. *Red, red, orange, green, yellow, black, tan, brown, brown, red! Where? Where is blue? Why no blue? Why, why, why, why, why, why?*

It hadn't been this bad since he'd quit three years ago. *You knew what you were doing; you're a doctor. You know your enhancements make you more prone to addiction. What the hell were you thinking, asshole? That I hate you! I hate you, Max! You destroy everything! You destroy everyone! Crimson doesn't like you. She doesn't even need you! She needs your brain, ignorant little addict. You should die already.*

Max began to cry and convulse. He hated that he craved the serenity boosts so bad. It came in waves. He wanted them; he didn't. He hated that they controlled him so strongly and not at all. He couldn't choose when he craved them; he couldn't choose when he didn't.

It was a true addiction. He really wanted free, but he knew the only thing that could heal him was time. *Sure, they can make us immortal these days, but they can't fix addiction. Maybe I should have gone into research. I wish I had never studied medicine! I wish I had gone anywhere in life except the path that would lead me to this.*

Max voluntarily convulsed on the floor as if he was trying to expel demons from his body. It was more than a tantrum a three-year-old would throw. Max knew what he wanted. He wanted freedom from slavery to chemicals. He'd had it. For three short years, he had been completely free, but one freak occurrence, one that wasn't even that big of a deal, had slingshot him back to this.

He rolled over to the metal pharmaceutical locker, sweating and writhing in both physical and emotional pain. He began to pound his head into the locker with a vehement rage.

He bashed his head into the metal one time and felt his skull absorb the blow with a large hematoma swelling under the skin. He fervently smashed his head a second time into the locker with all of his force. His vision dimmed and he heard a ringing in his right ear.

Once more. That's all you need to be free, Max, that's it.

He paused and choked. He started crying even harder than he had been. He could barely breathe through the tears and gasps. He wasn't crying from the physical pain he had dealt himself. He was crying because his mind was drawn to Crimson. *What if she does care about me? Even if it is just as a friend? Just a fellow soldier for a good cause? What if? What if nothing...*

A third tempestuous slam; it was hard. The metal rang out; his neck made a cracking noise. He had slipped a disk in between his fourth and fifth vertebra that would be a con- stant source of pain and aggravation. He had also caused a concussive fracture to his skull. His skin split open and his hematoma ran down his forehead into his right eye.

He couldn't see out of it anyway because of the swelling around his retina caused by his first blow. His right eye was most certainly swelling; he could feel it. He convulsed a few more times before dragging himself to a position on all fours. He hit the floor eight times with both fists as hard as he could. His knuckles were already swelling and would cause him horrible pain in the morning.

Finally, he stood on both feet and faced the locker. He kicked it as hard as he could. Still, his chest heaved as he sobbed, grabbing for air between whimpers. His lips quivered and snot ran down his nose. Blood and tears fell like rain on his shirt.

No sense in crying about spilled milk all night; time to get to work.

Max reached into the locker. *Yellow, non-addictive stimu- lant, like caffeine but stronger. I need to calm down, but maybe this will focus me and I can do something useful for a change.*

He pulled out an awareness boost. Dosage on all boosts were the same—a typical dose was point one of a cc. Most syringes were multiple use and held ten doses. This one still had seven doses to dispense. He stuck the needle in his arm and pushed the plunger without hesitation.

A smile widened across his face as the feeling quickly overwhelmed his body. *That's better, time to get to work.*

One

Psyker Scream

"It requires a series of injections, five to be exact. The needles necessary for each round are fourteen-gauge; you would think that they would have made them like most bots on the market. Other bots you can just swallow, or inject with something a whole lot smaller, but no, despite all of the modern technology available, they still ask me to skewer some of your larger veins with a needle the size of a steak knife.

"Each round of the nanobot injections takes at least thirty minutes of your time still. You can't move while the needle is in your arm; if it slips out of the vein, then the bots spill all over the dermis, or worse yet, the needle re-punctures you but strikes muscle, or worse yet, bone! Do you know what happens when these bots are injected into your bone? It isn't pretty," the doctor said dryly to Zarfa. "You know, you youngsters don't think of this when you come in here and ask me to do this to you... Psyker Scream, right? Right? Well, let me see your arms," he said from underneath his white paper mask.

The doctor looked Zarfa up and down his right and left arm. He was spindly; his torso was average, lean, hairless except a small patch that grew between his nipples. His skin was white—not snow white, more of a grayish white. His legs stretched down, the femur much longer than average. Even when he wore jeans it was noticeable. His feet matched his femur in that the meatus of the foot was enlarged, but the toes were average. His arms were long; he had a reach that nobody could imagine. In his years of life, he'd learned a posture to disguise it, but the tips of his fingers came to his patella. His body, though being lean, wasn't anything remarkable aside from his odd proportions.

He stared into2 the doctor's eyes as he made his reply. "Psyker Scream. Yes, that's it... I am sure you are getting tired of seeing 'us kids,' but please... Even if I'm the last...I am willing to sign whatever waivers you have. Give me the bots, please?"

The doctor took a deep breath and held it; the world could have stopped spinning in the time it took for him to release it. Finally, he did. As his breath extruded from his lungs, the lenses of his glasses fogged from the hot steam being caught by his mask. He paced about two steps toward Zarfa then stepped back, tapped his toe, and spun around, grabbing his clipboard.

"Yes, yes. I really am sick of you! I opened this clinic to help people. Instead, I get all of you!" the doctor yelled in exasperation.

He didn't dislike his patients, even if they were silly rave kids in his eyes, but he'd opened this clinic twenty years ago in the hopes of really making a difference. And now what was he doing? He didn't even know. Sure, he would occasionally diagnose a disease, make a few treatments, or sometimes save a life, but that was rare. Sure, he kept people well when they came in with the sniffles; a lot of his clients were of the lower class who couldn't afford nanobot immuno-boosts. He would do the rudimentary tests, diagnose what many would refer to as a "third world disease," write them an affordable prescription, or if they were really destitute, give them free samples and send them on their merry way. He was making a difference in his community, sure.

But what bothered him were these rave kids. They all had the same story; they all wanted the same thing. The bots he would put into them were a high risk and had no practical application. They were expensive. The first time a kid had come in and asked for them, he'd shooed him out of the office, told him he was here to make a difference, to help, and then balanced his checkbook. By the time the fifth one came in waving a wad of cash in his face, his only reason for turning her down was that he didn't have the goods; he began to re-think his outlook.

Sure, he was here to make a difference, but if one didn't turn a profit then one couldn't stay in business. If a person couldn't stay in business, they couldn't help. It was a vicious cycle. So, on the fifth one, he told her, "Come back in two weeks and I will have what you need." With a grin and a wink, he took out a loan, and the rest was history.

But that was five years ago. He was still treating the poor and making a difference, but these kids kept coming in, and what for? He'd taken an oath—do no harm. Was he? He couldn't understand. He hated that they would take the risk. He knew that twenty percent of them had died while his palms were greased with their cash, untraceable.

It was good for him... It was good for his community; he was helping... He was. That's what his mind told him, but his demons wouldn't let him sleep. This was the last one, he told himself as he handed Zarfa the clipboard with the waivers and consents all attached. Even if twenty percent died and he felt guilt, he wasn't stupid; those papers would keep him out of jail.

"Be sure to read every bit of both sides," he muttered.

Zarfa, as if without thought, began signing every dotted line with haste.

"Don't you understand what you are doing to your body? Don't you understand the pain you will feel as the bots mutate and transform your acoustic nerve endings and rewrite your brain to understand those insane high frequencies? *Don't you get it? That last paper explains if you stop the injections early, you will go deaf!*"

"Please stop yelling." Zarfa was cool, calm, and spoke as if he had the authority.

"It's so much pain... And what for? A shitty band."

Zarfa began to take deep breaths and tried to shut down his emotions; he tried to go numb. Pain... It was something he was all too familiar with. How was the doctor to know? "I am well aware of pain, Dr. Hall. Pain you probably couldn't imagine," he said as his mind began to wander.

Thoughts of his homeland flooded him—the city of Ilyeion, which had been founded about seventy-two miles to the south of the old world's Baghdad. Despite the fact that Muslim culture was all but dead, some things remained very much the same. Merchants and vendors lined the streets of Ilyeion, selling their goods and wares.

In the bazaars, one could buy anything from a slave to a

molded protein simulation of an apple to the most advanced weapons. Ilyeion had beauty and wonder, but it also had a darkness to it. Despite the darkness, it was Zarfa's home. He was a long way from it in the city of Alexandria, capitol to the country of Alexarian. His plan was to attend to business then return to Ilyeion as soon as he could.

The night that made him leave, that made him into who he now was—that was the pain he envisioned as the doctor grilled him with questions. On that night, the winds were heavy. No storms were predicted, no orders placed, yet the sky grew black with clouds—clouds of wasps, none of which had ever been known before the era of the Great Extinction. These wasps had been genetically created from the DNA of a common mud wasp that inhabited the Middle Eastern region. However, they were extremely altered.

The average one of these mud wasps was ten to thirteen feet in length. The average weight was four hundred kilograms. The stinger was about a meter in length. If the puncture didn't kill a person, the venom was sure to. They feasted upon the bodies of those they killed, but worse yet, they weren't wild creatures that could simply be exterminated.

The Faraza was at the heart of the swarm, or that was to say, the organization known as the Faraza. Their exact location was still unknown. All one had ever heard were vague reports of the wasp swarms returning to an underground entryway, down into the deep labyrinth that concealed them in darkness even during the day. The cult of the Faraza had an unaccounted number of followers and their secrecy was kept so close nobody knew how to join.

Many survivors who had seen some of their families captured, however, reported at times seeing a lost relative as one of the raiding party months after their kidnapping. The raiding parties were vicious; the wasps would swarm in with two to four riders each, dependent on the size of the riders. They would descend, silent wings with great fury, murdering, pillaging, and kidnapping.

These terrible menaces appeared with little warning. There were watchtowers with sky watchers, but they were only minimal help. The intense speeds at which these parties approached made any retreat seem futile. By the time their shadows blotted out the sun, it was too late. One was certain to feel the breeze pass by as one was slain, or worse yet...taken.

"Really? What's a punk kid like you know about pain? All of you Psyker Scream rave kids are all so mystical and totally emo. Give me a break."

Zarfa didn't say a word, only lifted his shirt to reveal a scar on his left side. A horrendous scar, one that yelled out, "I survived." It had glanced him, but it was enough to cause an evisceration. His intestines had flopped toward the dirty ground as he saw his sister taken into the clouds by a wasp rider. He had been coughing out blood and shoving his viscera back inside before he even realized he had just brushed with one of their massive stingers.

Tears had welled in his eyes and he lifted his hands toward the skies. His voice made noises, but the words were inaudible. He had been crying because of the physical pain, but even more so for the emotional blow that had struck him. *Sarah! Sarah! My sister!* was what he thought as he saw her taken so quickly.

She was beautiful, tall, elegant, graceful, a professional tribal dancer who once reminded their people of the old ways of the land. She was only sixteen when she had been taken. Zarfa, a mere young man, the age of twenty-four, quickly turned to a bitter soul that was ageless as his life threatened to leave him while his last remaining family member was so brutally excised from his life.

They had been in the market. She had been dancing, as she was hired to do by a wealthy merchant. Zarfa was standing by as her bodyguard, as he had always done. Zarfa took pride in being his sister's bodyguard. It got them by in life, enough to eat and have a home, but they were truly content with each other. His tender sibling love was gone in an instant.

"There is a story that goes with this. You are unworthy, doctor," he stated as he felt tears welling up and rolling down his cheeks.

He wanted to forget what happened next. Many times, he would lay awake at night after that awful day, wishing he had died then and there. No matter what he did, no matter how hard he cried, or pummeled himself, or drugged himself with alcohol combined with whatever depressants he could get his hands on, he couldn't make the dark vision go away. What happened next, he couldn't forget, and he wasn't even trying to hold on...

He stood, one hand holding in his organs, and he began to run toward the wasp that was gaining altitude. A rider to his right was coasting in alongside him to make its final strike. The rider made his command and the wasp obeyed. In one quick movement, like a beautiful flash of lightning in the night sky, Zarfa faced the rider head-on. He avoided another sting and clutched one of the paperlike wings of the wasp. Holding on as tight as he could, he began to ascend into the sky.

He struggled his way up the giant insect and to the rider. The rider turned to face Zarfa. He was wounded and certainly no match for a raider, or so the raider might have thought. Before he knew it, Zarfa had closed the gap between them and was struggling to throw him off his mount. The raider took his baton and clubbed Zarfa in the face twice. Bones cracked and blood flowed from his nose. Zarfa, nearly dead, grabbed hold of the raider's bludgeon and pulled it easily from his grasp. Zarfa had never seen himself as a mere man, but always a beast, and a fierce guardian of the ones he loved. A ferocious guardian fought to his last breath and a wounded creature was more dangerous than a live and healthy one. He was wounded, angry, and more of a creature than a man at this point. Nothing less than death or loss of consciousness would stop him now.

Before the raider even realized he was disarmed, Zarfa had struck a blow to his humerus so hard the bone shattered. As his hand lost hold of the reins, he grabbed for them with the other hand out of reflex. He should have put up a defense, but it would have done little good. Zarfa struck with another crushing blow; the wasp rider's other arm crippled under the force of his brutal strike. Zarfa then gave a push and the rider plummeted to the ground.

They were about seven meters from the earth when Zarfa grabbed the reins of the giant wasp. He looked around and realized his sister was gone. He also realized he didn't know the first thing about controlling one of these beasts. Without its rider, it was flying erratic. One of its wings had been ripped in Zarfa's maddened, adrenaline-filled struggle with its enormous body.

At this point, the blood loss and the crushing defeat had taken its toll. His last thought was "an eye for an eye" as the world went from color and light to darkness and the giant insect mount crashed head first into the ground. Zarfa lay there as if he were another corpse from the fierce battle. He has lost sight of what had gone on around him because he fought to live and to save Sarah, but there were corpses, both human and freakish insect, innocent and raider alike, scattered across the bazaar streets. He lost consciousness completely as the feeling of total defeat engulfed him...

Zarfa realized he was zoning out again. He often did when he thought about the past. He could feel his eyes dampening with more tears at the thought of his sister. He breathed in deep, then out so fiercely it was as if he was breathing out fire.

He looked Dr. Hall in the face. "Can we get on with this or what?" Zarfa questioned.

Doctor Hall swallowed as he looked at the scar. Most would have been killed by something so large without immediate medical attention. He began to get a bit nervous and started to sweat. If his patient was walking around safe and sound after such a mortal injury, he certainly didn't want to be on his bad side. Then he had the strangest thought. *Maybe I am helping these kids*.

He shrugged it away, cleared his throat, and said, "Well, I am sorry for the outburst. I really should work on my manners. If you are ready then, seeing as you have already signed the waivers, allow me to strap down your arm and we shall begin the first round of injections."

Zarfa regained his composure. Though he hadn't let out a sound, it embarrassed him deeply that the doctor had seen even a single tear roll from his eyes, let alone the many hundreds that now stained his shirt. He sat staring the doctor in the eyes for a brief moment, but one that must have felt like an eternity to the poor man in the white lab coat. His face was still hidden under the mask, but Zarfa could tell he had terrified him, even if he was a sobbing baby.

Without fear, without trembling, without hesitation, Zarfa

held out his long, lean, muscular arm. He eyed his own veins, wondering which the doctor would choose. What he was about to feel, he wouldn't even consider pain.

"Make it so, good doctor."

Doctor Hall took hold of his arm and set it on the padded leather arm rest. He then strapped him down to it. The straps weren't meant to be cruel, but he really meant it when he said it mustn't strike bone under any circumstances. The nanobots would begin mutating the bone rather than nerve and calcify the brain, killing Zarfa almost immediately.

"I don't know how this is helping any of you," Hall scoffed. "Psyker Scream... It's just a shitty techno, heavy metal fusion band, isn't it? There is a lot I understand in this world, but that will always be a mystery to me."

"Let's keep it that way."

Two

The Doctor

"Thank you, doctor," Zarfa said politely as the doctor pulled the heavy-gauged needle from his arm.

The pain was bad, but Zarfa was somehow more cheery now than he had been before the treatment. Dr. Hall could see it in his eyes; he was grateful. Zarfa then dug into his pockets and pulled out his bank chip. Dr. Hall held his bank chip out toward Zarfa.

"Okay, ten thousand credits transferred to your account, doctor. I look forward to seeing you again four more times. After that, no more," he said dryly.

"Any time. Give it a week, please, and I didn't introduce myself properly. Now that I am your doctor, call me Max, please. Max Hall, but just Max will do."

His demeanor had changed from the emotionally charged wreck that had been ranting at Zarfa earlier. It would be an understatement to say that Max was passionate about helping people. He'd really set out as a doctor to make a change in the world, originally. He was approaching his forties now, though, and felt as if he had changed very little. He needed a new scene. Somewhere he could make a difference.

"Will do, Max."

As Zarfa left the office, Max got the chills. It was as if someone had blown cold air right down his spinal column. He didn't understand it himself. He'd always thought these Psyker Scream fans were just privileged rave kids spending their trust funds on some new trendy band, but Zarfa, was different.

He was quiet, stoic, testy, sarcastic, stern, but what really stood out was weathered. His battle scars weren't fake, not some sort of masochism or self-mutilation. Not some sort of cult ritual. No, it had definitely been a battle.

But from what?

Max didn't have an answer, and he wouldn't rest easy until he did. There were no other patients to see him, so he sat down at his desk and pulled up the Synaptix Corp multi-processor interface. Back in the day, people were okay with calling it the "Internet," but these days, it was much more than a collective of web sites; it was practically a world that mirrored the physical world with its every day hustle and bustle.

Some punk hackers figured a way to link the Net with a human brain via a simple, small electrode implanted right behind the optic nerve. To see to it that this chip wasn't used to hack into someone's brain at any moment of the day, a safety protocol was put in place so that the chip would only activate in front of a terminal. When the user sat at a terminal and pulled up the interface, they were still aware of their surroundings.

They could see from the eye that didn't have the electrode; the other eye, however, would see a sea of information. The information was easy to navigate. All one needed to do was think of what one wanted to see. The first few times most people would get on, all they would see were lewd pictures or videos of people having intercourse, or sometimes of a cat chasing a ball, but with some practice and self-discipline, one could find anything in the vast sea.

The other additional advantage of the interface was that the brain could respond so quickly to the written word without interpretation being required from direct visual stimuli. Reading an entire book was nearly instant. These days, to spend the whole night on the interface was considered abhorrent. Nobody needed to be on that long; their brains wouldn't be capable of storing all the information one would see in an entire eve.

Max took a sip of his cold, stale coffee and began looking for information on Psyker Scream. He waded through information for roughly ten minutes. He had instantly *seen* four videos, two books, hundreds of web pages, and about a thousand pictures of them performing. However, he was no closer to understanding why Zarfa would possibly want the modifications.

Was he really nothing more than an emotionally scarred and angst-ridden fan of some trendy band? Was he beaten up so badly on the street one day that he became another kid who liked crazy screamer metal and deep techno beats? Max refused these conclusions.

Maybe the answer was in the nanobots, he thought to himself as he twisted his hair in his finger with his right hand, leaning on the desk. He searched and he searched, reading every specification, every design, every review, and all kinds of medical data on the bots. He knew more now than he ever had, but still, it wasn't adding up.

The unaltered average human could hear in frequencies ranging from twelve hertz or cycles up to twenty thousand. The bots, other than the high death rate due to complication, were rather pointless and benign. All they did was increase human hearing on the low end of the scale, or bass, to hear frequencies as low as one hertz. It also increased the high end of the hearing range to be able to include frequencies between ninety thousand hertz and one hundred twenty thousand hertz.

The bots left out all tones between twenty thousand to ninety thousand. The reason for this was because the tones in between were everywhere. Microwaves, plasma field generators, hovercraft, plasma energy lines, even lightbulbs produced noise frequencies between twenty and ninety thousand hertz, but dropped off significantly at the higher levels.

But why would someone want to hear such high frequencies, or such low ones, for that matter, as well? It didn't make sense; something still didn't add up. Max knew there was a much larger picture and he was missing it. Zarfa's remark wasn't made as an insult against a musically challenged older man; it was to keep him out of something... Something that he wanted to know about.

"Ugh, I've wasted so much time," he muttered.

The flow of information began to make his head hurt. He had already reached the limits of what a human brain could take in. Frustrated, he leaned back in his chair and finished drinking his cold cup of coffee that tasted more like battery acid than coffee.

Business was slow today. Sure, he had made more money today than in the last month with the one Psyker treatment, but he was getting bored. He usually saw several legitimately sick patients in his area of town, along with the few stimulant freaks and boost users, but they'd begun to avoid his office because of the reputation he had for the way he dealt with them. He sat there in his chair, zoning out with a mouthful of rank coffee, and let his mind wander.

He didn't know how much time had elapsed in his day-dream before he heard his door slam open. He jumped up, spitting out the coffee all over his desk and floor. The woman who had abruptly burst into his office like she was breaking in startled him in his dazed state.

She was tall, about five-foot, ten inches, and slender. She was wearing a very tight plasti-poly black and pink jumpsuit. Her eyes were striking and almost catlike—she had a dark line of black around her iris, the core of her iris was a deep blue color, and the trim of her iris around the pupil was bright yellow. Her hair was a striking red that contrasted beautifully with her pale, almost porcelain skin.

She wasn't old, but she wasn't young either. She looked roughly thirty-five, and her face spoke of experience...life experience, things that would wear a weaker person out. She had deep worry lines at the top of her nose by her eyebrows that told of a lot of heartache and pain. She was, however, beautiful beyond a doubt—a real woman, not a little girl.

"Tell me, doctor, what do you know of the Psyker treatments?" she questioned with a sheepish grin. Her canine teeth were slightly longer and more pointed than average.

"Well isn't that the popular question of the day? I know everything there is to know about how to administer it, everything there is to tell about how the bots are produced, and what they do. Yet, I still don't know much as to why everyone is in a rush to get them. If that's what you're asking," Max said in an exasperated tone. The adrenaline of the scare was starting to wear off, but a new type was beginning to kick in from her beauty.

"Heh, figures. I already know why I want them, but you just might be my man. Tell me, do you have the capabilities to modify nanobots? I need something like them only...different. What I need, they don't make. I heard you do the treatments, but can you modify them?"

"Modify an already extremely physically-altering, highly dangerous nanobot? Here? In my office? Are you mad, woman?"

"Maybe. Of what concern is it to you? I am sorry to have wasted your time, doctor. Good day," she said politely with a curtsey as she began to turn toward the door.

"Wait! You came through that door like you were being chased or were coming to rob me only to ask me a crazy question, and I don't even know your name. On top of that, you are the second person today to come into my office and inquire about the modifications. On top of *that,* you appear to be a splicer. Before you go, please, entertain me. What do you want to know about all this for? And why the need to modify the bots? That's a new one for me."

She smiled at him again and walked toward him. The skin-tight jumpsuit she was wearing was made for soldiers to fight without restraint from clothing. She was gorgeous, and every curve of her body was showing. She was clearly very sleek and muscular and even though the doctor had become accustomed to seeing patients naked, this one made his heart jump.

She walked right up to his desk and looked him in the eyes, let out a little purr, and reached out her hand to stroke his bangs. She took some of his hair and started twisting it in her fingers. Max stood there, annoyed. Despite her great beauty and the fact he was contemplating asking her out to dinner, he truly wanted answers to his questions. Also, he was wondering how much of a lunatic she was. He didn't even know her name and she was touching him like they were old friends...or lovers.

"Max, you haven't changed a bit. Silly boy, you don't even know the girl you went to school with? Let's see, I think we were in kindergarten together. Then again in the third grade and, oh yeah, all of high school. Was it all those years? I feel like I forgot one," she said playfully.

She knew his name. He had gone to school with her?

"Uhhh, refresh my memory," he stated.

"The name is Crimson. Crimson Rose. You recall every-one made fun of me in school? Said I was insane? Said I lived too much in fantasy and not in the real world? You remember now, right? You even made that little chant about me," she said, not angry, just matter-of-fact, then dropped her hand back down to her side.

He remembered. There was always something amiss with her. She had been strange in school... She was homely and always dressed in an overly innocent motif. He never thought she would bloom into this mature, beautiful woman he saw in front of him. If he had, he maybe never would have made fun of her.

"Yes, I remember," he said with a gulp. "Please forgive me. I was a child then. I was stupid—"

"Hell yeah you were, ugly too, so I didn't care about your little chant. The reason I am here isn't because of some score to settle or to rub anything in your face. I happened to be in the neighborhood and saw your office. I came in to ask if you could do the impossible, nothing more. Don't worry, you aren't the first doctor I have asked and, with your answer, you won't be the last. I have to hand it to you, though. Something must have changed you. You used to be rude, self-centered, care-less, crass, and well, let's face it, an all-around ass. But here you are, in the slums, offering free care. You've changed a lot, as have I. It's good to see you, *doctor*. Who would have ever thought, Max Hall! MD!"

"Speaking of change, you got gene spliced with a cat? Really?"

"Yes, really. Not a cat, though. It took a lot of work, but I got my hands on the genetics of a cheetah. Don't ask, I know most of them died out in 2064. Anyhow, can I go now? I feel I've played your little game enough."

"You can go any time. I can't detain you... A cheetah? How? Never mind. Like I said, you are free, but still, my questions—Psyker Scream, the modification to the bots?"

"Look, it appears you've changed, but people still think I am as crazy as I ever was. You want answers, come to a Psyker show tonight. Come see what you hear. They're play-ing in town tonight; not many people know, so the crowd won't be too big. Show me you've got an open mind and maybe, just maybe, I will let you know more."

"Come see what I hear? I think you've forgotten some-thing. I provide the enhancements. I don't have them my-self."

"And you forget, neither do I. Guess you don't truly want answers...too bad," she said nonchalantly as she began to saunter toward the door.

Max was going mad with questions; he had more now than when Zarfa had left his office. He wanted to pull his hair out. He had a bit of a temper and wanted to tackle Crimson and interrogate her. He would lose, if he could even catch her.

"Crimson!" he shouted eagerly.

She paused and turned her head with a devilish smile. "Yes?" she questioned, cocking her head to the side.

"Where is it? What time? But please tell me, what do you mean by come see what I hear?"

"Eleven tonight. I will be by to pick you up and you will just have to see what I mean, if you can see it."

"I close the office at seven, so how—"

"I know where you live; be home."

She was out the door quicker than he could say another word. If she had stayed, he would have been asking a myriad of questions. How did she know where he lived? Who was this girl?

He wished he had never been a jerk to her as a child. It seemed like she was over it, but he couldn't help but feel that this was all an elaborate ploy to get back at him. Who would get spliced with a cheetah? Even eerier, he thought, how? His mind started to simmer down as he was still standing behind his desk, befuddled.

He looked down to see the coffee he had spat out all over his desk and, suddenly, felt a wave of embarrassment. He didn't think he even stood a chance with this girl after she reminded him of the school days, let alone the fact she had probably seen him jump out of his chair frightened as a schoolgirl who found a mouse.

He was wondering by this point if he had spat any coffee on her... He didn't see any, and she started off a good distance from him, but in a time of shock and fear, who knew how far he could spit? His heart was still throbbing. This was, by far, the most excitement he'd had in a long time, all in one day.

Any semblance of calmness was now completely out the window. Any concentration he had on a single subject— shattered. Even if a patient were to come in now, he would probably misdiagnose them and be guilty of malpractice. He hated abusers, but he was in need of a serenity boost. He opened his stainless steel desk and pulled out a syringe; the fluid inside was only point two of a cc.

Holding the syringe, he stood up, walked over to the door, and locked it. He flipped around his little sign that said "out to lunch" and walked back to his desk. He sat in his leather chair and stuck the boost in his arm. After five seconds, he felt a normal calmness; after ten, he was oblivious, and after fifteen, he was unconscious.

It had been a long time since he had used a serenity boost. He hadn't expected to react so strongly. He should have only used a tenth of a cc. He knew that; he was a doctor. Those were the thoughts he had when he woke up at ten o'clock at night, still miles from home.

Three

Pilvikone

"The Solovox 5S-237 or 'Pilvikone,' if you will, offers the finest in weather selection for our most esteemed customers. Whether you want the perfect picnic in the park, rain for your crops, wind to fly a kite, or need snow for your favorite winter activities, we have you covered," said the Barometrics representative.

"Excellent. You know, it is hard to imagine that this technology really works. I know I have probably seen the fruits of all of your labors in my daily activities and never gave it a second thought. However..."

"However?" he questioned, pausing to allow the customer time to make a response.

"However, how do I know after I have handed over my credits that I will actually see the results of what I paid for? How do I know that the weather you claimed to have brought to your other clientele isn't just random weather patterns you have claimed to make? How do I know your device actually works and that this isn't some big scam? I mean, come on, with the secrecy waiver I have to sign and the laws being what they are, I could never try to sue you if this technology doesn't really work. Your office, though being grand and majestic-looking, could all be a ploy. Sure, you could have had a million clients all sworn to the secrecy that I had to sign in order to come in here, not to mention the contract I would have to sign to requisition your services. It's all so—"

"So unrealistic?"

For once, she was being cut off in conversation.

"Yes, I can see your concern, but rest assured this is no

hoax or scam. There is no smoke and mirrors here. In fact, our technology isn't even a secret. We are not well known because only an elite few can even afford our services. Laws and contracts and governments being the way they are, indeed. We have no competitor because the law doesn't allow it. It would generate chaos and, in this world, we do need stability of some sort. These machines are very expensive to make and maintain; there are currently sixteen active 5S-237 units active around the globe. They are able to project their effects more than two thousand miles from one another. These are all facts that are a matter of public record. Does this allay your fears of the company in the slightest?"

"It does, but why all the secrecy? Why the waivers?"

"Good question. It is because we can't be having our customers know each other's names. Weather is a funny thing. One person wants rain; another, sunshine. One customer wants snow, and another, wind. The first I described contradicts; the second doesn't. One customer offers to pay fifty thousand credits for a windy day; it is granted. On the same day, a customer offers the same sum for a snowy day. We can grant those both on the same day. The customers sometimes aren't fully excited about their purchase, but with all things, there is sometimes buyer's remorse. Furthermore, both truly got what they wanted.

"What happens, though, when the first situation I described is asked for? One client wants rain, one wants sunshine; both are looking to pay for a whole day. People are very temperamental when it comes to their weather. We don't want one killing the other to have less competition. You know assassination contracts are easy to buy these days and even legal in most cases," he stated.

"Right. So, what happens if two people want something different on the same day? With the secrecy, one can't offer the other a compromise, or even withdraw their bid on the weather. How do you handle it?"

"Easy, an anonymous bid. Sunshine offers thirty thousand credits for the day. Rain comes in with a bid, is then told what the current offer for the day is. Rain is then given an opportunity to counter offer, the company documents, and the offer is given back to sunshine. The first, sunshine, if you will, always has the final say. If he chooses to pay more, he has it, end of story. We do not want outrageous bid wars. Again! Order...in a chaotic world; that is our slogan. However, if sunshine decides the price is too high, he can decline a second bid and it is over. It is as close to 'fair' as we can be."

"Okay, here is another for you since you are obviously well scripted and nothing I have asked has even made you bat an eye." She paused.

"Yes?"

"Back in the centuries before we had this technology, naturally occurring weather patterns would arrive at the same point of contact, causing a disaster such as a hurricane, tornado, gale force winds, flash floods...need I go on?"

"Okay, destruction, disorder, chaos. I still don't understand your question."

"It's because I haven't asked it yet. How do you keep these things from happening?"

"It is easy. We check all orders, cross check all orders, and even triple cross check every order around the globe to see to it that no client conflicts occur. Additionally, even if there is no client conflict, we check with a discrepancy in weather patterns. As you probably know, we can't be having a fast moving humid hot front collide with rapidly moving cold front. It would spell disaster for us all. It would spell..." He trailed off.

"Chaos, I get the point. I am glad to see that you have a system to check these things. The last thing I want to do is fund a company that inadvertently was used by terrorists to kill us all!"

"We, as a corporation, concur. I can tell you they have tried, but with our security checks doubled with the high grade override systems that we have installed, it is impossible for anyone to abuse this technology, even its creators. Any further questions?"

"You've mentioned cost, all random numbers that didn't seem to indicate a base price. What is the cheapest your services come in and what are the increments of time?"

"All weather can be purchased in increments of one hour. Base price on the median is twenty thousand credits for an hour. Some requests are easier than others, so that's why I gave you a median. We have a spreadsheet that covers it all. However, if one is to make a purchase of a whole day and night's worth, with the exclusion of sunshine—we aren't gods—a discount then applies. Buying only one hour is always the most expensive route one could possibly assume. A twelve-hour package is typically the most reasonable. However, as I said, there is a spreadsheet that covers this all."

The answer was as well rehearsed as it could come. She scanned him up and down and remembered everything about him. From his navy-based, pinstriped blue suit to his late nineteen-fifties bowler hat. She wanted to remember him for her own purposes. This was a man that was obviously intelligent and filled with more information than he would divulge given this situation.

"In order for you to be a client, you have to sign this document, which as you pointed out, swears you to even more secrecy. If you are okay with that,"—he began to hand her a pen—"then all we need is for you to sign your name... What was it? I know I could look at the original documentation, but you must understand, I really am bad with names and I forgot what you said at the beginning of our conversation, terribly sorry really."

This excellent business man had lost his edge. He didn't remember her name. He had been pacing her so well.

"It's because I didn't say, and you didn't think I would be worth your time so you didn't even bother to look at my application or my preliminary paperwork. I forgive you; the name is Crimson. Crimson Rose."

She took his pen and signed her name. She was now a member of the Barometrics Corporation as a client. She could buy the weather she wanted. Some of her questions were satiated, for now. She, however, felt that it was time to leave; more of her inquisition would come later.

"Thanks for doing business with me, sweetheart," she said with a sly wink.

"Um, uh... No! Thank you for your business," he said unsurely, caught off guard.

"And your name was?" she said, smiling as innocently as a blushing virgin who had seen the man she lusted after naked for the first time.

"How rude of me. I must have never introduced myself properly to a woman of your caliber, as well as a potential client." He didn't know it, but he had already made several vital mistakes in his answer. "But the name is Brian Nash."

"Good meeting you, Brian," she said, turning toward the hallway that would lead her out of his office. "I hope to be doing a good amount of business with you in the future." She then sauntered down the hallway with a feline's grace. As she exited the office building and hit the streets, she cocked her head and spat, followed by a mutter. "God damn pig!"

She continued down the concrete sidewalk back toward her house on the west end of town; she would have to pass by the central slums to reach her home. She had more business to attend to today. The road to completing her vendetta would be long and bloodied.

I may as well continue to pursue my ruse since I am stuck walking, she thought to herself. She activated her Link System Communications Device and asked it to call Brian Nash. There were three rings. He undoubtedly had caller identification and knew it was her. Her final dealings with him must have had him confused; it's what she had intended anyway.

"Hello?" he asked, puzzled.

"Brian, I know I only just left your office, but I wanted to throw this out there. I do have half a mind to retract any thought of wanting to purchase your services by the fact that you didn't give me your all from the very beginning as you should have."

"You're right, I didn't. It was presumptuous of me to do so. I see so many people come in looking at our product and they never make the commitment. I judged you to be like them and I really wasn't trying to impress with my best of knowledge and expertise. I am really surprised you noticed. You are quite the savvy woman. May I ask, though? Why are you calling? You aren't retracting your request to be a customer, are you? As you know, we require a fifty thousand credit applicant fee that is non-refundable. Also, may I add, our services could be of much benefit to you in your line of work, Miss Crimson." He was a salesman all right. She could hear his cockiness coming back in his tone.

"You are correct, and I am a woman of reason. I hadn't thought anything as crazy as wasting fifty thousand. Additionally, please never pander me as to how useful the company's services—Barometrics' services, not your own—could be to me lest I forget my line of work. The reason I called was to offer you a chance to redeem yourself. I know that you make a commission and I can request a new sales representative at any time. So how 'bout it? Up for proving you aren't as useless as you seem?" Her questioning tone was subtly seductive, like a dominatrix calling a slave.

Brian's voice had a tone of confusion. "Well, what exactly did you have in mind?"

"Tomorrow, you take me to dinner. We meet at the Blue Nami on the east end of the city. If you don't know it, look it up. You're paying. I figure you can afford it after the commission of my applicant fee. If you can't stimulate me with an intelligent conversation then take me home. Even a girl like me needs to get plowed every once in awhile. Your body is good enough to do the job. If it isn't, I've got some boosts that will help," she said forwardly.

It was a risky strategy. If this guy had any common sense, he would feel a trap coming. If he was an ordinary man, he would let his male member do the thinking for him. Either way, she needed to use him like a chess piece and hoped he would take the bait.

"Well, Miss Rose... I don't know what to say. Under normal circumstances, I would be offended by your outright demands, but seeing as these are anything but normal circumstances...I accept. I will see you tomorrow at the Blue Nami. What time works for you?" She could tell he was already envisioning himself panting over her sweaty body.

"Eight," she said, then disconnected.

Men are such easy marks. All you have to do is offer sex and they will do about anything. If that doesn't work, cry. She had been so wrapped up in her conversation that she hadn't realized she was already in the slums. As she looked around for a landmark she could identify, she saw a bald-headed, grey-skinned man stumbling her way.

He was either intoxicated or had obviously undergone recent nanobot modifications, and he had the appearance of a Screamer. As he stumbled closer, she made eye contact with him. He looked at her with a strange, inquisitive expression. She was known to turn many heads with her beauty, but his countenance wasn't lustful. It was...as if he had seen something familiar to him.

"Excuse me, sir, but is there a clinic around here? My head hurts something awful and I could really use a doctor's attention," she said to him in an almost southern belle accent.

He stared at her with a complex expression in his eyes. His body was quivering, his lips were trembling, and when he spoke, his voice was distorted. "There is. Keep heading north for about six blocks, east two, and you will see between a café and an abandoned building Dr. Max Hall's office. He can help."

"Thank you, kind sir," she said, still faking an overly sweet persona. She had to play so many roles in life that she did so naturally. She sometimes didn't even realize it when she wasn't speaking in her own voice. Sometimes she forgot which of the voices she used actually belonged to her. All that she really knew was she had a purpose and nothing would stop her from fulfilling it.

"Not a problem," said the awkwardly-proportioned stranger.

Before he could say anything else to her, she had begun a hasty stride in the direction of Max Hall's office. She was curious as to how he was doing, if he was the same Max she'd known so many years ago. She passed by many seedy characters as she made her way to the office.

She was certainly out of place by the looks of her—her skin tight black and pink combat suit, her flowing red hair, her striking eyes, and her angelic skin tone. This was a destitute part of town and if it wasn't for the fact that she was moving faster in her walking pace than most people jogged, some of these unruly hoodlums would have likely tried to have some fun with her.

She rounded the corner and stood near a green dumpster. Exactly as the stranger had described to her, there was the café, Floyd's. Then there was a tacky neon sign half burnt out and flickering. Below it was a black cast iron door with a gauss weaponry resistant glass window that read, "Doctor Max Hall." On the other side of that was an abandoned building that should have been condemned. There was no doubt a bunch of boost addicts squatting in there.

She flipped open a bangle she always wore on her wrist and revealed a portable Synaptix Corp multiprocessor interface. She pressed a side button and turned it on. She stood staring into space for about fifteen seconds. By the end of it, she had confirmed this was in fact the Max she had been in school with as a child.

She also confirmed his birth date, home address, blood type, portfolio, specialty of medicine, every test score from youth through his college days, how many women he had been with, as well as any crime he may have been suspect or convicted of. Nothing was sacred.

She closed her portable interface and took in a deep breath. She exhaled it out of her mouth and at the end, let out a girlish giggle. She regained her composure then said aloud, "This is going to be fun."

In an instant, she bolted off at lightning speed toward the black cast iron door. She knew it was going to make a rumble that would shake the building and those inside the office.

Her speed was unmatched and her strength inhuman; she might even unhinge the door when she came into contact with it. He might have patients in there now that had weak hearts. He might even become startled and wet himself. She hoped these things would all come true. It would give her a good laugh.

Right before impact, she had to wipe the grin she was wearing off her face. She had to be cool, calm, assertive. She had to be in command. She couldn't be this little girl running in the street about to barge through the door hoping to scare someone. She had to go back to being a woman. She had to go back to playing roles to get what she wanted to fulfill what she needed to do. It was time to get real, time to be serious. But for those few brief seconds that she could be a child, and the memories she would hold of them after? Well, damn, they sure did feel good.

Four

Back Alleyways

After paying, he stumbled out of Max's office. He had felt pain before, but never quite like this. The large, hollow bore needle into his brachial vein was nothing compared to the migraine associated with the nanobots demyelinating the sheaths around his acoustic nerve and portions of his brain then reconstructing them to hear and understand new frequencies.

He was stumbling down the streets of Alexarien looking like a junkie; his balance was off and he felt sick to his stomach. The things he heard around him weren't quite the same and he kept hearing deep rumbles followed by screeching pieces of high frequencies so intense he thought his eyes were going to burst.

The pain made him sick to his stomach and he couldn't remember where the apartment was that he was staying at. His vision was blurring and he began to sweat like a booster suffering from withdrawals. He had been so smug back at the office. He did know pain of all sorts that most humans could only imagine in nightmares; this was worse.

He had talked to himself in his head, though; he re-established to that this was necessary. Even if it wasn't, there was no going back now. He'd signed the papers and once the series of injections was started, it could be detrimental to stop. Everything he read on the net said that the first shot was always the worst.

He shook his head, kept stumbling, and crossed the street. He was trying to go by memory, which was now clouded by flashbacks and pain. He thought he was headed the right direction toward home when he saw her—Sarah.

No, it wasn't her; she was much too old. She would only be about nineteen, and a little bit taller. Her hair would be black. *You can change that,* he thought to himself. Her face, though, had a similar character, something familiar.

Her multi-colored eyes were the same as his sister's, how? Nobody had eyes that revealing, that piercing, that striking. Who was this demon headed his way? *Doppelganger*, he thought.

The way she walked and the air around her made him forget his pain, forget Sarah had been kidnapped. He felt the urge to ask where she had been, but he knew this wasn't Sarah. *She'll think I am a lunatic.*

"Excuse me, sir, but is there a clinic around here? My head hurts something awful and I could really use a doctor's attention."

Ironic, so does mine. Who talks the way you do anymore? he was dying to say. "There is. Keep heading north for about six blocks, east two, and you will see between a café and an abandoned building Dr. Max Hall's office. He can help."

"Thank you, kind sir."

"Not a problem." He was burning to say something, to ask about his sister, but before he could say another word, she was gone with a stride so swift it appeared she was floating, drifting on the wind. The way his sister used to move.

He clutched his forehead and, strangely, the pain was gone. He could see straight. He heard her fine despite being dumbfounded. Perhaps the pain was over. Perhaps the bots took a break from their task. Maybe he had become accustomed to the pain now. Zarfa didn't know, and he didn't care either.

Dazed by the surreal reminder of his sister, he looked around. Despite stumbling nearly blind, he was headed the right direction of the apartment he'd taken a few months lease on. He needed to get home and rest, so he continued to travel down the streets of the slums.

He noticed that this area of the city was a breeding ground for delinquents. He had only been in the city for a brief period of time. Zarfa had heard many tales of Alexarien as a child, and even more when he began his journey to the city for his treatments. He didn't know how much of what he had heard was rumor and what was true.

So far, he had only seen the run down districts of the city, and all that he had been told was true. The streets were dirty; there were homeless, gangsters, and punks riddling every street corner and sidewalk. Addicts were everywhere, boosters and stimulant junkies alike passed out or shaking in every alleyway, lying in wait for someone to come by that they could rob for their credits in order to score their next hit.

He had to be here. He had to receive the treatments, and then he was destined back home to Ilyeion. He knew he couldn't stand to live in a place such as this. He thought the crime and poverty in his city was awful when he was there, but this was inexcusable.

Since this was exactly the vision every rumor of the slums conjured before his visit, he could only imagine what the west end of town was like. He had heard of the luxury, elegance, and decadent lifestyles that were held there. He heard of the slavery—anyone could be bought or sold for a price if they didn't have the money to support themselves.

Work was scarce. Zarfa was barely getting by with his job fighting in the pits. He began to ponder whether or not he would be able to fight tomorrow night and earn his keep. For now, the pain had subsided, but what if it came back?

What if he was in so much pain that he had to tap out on the fight, or his enemy got the advantage and won? The rules were to the death or surrender. What if he couldn't even stand? He had a lot on his mind and was beginning to feel overwhelmed. The only thing he wanted to do was rest, and he was getting close to home.

His residence was in an alleyway up ahead. Typically, there were a few junkies huddled around a garbage can chatting about how great life had been before they were on the street and how it was everyone else's fault that they had gotten here. Perhaps it was, but from Zarfa's vantage point, it most likely was their own.

Zarfa stood at the entrance to the alleyway and saw the same people he had always seen for the last few weeks. The same junkies and the pimp who had taken a liking to this location. By this point, he was glad his pain had gone. His vision was good and he could see clearly again. One didn't want any disadvantages when he or she was standing in an Alexarien slums alleyway.

He hadn't been given any trouble as of yet, but who knew? This could be his lucky day. He proceeded down the alleyway as usual, passed by the junkies reminiscing by a garbage can that still stunk of the fire that had been glowing in it last night to keep them warm.

They asked for spare credits as he walked by—typical. He told them no, as he always did. He knew they would only spend it on boosts or stimulants. It might bring them some happiness, but it wouldn't fix their problems. Plus, he was on a mission in life. He needed money to accomplish it, and though he had saved enough for his first series of bots, he would need four more rounds, and a week wasn't sufficient time for him to save. He didn't know what he would tell Max when he returned.

For now, though, he didn't worry about his finances. He figured he would come up with something. Max seemed like a good man, and he had taken an oath to do no harm. He couldn't sit idle and let Zarfa die, could he?

As Zarfa arrived at his apartment door, he got out his keycard and reached out his hand to swipe it. He expected to hear the buzz followed by the click, but instead, he heard a ringing in his ear. *These damn side effects*, he thought to himself. It took a second for him to realize he had been hit in the side of the head and that the bums in the alley were screaming and fleeing.

Zarfa fell sideways and his head made contact with the pavement that had been only seconds ago under his feet. He felt the asphalt dig into his cheek. Who'd hit him? He hadn't seen anyone unusual.

He jumped to his feet, spinning to face the side where the blow had come from. There was already a leg coming at him for a strong kick. The opponent had no doubt launched it at him while he was on the ground. It was a good thing Zarfa's reflexes were quick and fluid or else this kick could have caused some pain.

Zarfa jumped. The kick was aimed low and he cleared this behemoth of a man's leg with his evasive maneuver. As the man began to retract his attack, Zarfa launched a counter with his own heel aimed at the man's knee. It landed— Zarfa could hear it, and feel it too. It made a snap as his counter attack broke this beastly figure's tibial plateau. Despite the utter pain his enemy must have been in, he stood there in a guarded position, preparing to fight.

Zarfa stood at about six-foot, one inch in height; his unnamed enemy was at least a foot taller. Zarfa, however, had comparable reach with both his arms and legs. It was the reason he had been Sarah's bodyguard. It was the reason he had taken a job as an entertainment fighter in this God forsaken, dank hell of a city.

"I don't want trouble and I will kill you," Zarfa stated, giving the most searing expression he could muster.

"What makes you think you can?"

"The fact that I just broke one of your legs. Impressive you are still standing on it, but it is broken. You are still in pain, and I am faster. Walk away."

"I can't, leg's broken, remember?"

This monster was huge. Not only did he tower over Zarfa, he had to have had at least a hundred pounds more muscle than he did. Zarfa was shocked that he hadn't been rendered unconscious with the sneak blow the man had launched on the side of his head. How had he snuck up on him? Where had this beast been hiding?

"Your ear's bleeding, kid. That was a good counter attack. I underestimated you, but I won't again," he said as he hit a button on a device that was worn around his wrist.

Immediately, he disappeared. Zarfa's heart began to race so fast and so hard he believed it would burst forth from his rib cage. He had seen nothing like it before. *How did he disappear into thin air like that? Nobody has tech like that in Ilyeion.*

Zarfa drew a breath and began to concentrate on relaxing. He needed to not be tense. He needed to flow. Like a waterfall, he needed to be fluid to come crashing down. An early martial arts master had taught that principle centuries before, and it worked equally as well today as it had then...when you could see your enemy, that is.

He listened for movement, for breath that wasn't his. He didn't hear a thing. Had his enemy moved? Was he still standing there sizing him up? Why was he being attacked? At these thoughts, he heard a high frequency screech, not in his ear but in his brain.

Had the sneak attack damaged his eardrum? Was he de-

veloping a hematoma pressing on his brain, causing him severe discomfort and eventual death if he didn't get away?
Was it the Psyker treatment? Why now?

The alleyway was empty. The moment this goliath had
appeared to slay the proverbial David, the junkies and bums
had scattered like cockroaches in the light. The pimp who
had taken up station in the alleyway, always offering his
goods, was nowhere to be seen. Zarfa was alone, not that
those shady characters would have offered him much refuge
anyway.

He ran toward the entrance of the alleyway as fast as he
could. He didn't need to be here; there was no shame running
in order to fight another day. Especially since he was fighting a
phantom, an apparition that sought his blood.

His footsteps clattered loud, heavy, and fast as he ran
toward the street. He was almost there. Once he made it, he
would take a sharp right and hightail it back toward Max's
office. They weren't exactly friends, but neither was he and
his employer, who was much farther away. Other than those
two, he didn't know anyone here.

He felt security that came with the relief he had gotten
away, then he felt a heavy blow to his throat. His trachea
was going into spasms; he couldn't breathe. His body
screamed it was his end while his mind told him to relax; he
wasn't done yet. He was fortunate the blow hadn't crushed
his trachea entirely, but it had knocked him to the ground
again.

His enemy was still here, and the ringing in his head was
growing ever louder. Worse yet, he couldn't scream for help,
and he couldn't see who was inflicting this pain any longer.
He shouldn't have hesitated; life should have taught him that
by now, but he was stupid.

His stupidity would be his demise this day. He was sure
to be dead in a matter of minutes. He should have struck fast
as lightning and broken the man's neck the way he'd broken
his leg. He'd had his chance and he passed it by, why? Because he wasn't a killer? He had killed many.

Coughing and gasping for air, he stood again, recovering
as quickly as he could. Looking around, Zarfa thought to
himself, *Look for something, movement, anything that tells
you where he is.* Out of the corner of his eye, he saw a can

of spray paint by the burned up garbage can. It wasn't much, but it was all he could think of.

In one swift move, Zarfa rolled toward the can of paint, hoping and wishing that it wouldn't be empty. As he came out of his roll, he snatched the can in his hand and felt wind above his head. Any lower and he would have caught another strong, swift blow, one that might have done him in.

His throat had stopped convulsing and he could breathe again. He was still in a crouched position from the rolling maneuver he had quickly completed. He hoped his ears would help him in this wicked battle, but they were still failing. His eyes were fine, but he could hear nothing but a loud screech drowning out all noise.

As he felt the blow glance over his head, missing him, he performed a back flip. The best he could tell, his opponent's blow had come from in front of him. How could he be moving so quickly? He was sure he had broken his leg with his counter.

Standing, he sprayed the paint from the can in a wide angle in front of him. The yellow paint misted the air and he could see an outline of a person, much smaller than he had remembered. This outline stood at merely five-foot, five inches. It was directly ahead of him.

Without hesitation, Zarfa launched forward a blow with his left hand, hitting approximately where he assumed this enemy's eye would be. It landed. There was a scream followed by blood squirting on his hand. Zarfa pulled back from his attack and took a defensive stance. *How many are here?*

Before, his ears failed him; he hadn't heard the big one move because of the unbearable screeching. His ears began to relent as, slowly, sounds began to distinguish themselves once again. He was being tag-teamed by these specters of death. He still didn't know why. He had only been in the city a few weeks, surely not long enough to make enemies.

The little one was no longer invisible to him. Between the yellow paint and the blood trickling from his face, he could make him out. The time for questions and games was over. It was time to end this.

Zarfa sprayed around himself again. This time, he pivoted on his heel and in one swift motion, had sprayed a cloud of detection three hundred and sixty degrees around his body. This move revealed that the large one was sneaking up behind him, no doubt to try to hold him or perform another sucker punch.

"I'll start with you," Zarfa said aloud. He heaved the can at the small enemy's head while simultaneously throwing a powerful haymaker and leaping toward this cloaked figure. They both connected. First, the can hit and echoed a loud pinging noise. Second, his haymaker landed square in the ear of the little one, surely blowing out his ear drum.

This enemy that had been besting him hit the ground so hard he took an additional blow to the head when it connected to the pavement. Without letup, like a furious tempest, Zarfa threw a low kick where he expected the little enemy's neck to be. It was there—he felt it connect with all of his fury and force. This vindictive blow proved fatal. He could barely hear it as noises continued to differentiate, but he felt as his shin connected with the neck of his foe. He felt as cervical vertebrae separated and shattered from one another and the enemy went limp on his leg.

Quickly, he switched stances and turned to see the behemoth. He knew the jig was up when he had been sprayed with paint. By now, he'd dropped his cloak and Zarfa could see him clear as day. No more games, no more tricks.

"*Who are you?*" screamed Zarfa, spit coming from his mouth.

The ringing was beginning to fade. *These damn bots are more trouble than I thought.* He may not be able to hear clearly yet, but he planned to extract answers one way or another.

"I am Faraza," the giant said, pulling out a pistol and aiming it at Zarfa. "And on that note, you are dead." He squeezed the trigger and fired three shots.

Zarfa ducked the moment he saw the gauss pistol drawn. The projectiles missed and he could hear them clear as day make contact with the alleyway behind him. His hearing was back; he was happy about that turn in luck. Now all he had to do was avoid being shot.

He was in a crouched position like a sprinter ready to come off the line. The first barrage of bullets he had been quick enough to avoid; he only hoped to be as lucky with the next. In a split second, the man had changed his aim and was firing upon him again. Bullets were fast, but Zarfa could see their paths; his eyes were quicker.

He took off from his crouch and was closing the ten-foot gap quickly toward this beast. *Faraza—what are they doing here? How did they know where to find me?* Rage welled deep inside of him as he remembered, once again, the day Sarah had been snatched from his life.

In the two seconds it took to close the gap, he relived the battle in his mind. It then trailed to the woman who had asked him directions only an hour ago. Seven more shots had been fired in haste. One went under his armpit and glanced his ribs, fracturing two of them on the right and causing blood to spit from his wound.

He tried to dodge them all; he was fortunate that this was a mere flesh wound, barely deeper than the surface, not fatal by any means. He grabbed the Faraza agent by the wrist. With his right arm, he pulled the man's arm down and forward. With his left, he sunk his elbow into the wrist of the assassin. Like a tree branch under the foot of a large man, he heard it snap. The bone protruded from the skin and blood flowed forth. He dropped the pistol and it hit the ground; it was on a hair trigger. The impact caused it to bounce backward with the barrel facing his enemy. It fired again. The bullet missed Zarfa and struck the calf of the assassin's unbroken leg.

His enemy and would-be killer fell to his knees. Switching his grip to the man's left arm, he pulled it forward and kicked his shoulder, dislocating it. This man on his knees was still at about abdomen height compared to Zarfa. Zarfa jumped into the air with great agility and planted both of his feet on the Faraza, launching off from his chest in another great back flip.

Zarfa landed on his feet as the Faraza sprawled on his back, nearly dead but still conscious.

"Faraza? I thought I left you all back in Ilyeion!" exclaimed Zarfa. His rage was wearing off, but he wasn't going to make this easy. He needed answers. He demanded answers.

"I'll bet you did. Looks like you really got the best of us. What is the body count now? Into the hundreds, I imagine. You left quite the wake of destruction before your exodus."

"What's it to you? You're all evil. You nearly killed me, kidnapped my sister, and pursued me with a vengeance for killing one of your men in a raid. You expect me to show you mercy or concern? I want answers and I will torture you if I have to in order to get them!"

The Faraza was laughing maliciously. "I know you will, boy. Are you stupid? Do you know why we pursue you? If you did, perhaps you would have allowed us to capture you today. Then again...maybe not."

"Enlighten me; why do you keep chasing?"

"Sarah."

The world grew black. It made sense that he would know, but what was she to them? To them, she should be just another captive. To them, she should be another one of their mindless minions. She had her name intact?

"What of her, swine? It didn't seem like you were trying to capture me. It seemed as if you were trying to murder me."

"That first hit was intended to knock you out. Sarah wants to see you. That's why you're here, right? So you can find a way in? We would have let you in, idiot."

"What do you mean she wants to see me? Stop being cryptic and be straight with me, lest I start removing precious appendages."

"I'm not trying to be cryptic," he let out, writhing. The adrenaline had worn off and his body was wracked with pain.

"So what then? You expect me to believe that my sister, one of your drones, wants to see me?"

"Drone? Ha! Far from it. Are you daft, boy? A talent like that would be a shame to erase and turn into a drone. She holds an esteemed position. I assure you." His tone sounded smug; he knew more than Zarfa and he knew it irked him. It seemed as if he enjoyed taunting him. He was already in agony. He already knew he was going to meet his demise; he had accepted it. He was drawing his last breaths, so now it seemed as if he would try to sow doubt in Zarfa's mind. The last bit of joy he would derive would be in taunting Zarfa.

Zarfa couldn't help but feel sick. His composure was calm. He had won the battle; there was nothing left to do but extract information. However, with each sentence, he heard his heartbeat grow rapid and more tense. He hadn't seen his sister since she had been taken three years ago. *To think, is she still alive? Intact?* Couldn't be. This was some sick game. Everyone who had ever been seen alive after the Faraza had kidnapped them was always a twisted drone that had no resemblance of their former selves.

"Shut up about my sister. I know she isn't dead. I know she is with the Faraza, but she is nothing more than a minion, one of the drones now. Last I saw her, her eyes were dead, lifeless. She was nothing but a shell. She isn't asking for me by name, giving commands anywhere. You're just angry I've been killing you off left and right."

"I can't help it if you choose to believe that. Don't worry, you will see for yourself."

"Damn right I will. As soon as my business is done here, I'm returning home and I will kill every last one of you if that is what it takes."

The Faraza assassin was laughing as blood trickled down from his injuries. The pain he was in must have been unbearable. Zarfa stood there sizing him up as he held his side that had been grazed. Blood flowed from between his fingers and his body ached from the shattered ribs. He knelt down and picked up the gauss pistol that had been used against him. He looked in the magazine and there was one bullet left. Methodically, he loaded it back into the gun and aimed it at the Faraza. "Any last words?" he asked dryly.

"Would you believe them?"

"Probably not."

The shot rang in Zarfa's ears. The bullet went clean through this fiend's head. He no longer laughed at the frustration he caused Zarfa. He no longer writhed in pain. He just lay dead, rapidly cooling on the sidewalk near the entrance to the alleyway. *Where are the police?* Zarfa thought to himself.

He holstered the newly acquired gun into a pocket sewn into the inner seam of his pants. It wasn't comfortable, but it would do, and it was less visible than a side holster. He then took off the cloaking devices he had seen his would-be killers use from off both their wrists. He had no idea how to use such a device, but he was sure it would come in handy if he had them.

After looking around for a few minutes, assessing the world around him, he realized that this type of battle wasn't uncommon to these people. The moment the violence had ended, the cockroaches had made their way back to their assigned spots in the alley—not like Ilyeion at all.

The world in general was a harsh and cold place to live, but this was hell. There appeared to be no law; it was practically anarchy. He could have died in the streets this day. Justice would never be found for him and the human carrion birds that surrounded him would probably rustle his every pocket to make sure everything of value was stripped from his cold, dead corpse.

But he hadn't died. He was the one walking away. He wasn't sure how he would fight in the pit tomorrow, wasn't sure if he should go back to the doctor to have his bullet wound tended to. He remembered he had an antiseptic spray in the apartment, and he was only steps away from it, so he decided to continue as if he hadn't been attacked.

He stepped inside his apartment and closed the door behind himself, locking it. He walked across his shiny hardwood floor; his steps echoed in the cool air of the apartment. Cautiously, he peeked his head into the bathroom, inspecting it to be sure there weren't any more battles waiting for him. He found nothing, but that didn't reassure him. His enemies could apparently do the impossible and become invisible.

He walked over to his bed and sprawled across it, lying on his back. It was merely two in the afternoon, but it had been a long day. He closed his eyes and, as his mind wandered off, he couldn't help but think of what had just happened, what had been said. Memories of the last few years kept striking his mind like lashes from a tormentor's whip. It was what drove him, but he didn't like dwelling on it.

Too late. He would have to face his memories tonight.

Five

Getting to the Show

How long have I been out? Why is it so damn hot in here? Why am I shaking? What is this I feel? Max awoke at his desk, sweating profusely and feeling nauseated. He could vomit at any second and his vision was blurred. It had been a long time since he had used a boost. *I am so tense,* he had reasoned before he had pushed down the plunger that would re-ignite his nightmare.

Back in college, he had been equally as neurotic as he was these days. He worried over everything. Whether he had passed the test or not. What girls liked him? What teachers hated him? Even stupid things like what he would have for lunch he stressed about.

Max was intelligent, maybe too much. It's what caused his deep-seated anxiety. He couldn't shut off his brain; he couldn't sleep. He was unnatural in his ability to work on complex projects and thoughts. As a child, his parents had him "upgraded" with every last intelligence booster Synaptix had to offer, so it was a terrific understatement to say he was smart.

As he progressed in school, the learning and the practical application were a breeze to him. What was difficult was not stressing over whether or not he had stepped on that flower on his hurried way into the classroom. Complex issues were a breeze, but daily life for him became torture. He had to tie his shoelaces "the right way." Sometimes, this meant he would tie and retie forty, fifty, sixty times to get them exactly "right."

The neurosis started taking over his life. That's when, at

the ripe age of twenty, he was introduced to stims and boosts. Stimulants—or stims for short—were drugs one could purchase anywhere—grocery stores, plasma shops, or even vending machines. They were used to treat a variety of issues. Anything a person wanted, he or she could find—muscle building stims, relaxing stims, concentration stims, agility stims; you name it, they could be found.

They often came in generic-looking bottles with only one or two words on the label telling what they were for—strength, mass, tone, speed, concentration, relaxation, joy, and the list went on. They were color coded so that nobody mistook one for the other. Really, even the biggest simpleton could find what they needed and use it, absolutely legal. However, not without risk.

Stimulants had to be taken daily and took about a week to build in one's system to achieve the desired result. There was a list of side effects and warnings on the back of each bottle due to the fact that it was required to be printed. Full disclosure was the only law companies had to follow these days. Stims were typically pretty benign with the side effects; however, they were still addictive.

The typical case of stim addiction took about six months of use followed by the user trying to quit cold turkey; cold turkey was never advised. The discreet user of stims knew to give their body frequent breaks to avoid addiction. Also, the use of a boost with the same effect as a stim was never advised. The drugs metabolized in such similar ways that it would cause an amplification effect that the body, although being able to process it, would begin to wear the user down and cause an early demise.

Stimulants, kept in their place, were great for anyone seeking an easy solution to a result they desired. They were relatively safe and effective. They were intended for the patient user who didn't mind waiting for the results and who didn't mind the results being often times subtle.

That wasn't Max's style, however. He wasn't patient when it came to the things he wanted. He wanted peace. He wanted to be able to shut down his brain and relax. Every waking second, he heard his own voice reasoning on a hundred different things. He always felt sick from lack of sleep and he didn't know how to control his creativity or his intellect properly.

His obsessive-compulsive behavior was all-consuming and he wanted a quick fix; he didn't want to wait. Even more, he didn't want a subtle change that helped him turn off his brain. He wanted something fast, nearly immediate. As quickly as his brain worked on and processed information, he wanted it to shut off at command even quicker. He couldn't do it on his own, though.

That's when he turned to boosts. Twenty years, one month, seven days, thirteen hours, eleven minutes, and thirty-three seconds. That's how old Max had been when he injected his first boost. He had been counting his age in his head right before he slipped the needle into his arm.

It was glorious; it was everything he had imagined. He had been standing in his room right near his bed, pacing back and forth. *Another sleepless night,* he imagined. He couldn't take it. If it continued, he would jump off a roof. So he did it, a tenth of a cc of serenity straight to his arm. It was the lowest dose available; there was such a small amount of fluid in his syringe he doubted it would be enough.

He was already in medical school and he thought that the drug would only be absorbed by capillaries in the muscles and dermis and not even be able to circulate in his system. He didn't think it was possible that five seconds later, his legs would drop him to the floor. He hadn't studied pharmacokinetics or pharmacodynamics yet. He ignored the warnings that boosts were highly addictive even on the first use; he was ignorant. That had been fifteen years ago now, roughly. He was much more informed; he should know better.

"God damned addicts," he muttered aloud, confirming what he was to himself.

Max stood. His shirt was covered in sweat. His body ached. It hadn't felt a boost for years and now all the cravings he had subdued came crawling back under his skin. He tossed his used syringe into a garbage can and shook his head violently; it throbbed.

He pushed back in the drawers of his desk that he had left open before he had abandoned himself to the effects of the serenity boost. His legs were still shaky; his body wasn't as good at processing the drug as it had once been. He looked at the clock on his desk and saw that it was ten at night. He needed to be to his house, which was miles away, in an hour to meet with Crimson.

He stumbled over to a mirror to check his appearance. He scanned his figure up and down. He was short, about five-foot-five. His hair was short and blonde, looking quite disheveled. His forehead was decorated with thick beads of sweat and his face was flushed from his cells rebelling against his will, craving more of the drug. He remembered this feeling, the slavery, the lust, almost always ending in him abandoning himself to the boosts once more.

He looked down to his hands; they were veined and masculine. He had a working man's grip and musculature to go along with it. This, he had worked for, not cheated to get with stimulants or boosts. He couldn't stop his hands from having violent tremors, another effect of addiction.

"*I hate you!*" he screamed at himself in the mirror.

His voice mixed with the sound of glass shattering as his scream echoed throughout the small office. Before he had even realized he had done it, he had struck the mirror with a closed fist in a tantrum of self-loathing. The glass had shattered at the force of his blow with his right hand and lacerated his knuckles. He was fortunate to not sever any digits.

Blood flowed from his hand profusely; he should have stopped to treat it, but the adrenaline was taking over and overriding the after effects of his bad decision to use a boost. He didn't bother to wrap his hand in a bandage. He just looked at it and thought, *And then this happened.*

His mind was raging. He had already made a fool of himself in front of Crimson. He already looked like an idiot. What more harm could arriving late and bleeding do? *None. She'll understand, maybe.*

He grabbed his keys and his credit chip and stuffed them in his pocket with his left hand. He was bleeding all over his office floor, but his obsessive nature couldn't handle the thought of any of his blood staining his clothing. He opened the large, black security door that led out to the slums. They were always dangerous, but even more so at this time of night.

He slammed the door behind himself and locked it. He looked into the direction of his home, about three miles to the west of his office. He could make it well within time if he ran. He crouched low with one knee to the ground, the other to his chest, and both palms on the concrete sidewalk. It was the same stance an athlete would take before hearing the shot that would signal the start of a race.

Zarfa woke in a puddle of stale, sticky, stinking blood on his bed around him. The shot had grazed him a little harder than he had imagined. He still couldn't tell if he was awake or dreaming. He was discombobulated and wasn't even sure where he was. He had gone to bed at two in the afternoon. It was now nine.

The last seven hours had felt like an eternity. His mind had been racing with thoughts of his recent fight, the events at Max's office, the woman he had seen on the street, his sister, her abduction, and the death of his parents at the wasp raiders when he and Sarah had been mere children.

It was torment, one flashback after another. *This is hell. I did die.* But he shrugged his shoulders and twisted over to his right side, planting the palms of his hands on the bed and pushing his upper body up. He could feel the blood. His brain had a hard time grasping where it had come from. Finally, he realized it was his.

He slung his legs over the side of his bed and felt a sharp pain from his side where the bullet had glanced him. He put his hand on the wound; the bleeding had slowed and his shirt was ruined. His fifth and sixth ribs on the left side were fractured and no doubt oozing blood. They ached as he took every breath and tortured him.

I should have asked for painkillers while I was at the doctor's.

He drew his hands to his sides and planted his feet on the floor in front of him. He looked down at his feet. No wonder they were sore and felt sweaty. He hadn't even taken his boots off before he passed out. His mouth was dry; the blood loss and the hours without fluid had dehydrated him. He stumbled over to his kitchen sink and filled a glass from the tap. He gulped the water down as fast as he could. It tasted metallic and was repulsive unfiltered, but he was *so* thirsty. He poured another. As he finished drinking, he looked down at his side. He couldn't see much through his blood-stained, torn t-shirt, but it looked bad.

That's going to get infected, and it hurts like hell. I'd better see if the doc is still around.

Zarfa filled his glass a third time, drank it down as fast as he could, and prepared himself to go back to the clinic. He had no idea if Max would still be around, but he had to try. He felt the inner seam of his pocket. He had passed out with the gauss pistol still holstered there. *Stupid*. If the gun hadn't have been empty, he could have blown his leg off in his sleep, or worse.

He went over to the bed, picked up the two devices that the assassins had been wearing, and put them in a small backpack lying by his bed. He assumed them to be cloaking devices and probably of some value, even if he didn't know how to activate them. He had never seen some of the technology that prevailed in Alexarien. He couldn't be faulted for being ignorant as to how it functioned, but one thing he knew well from his home was the art of bartering.

Zarfa slung the backpack over his shoulders and winced. It hurt moving his left arm. He was glad he hadn't been shot on the right. He was ambidextrous, but he did tend to favor using his right. He looked around the make sure there wasn't anything else he thought he might need to take with him. He didn't see anything. Considering his condition and the part of the city he was in, he began to wish he did know how to use the cloaking devices.

"Oh well." He sighed to himself as he walked out the door.

"Where ya goin,' docta?" questioned the leader in a group of five men approaching Max.

They were obviously a gang and out seeking some easy money. Max thought he could hold his own against one if he was in peak condition, but right now, his body was wracked with the effects of a boost addiction.

His heart began to pound; he was afraid. It felt as if there was a stone beating against his rib cage. He no longer worried about getting to his house on time. He was now worried about getting there alive.

Why did I lock the door behind me? Why didn't I look around more carefully? I know it is dangerous out here.

"Only trying to get home and see a girl, gentlemen. No need for violence and robbery."

He didn't stand. He stayed in the position ready to sprint, wishing he had done so only moments earlier.

"Who said anything about that sort o' nonsense, doc?" the leader questioned, approaching Max at a calm pace.

There was still some distance between Max and the gang. He didn't recognize these men as any of the junkies he had shooed away. He didn't know them at all. *The only reason they know I'm a doctor is the big, stupid neon sign right above me. Curse my luck.*

These men feigned innocence, but they had a threatening semblance. They appeared as a pack of wild hyenas smiling, laughing, goading as they approached, waiting to encircle their prey. Two of them were fat, merely bloated bodies to add intimidation by numbers. The leader, however, was well muscled and carried himself like a leader of vermin would. He appeared to be fast; his stature seemed strong. The other two men in the group appeared to be his support, and all of these three apparently had seen their fair share of fights, or muggings anyway.

"Looks like you should see a doctor," the leader said with a chuckle, his eyes resting on Max's right hand.

"You're right, I should. Why, I hadn't even realized I was injured," replied Max sarcastically.

The men in this gang were grinning wide, evil smiles. Smiles of destruction, smiles of executioners. Despite the playful banter, Max could tell they weren't in the business of leaving men alive.

Enough games, it's time to leave them in my dust.

Max took off in a sprint, running to the right of this pack of evil men. He was trapped on his left because the buildings lined the sidewalk, but to the right was the broad, open space of the road. Hovercraft passed by at an alarming speed, but the streets were far from crowded right now and he felt safer taking his chances there than on the sidewalk with those five rabid dogs who claimed human suits.

The burst of energy let forth from his leap off the ground

was enough to get him going at a good running pace from the get-go. He ran down the street, avoiding the men entirely. A hovercraft passed between the group and Max right as he had started his run toward freedom.

Hopefully, they won't chase.

Max turned his head to look behind and saw he had no such luck. The two fat ones stayed behind, but as for the leader and his two cronies, they were in hot pursuit of what they saw as easy prey. In only seconds, Max had made it to the end of the block and hooked a sharp left at the intersection. This turn would take him toward the direction of his house and a better part of town. One where there would be a police presence that would stop an unseemly affair such as what was going on here in the slums.

Only three more miles of this. I can do that.

Suddenly, his optimism left him as he felt a rope wind around his feet. One of the men was an expert with throwing weapons and had a shiruken-type device with a rope on it. As the rope wound and twisted around both of Max's feet, he tripped. Everything felt like slow motion as he began to fall.

His head, face first, struck the concrete with a strong force. The blow dazed him and he felt as if someone had kicked him in the head. He tried to shrug off the pain and get back up; it was hopeless. His feet were bound and he barely managed to roll over onto his back by the time the three had caught up with him.

"Here's for trying to run," one of them said as he dropped to the ground beside Max and punched him square in the nose.

The man then climbed on top of Max and proceeded to hit him in the stomach. If he wanted Max dead quickly, he would keep working his head. He didn't. This sadist wouldn't be happy until Max's internal organs were liquefied from his violent pummeling.

Then suddenly, a crack. *It sounds like lightning. Great, I get rained on when I die.* New pain was no longer upon Max. Just the dull ache from falling and taking several blows. The man who had been hitting Max was now lying on top of him, limp. Lifeless.

Max had no idea what was going on. He was confused by the unpredicted onslaught of the ambush right outside his clinic. He was baffled by how quickly he had been caught. He was thrown into utter bedazzlement by the rain of blows he had suffered, and now, the man dead on top of him didn't make sense.

Did I kill him with my mind? What's going on?

"Unless you all want to die like your friend here, I suggest you leave. He makes the third life I've taken today. *I'm not afraid to go as high as seven!*"

The voice of a guardian from the void, of a stone cold beast, of a dark mystery that had seen horrors Max couldn't even imagine. A voice of familiarity even though he had only heard it speak a few times earlier that day.

"Zarfa?"

"Yeah, Max. Stay down until I tell you."

Max peeked out from under the corpse of the man on top. *How did he kill him so quickly?* Zarfa stood like a gargoyle ready to fend off any evils that may approach. Max couldn't have had been more grateful in that moment.

Another crashing crackle came and the sky lit up with magnificent white light that revealed to Max that Zarfa was injured. This time, it *was* lightning, which meant one thing. *Rain, great. I do die in the rain.*

The remaining four approached Max and Zarfa, intent on killing them both. They most likely weren't going to let Max live before Zarfa's intervention. However, any chance of a peaceful resolution was completely gone from sight. Zarfa took a relaxed stance and seemed to be leaning back with his hips jutted forward and his shoulders slinking back. Max thought it was a bizarre way to be standing if you valued your life.

The leader of the gang and the other fit one were rushing at Zarfa with murderous intent. The two fat ones were trailing behind. It had only been a block and a half run, but they were already winded. As the two fighters closed in on Zarfa, they split directions at the last second, one to Zarfa's right, the other to his left in an attempt to flank him and sandwich him in an attack.

It failed. Zarfa jumped straight into the air and did the splits, sending fierce kicks with his boots into both of his enemies' throats. His movement was so fast, so elegant, so graceful, even a martial arts master wouldn't have seen it coming. The two men dropped to the ground clutching their throats, gasping for air. He had no doubt crushed their wind pipes, but Zarfa wasn't the kind to take chances.

He quickly dropped on top of the leader's neck with both of his knees, then in one quick movement, jerked his head to the side with all the force his legs could muster. One loud pop as rain began to pour on them all. The leader was dead and the two fat men who had caught up began to slink away. There was no way they were going to fight Zarfa if he didn't press the issue.

"Four," Zarfa said matter-of-factly as he walked over to the other man he had dropped with his double-kick counter attack.

This man was obviously the throwing weapons expert who had managed to entangle Max. You could tell by the variety of objects he had strapped to and hanging from his outfit. Knives, axes, darts, and tools of entrapment. He was still gasping for air; the blow must have collapsed his windpipe.

Zarfa removed the gun from his inner seam pocket and shot an evil stare over at the two fat cowards still worming their way backward. Rain poured down on all of them and lightning flashed again.

"*Five!*" Zarfa screamed as he pistol whipped the back of the man's head.

The first blow made a thud, the second a wild crunch, and the third revealed blood, bone, and grey matter. Zarfa removed two throwing axes from the man's body and stepped toward the fat henchmen.

"I've had it with this damn city, the dogs and filth never sleep here," he muttered.

Terror consumed their faces and death had already glossed over their eyes. They knew their fate was close at hand.

Zarfa dropped the pistol and kicked it straight up in the air, sending it launching into the sky. In almost the exact same instant, he threw an axe with each hand. Both axes hit their marks nearly simultaneously right in the center of the henchmen's flabby chests, burrowing through the sternums and splitting their rib cages. The gauss pistol came falling right in front of Zarfa's face and he grabbed it midair and shoved it back into his pocket.

He walked over to the two fatties lying practically side by side, and after clubbing them both in the throats for good measure to be sure they were dead, he stood and triumphantly, proudly stated, "Seven" loud enough for Max to hear despite the noise of the rain drops falling all around them.

And then, silence. The rain still fell and made pitter-patter noises on the concrete and asphalt. The thunder rolled and boomed in the sky; the lightning cracked with an intensity that displayed immense power, but as Max crawled out from under the first of the gang that Zarfa had killed, it seemed to him as a symphony of silence.

By the time Max freed himself from the corpse and stood, Zarfa was at his side.

"I thought you were a well-respected doctor and an asset to your community. What's this all about, doc?" Zarfa asked, raising an eyebrow.

"Greed, I suppose. I don't know these men at all."

"It's a good thing I needed to see you. I get the feeling you usually aren't around this part of town this late or else you'd be smart and carry protection. I couldn't help but notice on my way over this area is riddled with killers, junkies, and prostitutes, either of their own volition or their pimp's."

"Yeah, this 'fine' area is home to a lot of 'winners'... It has real heroes here, too, though. People working minimum wage to keep their families fed. People who show love and natural affection to their own and even strangers in a world that is severely lacking. That's why I opened my clinic. I see you've been wounded...again." Max's last statement was referring to Zarfa's new wound, as well as his already healed battle scar.

One of Max's eyes was swelling from the beating he'd taken, he was in severe pain, and though his mind was still racing about his meeting with Crimson tonight, he couldn't help but give attention to Zarfa's condition. Max was, first and foremost, a doctor. He cared about people, even when he didn't want to.

"This? Old woman with a bad aim tried to take me out for grocery money," Zarfa said with the slightest note of sarcasm.

"Oh, really? Must have been one of those heroes I told you about. I'll bet her family is starving."

"Must be."

"Let's get you back to the clinic. It's only a block and a half. You look like hell and it's the least I can do," Max said, offering his shoulder as a crutch.

Zarfa may have recently killed five more men and made it look easy; he may be a ferocious wounded animal with no regard for lives other than his and the ones he was seeking to protect, but he was still human. He saw Max's kindness and put his right arm around his neck, resting his hand on Max's right shoulder. "Thanks, doc," he said solemnly.

"Don't worry about it. I'll bill you for personal assistance," Max said, smiling.

Zarfa sucked up the pain and didn't so much as limp or gasp on his way back to the clinic. He couldn't help but notice the lacerations on Max's hand as they walked back. The rain had washed off all of the blood and it looked like gaping chasms of skin leading to his tendons.

Max unlocked the large, black iron door that led into the clinic and made Zarfa stand on his own as he pushed it. As the door creaked open, Zarfa saw the glass scattered on the floor and the blood trailing to the door. It looked as if someone had robbed the place, but he knew no one had. They both stepped in and Max turned on the lights.

"Looks like they tried to jump you in here, doc."

Max paused. "Nah, I was struggling with myself. Something I thought I had conquered... Guess not."

"Yeah, I'll bet there is a story that goes with it. I'm probably unworthy," Zarfa said in all seriousness.

"Nah, you aren't unworthy. But it really isn't worth your time. It's pathetic and not worth anyone's time. Now, let's get some medifoam on that injury of yours."

Max had already gotten a can out and began to shake it. Zarfa tensed up. He had been through a lot of pain in his lifetime, but he still hated the sting of medifoam.

"Not to sound gay or anything," Max said sarcastically, "but I really need you to take off your shirt for me."

Zarfa smiled slightly; he respected Max and even tried to banter with his humor earlier. He felt as if he failed. He didn't know Max well enough to know if he truly saw or appreciated it. As he peeled off his shirt, he let out a sigh and his mind wandered.

This has been a bizarre day. I hated this guy and his fake sincerity earlier today, but I think it is real now. Damn idiot would be dead, though, if it wasn't for me. Maybe he will give me the next four treatments free. I don't know, what's the harm in asking?

Zarfa threw his shirt into the trail of broken glass on the floor; he didn't care. It had a hole in it and was covered in more than his own blood. He would leave it. He raised his left arm and got ready for the medifoam. He drew a long, deep breath and held it.

"Fire away, doc," he said.

Without the least bit of hesitation, Max stuck the nozzle into the wound, touching one of the broken ribs. He pulled the trigger and the stinging bite of the medifoam struck Zarfa with an intensity that he wasn't prepared for. It wasn't a high level of pain, but it reminded him of the way the sting felt from the giant wasp that had nearly killed him. The pain he felt that nearly crippled him and stole his breath was emotional trauma, and no matter how many times he tried to prepare for it, he was never ready.

"Done, and done," Max said as he pointed to a bed on the far side of the room near the waiting area. "Lay over there, get some rest. There is a mini-fridge under the desk. Help yourself to whatever is in it, get lots of water. Thank you for all that you've done and I really hope I don't seem ungrateful, but I need to run. It's ten-forty-five and I was supposed to meet someone at eleven. I am so late and I hope she is there. Really! Thanks! I mean it, and I know I am in an awful condition, but you will be better in the morning. I will tend to mine then; it will all work out. I have to meet Crimson."

"You have a dying patient and you abandon him for a date?"

"You aren't dying. I diagnosed your wound and it was pretty peripheral. You will be healed by the morning with the foam."

"She must be special."

"It isn't like that."

"No?"

"No. She is beautiful, but she promised to answer questions that you wouldn't, so I am off to discover."

"And what if I rip you off and steal everything while you are away?"

"You saved my life; you earned it."

"Take this. You need it more than I do," Zarfa said, handing Max the gauss pistol.

"It isn't even loaded. There are no bullets in this thing."

"Just wave it around. Trust me, it makes a lot of folks jumpy enough they won't try anything."

With that, Max was on his way out. As the black door slammed shut behind him, Zarfa could barely see him sprinting with all of his might off into the darkness and the rain.

Max lived three miles from his clinic. No matter how fast he ran, he wouldn't be there in time.

He arrived at his apartment half an hour later. It was roughly eleven-fifteen and he hoped Crimson was at his door. He hoped she wasn't a stickler for time. He hoped Zarfa didn't really rip him off and take everything out of the clinic.

As he rode the elevator, noticing he could only see out of one eye, his mind raced. His day had been crazy, so much excitement, so much near death... Then it hit him—anxiety and craving. The same as before. He was anxious and he craved a boost. He could tell his mind would continue racing.

You've been clean almost three years before today. Come on, think! Relax. Breathe. You don't need a boost, Max, you don't. Your cells are telling you that because they are weak. Just...breathe.

Max took a deep breath and, determined to calm down, held it until he heard the elevator ding. Sixteenth floor—it was his stop. He stepped out and looked down the hallway toward his apartment, 203. The hallway was well lit and he saw nobody. He let out his breath and came to grips with the fact Crimson had left.

He walked sullenly down the hallway to his door.

It wasn't his fault he was attacked by a gang of lowlifes. She didn't know that, though. Maybe she didn't even know where he lived in the first place! Maybe it was all a joke! Maybe she was at some other random Max Hall's apartment waiting for him.

He had reached his apartment door, but his thoughts continued like before, racing and contradicting. He was tired and defeated. He was going to go in and sleep. He felt sick to his stomach and the sweating and tremors had started again. He cursed the day he ever took his first boost.

He swung the door open and, dripping wet from the rain still, stepped into his apartment. He fondled the wall, searching for a light switch as he closed the door behind himself. There was a brief moment where the light from the hallway was extinguished behind the closed door and it was utter blackness before he flipped the switch. As it flashed on with a flick, he was blinded again from his eyes adjusting to bright white radiance.

"Hey there," she said, lying on the couch with a totally bored look on her face. "You're late!"

Max panicked and, out of reflex, threw himself backward against his door, catching a doorknob to his left kidney. He writhed in pain and flopped himself face-first onto the floor, battering his already agitated bruises. He rolled around for a second then crawled to his knees and looked up toward Crimson lying on his grey suede couch.

"Oh, so you've been doing antics like that all the way here? No wonder you're late, and no wonder it looks like a crowd walked on your face. I would have thought you had been attacked, but after that showy display, I think you just walked into every blasted sign on the way over!"

Crimson stood from the couch and Max couldn't help but notice the white leather high heels she was wearing. Her peach dress with white Celtic knots complemented her hair, eyes, and skin. There he was, bloodied, bruised, and dripping with rain, feeling as if he had stood a date up at a fancy restaurant. Even more confusing, they were on their way to Psyker Scream.

"I was attacked," he muttered out, feeling stupid after his frightened display.

"I'm sure you were. We are already late and I am doing this for you. How quickly can you get changed?"

"Five minutes."

"Atta boy! Go make yourself pretty for me. I'll be waiting," she said in a tone Max couldn't decide was seductive or not.

When he returned three minutes and twenty-six seconds later, he was washed, smelling nice, and wearing a paisley-patterned silver and black button-down shirt that matched his form nicely, as well as a pair of blue jeans and black combat boots. He was hoping that he wouldn't fight any more this evening, but he no longer knew what to expect. His eye was swollen and throbbed. He wanted to sleep, even though he'd spent most of his day in a drug-induced coma.

"Well, after seeing you, nothing I can do would compare," he said with sincerity.

"Don't suck up for our school days, Max," she scoffed.

"I'm not. I mean it. I didn't even expect you to be here when I didn't see you in the hall. Thus, the frantic throwing myself into the doorknob. You know, I don't make it a favorite pastime to do activities that will make me piss out blood in the morning, right?"

She let out an innocent giggle and smiled with her feline teeth glinting in the light, inviting him toward her. "The way you threw yourself into that doorknob, you could have fooled me," she said with a smirk.

"I was trying to. By the way, not that I am complaining or anything, but how did you know where I lived? And how did you get into my apartment?"

"Wouldn't you like to know?"

"That's why I asked."

"Too bad. You ready to get a move on or what?"

Completely perplexed, Max just stared Crimson in her majestic eyes. He thought about saying nothing, but then decided against it. "I'm locking it behind us. Unless you know some reason I shouldn't."

"I don't know anyone dumb enough to not lock their door when they aren't around. Even in this nice neighborhood," she said with a smile. "Now come on before it's over. You have to see this."

At that, he locked the door, she took him by the hand, and down the hallway they strode.

Six

The Show

"So, tell me...what do you hear?"

"Hear? Are you nuts? I give the Psyker Scream bots at my clinic. I've never even dreamt of giving them to myself."

Crimson and Max had shown up late to the Psyker concert. The fans were in the audience, not behaving the way one would think for a metal techno fusion band that boasted the world's most amazing and bizarre acoustics known to man. Instead of the crowd shoving, moshing, hopping, and crowd surfing, they were standing there doing nothing but staring at the stage. Some of the fans were staring at each other, but nobody was acting rowdy.

It was surreal. The band members—Surge, Zax, and Badger—were all on stage. They were apparently playing their instruments. The set had started about an hour before Crimson and Max arrived, but nobody seemed to respond to the music; nobody showed any form of excitement.

"So, you don't hear anything? Nothing at all?" Crimson asked, staring intently at Max.

"No."

"Close your eyes; try harder."

Max looked at Crimson as if she had lost her mind completely. How many times did he have to tell her that he didn't have the modifications? There was no way for him to hear the music. He drew a breath in deep. He was in pain from the beating he'd taken earlier; his eye was still swollen, and his hand had a stinging pain from the cuts he'd inflicted on himself. He held his breath for a count of five and closed his eyes as he released it. He concentrated on trying to hear the guitar.

"Where. Was. The. Blind. Guard. Tree. Yellow."

Max opened his eyes and looked at Crimson; he gave her a befuddled expression. "What did you say?" he questioned.

"I didn't say a thing, big boy." Her tone was purposely seductive and condescending at the same time. "So, tell me, what do you hear?"

"Words. They don't make any sense, though. They're just...swimming, disconnected. I don't know how to describe it other than that. They're in my head. It sounds like switching between broadcast signals very rapidly and all you catch is one word on every station."

"Keep listening, keep trying to hear," she said in a soothing voice, running her hand in a downward stroke from his forehead to his chin, closing his eyelids.

It would be nice if you told me what I was trying to hear.

He kept his eyes closed and tried to clear his thoughts. He could feel that Crimson had moved her hand back to his forehead and was resting it ever so gently on him. He kept hearing words. None of them made any sense; none of them conjugated. Then, suddenly, he felt a deep reverberation shaking him. It felt as if his bones could hear thunder rolling though his body.

He couldn't hear the tremendous bass that was rattling him, but he sure could feel it. He wasn't even sure if it was real. He wasn't sure if he opened his eyes that he would still hear it, so he kept them shut. Suddenly, he heard a buzzing as if it was piercing through his head; the noise didn't hurt, but it felt awkward and intense.

"What does it sound like?"

"Droning, it sounds like droning, but I can't hear a thing."

"Wait for it."

"Wait for—" He let out a scream of agony as he clutched his head and dropped to his knees. A screech more intense than anything he had ever heard before pierced through his head and shattered his nerves. The noises he felt and heard, the voices in his head, all disappeared and it was back to the way it had been the moment he walked in with Crimson. There was nothing he could hear other than her.

"Want to know what that was?" she inquired of him.

"Kinda .It hurt like hell whatever it was."

"I'll tell you, but not here; it isn't safe. Let's head back to your apartment."

Not safe? Great, I've only been attacked by five men to-night. What else could possibly go wrong? What world does this chick live in? What is "unsafe" to her?

"What do you mean not safe here?" he asked as he rose to his feet. Max glanced around to see that most of the fans were beginning to open their eyes and look around. The three band members were staring right at Crimson and him, no longer playing their musical instruments. He suddenly felt very, very uneasy. The crowd of thousands was turning, facing the two of them.

"Uh...Crimson? I feel as if we might be unwelcome at this party. They seemed to have been enjoying until we arrived. Perhaps we should go."

"Start walking toward the door. I know the drill by now. We should be fine."

"Should be? Why can't we just be fine? How about that? I like that idea."

"Shut up and start walking."

She placed her hand on his back between his shoulder blades and drew his body into hers, spinning him to face the exit. They were walking across a concrete floor and her heels were making what seemed to be an awful racket in the dead silence of the crowd. He could feel the eyes burning their skin as they walked, like prey waiting for an attack.

"If it isn't our friend Crimson!" one of the members shouted from behind them.

"It's Badger, their vocalist, keep walking," said Crimson under her breath.

Max didn't have anything funny or sarcastic to quip back at her with. He was genuinely afraid, even more so than he had been earlier that day.

"Stop them!" Badger commanded.

At his command, the crowd rushed up the stairs. In a matter of seconds, they were surrounded by a mob. Every face was glaring at the two of them with intense anger and hatred. It sent shivers down Max's spine. Crimson could feel it, but she kept breathing normal as if she wasn't even phased.

"They're going to kill us, aren't they?" Max questioned.

"Probably."

How does he know I'm not going to rip him off? Or rav-age his place for the fun of it? He doesn't know me, and he trusts me like this?

Zarfa's thoughts were hard for even him to imagine. As long as he had drawn breath, he'd never known trust. Maybe he had...before his parents had been taken. Maybe before then he'd had trust.

He had trust that when he came home his parents would be there. He had trust that his sister would be in the crib as usual; his mom would feed him a snack when he got home from school. Because, in thousands of years of history, some things had never changed. His father would be at work when he got home; his mother would be there to attend to his needs as she had done to Sarah all day when he was at school.

But trust now? Trust was gone. Trust had vanished the day his parents were abducted by the raiders; it died the day Sarah had been taken. Trust wasn't a thing he gave out freely. Protection, yes. But trust? No. He didn't trust anyone, and with his less than amiable demeanor, nobody trusted him. People in Ilyeion had seen him kill over a drunkard try-ing to get fresh with his sister. And not only the drunk... His friends too.

So why did Max trust him?

Why did Max trust me enough to leave me here? For all he knows, I could steal all of his stuff. What was he in a hur-ry to do? He left with such haste.

Zarfa wanted answers, so he began to look for clues around the office. He stepped over the broken glass strewn on the floor. It crunched under his boots, making a soft crackling noise. Zarfa approached the desk Max had closed in a hurry and noticed the serenity boost in the waste basket.

Nothing was out of the ordinary other than the broken mirror and the blood mixed with glass trailing to the door-way. It looked as if the battle with the five gang-bangers had started here. He already knew it hadn't, which made him all the more eager to investigate further. He gazed around the clinic, which was really only a small room with a sub-divider marking the waiting area and entrance from the office and diagnostic room. Privacy wasn't much of an issue in the slums and, if it was, Max could ask the other patients to wait outside of the building until their turn. His gaze fixed solidly on the Psyker bot injections Max had lying on the counter of the exam area.

It isn't theft if I pay. I don't know what these cloaks are worth, and for all I know, it will cover it. Plus, I gave him that gun.

The fact he'd saved Max's life barely crossed Zarfa's mind. He was about to steal his next four treatments then finish the night by rooting around for some painkiller boosts. He knew that the treatments for the Psyker bots would cost another forty thousand credits he didn't have and would take awhile to raise fighting in the underground. He also knew he had a fight to perform at in roughly eighteen hours, and he reasoned a guy like Max would know what these two devices he had in his bag would be worth. For all Zarfa knew, they were worth way more than what he was taking.

Zarfa opened his backpack and left the two cloaking devices on Max's desk. He then went over to where he saw the Psyker injection ampoules and stuffed four into his backpack. He was far from greedy. After having such a violent reaction to the first round of treatment, Zarfa was nervous at the least, but confident that he had observed what Dr. Hall had done to him well enough that he could do it to himself.

After putting the treatments in his bag, he zipped it tight. Zarfa thought about putting the backpack on and going back to his own place. The medifoam had begun to regenerate his tissue and ease his pains. In no time at all, he would be healed. He could hear it raining outside still, however, and the thought of walking shirtless with a backpack that had uncomfortable straps in the cold rain was less than pleasurable.

He saw his old bloody, wet, tattered shirt lying in the trail of glass where he had thrown it. He let out a sigh and decided to rummage around. He found a green t-shirt with grey trim in a hamper against the wall in the corner behind Max's desk. It smelled dirty, but he put it on anyhow. It was too short and his midriff showed like a skanky teenage girl who had grown too large for her extra-small-sized shirt, but he wore it anyway.

Zarfa looked at himself in a small mirror on the counter by the sink in the section of the room Max did examinations and decided he didn't care. If anyone questioned it, he would kill them. After deciding that his pseudo payment was good enough for the injections and the shirt, he grabbed his backpack and headed out the door. He was sure to close it behind himself. He felt bad that he couldn't lock it to keep all of the lowlifes in the area from easily getting into Max's office and making off with his goods, but he didn't have a key.

I knew there was something I had forgotten. Recruitment is tonight.

Zarfa's mind raced as rain came down upon him. He had his own reason for doing what he had been doing, but he thought it would be good to go to recruitment night anyhow and see what they had to say. Maybe his cause was the same as their own; maybe he would find allies in this battle he was fighting by himself. How would he know if he didn't go to the event?

What have I got to lose? If I don't like what they're all about, I can simply walk away and do my own thing. But the saying goes, "My enemy's enemy is my friend."

"We thought we told you to stay out of here," stated Badger.

Crimson smiled wide and scanned him up and down. Her mind raced as she thought of the best way to deal with the situation. She had done some spying into the Psyker Scream phenomena and she'd gotten too close to the truth without joining them.

"You did... I kinda thought that maybe you would be lenient with me since I brought a guest," she said sarcastically.

"Oh? So now I have to kill the both of you? And this poor sap probably doesn't even know what he has gotten into with you."

"I don't! Take the girl," Max said to lighten the mood, half joking...half not.

Crimson glanced over at Max, half annoyed, half impressed. She expected him to be wetting himself like a school child. She could feel that he was afraid, but by this point, she figured they would leave alive since Badger hadn't ordered them killed yet.

"Let's face it here; the only three of you who can really fight at this place are you, Surge, and Zax. This is only a base recruitment, and all of these guys are green. I can tell by looking. Max here can't fight; you can tell by his face..." She lingered in her sentence. "So let's just say you let us off with a warning? I know you gave me an ultimatum last time—join or die. Be fair, I may not join you, but Max here has no clue what is going on. He may very well join you."

Her speech was clear and firm; she spoke as if it weren't for the three that comprised Psyker Scream, she could kill everyone in that room with ease. She turned her gaze from Max back to Badger. She wore a crazed look, trying to stab through Badger with an evil gaze. Her hair had gotten wet and was frazzled and flopped over her face. As she spoke, she began grinning wide. Nobody would have taken her seriously except those who knew her reputation.

"He doesn't know a thing, huh? And you brought him here? Why?"

"You could call him your biggest proprietor in the slums. He is practically handing out the bots, which you should be ecstatic about. You know those bots cost a pretty penny, but Max here will let people pay in increments if only to have the pleasure of hearing your beautiful...*music.*"

Crimson didn't know if it was true or not. She hoped that Max would pick up where she left off if they questioned him. He stared Badger in the face as she spoke, not saying a word. His expression, if he was giving one that would give him away, was unreadable due to the beating he had taken earlier.

"Really? You have been treating people even if they can't pay in advance? And you don't know anything at all. Tell me, what did you hear tonight?"

Max sighed. "What is with that question? All friggin' night I hear that damn question, what did I hear? I'll tell you! A bunch of noise, noise that almost deafened me! Noise I couldn't care less about, and yes, I am handing out your bots with no regard. I know twenty percent die, which just means I need to take an educated risk. I need money to stay in business and treat my patients in the slums, even if ingrates live there that would slay me for whatever gain they could possibly take from me. But Psyker patients are some of my only paying clients. Sometimes a patient comes in who can only afford the first treatment. If they come back for the second, I finance them up front as long as they sign a contract stating that they will pay me back in a reasonable time. So I don't have a damn clue what the hell it is your little club is doing. I wasn't that interested before and I am even less interested now! You leave us be and I'll keep doing business at my practice the same way as I always have. It seems as if it is benefitting you, so killing me would be to your disadvantage, it appears. Not that it will deter you, but it is certainly worth thinking about." Max stated it all as if he had authority to command the whole crowd.

"You've got some balls, Max, and you don't know who this woman by your side is at all, do you?" Badger questioned, raising an eyebrow and giving Crimson a look that could kill.

"Me? Ha! I've known Crimson since kindergarten. She was a mystery then and always will be. I don't really know her, but she came in today as a patient. I had a patient earlier that had received his first treatment for your little bots and I wanted answers because he was acting so...secretive. She offered to explain things a little. Now that I've seen this, I wish I had never asked."

"All right, let the doctor go. Take her to the back for interrogation and possibly execution. Max, forget what you've seen or heard here. This didn't happen. The second you say it did, you will suffer a worse fate than Crimson here."

Max was shocked; he hadn't expected his response to get this reaction. He had a sick feeling in his gut. He'd envisioned himself and Crimson either dying together or walking out together, not this. He felt as if he had done something wrong, as if he should do something else to save her. He looked at her frantically, terrified.

Crimson, still smiling, still looking insane, stared into his eyes and nodded. She didn't look worried at all. She looked as if she accepted her fate. She didn't look like someone who believed she would be executed.

"But—" Max began to object.

"Max, old friend. Please shut up. Do as the nice Badger-man says. They only want to have a friendly chat with me... He, his band, and these few thousand admiring fans, that is. Trust me, this is a mere tryst in the park for a girl like me. I'll be fine." There wasn't the slightest tone of fear in her voice. She either had a secret plan or really didn't care what happened to her.

Max couldn't help but wonder what would happen as he was thrown out into the rain in the back alley. The three men they had escort him hadn't been particularly gentle, and when they threw him out, they made sure to toss him on the ground and kick him in the ribs a few times. He would definitely hurt in the morning.

He stood after they left; he didn't want to get up too soon and risk another beating. He knew these men were vicious and meant business. He felt helpless, but like he wanted to help Crimson. What could he do? Walk back in waving a pistol?

Shit! Why didn't I draw it? Sure, even if it was loaded, I could kill only a few at best before they took us down, but if I reversed it and took Badger prisoner, they wouldn't kill us. They'd let us be until we could get far enough away to outrun them.

"Funny seeing you here."

Max heard Zarfa behind him. It was total déjà-vu. He should have felt relief—Zarfa had saved him only hours ago—but he didn't. His stomach twisted in knots. Zarfa, as far as he knew, was one of *them*.

"I could say the same," Max stated, not turning around to face him.

"You could? Why? Because I've never had Psyker bot treatments? Oh wait..."

Max realized how stupid he sounded. He didn't need it rubbed in. He was nervous and thinking about too many things. Right now, he had been pondering over fifteen different plans to save Crimson—his wave a gun in Badger's face plan seemed the least stupid—and now he was trying to hold a conversation with someone he didn't know whether to count as friend or foe yet.

"I didn't know they would accept you after only one treatment?" Max questioned.

"They might not. I don't even know if I want to join them

yet."

"Then why the treatments if you don't want to join the rest of the 'Psyker Scream fans?'" Max asked. After the display that led up to him being kicked out of the warehouse, he assumed that there was more to this than them being a band.

"They are necessary for me to find my sister. People where I come from can see the raiders as they come down upon us from the sky. By then, it's already too late. I intend to be the only one who can hear them before they come...where they hide."

Max stood there agape. He couldn't believe Zarfa was letting him into his history, his psyche. He knew he needed to be cautious, but for now, he may as well consider Zarfa a friend, even if he did go with the whole "take a prisoner with an empty gun" routine. He didn't think Zarfa would rat him out.

"*Because it's mine...yellow...kitten.*" The words sang clear in Zarfa's head, but didn't make any sense. "What was that, Max?"

"What?"

"I thought you said something that didn't make any sense. Must have been my imagination."

"Perhaps."

"*It is in the...fifty-six...what about...midnight.*"

Zarfa shook his head. His vision was getting blurry like earlier that day. It wasn't pain; the medifoam had almost completely healed his fractured ribs as well as the soft tissues. He didn't hear the deafening pitches he had heard earlier, but he did hear chaos and confusion. It would come and go, sometimes up to a hundred different voices flooding his head.

"Max, I hear voices. They're in my head, but I can't make out what exactly is being said. Some are like whispers; others are screaming. None of them are talking to me, but all of them are talking to me! *What is this?*"

Max began to get more nervous than he already had been. His first thought was of a serenity boost, but he quickly pushed it out of his mind. *You don't need it, Max!* Then he thought about, only minutes ago, what Crimson had asked him, what he heard. He remembered hearing words in his head. Disjointed, unrelated words...only in his head, not in his ears.

"That's what she was trying to show me...but how?" Max pondered aloud as he looked at Zarfa in amazement. Max stepped over to Zarfa and rested a hand on his shoulder in a comforting manner. "Zarfa, breathe. Stay calm, I need you right now. Close your eyes, listen. Lock onto a voice and try to ignore the others. Tell me what you hear."

Zarfa was unnerved. He had never had voices in his head before. To make it worse, he had more voices than he could count at this point, some screaming, some whispering, others having a nonchalant conversation. He closed his eyes and did as Max instructed. He chose a voice that he found distinct and focused on it and only it. Slowly, the other voices began to fade, and Zarfa could now hear only this one man's voice clear as if he were talking to him in person.

"I hear a single man talking now," Zarfa stated. His voice was shaky.

The rain poured down upon them; the sky flashed with a brilliant, radiant white light. Thunder boomed and roared as the electricity arching from the ground upward hit the clouds and crackled. The raindrops splattered upon the concrete and asphalt that surrounded them and that fresh, clean smell filled the air. Despite the distractions of this and Max's voice, he held his thoughts on the lone voice now echoing in his brain.

"What's it saying, Zarfa?"

"He...it's a he. He is saying..."

"Looks like we have another visitor tonight! Not backup either, poor Crimson doll," Badger said as he backhanded her so hard across the face the room spun and a bit of blood trickled from her lower lip.

"Aww, too bad. I really thought a white knight was going to come and save me too," she said as she giggled like a little girl.

She stared into Badger's deep blue, almost purple irises. He stood several inches over her and was close to three hundred pounds. He wasn't fat by any means; he had a very muscular frame covered by only a thin layer of fat and a small paunch on his belly. He was one of the hairiest people one would ever lay eyes on; thick black and white hair peeked up through the collar of his tank top and caressed his chin, which displayed a neatly-kempt salt-and-pepper goatee.

His arms looked like a werewolf's; the hair was so thick one could barely see any skin. It crept all the way up his forearms and to his knuckles. One could swear he looked like a wombat who had put on a poorly crafted man costume. The hair on his head was wiry and wild. It looked as if he hadn't combed it for a week. Judging by his wrinkles and hair, he looked to be in his fifties, not your typical rock star these days. Then again, it wasn't your typical rock star that played music a person had to get his or her nerves modified to hear. It also wasn't the typical rock star who could command his fan base to do whatever his wishes were.

"We will see how funny you find this all when I use whatever means I see fit to extract information from you," he said as he uppercut Crimson, his blow striking her diaphragm.

Crimson fell to the ground, her diaphragm in spasm from the strength of the blow. She had been winded by his brutal attack and could barely breathe. She would have tried dodging it if she even had the faintest idea of how to get out of here alive. She wasn't a quitter, but she was smart when it came to being obstinate. No need to completely anger the dangerous man in front of all of his adoring fans, or fanatic army.

"Surge, Zax, take her to the back room. Chain her and guard her. She is more dangerous than you could even imagine. Don't let her get away. I want to know what she is planning," Badger commanded his lackeys telepathically.

Crimson knew he was doing it. She knew if her mind wasn't so clouded from the pain, she could make out some more of what was going on. As it stood right now, she couldn't concentrate enough to get more than faint, crossed signals and the occasional intermittent sentences. She was barely beginning to recover her breath when she was hoisted up by Badger's two cronies and taken away.

"Well, ladies and gentlemen," Badger said as he clapped twice, "open up the door and welcome our new guest."

Right as he finished his grandiose introduction, the doors swung open. They made a slight creaking noise as they did. In the doorway stood two shadowy figures; flashes of lightning illuminated the imagery behind them. The dim lighting inside the warehouse didn't do much to immediately reveal their faces. As they stepped forward, the crowd could see that there was a new face, as well as one they had told to get lost only ten or fifteen minutes ago.

"I thought I told you to get lost and forget about your friend...the girl."

"You did. I thought you would forgive me, however, seeing as I was coming with a guest of honor. I treated this man with the Psyker bots this morning. You see, he wanted to know where you all were so he could join your little club, and that's why I teamed up with Crimson to come here." Max had come up with that little lie on the spot and hoped Zarfa wouldn't fail him.

"Well, he is of no use to us yet...*doctor*. You see, we can sense him right now, but he can't sense us. He would have been able to find us on his own once he had completed his last round. So if you think you're helping by bringing fledglings that are still wet behind the ears, you're not. Make this one your last, or we will."

"I heard your voice from outside! Badger, right?" Zarfa piped up.

"Aww, how cute. The neonate heard his first words. Has he yet to speak any, though? I'll admit, this is impressive you selected a voice so easily, but you still aren't past the most dangerous part. We all know it is the third round of injections that has the highest mortality rate. How about you come back here once you've shot in all five? Okay? Now, *scram!*"

"How about a deal? I'll come back after the next four injections are done and join you? All I ask is that you let my doctor's friend go, fair?"

"Ha! Fair? You don't know what that woman is capable of, do you? Not surprising. Sorry, but I need her, or the information that she has anyhow. My offer is this, turn around, leave, and don't suffer the pain of being beat to death by an angry mob."

"Where is she?" Max demanded.

"Cute. She did mention a white knight coming to her aid; too bad it's you. I'll tell ya where she is, and what I plan to do to her too..."

Surge and Zax weren't too gentle as they threw her to the cold floor of the tiny back room. It couldn't have been more than ten-by-eight feet. It had a single bare bulb dangling from the ceiling keeping the room barely lit. There was a chair placed over the top of a drainage grate sitting as the center-piece of the room. The chair had leather straps for the hands and feet, and a chain collar connected to the ceiling and dan-gled down to the seat of the chair.

Surge kicked Crimson in the ribs to usher her to her feet; it worked. The pain prompted her to jump up from all fours to a standing position. She knew what they wanted. For her to sit in the chair. *Screw that.* Her eyes went wild, like a beast cornered. These two seasoned henchmen could see that she was still in control of herself despite her wild-eyed, crazy-looking mannerism.

Surge grasped at her wrist as fast as he could. He thought it would be as simple as pushing her down into the chair and overpowering her. She dodged backward as quickly as possi-ble. His movement seemed like a geriatric trying to catch a fly. Before either he or Zax realized it, she was behind the chair and had already thrown it at his head.

Her aim was true; the chair rebounded off of Surge's head, dropping him like a sack of bricks. Zax still barely realized that a fight had even begun. He pulled his pistol and aimed it at Crimson. In the time it took for him to draw his weapon, she was already flying in his direction, swinging on the chain that connected to the ceiling, using the steel collar as a foothold to gain momentum and balance.

As he raised his gun, but before he could shoot, she had already closed the gap and was sending the toe of her white leather lace-up heel straight into his temple. He dropped to the ground in immense pain, his pistol sliding across the floor. He wasn't unconscious like Surge was already.

He stumbled as quickly as he could to his feet, muttering profanities. Before he could even launch an attack of his own, she had managed to get behind him and put him in a sleeper hold. He shook wild and viciously with all of his strength, slamming her into the wall to get her off of his body. He couldn't, and, in seconds, he too was unconscious.

It isn't time to start a war yet. I'll leave them alive.

Crimson ran over to where Zax's gauss pistol had slid and picked it up. She didn't have any pockets in this dress to discreetly hide her newly acquired weaponry.

What the hell, I guess I will just have to run out toting two of them as accessories to my lovely ensemble.

Before stepping over the unconscious Surge, she stopped to examine his forehead. The chair had gashed it pretty hard and he was bleeding profusely. *He won't die from this, just be a little uglier.* Without hesitation, she removed his pistol from his person and held it in her other hand, dual wielding like a maniac one would see in some kind of comic book.

Her red hair was frazzled and flowed down to right past her shoulders. Her wild eyes darted mischievously, examining for any hidden trap, ambush, or enemy. Her muscles rippled as she hurried back toward the front entrance. Her cute party dress swayed over her toned physique as her heels clattered on the hard floor in the room that would be otherwise empty if it weren't for the nearly two thousand fans standing behind Badger. Someone other than her was currently holding their attention, but not for long.

Before the clatter of her heels had even registered as a noise out of the ordinary to anyone, two gun shots that definitely were unexpected rang out, causing everyone, including Max, Zarfa, and Badger, to jump. There was a clamor of swearing and remarks as the crowd turned to face Crimson. She saw that Badger, too, turned to face her. It took a few steps to get from the pit where she was standing up to the entryway where the doors were. He was elevated barely enough above the crowd that the two of them could look each other in the eyes.

"Your cronies are still alive, dick weed! That's what you get for trying to interrogate me. Next time, skip the theatrics and put a bullet or two in my head! Cut off my arms and legs or something! Give those guys a chance to handle me, all right?"

"Very well! Are you ready to fight my horde of faithful fans?"

"Think again," she screamed as she fired a warning shot that grazed Badger's ear.

Badger grabbed his ear as Max screamed, "Crimson!"

"That was a warning. I didn't come here looking for a fight. I didn't come here looking for a war. I came here to show Max some answers. I believe we have all we came for. Let us go or your brave and fearless leader Badger here will catch a double tap to the head. After that, I don't give a damn if you stomp me into the floor. At least I'll die happy!" Crimson ranted.

Her eyes were crazy as ever and now she had a wide grin on her face. If Badger didn't know any better, he would think that she was about to bite out his throat with her elongated feline-looking eye teeth.

Badger raised his hand and signaled for the crowd to do nothing, his other hand still pressed tightly to his bleeding ear. He didn't savor the idea of losing this fight, but he didn't savor the idea of losing his life either.

"Let them go," he said sternly.

"Oh, how kind of you, sweetheart," Crimson said with a chuckle as she made her way across the warehouse, up the few steps, and stood between Zarfa and Max.

Zarfa was on her left; Max was to the right. Both were shocked at what was going on. Zarfa hadn't planned for this to happen, neither had Max. Max was relieved they would all be leaving in one piece. Zarfa still wanted to know more, but assumed it would be better for him to come back after he finished the injections rather than press the issue tonight. Crimson knew she shouldn't test her luck and spark an outright war with the Psykers this evening, but her fingers were twitching on the triggers of her acquired pistols as if she wanted to unload every round into Badger's body.

She ran her tongue across her lips and tasted the blood from the split she had on her lower lip. "Call that graze on your ear even for the mark on my lip, *friend.* I'd love to kiss and make up, but I've got my hands full. On that note, I say g'night, pal. Don't even try to retaliate. You'll regret it."

Badger didn't say a word, just stared at her with the occasional glances over to Max. His solid expression screamed one word—murder. He would gladly do it the moment the time was right. He knew, too, that if he so much as gave her an inkling, she might die tonight, but so would he.

"'Til we meet again, love," he said with a wink.

At that, the three of them were off into the night. The darkness and the rain quickly shrouded which direction they headed. Their pace was quick until they were back into Crimson's part of town. It was about three in the morning. It was still dark, but the rain had subsided. They all looked tired and were still sopping wet.

"Well, doc. That wasn't how I thought my night would go at all. Look, in this backpack here, I've got the next four treatments. I watched you well enough I think I can give them to myself. I left two pieces of tech that I found on your desk as payment. I think they're cloaking devices, but I'm not sure. I've never seen tech like that. It's a long story, one I don't have time for now," Zarfa said as he turned his back to them and began his journey down the road.

"But! Wait!" Max shouted.

Zarfa hesitated then halted.

"Look, I'm grateful to you. You can have the bots, I don't care! You saved my life. I don't need your money. But re-think it, please? Didn't you see what was going on in there? The Psyker Scream phenomenon isn't some mere craze over fad music. It has to be something deeper."

"I'm already involved in something deeper, but thanks for the concern, doc."

"Max is right, you know. You might want to reconsider. If you don't choose wisely, you may wind up on the wrong side of a war that is about to begin. That isn't a threat, just a fact. Look, I would love to explain, but after tonight, I am quite tired and need to get my beauty rest. Zarfa? That's your name, right? Look, I recognize you from earlier today. I saw you stumbling around. First treatment today, right? You can't do another for, at the minimum, five days from now. Meet me tomorrow, mid-day at Max's clinic. I'll explain."

"Fine," Zarfa said, then proceeded to make haste in the direction he had originally started walking.

"You're staying the night with me," Crimson said with an eyebrow cocked.

Max's heart began to race and thump. He was nervous. The night had already been unpredictable, and now he had a beautiful woman not asking, but telling him he was going to stay the night? A beautiful woman still holding two loaded guns like they were toys. A beautiful woman who could kill him with ease regardless of which of the two of them were holding the pistols.

He cleared his throat and said with his voice crackling, "I am?"

Crimson could tell he was blushing, even if it was dark out. His face was a dead giveaway that he had taken her wrong. "Yeah, you are. They know you're Max. They know you're a doctor. They know your clinic is in the slums. Whether you're helping them or not...you've been seen with me; that makes you their enemy. I would say sorry, but you are the one who wanted answers."

"So you're protecting me?"

"I'm protecting myself. If they got to you, they would use you like a bartering chip to get me. I sorta like you. I don't want to kill you unless you give me no other option. So, you are staying here until I can escort you back and watch you. Once I explain it all, you will have to make a choice."

"What choice is that?"

"To make a difference, like you've always wanted to."

"And if I choose wrong?"

"You'll die, sooner or later. But hey, even if you choose right, the outcome will be the same. So don't let it get you down, chump."

They stood there staring at each other for awhile before Crimson turned toward the building that her apartment was in. She pointed to it and Max thought it was a joke. There was no way she could afford an apartment in this building. It was on the upper west side; this skyscraper was home to some of the richest individuals in all of Alexandria, let alone Alexarien.

"Right. You realize that apartments start at about a billion credits a month in this building? It's known to be a hotspot with every amenity anyone could want included in the fee. The person who built this was a genius."

"I know she is," Crimson said slyly with a Cheshire grin.

It took a moment to register in Max's brain. He felt the blood drain out of his face as he pondered what she meant. Finally, he opened his mouth. "You mean to say you built this?" he questioned.

"Exactly," she said, pointing to the top floor. "I own this whole thing, and I live on the top floor. So, you coming up of your own volition or am I going to have to make you?" she asked, placing the barrel of one of the pistols to his stomach and raising her right eyebrow in a playful manner.

Max's heart was fluttering and he was definitely overly excited about everything that had taken place in the last day. His life always seemed so dull and boring, but now, in mere hours, it seemed to be getting turned upside down.

"I guess I have no choice. Some mad woman wants to take me hostage as a sex slave," he said, smiling.

"Watch it, buddy. I can pull this trigger with ease. Now come on, let's get off the street and get dry."

The two of them rode her private elevator to the fifty-seventh floor. She had to swipe a key to get into it and it let them off right in her living room. The apartment was massive. It appeared to take up the entire top floor of the building. If she didn't own this building, it would have cost more than any sane human would pay to live in a high-rise complex.

The moment they stepped off the elevator, Crimson tossed the pistols across the room, pulled her dress over her head, and tossed it as well. With her back facing him, all she was wearing now was a pair of thong underwear and her white leather high heels. His heart began to throb, and he was clearly aroused. He let out a slight gasping grunt that caught her attention. Crimson turned her head and stopped to look at him as he stood there, awkward and confused.

"What? You've never seen a naked girl before? You're a doctor, right? And I was wet, give me a break. I'm going to my room to get something dry and comfortable. I'm sure I've got something in one of the guest rooms you can wear."

"I've seen naked women before socially and professional-ly. It's just...you're beautiful, and I didn't expect you to rip your clothes off like it was nothing."

"Oh really? You think I'm beautiful?" she asked rhetori-cally.

Before he could answer, she had turned and started walk-ing back toward him seductively. Her stomach was firm and cut, sleek and muscular. Her skin looked soft, and while and her breasts were small but perky, Max hadn't noticed earlier that she wasn't wearing a bra. He definitely noticed now.

He was nervous and embarrassed, as she slunk back to him. She stood only inches from his face and reached up, stroking her hand across his cheek and to the back of his head. She grabbed onto his hair and gave him a hard tug, pulling his head backward, and kissed his neck. It sent a shiver down his spine and a tingle across his legs.

"I'm nothing more than a terrible tease, Max. Pretend you only got to see me naked in a professional sense. I'm not going to sleep with you...tonight anyway," she said as she softly kissed his lips and let go of his head.

"I barely know you and I've already felt the full spectrum of love and hate for you in such a short period of time. I can only imagine if I pick the wrong side and wind up your enemy."

"You'll be dead too quickly to worry about it." She said it dry, flat, matter-of-fact.

At that, she turned and went into her bedroom. Max, still confused and feeling a bit used, stared at her and took note of how the muscles on her back and shoulders moved as she walked. The way her hips swayed—he couldn't tell if she was trying to be seductive or if she was so naturally. He wished he knew whether she was actually interested in him or only playing some sort of game.

"Besides, Max," he heard her holler from her bedroom, "it would be awful of me to take you to bed tonight when I've got a date planned with someone tomorrow."

"Right, I should have known. You have a line of men waiting to pleasure you." He said it sarcastically, but he was serious.

"You could say that."

When she returned, she had already gone to another one of the rooms and brought him out some new dry clothes. She was holding some comfortable plaid pajama pants and a black t-shirt for him to wear. She, herself, wasn't wearing anything fancy. Just some fuzzy white pajama pants with cargo pockets and a heavy metal band t-shirt that was too big for her.

In moments, she had transformed herself from a seductive vixen to a frumpy-looking housewife. She no longer looked crazy or untamable. She no longer looked like the wild woman who had almost gotten them killed and then subsequently rescued them in the same night. She no longer looked like the gun-wielding devil he had seen earlier. She now looked tame, domestic. She looked human to him. No longer did she look like an indestructible heroine from a comic book.

"Here, put these on. If you need your privacy, you can change in the first room to the right. It is one of the guest rooms," she said, throwing the clothes to him and pointing down the hallway she'd emerged from.

"Thanks," Max said.

She had been pretty open with her body, but Max was feeling insecure. He decided to take her up on the offer of privacy. He walked down the hallway and went into the room she had described. It was simple. It held a queen-sized bed on an oak frame and an elegant carbon fiber dresser. The room was simple, but felt comfortable and cozy.

He finished changing and turned around to walk back to the living room, only to be startled by Crimson standing in the doorway. He jumped a little, and wasn't sure if he was more startled by the fact he hadn't heard her creep up or the fact she was holding the pistols again. She had a smirk on her face. She no doubt saw his jumpy nature bleeding through into his every action.

"Don't worry, I only saw your back. To my disappointment, you already had the pants on by the time I came in."

"A pity for you."

"Indeed."

She handed him one of the pistols and stated, "One under your pillow, one under mine. The safety is on if we are attacked; don't forget it. I'm sleeping in here with you, so don't get any ideas. It's purely because it is safer to be together."

"Okay, I won't. Why don't we go to your room?"

"Nobody but me goes to my room. Now get in bed, Max, and let's get some rest."

As they lay in bed together, he couldn't help but realize they both smelled as if they'd had a hard day. It was a mixture of body odor and that smell rain and asphalt had when it mixed. It wasn't particularly bad, and there was a good distance between the two of them.

"Max?"

Her voice sounded soft, not like he had heard before.

"Yes?"

"Don't get the wrong idea, but can you hold me, please? It's been awhile since I've had company."

"Okay," he said as he nestled close behind her, putting his head on her shoulder.

"Thanks."

Crimson sighed and felt comfortable. She wasn't impervious; she had emotions and needs, even if she didn't show them, even if they were erratic. Her breathing began to deepen and match Max's. Before they knew it, they were both deep asleep.

Seven

You Say You Want a Revolution?

"Wake up, Max darling, wake up," Crimson said, her voice as soft as silk as she gently shook his shoulders.

She had been awake since seven that morning. She didn't need much sleep. She had already attended to some business, gotten dressed, and started breakfast. It was now ten o'clock. She tried to look as sweet as possible as she gently woke Max, and knelt next to him on the bed.

Max wasn't one for the morning; he hated waking up. To him, mornings were something to be loathed, not embraced, which was funny seeing as he routinely woke up at six every morning to open the clinic by seven. He grumbled under his breath and swatted at Crimson. He was lucky she didn't retaliate.

He stretched and sprawled, contorting his body in all sorts of unseemly positions as he made awful grumbles and hisses. At one point, Crimson swore he was cursing at her, but the words were barely audible and unrecognizable. She stared at him for a second. If the gentle approach wouldn't work, she would have to get rough.

She yanked the pillow out from under his head. His head flopped back and hit the gauss pistol she had instructed him to leave there during the night. It caused minimal discomfort, not enough to awaken him. Before he knew it, however, Crimson was raining down blows upon his face with the down pillow that had earlier been caressing his head, beguiling him with thoughts of more sleep.

"Wake up, sleepyhead! Wake up! Wake up! Wake up!" she shouted playfully, hitting him over and over.

Max grumbled and roared. He propped himself up quickly and was facing straight forward. He still was barely able to make words. They all sounded like noises a grumpy bear would make upon waking from hibernation. Signs of his waking didn't satiate Crimson's playful nature, however, as she blasted him straight in the face with the pillow so hard that it knocked him back to a laying position.

"C'mon, sleepyhead! Wake up!"

"I'm trying to! Stop hitting me, you frickin' lunatic! Damn it, you can be a beast!" he shouted back, less than playful.

"Yep, I sure can. Now, get a shower and change. There are clothes that might fit in the dresser across the hall in the guest room. I've started breakfast and I need to get back to it before it burns. What if I was an intruder, by the way? You would be dead for certain. Some good that gun would have done you under your head."

"When you shook me awake, I knew it was you! Of course I wasn't going to go for the gun. Knowing you, you would have had me disarmed and been pistol whipping me with it before I could even take the safety off!"

"True. Now get showered and dressed. You've got a big day ahead of you, *Doctor Max Hall, MD.*"

"I get the feeling you're making fun of me when you say *Doctor Max Hall,*" he said as he rolled his legs over the side of the bed and stood.

He opened his arms wide one more time, letting his pectorals stretch. He yawned loudly and bent down to touch his toes. He despised mornings, but somehow, yelling at Crimson had put him in a better mood to face the day. He'd started out angry when she was hitting him with the pillow, but as he yelled, he began to feel playful, almost like he should hit her with a pillow back in good spirits.

Max was always awkward, though, and didn't quite know how to treat girls who roughhoused with him. He liked Crimson; it was obvious, and he was beginning to feel a bit like a jerk for yelling. He knew he'd sounded gruffer than he meant.

As he continued to stretch, Crimson proceeded on her way out of the room. She was wearing tight blue jeans with a pattern on them of flames and dragons. She had on a short, camisole-styled shirt that was burnt orange in color that showed her midriff, and a tan shawl that covered only her shoulders and the upper portion of her chest.

Max loved her style. It was always unique. He had already seen her in three completely different outfits and he couldn't help but imagine what else she might have in her wardrobe. As she got close to the doorframe, only about a foot away from him, he was overtaken by a sudden spark of playfulness. Without warning, he leapt toward her, tackling her to the floor unexpectedly.

They both hit the short blue carpet that covered the floor with a thud. The breath was slightly knocked out of Crimson. She would have retaliated quickly and put him in his place if it wasn't for the fact that he was giggling like a child on top of her. She contorted her body and rolled, facing him.

"Guess I deserved that, eh, doctor?" she asked, eyeing him playfully.

"Sure did. Sorry for being so grumpy, but you woke the beast in his cave."

"Good to know the beast takes a long time to awaken before he pounces. Not to kill the playful atmosphere or anything, but I need to go attend to breakfast before it burns."

"Nope. You're at my mercy now," Max said as he got his hands ready to tickle her.

Without warning, she leaned up and bit his bottom lip—hard. "Unhand me or else I'll show you a real beast," she mumbled, her words muffled by the fact she had his lip between her teeth.

"Okay, okay," he said, putting his hands up in surrender as he tried to stand.

She clung with her teeth to his lip until she had it stretched as far as she could. Right as he reached the threshold, she released him, allowing him to stand all the way. With that, she extended her arm and Max helped her to her feet. He showered and she finished cooking breakfast.

When he came out to the kitchen, he wore a pair of tan slacks he had found in the guest room and a collared button-down blue shirt with white pin striping. It was simple, comfortable, and looked professional enough for his clinic. Not that any of his patients would even care, but he did.

They sat at the table in the living room. It appeared to not get a lot of use. There was room for about six people to sit, however, there were only two plates of food out on one corner of the table. Crimson had already devoured most of her food and he felt as if he had some catching up to do. He sat down and began eating. It was still warm, so he knew he hadn't delayed too long in joining her. *She is a really quick eater*, he thought.

"So, I knew you in school. We even had two years at the same college. You never paid any attention to me. You were always popular, and you never seemed to care for anyone but yourself. What made you change, Max?"

"Who says I've changed?"

"I do. You were known to be the smartest kid in the school no matter where you went. Everyone knew your parents gave you a boost up in life; every bot Synaptix made for intelligence, memory, critical thinking, and more, you had them all. It was no secret your parents wanted you to be smart enough to change everything. You knew you were smart and you were cocky and self-absorbed, the most likely to be some big researcher and make billions. However, you opened a clinic in the middle of the worst area of this city. A clinic that treats the poor who can't afford all of the modern cures with patients who can barely pay you enough to keep your doors open. How do you explain this? Why not be out there researching more cures and ways to advance mankind? Why not make a big change?"

"Would I really be making a big change if I were a researcher? Sure, I could come up with a new treatment for some disease, but only the rich could afford it. Am I really changing anything if I do that? What if I make billions and, with the money, open a charitable clinic like I have now to treat the poor? Would the person I put in charge really care for the people who come in? Or would they do it out of a mere obligation to get a paycheck? If you ask me, I'll leave the research to the greedy, let them 'better humanity, make a difference.' As for me, I would rather be on the front lines. I would rather be the one treating the afflicted with my own hands.

"It's no secret I lived a life of luxury growing up. Even now I have a portion of my parents' wealth that gets me by. I was self-absorbed. I didn't care. I did want to be rich... But then I walked through the poor area one day and the things I saw struck me. I know it sounds corny, but I thought to myself, 'how could I ever be happy with myself knowing there are people who deserve to be cared for dying in the streets, in my very own backyard, so to speak?'

"Alas, I've been thinking lately, and I've realized over the last five years, I haven't made the change I want to. I don't know what it is, but there has to be a better way for me to help everyone; not just the rich, not just the middle class, not just the poor...but everyone."

His eyes were deep hazel in color and burned with a reflection of sincerity and passion. He meant what he said, and though he had already spoken for a couple of minutes, Crimson could tell he had a lot more to say. There was more to his story; there was more to his passion, but for now, she would leave things as-is.

"Very impressive, and it wasn't bullshit like I was expecting. Well, later, when we meet up with Zarfa, I'll explain what I am trying to do. Maybe you can make a big change."

Crimson finished her last couple of bites, stood up, walked over to the sink, rinsed her plate, and left it there. "Just leave it there when you're done," she said as she disappeared down the hallway where he knew her bedroom was located.

When she came back, she had a gun on her hip and a plasma dagger in its sheath on her inner right thigh. She was holding another longer plasma blade in its sheath in her hand. Judging by the sheath, it was about the same length and shape as a wakizashi sword.

"A present for you; you may need it. Knowing me is a health hazard," she stated, tossing it in his direction.

Max grabbed it in the air and smiled. "Like I could even use this thing to defend myself."

"You use a scalpel sometimes, don't you?"

"It isn't the same. The patients usually aren't moving, and they usually aren't trying to kill me."

"Well, at least you know where to aim to kill someone who is trying to kill you. Let's go, I told Zarfa mid-day and it is already ten-thirty. If we leave now, we can make it to the clinic by eleven. Plus, I am sure you've got some patients that would like to see you."

"You would think, but even practically free care isn't being used much these days. It seems strange. When I first started, I treated diseases and conditions daily. Now, it seems like nobody needs me, but I know these diseases haven't disappeared, only the patients have."

"*Strange,*" she said, as if she knew the answer why.

When Zarfa woke in the morning, he was lying on the couch in his living room. He'd slept there because of the sprawling puddle of dried, rotting blood on his bed. His nose and stomach revolted at the stench of it decaying on his sheets; the flies buzzing around his apartment had no doubt been laying their eggs in it all night long.

Of all the things we killed in the Great Extinction, why couldn't flies have been one of them? He gagged on the thought of maggots wriggling around all over his bed. He glanced over to the doorway and saw his backpack with the Psyker nanobot treatments there. His mind raced back to earlier that morning. It seemed like a lifetime ago when he recalled all that had occurred.

How did I hear Badger before I had even met him?

Zarfa stood and looked at the alarm clock by his bedside. Ten-twenty-two; it was about the time he always slept until. With his job of fighting in the underground matches, he usually didn't finish work and get to bed until two or three in the morning, so even though he was exhausted from his now healed injuries, he really hadn't stayed up much later than he was used to.

Zarfa walked over to his bedside and opened the drawer to the nightstand that his alarm clock rested on. Inside the drawer was an array of boosts—he used them on occasion and felt it best to have one of every sort lying around. He reached in and pulled out a neon yellow one clearly marked "energy" on the label. He popped off the cap, stuck the small needle into his arm, and shot it in.

Immediately, his body began to surge with an almost electric energy. He didn't feel jittery or shaky at all; he felt rested and ready to take on any challenge that might come his way. First, he had to deal with this stench. He couldn't handle it any longer. He stripped off his sheets and threw them in the alleyway outside.

They aren't worth the hassle to wash. I have half a mind to burn the whole damn bed.

He examined the mattress. His blood had soaked through and deeply stained the material. He knew no matter what he did to clean it, there would be no way to get the blood out, so he flipped the mattress and reminded himself he wouldn't be living in Alexarien much longer. The smell was already better, even though it still lingered in the air.

Zarfa made haste to get showered and change into some clean clothes. He checked the clock again. It was about eleven. He figured he could go by Max's about noon and hear what Crimson had to say. Right now, however, he needed food. His stomach was still revolting over the stench in the apartment, but he could also feel his digestive acids eating the lining of his churning stomach.

He grabbed his banking chip and headed out, locking the door to his apartment behind him. He made his way through the alley cautiously. He knew that he would now have not only the Faraza looking for him, but the Psyker Scream crew as well. He didn't want a repeat of the stealth assassins; he had barely managed to win that battle.

He found a small café around the corner from his home and went in to get breakfast. He connected to a multiprocessor interface access center that the café had available to the public and looked up records on Psyker's leader, Badger.

None of the information he could find on him was of any use. Most of it was peripheral junk that fans of any rock band would eat up. The deepest thing he could find on the man was that his real name was Coy McRodger. Subsequent searches of that name yielded no fruits. He'd gotten the stage name Badger in high school due to his awkward face and the wiry hair that covered his body.

Frustrated, Zarfa shoveled his breakfast and left the café. If his job wasn't to knock people around all night in a cage, he would be seeking a fight. It seemed to him as if there was too much going on in his life—the Faraza, Psyker Scream, and Sarah. He knew Sarah was still alive; he had seen her in a raiding party before he left Ilyeion.

She remembers me? She's a person still? Yeah, right!

It wasn't uncommon for loved ones to come back as raiders. However, when they came back, they were never themselves. When the parties first started showing up, an attempt was made to try to capture live ones that were recognized. Many families had retrieved their loved ones only to be left with even more heartbreak.

There wasn't one successful case of retrieval. Nobody was certain as to how they did it, but the Faraza always controlled those who had been captured. Their victims never remembered who they were; they usually didn't even remember how to speak. They would fight at every chance they had to escape.

Ultimately, the efforts to retrieve people who were recognized were stopped. The ones who had been retrieved and reunited with their families more often than not were successful in killing their family that wanted nothing more than to rehabilitate them and ease their suffering. Those who weren't killed were maimed and sadistically tortured. Nobody was sure how the Faraza was brainwashing them and turning them into these mindless drones of destruction, but they were, so efforts to capture and rehabilitate stopped. That was why when the assassin told Zarfa that Sarah wanted to speak with him, he was incredulous.

There is no way. Of course he knows about Sarah. I'm somewhat infamous with the Faraza. Why would he lie? What was his motive? To get into my head?

It worked. Zarfa began to think of all that had happened before he left Ilyeion. He was hailed as a hero and a champion there. In the years since his sister had been taken, he had killed raiders into the thousands. When they attacked, he had organized a small band of those agonizing over the loss of their loved ones. They would suit up for battle and head into the streets. They called themselves "Legion Nine." Originally, Legion was given as a nickname to Zarfa because he fought like one by himself, and the number he slew grew to match it.

He started with eight strong supporters that followed him into the first of his counter attacks against the Faraza. A year later, they had grown to roughly two hundred soldiers, and their ranks grew each day. Though they were gaining in numbers and strength, these soldiers faced loss at each battle. Of Zarfa's original eight, only two remained alive, and one of them was crippled beyond the ability to fight.

Despite the danger, despite the loss, whenever the swarm arrived to ravage Ilyeion, Zarfa would send the call, and his warriors would heed it. They would clad themselves in whatever armor they could afford or make, and take up any armaments they could get their hands on. Some had rifles, pistols, and bows. Others could only muster a crude makeshift weapon or plasma blade. Some took trophies from the weapons the raiders had used, gaining pleasure in crushing them with their own instruments of destruction. Zarfa always took a backup plasma Tanto blade and a gauss pistol, but he preferred to kill with his bare hands if he could.

He remembered his army back at home waiting for his return, all of their hopes resting upon his shoulders. He carried a great weight; he vowed to bring the Faraza down. He was resolved to do that now more than ever, but what would he do when confronted with his sister?

What if that man wasn't lying? Why would she want to see me?

He called to mind how it seemed that, when raiders saw him, they would concentrate the attack, almost as if they were intent on capturing or killing him. He always thought that this was because of the trouble he was causing them. He thought it was because he was infamous amongst the Faraza for killing so many of their men.

What if it was an order from...Sarah?

He shook his head in disbelief and exhaled a breath he felt he had been holding for the last couple of blocks. He was so lost in thought he didn't even realize how tense he was. Now, he stood outside the big black door that led into Max's clinic. He took a couple of deep breaths to relax and tried to shake loose his tense muscles. He really didn't want to hear what Crimson had to say, especially since something of her reminded him of his dear sister.

This bitch had better not mention Sarah too, or I'll kill her with my bare hands.

Zarfa opened the door calmly and glanced around the room. There they were, waiting for him. He was already on the offensive and he hadn't even heard what either of them had to say yet.

"What do you mean he killed the two we sent? They were two of our best. They even had tech on them nobody had seen before. We knew he was dangerous, but this? We can't afford capturing him. We either let him be or we kill him," said Ghast, commander of the Faraza.

"You said if I helped you that you would deliver my brother. I've made good on my end of the bargain. It's about time you make good on yours."

"That I make good on mine? Dear Sarah, don't forget who made you and gave you strength, lest you lose your head, fledgling."

Ghast glanced over to the messenger in the room and thought it would be best if this dispute between himself and Sarah were handled with no eyes or ears on them. He waved him off then glanced down at his gun in a contemplative manner so as to send the hint that if he didn't get out quickly, he would shoot the messenger. This underling valued his life, so he made haste out of the door while Sarah stared at Ghast, enraged with his proposal.

"You dare to make me look weak in front of a low-ranking solider such as that? Neither of us even know his name. He is that valueless. They always send the nothings...you know my temper, being what it is," Ghast spat out.

"That I do, *master*," Sarah said condescendingly, "but stop trying to distract my attention from the real matter. Zarfa is powerful; it is why we want him on our side. What is the toll up to? How many has he killed of ours in battle? One, two, three—"

"He has killed roughly two thousand; stop trying to exaggerate his greatness."

"Oh yes, *only* two thousand...with his own hands. Did you forget Legion Nine? How many thousands have they killed?"

The room was silent. Ghast and Sarah could hear each other's breaths. Only the two of them stood in the room, his office in the underground catacombs carved out by the mud wasps. He sat behind a small desk made of dried mud, which had been crafted by the wasp drones. Sarah stood as an ominous cloud staring into his eyes with rage.

"And that is exactly why I sent the two. That is why their orders were to take him dead or alive. They had every trick up their sleeve to use, even tech that hasn't been released to the market yet, and still they—"

"Failed! I know, so now you send ten, twenty, thirty at a time! However many it takes! I want my brother and I want him here. I know we will have to condition him at this point or else there is no way that he will join us; he is too idealistic. However...and you had better be listening to me, I want my brother to be recognizable. I want my brother alive. I want him as my protector again in some way, shape, or form, but I don't want him to be a drone. His power lies in his emotions and his feelings. What kind of a protector would he be if he didn't love me as he once did? Let's face it, even if you had taken him the day you took me, he wouldn't have joined our cause. He is going to be stubborn. He would rather die than be a member of the Faraza, even if it means he can have me back. In his mind, when he meets me again, I won't be his sister. I'll be his enemy. He was damaged too much when Mother and Father were '*taken,*'" she said.

"If it wasn't for your father, I would have you killed. I know he heard me say that in one way or another, but it is true. He values me only slightly above you, but I will not forget my place, and you...you had better not forget yours, worm," Ghast spat back.

"You are very wise to know no conversation between you and I is confidential. Down here, nothing is sacred. Someone is always listening, and that someone is ultimately my father. So, even if I am under you...get Zarfa back. Plain, simple. Got it?"

Ghast was outraged. If he weren't sitting behind a desk, Sarah would see his legs trembling with anger. It was all he could do to keep his hands from quaking the same way. He had been the leader of Faraza for the last twenty years—he still was. However, three years ago, when he had received the orders to capture Zarfa and Sarah, he had begun to see his end was close at hand.

Their father, Thomas Cudrow, was at the heart of Faraza. Ghast, although being first in command and public figurehead of this cult of raiders, was merely a puppet following orders from Sarah's father. Ghast viewed the capture of Thomas' children as a threat to his power and authority. He would rather see them dead.

"I got it. If I don't get your toy back, you're going to go tell Daddy on me...grow up," he said. He looked to the ceiling, where he assumed a bug to be spying, and gave a wink.

"Don't forget it, love," she said as she stormed out of the room and slammed the door.

"He is in the slums. I can hear him faintly. He doesn't even know he is speaking to the network, but he is there...listening to what she has to say," said Zax.

"Crimson? The bitch who damn near shot my ear off?"

"Yep, her. He's hearing her out...appears they aren't allies...yet. I'd like to tell you what exactly is going on, but he has only had one treatment. I'm surprised he is broadcasting a signal this strong. If he has all five treatments and is trained...he may be a better solider than you, Badger."

"I see. Give me details as they come in. Also, send ten men to Max's. Give them the order shoot to kill, except the bald one. Take Zarfa alive if we can. We don't want Crimson corrupting his mind. She knows too much about us, and whether she intends to fight against us or not, we don't have the time to wait and see."

"Understood, sending out the order now to our top ten soldiers."

Badger paced back and forth in the room, clenching his injured ear between his index finger and his thumb. He still wasn't quite sure how this disorganized threesome had outwitted him and his psychic army the night before. He knew that Max and Crimson could hear a little of their broadcasts without having Psyker bot treatments, but so could anyone.

The bots made it so that the recipient of treatments could pick up on the unconscious brainwave resonation that every human produced. On top of that, it would make those who had received treatments resonate stronger. Zarfa had to be an anomaly because nobody was able to broadcast from that far away after one treatment. The fact that they could track him twenty or more miles across town meant by the fifth treatment, he would hypothetically be able to converse with other Psykers around the globe.

This thought frustrated Badger for two reasons—one,

Zarfa would be a dangerous enemy if left unchecked; two, Badger had received orders from the top to let him live until he had made his decision resolute. Even if his decision was to go back to Legion Nine, Badger was to leave him alone.

"How long until our men reach Max's office?" Badger asked Zax.

"With hovercraft congestion on the airways the way it is right now? Forty-five minutes at least."

"Punctual, I like it," stated Crimson with a smirk.

Zarfa said nothing in return. He glared at her as thoughts of his sister invaded his mind. For some reason, he could see Sarah in Crimson and he both loved and hated it. He probably would have appreciated it more if it weren't for the fact that he had earlier been introduced to the thought that Sarah might still be herself, and working with the Faraza of her own volition.

"In all fairness, you did say afternoon, so would I still be punctual if I arrived at three?"

"Yes, less punctual, but still punctual. The fact that it is only a minute past twelve screams punctual. Like a solider, like a...*commander* even," she said with an eyebrow raised.

Zarfa stood only a few feet inside the doorway. He closed the door behind him. He knew it absurd, but he didn't want anyone passing by to hear this conversation.

Max sat behind his desk at the far end of the room with his hands folded in front of him. He still hadn't cleaned up the broken glass from the night before. Neither had he patched his injury with medifoam. *Strange,* Zarfa thought.

Crimson sat in front of Max on his desk and to his left so as not to obstruct Zarfa's view of Max. There was a chair seated in front of both of them with a small table next to it. On the table, Zarfa could see that it was their attempt to make him as comfortable as possible. They had placed some water and snacks on it for him.

"Please, have a seat," said Max.

Zarfa walked over and plopped himself down in the chair. It was comfortable, but he felt as if he were being interviewed, and he still didn't trust that the food and snacks weren't laced with something.

"Why is it I feel as if the two of you are teaming up to tell me something I don't want to hear?" Zarfa asked.

"I assure you, Max knows as little about why we are here as you do. I refrained from telling him anything until you arrived for that very purpose."

Max nodded his head in agreement.

"So, what is the meaning of this? You said there was a war coming, then tell me. When? Where? Why? What does it have to do with us?" Zarfa was monotone, but with a slight glint of aggression.

"Before I do, please let me preface all that I say with this—first off, Zarfa, I've done my homework on you. I know you lead a small army, Legion Nine, as they are called, and it is quite impressive. Little to your knowledge, the fact that you are fighting against the Faraza makes us allies. Furthermore, I know why you are here. I know why you are getting Psyker treatments. However, you have been misinformed. If you do modify your hearing, your scheme will work. You will be able to hear the wasps before they emerge from the earth, and you will be able to track them back to their lair... However..." She lingered for a moment because she could tell Zarfa's curiosity had been piqued.

"However what?" he asked, not even bothering with such things as how she had known he was planning an offensive strike after he returned.

"Why do you think that so many young adults have decided to get the Psyker treatments despite the high risk? Despite the pain? You aren't privy to this, but have you seen the commercials run in Alexarien advertising Psyker Scream and the modifications required to listen to them? They are blunt, honest, and hide none of the risks. However, what they don't have to tell you is these commercials have an encrypted frequency that transmits directly into the amygdala and cerebrum of the brain. They send a message silently right to the viewers' emotions and thoughts.

"Granted, this brainwashing technique works best on young adults, particularly females, however, nobody is immune to it. If it were a perfected technology, they would have no use for the bots. First, they snag their audience with the signal, then they gut them with the bots. When those bots rewrite your brain to hear the higher and lower frequencies, they also remap your entire brain so that you can hear the thoughts of those whom your brain resonates with clear as day. This enables telepathic communication within what is ultimately Synaptix Corporation's army they disguise as the band Psyker Scream.

"Badger is their leader and Surge and Zax are his right and left hands. Once anyone has had all five treatments, not only can they communicate telepathically, but they are completely open to any form of suggestion that comes from the base source. I am not sure how many base sources they have, but I do know that the three that comprise the band aren't under anyone's control but their own. However, they are extremely loyal to Synaptix.

"They can control their 'fans' by merely sending them telepathic commands. Those things you heard when you went to the concert were signals you were picking up from the thoughts of the audience. If you go through with the treatments, you will be able to communicate with them. You will be their ally, as well as my own in that Synaptix, myself, and you all want to end the Faraza, but you will be susceptible to being one of their little puppets...which would make you my enemy."

"So you're telling me if I follow my goals, we are going to be enemies? Why don't you go ahead and kill me right here? Or try anyhow."

"Because it isn't my style to do so. They can't control you yet. You still have time to decide. If you stop the treatments now, you will go deaf, also one of their tricks to make sure they build their army of brainwashed slaves without letup. Being deaf isn't so bad, not compared to being a tool of Synaptix."

As Zarfa sat in quiet contemplation, Max's mind was running a mile a minute. "Hang on, it wasn't only Zarfa who heard voices, though. I did, and I am willing to bet you have too, Crimson. How is that possible if we don't have the nanobots in us?"

"Our brains, even without modifications, naturally resonate between one and thirty hertz at any given time. You should know that, *doctor*. We were standing in a mass concentration of people whose brains have been modified to amplify that resonation, so naturally, we would receive bleed through messages. Of course, we could never communicate back. We would never be able to spy on them and figure out what they were saying. We would only get garbled voices and random words that meant nothing. Zarfa, on the other hand, had already had some modification, which is why, with a little focus, he could center in on Badger's 'voice.' Consequently, Zarfa, they can now track you wherever you are until you either go deaf from complications or become one of them and don't care any longer if they are tracking you or not."

"I see," said Max, nearly dumbfounded.

"So you are telling me that my brilliant idea to be able to go on the offensive with my army was the worst strategic plan I could have made if I wanted to remain myself and take down the Faraza?"

"Correct."

"Then I guess it's a good thing that my hatred for them is so deep that I don't care if I live or die! I don't care if I become a puppet of Synaptix, just as long as the Faraza are destroyed."

"Did you miss the memo when I said I seek to destroy them as well? I have higher goals. Don't be stupid; hear out the rest of what I have to say, and then decide, please."

"Don't tell me what to do. You don't know me! I don't care about *yours,* just mine."

"We have the same goals! Mine, however, include destroying Synaptix as well. You see, the Faraza are the henchmen of the Polyhelix corporation. They kidnap and spirit away people to experiment their gene manipulation further. This, *Max,* is where your patients are going. They are taking them from poor-afflicted areas such as the slums, or places that don't govern themselves the way Alexandria does because they can get away with it. They are equally as sick, if not more so, than Synaptix. The point is, both are planning to raise an army and dominate as much of this planet as they can. It isn't man's place to play God such as this. Mindless armies on one side being controlled by nothing more than, to put it simply, radio transmissions. On the other side, a corporation with no soul that is building an army of chimeras out of people whom they've kidnapped. Both sides have, in the past, contributed to the betterment of man, but today, they have made themselves idols and gods to the people. My goal is their utter destruction. So, Zarfa, are you content to destroy only the Faraza, which is nothing more than the tail of the beast, or will you strike its head alongside me? I could use you; I could use your army."

"Use, how appropriate. I thank you for telling me all of this, but it really seems as if you are simply saying, 'don't let someone else use you and manipulate you; let me do it.' No thanks, I'll take my risks doing my own thing," Zarfa said calmly as he stood and faced the door.

"I am sorry that it ends this way. The next time we meet, we will most likely be enemies. I do hope, though, that I am wrong and that it will not be so," Crimson said, sounding a bit hurt by his decision.

Zarfa began walking toward the door.

"Zarfa! You won't bring them back," she said.

"Oh? And who is it you speak of?" he asked, aggravated.

"All the loved ones they took. I read it in the missing persons section of the Ilyeion post the day after you were almost killed. I know they took someone from you, someone you cared for deeply."

If she doesn't goad me any farther, I can let this go. She hasn't harmed the memory of my sister any. Face her and tell her how it is, let her know you mean business. All this talk of enemies. She needs to know that I will fight her viciously if need be.

Zarfa turned to face Crimson, preparing the most dangerous expression he could conjure. In his head, he had even composed a mildly threatening speech and was ready to give Crimson a piece of his mind. But it all fell flat when he saw her soft face staring back at him.

She had so much fire, so much passion. She really believed in what she was doing, the way Sarah had when she used to dance the dances of the ancient days. Sarah believed she was preserving the culture of their people, something their parents had failed to do when they had Zarfa spliced with rhinoceros DNA as a child to make him stronger than average.

All of this desire to do what was right, spark a revolution, and give the poor working heroes a fighting chance to be free of their slavery and bondage. He knew that even if she succeeded, there would be much change to be made still, but it was at least something.

He was disarmed. Her fire, passion, zeal, care, and idealism melted him away. When he looked at Crimson, he saw Sarah standing there, requesting his aid in an oncoming war. His countenance dropped and his face softened back to the typical indifference he usually wore.

"They took her. Her heart beats, but my intent has never been to bring her back. It's impossible. The things they do to the ones they capture make it so," he said, sounding defeated.

"Oh? So what has your purpose in finding her been all along?" Crimson questioned.

"To see her dead."

He was as curt as possible, and the moment he finished his sentence, he returned on his way out the door. He remained calm, in control. He usually didn't allow anyone to mention his sister. The room remained silent as he passed through the door and back onto the street.

"Damn, he is moving away from the office," said Zax.

"How far is the reconnaissance team from his location?" asked Badger.

After a brief communication telepathically with the team, Zax answered, "About ten minutes. Between my tracking skill and theirs, he should be easy to find."

"Stay on his trail, intercept him, bring him here. I will probe him with my mind and see what he knows. Should be easy since he has had a round of the bots already."

"Affirmative, sending the command. What will they do about Max and Crimson?"

"They've done all the damage they can do for now. It appears to not be as drastic as I thought it would be. Leave them be for now. We can stop them whenever we want. We could easily call ten thousand soldiers to our side at any given second if we use the frequencies; they pose no real hazard to us," Badger said authoritatively and brimming with confidence.

"The team has received the message. They are changing course to meet Zarfa and bring him in."

"So, I bet you were expecting that to play out a little differently, huh?" asked Max; he was never one for tact.

"Yeah, I did. Oh well, things might change," Crimson said in an annoyed tone.

"Well, you explained to him why you were interested in him. I guess I know what's going on now...what does it have to do with me? Why are you interested in me? I'm a simple doctor whittling down his time in the slums."

"What it has to do with you, Max, is the fact that you aren't content. You want to make a change; that is why you are here. Your patients are disappearing from the area because of the experiments that Polyhelix is kidnapping them for. Before long, if they get their way, you won't have a life here. You will be a slave to their corporation."

"Great, so you want a personal doctor to keep you safe and healed while you go off and fight for freedom? Terrific, sounds boring, and you don't even have an army. I don't mean to be rude, but it sounds as if you're going to fail. I can't blame Zarfa for rejecting your offer."

"Oh I've got some tricks up my sleeve, and I will be recruiting an army soon enough, and not with brainwashing or kidnapping the way the other two factions do business. I'm not that low of a human being. Look, I've got a plan and I am sure it will work. Furthermore, I am offering you the chance to take a stand in a revolution that will change the lives of the people not just in Alexarien and Ilyeion, but across the globe. These companies won't be content if either of their plans for domination work in just these regions; they will take it to a global level. Whoever said anything about me wanting a personal physician?"

"I guess I just assumed. So what then? What do you want from me if not that?"

"You and I know you have an intellect that surpasses many other doctors. You were smart naturally and science made you even more intelligent. I want your brain. I want you to design something for me. The task will involve you reverse engineering some nanobot technology for me then rebuilding it with a bit of an upgrade to both its hardware and its software. Interested?"

"And you think I'll be able to do this?"

"I know you can. The question is, will you try? So how about it? I have all the facilities you will need back at home. That's my main base. It also explains why I reside in the entire top floor of a high-rise complex. Everything you need will be taken care of; I have the credits to back it. So, what do you say? Want to make a revolution happen? Want to save more than you ever would in this small clinic?"

Max thought about it, thought about who he was and the reasons he was staying in this clinic helping the innocent and poor. He had seen death, but never caused one, even recently. There were times when he wanted to fight for a purpose, like last night at the Psyker Scream "concert."

He thought about what accepting her offer meant. It meant killing either directly or indirectly. Some of those whom he would have to kill might be people he once recognized from around his part of town, maybe even a patient he swore to care for. *Are they really still my patients if they've been brainwashed or mutated?*

He thought about Crimson, who she was, what he knew of her. Not much, but she seemed trustworthy, and it didn't hurt that he longed to be with her. She was beautiful outwardly and, in his eyes now, inwardly as well. He pondered for a good twenty minutes in silence as Crimson stood by not saying a word, letting him think.

She was standing on the other side of his desk, no longer leisurely sitting. She was staring at him, but her face was warm and inviting. Her piecing feline eyes somehow managed to seem warm and soft. Her bangs all hung to one side, swooping over the side of her face. As he got ready to speak, she wore a slight smile, revealing her overly exaggerated eye teeth.

"I barely know you, but I feel I can trust you. I'm in. However, I feel like you should train me how to use these," he said, glancing to the floor beside him where the weapons she had given him earlier were propped against his desk. "It seems as if being your friend comes with some added danger to my health."

"Without a doubt, friend. Also, the bots I need you to make changes to are the Psyker Scream nanobots. If you have any left around here, bring them," she said, her smile growing even wider. "You know you can never return to this life now; this office needs to be demolished. Gather the things you might need and we shall go."

"Why does it have to be destroyed? Why can't I just leave and stop paying rent?"

"There is no doubt personal information strewn in the things here that the enemy will use against us. I want to see to it that we take every precaution to make sure they discover as little as possible about you. Additionally, after I do what I'm going to do to this place, hopefully the enemy will think you said no and I lost my temper." As she finished her sentence, she reached under the back of her shirt and pulled out a device. "It's a cluster plasma grenade. It blows apart into several smaller explosives seven seconds after I pull the pin. Everything in here will be vaporized."

"Wow, you never fail to surprise me."

This woman is an absolute lunatic carrying a weapon like that! What have I gotten myself into? I really hope I don't regret this. She might be more volatile that I had ever imagined.

Max did as he was told. He looked around the office. He checked the exam room for things he thought he might need to take with him, but there wasn't really much. In the end, all he had grabbed was a series of Psyker Scream injections.

He went back into the main office and looked around. He really liked his desk, as well as a lot of the things he decorated this room with, but he failed to see the purpose in bringing any of that sort of thing. He stepped over to his desk and rummaged through the drawers. Finally, he opened the bottom drawer and looked inside.

Inside were several serenity boosts that he had yet to use. He craved one even now as he looked at them. He reached his hand inside and ran his fingers over the glass syringes they came in. He lifted a handful of them to reveal one orange strength boost he must have had from when he'd had to rearrange his office.

He pocketed the small orange syringe and dropped the blue ones back into the drawer. His hand trembled and his forehead began to bead small drops of sweat.

Not today. I am making a big change in my life. I have no need of the past.

Max kicked the lower drawer closed and, after grabbing his weaponry, looked up at Crimson who had not moved. She leaned over the desk and picked up the two strange devices that had been lying there.

"Having second thoughts?" she asked, genuinely concerned.

"Nope, just realizing what this all means. C'mon, let's go."

As they stood at the doorway, Crimson let Max pull the pin on the grenade and toss it into his clinic himself. Max did so and slammed the door shut behind them. They started walking down the street before they even heard the blast, but before they were too far away, they heard a slight bang followed by a terrible fizzing hiss. That many particles being evaporated at once sounded like war. It sounded like a new beginning.

When they got back to Crimson's home and base of operations, Crimson showed Max around. She showed him his lab area and all of the equipment she had already purchased. She didn't explain exactly what she wanted him to do.

Last, she led Max to his bedroom. "You look tired. Get some rest. I will show you more and explain more later."

He took her suggestion and collapsed onto his bed. He was fast asleep in seconds.

When Max finally woke from his overly long nap, it was about six-thirty in the evening. He wandered down a small hallway and back into the main room where the kitchen and living room were situated. Crimson was standing there in front of a mirror, fixing the wrinkles on the tight, red silk dress she was wearing.

"You look great. Where are you headed?"

He could see her face in the reflection of the glass as she answered him with a smile. "I've got more business to attend to. Don't wait up. It may take me some time."

"Oh, I see, a date?"

I told you that you misread the situation yesterday, idiot. She doesn't like you like that. You are nothing more than her fellow freedom fighter. But what the hell is she doing dating at a time like this? Right before she declares war. I hope I didn't buy into her for nothing.

"That's what he thinks it is. Trust me, Max. I wouldn't be so dumb as to be trying to find love with some stranger at a time like this. What do you take me for? A normal girl who is about to start a war?" She couldn't contain a small chuckle that trickled out of her mouth.

Yes! Stupid! Of course she isn't going on a date. I am so dumb.

"No, I didn't think that for a second. Just curious is all. See you tomorrow then?"

"See you tomorrow. Enjoy this day. It will be the last one of rest you see in quite some time."

Eight

Night at Blue Nami

"I'm glad you could make it tonight. I'm not a girl who likes to beat around the bush or pussyfoot about what I want. I had many questions back at the Barometrics office, but I know due to the nature of your job that your office would be filled with bugs. I am just a client who wants some answers. You could call me a humanitarian, in all reality. I don't want my weather orders to be affecting some poor souls to the south of us in Durban or something of that nature, so I have many questions regarding how exactly your technology works. It has been a mystery for the last hundred or so years since your CEO invented it.

"Let me preface this by saying that I do not desire to sabotage you. I am no terrorist. I realize that globally, all forms of government have passed a law stating that only one corporation could possess this technology and use it or else the whole world would be thrown into chaos! I understand all of this; however, I want to know, what is at the root of this device?" Crimson leaned over the candlelit dinner table and narrowed her eyes at Brian.

"At the root of it? I'm sorry, I don't believe that I grasp the meaning of what you're asking," Brian said as he cut his steak into bite-sized pieces.

"Okay, I get the point. What I mean is this. How do you prevent the storm, or lack of one, in one part of the world from affecting another part of the world? I heard your answer back at the office, but there are no bugs here. This isn't a press conference. I want some truth."

"You mean our service areas? Well, that is easy—things

are all mapped out quite precisely. The affluent nations who offer a populace that can afford our services are completely protected. We have ensured that 'remnant storms' won't occur and ruin anyone's day or cause a big disaster," he said, stuffing a large bite of meat into his mouth.

"I don't mean your service areas. I mean the rest of the globe. The blue zones, as our Alexandrian government like to call them. How do I know my selfish desire for a particular weather isn't causing a disaster elsewhere? In an area outside of your service area?"

He chewed as he spoke; he was far from graceful. Crimson couldn't understand how this guy was even a salesman for the Barometrics company with services as expensive as theirs.

"Well," he began to say as a small piece of meat fell onto the table, "if you read the contract carefully, we only promise for your orders to not affect any of our service areas. It isn't illegal. Some countries are better than others—some people's lot in life is a slave, others are billionaire assassins with an economic dynasty large enough to purchase our services. I am sure *you* understand."

Despite his lack of grace, he still spoke like a true salesman. No soul, no care, no driving force other than greed. He tried to lead his audience into his train of thought and was no doubt very successful most of the time.

"Why would *I* understand? Because I hold a black license? Because I kill others to make a living? Did you even bother to investigate who my clients are, or did you just see that I hold a license on the application and assume I was a mass murderer and that was how I managed to amass my large sum of credits?"

Brian choked on his bite and proceeded to speak, spitting chunks of it in her direction. "I'm so sorry, did not mean to offend, all I meant was—"

"That I am some soulless killer who could use your company's services to create cover for myself as I slip into an innocent's home and slaughter him or her like a defenseless child? I take no offense to what you think and say; you have a right to be ignorant and I, for my part, accept that you are. What I am offended by, however, is that you spit your food halfway across the table at me."

"Sorry," was all he could manage to say as he wiped his

mouth with the tablecloth.

"I am sure you are, *Brian,* but right now, I really don't care. I've lost my appetite," she said, pushing her plate of food away.

"Sorry, again. Please tell me, how can I make it up to you?"

"Go pay our bill and take me home. I really can't stand you and don't expect to have any dealings with you other than professional ones from here on out, but a girl has needs."

"Okay. So you are saying that I haven't lost your business?"

"Not yet," she huffed, annoyed.

Brain stood from the table, and found the waitress to pay. As he walked back to the table, he couldn't help but notice that Crimson had downed both of their drinks.

"Thirsty much?" he asked playfully.

"Yeah, are we ready? Let's go back to your place."

Max didn't know what to do with himself. Crimson had gone and he was full of energy. His lab looked awesome, but he didn't know what to do with it. He didn't know what Crimson wanted him to work on exactly, or else he would have started.

He was hungry, but he didn't care about food. He had an impulse raging in his brain stronger than any legitimate physical need. *Feed me.* It seemed to repeat in his brain. *I don't want to!* Max kept fighting back as he trembled and sweated, his body craving the toxic bite of a boost.

He spotted a pharmaceutical locker on the far end of the lab and decided to investigate. *Red, red, orange, green, yellow, black, tan, brown, brown, red! Where? Where is blue? Why no blue? Why, why, why, why, why, why?*

It hadn't been this bad since he'd quit three years ago. *You knew what you were doing; you're a doctor. You know your enhancements make you more prone to addiction. What the hell were you thinking, asshole? That I hate you! I hate you, Max! You destroy everything! You destroy everyone! Crimson doesn't like you. She doesn't even need you! She needs your brain, ignorant little addict. You should die already.*

Max began to cry and convulse. He hated that he craved the serenity boosts so bad. It came in waves. He wanted them; he didn't. He hated that they controlled him so strongly and not at all. He couldn't choose when he craved them; he couldn't choose when he didn't.

It was a true addiction. He really wanted free, but he knew the only thing that could heal him was time. *Sure, they can make us immortal these days, but they can't fix addiction. Maybe I should have gone into research. I wish I had never studied medicine! I wish I had gone anywhere in life except the path that would lead me to this.*

Max voluntarily convulsed on the floor as if he was trying to expel demons from his body. It was more than a tantrum a three-year-old would throw. Max knew what he wanted. He wanted freedom from slavery to chemicals. He'd had it. For three short years, he had been completely free, but one freak occurrence, one that wasn't even that big of a deal, had slingshot him back to this.

He rolled over to the metal pharmaceutical locker, sweating and writhing in both physical and emotional pain. He began to pound his head into the locker with a vehement rage.

He bashed his head into the metal one time and felt his skull absorb the blow with a large hematoma swelling under the skin. He fervently smashed his head a second time into the locker with all of his force. His vision dimmed and he heard a ringing in his right ear.

Once more. That's all you need to be free, Max, that's it.

He paused and choked. He started crying even harder than he had been. He could barely breathe through the tears and gasps. He wasn't crying from the physical pain he had dealt himself. He was crying because his mind was drawn to Crimson. *What if she does care about me? Even if it is just as a friend? Just a fellow soldier for a good cause? What if? What if nothing...*

A third tempestuous slam; it was hard. The metal rang out; his neck made a cracking noise. He had slipped a disk in between his fourth and fifth vertebra that would be a constant source of pain and aggravation. He had also caused a concussive fracture to his skull. His skin split open and his hematoma ran down his forehead into his right eye.

He couldn't see out of it anyway because of the swelling around his retina caused by his first blow. His right eye was most certainly swelling; he could feel it. He convulsed a few more times before dragging himself to a position on all fours. He hit the floor eight times with both fists as hard as he could. His knuckles were already swelling and would cause him horrible pain in the morning.

Finally, he stood on both feet and faced the locker. He kicked it as hard as he could. Still, his chest heaved as he sobbed, grabbing for air between whimpers. His lips quivered and snot ran down his nose. Blood and tears fell like rain on his shirt.

No sense in crying about spilled milk all night; time to get to work.

Max reached into the locker. *Yellow, non-addictive stimulant, like caffeine but stronger. I need to calm down, but maybe this will focus me and I can do something useful for a change.*

He pulled out an awareness boost. Dosage on all boosts were the same—a typical dose was point one of a cc. Most syringes were multiple use and held ten doses. This one still had seven doses to dispense. He stuck the needle in his arm and pushed the plunger without hesitation.

A smile widened across his face as the feeling quickly overwhelmed his body. *That's better, time to get to work.*

As they walked back to Brian's place, she could tell he was feeling awkward. He had displayed complete ineptitude. She wanted him to feel inadequate and weak. She wanted him to know his place, and to have no doubt that she was only going back to his place for her primal urges to be satiated.

"So, who do you kill then? If you don't mind me asking?" Brian asked hesitantly, his body language completely awkward.

"Oh, so now you want to do your homework? Don't you think you should have done that before I came to the office? Don't you think you should have done that before dinner? I gave you a whole day to prepare."

Brian was quiet, staring straight at his feet as he walked. "I blew it with you, I know. It is just that the company pawns so many of the small-timers off on me. I used to be an engineer. I maintained the machines, but it seemed like too much stress. I applied for a position as a sales rep and they gave it to me, but I feel like they give me all the small fry accounts. The one-time novelty buyers, you know? So I didn't do my homework on you. Do you know how many people have passed through my door carrying a black license? More than I could count. I'm sorry, I looked at your application; you looked the same as the others. I'm sure that's the only reason they passed you on to me. Sure, you have a large fortune, but so do a lot of other assassins.

"Killers don't buy sunny days, typically. They buy the weather they need for one job that will cover them, then usually we don't ever do business again. Either due to death, or they quickly realize that fog, rain, wind, whatever they order, didn't help them that much. You talk like you are going to use Barometrics services a lot, but I still doubt it. I'm sorry, but history has proven you to be false already. I am sorry, but now I am curious. Who are your clients; who are your targets? Enlighten me."

"My clients are the families that other license holders have ravaged and stolen from. My targets are assassins, typically big names with even larger reputations and egos. I do a little information gathering. I find out what families they've robbed from. Then take about a hundred payments on the same target and go in for the kill. So, in the field that I've chosen to pursue, every advantage matters. I will use your services more than once. What I need will be different each time. So, start treating me like a good customer and we won't have any issues. And let's be clear about one thing. I kill the bad guys; I'm not one of them."

"Okay, I'm sorry. My apartment is up ahead," Brian said, and pointed to a rather bland building.

The rest of their walk, which was six more blocks, was awfully awkward. Crimson began to think he had only pointed out the building so soon to avoid further conversation. As they walked up the staircase to his doorway, she shot him an evil smile, one that intentionally spoke more synonyms than she believed Brian even knew for "seductive."

"It's on the fifth floor," he said in a tone that almost sounded guilty.

"Let us both hope my night isn't a waste," she said as she leaned in on him and bit his lower lip. "Or else I might have to make you scream from more than pleasure."

Brian didn't say anything back. He could do nothing but breathe heavy, hot air into Crimson's face as he pushed the button for the elevator. It was there before he even realized it. Crimson was still sucking on his face and scratching the back of his neck.

She shoved him inside the doors and they began to close while she was still standing in the hallway glaring at him lustfully. Brian cast an eager glance, as if he was worried she was going to leave him in the elevator longing. Before the doors closed shut, she darted between them and clung onto Brian's body.

"Miss me much?" she asked as the doors closed and the elevator sounded a ding.

"I thought you were going to leave me with blue balls," he said sarcastically, trying to make a joke.

"If you disappoint, I'll leave you with none."

The SCARA type articulated robotic arm sat in simple complexity upon the mounting pedestal before Max. He knew the arms weren't hard to come by, but they were certainly expensive, so naturally, he was having difficulty understanding why anyone would purchase twenty of them to have in their home.

They ranged in sizes, pairs—the largest could assemble a military tank and the smallest pair a nanobot smaller than legal by both the laws of the affluent governments and the corporations that truly ran them. For this first construction, he would only need to use six of the twenty pairs he had at his disposal. They were beautiful, majestic, and Max had finished programming the last of the pairs that he needed.

As he laid the parts on the assembly line, his mind began to go wild. *I know she's going to love this! Oh she will be so impressed. She has no idea my level of brilliance. If a scientist and a research doctor is what she wants, that is what she will have. If she needs a fierce warrior and protector, she shall have that too. Oh, I can't wait!*

Max double checked his calibrations as he walked up and down the assembly line. His high from the boosts was still well in effect, and was causing him to sweat more than he should. He was already a hyperactive person in general, which was one of the reasons he'd become addicted to the serenity boosts so easily.

He should have been shaking too badly to get any work done, but he overrode the impulse he was sending subconsciously with his conscious thoughts. He felt as if he could do the work of a hundred people himself, and with the robots helping, a thousand.

His checks were all complete, the parts he needed all on the line perfectly. Now all he had to do was sit back and watch the beautiful machines work intricately to his exact commands. As he pulled the switch, he was amazed at the precision of such arms. He had seen them used in college and was even trained on how to program them some.

The rest of what he had learned about using them had been from the interface in moments of boredom back at his clinic. The robotic arms were beautiful in his eyes as they maneuvered their one hundred or more joints precisely to his very exacting commands. He could see them taking shape, his children of the mind. Sure, people had dreamt this dream before; however, he re-imagined it.

I'm not sure why she had those components laying around. I sure hope she doesn't mind me using them. Of course she won't once she sees what I've done. Oh so lovely, I like them more than the originals... I really hope she isn't mad at the expense I've already accrued, and it isn't even the project she wanted me to work on. Oh well, what is done is done.

What's she going to do? Fire me? Kill me?

Max began to giggle vigorously in almost a maddened way. As his work completed before his eyes, his giggle turned into a thunderous laugh. He was happy and also slightly unnerved they had come out exactly as he had intended. He felt proud, almost as if he were a parent.

Well now, there is only one thing left to do.

He removed his new creations from the assembly line and set them on a workbench as he began to reprogram the robotic arms again. This time, his calibrations were more precise, more demanding. This time, he would require arms that started at the littlest and most precise and go up to the mid-ranged size.

Once he was done reprogramming the software on each pair of arms, he double checked himself. Then triple checked himself, and for a matter of safety, checked again. Almost everything was set and ready to go.

Oh, one last thing.

He had almost forgotten to reset the direction of the assembly belt. Once he started it, it wouldn't have caused any real damage, but it would have made him look like a total fool.

Why would I care? I'm all alone. Sometimes you are such an idiot, Max. No wonder they all leave you no matter what you do! But not this one, not this time. She will be so impressed.

Max picked up his new inventions and carried them over to a mirror. They were perfect, glistening, sleek, manly, and delicate all at once. As he held each one individually, he mapped out their placement with a marker on his sink.

This is going to be remarkable! She is going to love it, I know it. More than a doctor and researcher indeed. I've been wasting my brain for too long now.

Max still had a high from the energy boost he had taken earlier, but it was beginning to wear off and he could tell he was in for a crash soon. He was happy that these boosts were non-addictive. He re-checked his calibrations and tweaked in a few dials until everything was perfect.

After placing his newly crafted inventions in the hand part of each of the larger robotic arms, he walked back over to the pharmaceutical locker. He had left it open and in a bit of a disarray, but he spotted what he was looking for right off. A small, white syringe, a non-drowsy anesthetic that would last about ten minutes. He knew he was going to need it.

He walked over to the starting section of the conveyer belt of the assembly line. His body would pass through all of the robotic arms on the conveyer belt and it wouldn't be over by the time the anesthetic wore off, but he was confident he could endure it. He stuck the needle for the boost in his arm, but refrained from pushing the plunger just yet.

Holding the syringe in one hand, he pressed the button to start up the assembly line with the other. The arms began ticking and whirring as they warmed up. The belt slowly began to spin, and the computers started clicking and processing the data he had input.

Five...four...three...two...one.

Max pressed down the plunger and laid on the belt. There was no pain as the plasma scalpel sliced off his right arm, and then his left.

"My humble abode," Brain said smugly as he opened the door to his apartment.

Crimson glared at the back of his head. If he could see it, he would know he was in danger. She was annoyed. Not only was he a bad, cocky salesman, but he was also arrogant about his living quarters. He clearly didn't quite appreciate that she stood heads above him in every aspect, including financially. If he was trying to impress her, he was picking the wrong things and doing it poorly.

"Oh my, you must make a lot as one of Barometrics' sales representatives," she stated in a sarcastic, unimpressed tone.

"I do, okay?" he said as he stepped into the apartment. "Even if they do give me all the low level clients; thanks for changing that for me."

He sounded sincere. Perhaps he really was doing all he could. *Who cares?* she thought. *He is still an incompetent buffoon.*

"Care for any wine, scotch, beer, well, really anything... Care for something?" he asked as he walked into the kitchen, leaving her to shut the door.

"Sure, why not pour me a scotch and whatever you'd like, big boy? I need you relaxed, no stage fright or anything that might hinder your...*performance,*" she said, closing the door and slinking over to the couch.

She kicked off her shoes and laid on her back on the couch as Brian brought over the drinks. He had poured two scotches, both straight; his was a triple, hers a double. He sat at her feet as he handed her the glass.

"So," he began as he started to stroke her calves gently, "what exactly do you have in mind for me tonight?"

She slugged back half her scotch before she answered. It was good stuff, obviously meant to be sipped. "I was thinking you could be my slave?"

"Oh yeah? What would being your slave entail?"

"Well, first," she began to say, only pausing to drink the rest of the scotch and set down her glass, "it would require you passing the amount I've had to drink. What's wrong? Sensitive stomach?"

He smiled devilishly and drank about two thirds of his glass in one gulp. "Not a problem, mistress. What else?"

It sounded as if he had done this before; maybe he had. Maybe he was used to it. It would explain his competence, always being the slave, never being the one in charge. He tried to wear a man suit, but Crimson knew he was only a weak little boy.

"Then you do what I say. I am your master. I might call you names and get a little rough—no crying, got it?"

He nodded and finished his scotch. "No problem, mistress."

He sounds so whipped, like there isn't even any fight in him! I hope this doesn't hinder my plan. This guy makes me sick. He is such a typical man with an extra dose of wimpy on the side. What a joke.

She stood up, reclaiming her legs from his light grasp, and pushed him back into the couch. She leaned forward, grabbed his jaw, and pulled it close to her face. She spit lightly in his face to mark him as hers.

"Take off your clothes," she demanded.

Brian didn't so much as wipe any of her saliva off or even give her any form of verbal answer. He obeyed like a true slave, one who feared his master's scorn.

"Don't touch, just watch," she commanded again.

She pulled her dress up over her head, revealing herself to be wearing only a garter belt, some black stockings, and a black thong. She reached behind her left leg as if she was undoing the clasp on her stocking that affixed it to the garter belt.

"Close your eyes, and don't respond to my touches. You're mine—you do what I say when I tell you to."

Brian's cheeks were getting rosy. She could tell the alcohol was affecting him. He relaxed his arms and stayed in the leaned back position she had put him in. He closed his eyes like a perfect submissive. "It should be easy to do, master," he said.

She slapped him hard across the face and he winced without opening his eyes. "Don't speak unless I tell you. I don't want a sound from you. You make me sick; you are here to do as I say and nothing more!"

He nodded his head and kept his eyes closed, breathing softly out of his mouth. It must have taken some self-control to not scream when she slapped him. Crimson could hit harder than a lot of non-spliced men.

Crimson pulled a glass syringe from the stocking on her left leg where she had been fidgeting. Inside the syringe was some clear fluid with a small microchip about the size of a grain of rice floating in it.

She slipped an eight-gauge needle out from her right stocking and screwed it to the syringe. It looked like a spear. If Brian were to open his eyes, he would run in terror. It didn't matter how submissive he was. If he saw this, he would run.

She hid the syringe behind her back with her left hand and leaned down, placing her right hand on his chest. She began kissing and licking his thighs sensually and worked her way up to his neck. She scratched him across the chest and bit his right ear at the same time.

"This might hurt a little," she whispered, tilting his head back with her right hand.

He tried to nod, but her grasp kept his head from moving. Before he even knew he was in danger, she had shoved the needle through his right nasal passage and past the sphenoid bone. The needle entered into the brain and in one flawless, liquid motion, she had injected the chip.

He barely even flinched. In a matter of minutes, "Brian" wouldn't exist. He would still call himself that, but he would be nothing more than a mere minion under Crimson's electronic command.

The chip, upon contact with cerebral spinal fluid, extended tendrils and entangled itself throughout his brain into every lobe. The tendrils even wrapped around the brain stem.

His every thought, every function, was now under her command, but he wouldn't even know it when he came to. When he awoke, he would barely remember a thing.

Crimson slipped back into her dress, disposed of the syringe by hurling it out a window onto the street, and poured another scotch. She sat on the couch, sipping it until the chip had completely done its job and he awoke to her scowling at him, tapping a foot impatiently. She was fully dressed when he came to. He was naked and apparently still ready for some much promised action.

"What was that?" she asked, seeming to be annoyed.

"What happened?"

"That is exactly what I was asking you. I slap you once, start to mess around with a little foreplay, and you pass out on me? How much did you have to drink?"

Brian smacked his lips, tasting his mouth. "Ugh, I don't remember, but it tastes like a lot."

"Figures, you're drunk," she said, standing, still sipping scotch.

"Why are you dressed?"

"Because you can't perform," she said, finishing her scotch and leaving the empty glass on his kitchen counter.

"Sure I can! I'm awake again. I'm sorry I passed out, but...look! I'm still good to go," he exclaimed, looking down at his swollen member.

"I've seen bigger on schoolgirls, not impressed. Also, passing out while I'm kissing on you really doesn't do it for me. I'm out of here. Think about me when you go into the office tomorrow. You're useless, but I still need your company. I don't see a point in trading you for some other rep. In the future, however, try to do your job better than your attempted trysts and we will have no issues."

"But—" he started to say, but she was already out the door.

Crimson stood in the hallway waiting for the elevator, giggling like a child.

The machines stopped whirring and humming. The conveyer belt had gone to standby. The job was finished. The last ten minutes of the process were extremely painful for Max because the anesthetic boost had completely worn off, but he kept himself from flinching throughout.

He climbed out from under the robotic arms, careful not to smack into any of them and break any of the delicate working parts. He felt lighter. He looked over to the starting point of the belt where his arms lay on the floor, lifeless. There was barely any blood anywhere; the plasma scalpels were great at stopping blood loss as they cut.

There was still a haze of smoke and a sickening smell of burned skin, blood, muscle, and bone in the air. As the device cut, it vaporized the tissues. No matter how precise and accurate it was, there would always be that to deal with. It would be centuries before every vaporized particle of Max was scrubbed out of the room.

He was beginning to crash. All of the energy boosts were wearing off. Even though it had been a success, his body had suffered a large albeit controlled trauma. He staggered over to the mirror to investigate. He liked what he saw.

It's clear they're fake; everyone will see that, but I was working on a tight time frame so I've got to cut myself a little bit of slack. They look good. I know they're at least fifty times more powerful than they were before. Steadier than any flesh and bone. Perfect, lethal, stable, powerful. A nice fit indeed.

Max's legs began to buckle. He was tired and sick of fighting it. He flopped down onto the ground and curled up into a fetal position. He took two deep breaths and then was fast asleep. The other project he had in mind would have to wait.

From the time Crimson had left her home to now had only been roughly four hours. She figured even though Max was roaring and ready to do something when he awoke, he would surely have found something to keep himself entertained. She rode the private elevator to her home and stepped off.

She smelled something bizarre in the air. She couldn't quite put her finger on the scent, but it made her a bit nauseous. She felt something was amiss. She proceeded with caution in the direction of the smell. It led her toward the lab.

This isn't good. I hope he hasn't made some chemical weapon that will kill us all. What is that smell anyways? Burned hamburger and women's perfume? I hope it goes away or else Max is getting a serious lashing.

The smell was strong outside the door of the lab. Crimson didn't have a weak stomach by any means, but it was still making her sick. Partly because of the worry that something had gone terribly wrong and what she may be breathing was toxic fumes that would kill her.

As she opened the door, she scanned the room cautiously with her eyes, looking for anything out of the ordinary. Quickly, she spotted something.

Dismembered arms. I knew I shouldn't have left him alone.

She recognized the arms—they belonged to Max. She still couldn't see him and began to think the worst. Her pulse quickened and she took a stance ready to fight. She hadn't taken any weapons with her tonight. She didn't think she would need them, especially in her own fortress.

Calm down, if they were assassins, how did they get in? What are they using? Plasma blades! I knew I recognized that awful smell. Okay, so where is Max? I need to go in and investigate.

She slowly peeked her head around the other side of the door and scanned more of the vast room that she couldn't see from the hallway. She saw a body on the floor lying in front of the mirror. She slowly crept inside the room, still vigilant.

If those arms belong to Max, who is that body?

As she approached the mysterious body, she began to relax. There were no clear signs of anyone else in this room. It was just her, the corpse at her feet, and the creepy severed arms. The body lay there, seemingly lifeless, with one of its arms draped over its head, obstructing her view from seeing who it was.

She nudged it—no movement. Still cautious and not wanting to risk a sneak attack, she kicked the body as hard as she could in an attempt to roll it over. It worked—the body jumped to its feet screaming.

Before she even heard the words, she reacted, jumping

on the man, attempting to pin him to the ground. He was fast and strong and grabbed her midair, tossing her across the room. She landed hard on the ground and sprung up as quickly as possible, ready to charge, when it registered in her mind.

That's Max's face...how the hell?

"Damn it, you crazy-ass woman. What the hell are you doing to me?" he blurted out, rubbing his side where she had kicked him.

"Max! What did you do? I thought you had been murdered in here!"

"What gave you that bloody idea, you lunatic?"

"Oh, I don't know? The fact your arms are lying on the ground over there, perhaps!"

She pointed. He remembered, and realized that maybe he shouldn't have left them lying around. "Well, my *love,* it's fine!" he yelled sarcastically, wildly motioning his new prosthetics.

"I can see that! I left you alone for four hours and you were exhausted. How was I supposed to know you were going to go wild, make yourself some kind of freakishly strong robotic prosthetics, and perform the operation on yourself? Did you somehow hint in your conversation before I left that you had this in mind? No! I thought an assassin came in, cut them off your body, and you somehow..." Crimson started to trail off as she realized that what she thought may have happened was equally as preposterous as what had actually happened. "Look, Max, I didn't mean to hurt you. I couldn't see your face. Your arms...were lying on the frickin' floor! I didn't know who you were, so excuse me for kicking you! Maybe you should sleep with a combat suit on."

"Not a bad idea since rolling me over gently clearly isn't an option! Damn!"

The room was awkwardly quiet as their childish altercation came to a halt. The air still smelled awful and Max's face looked awful. She couldn't help but notice he could only see out of one eye and that boosts used and unused were scattered all around the floor.

"What made you do this to yourself?" she asked, sounding concerned.

"Boredom and loathing to start... Then I thought to myself, why not be more than your mad scientist brooding away in the corner of this coming conflict? Even if I am stuck in a lab this whole war, I am going to need defense."

"I gave you a gun and a plasma sword."

"Yeah, you think I know how to swing a sword? You think I know how to shoot a gauss weapon? I'm a doctor. I fix people, I don't break them. But if I'm going to help you, I need to be self-sufficient. So I made these; they were really easy. I went onto the net, got the blueprints for what the military uses on their soldiers, then made some modifications for the better.

"I still need to replace my busted eye, however, with a robotic. That's the next project. Complete with a targeting system. Both arms can shoot four miniature cold fission warheads each. They pack a punch, could destroy a building or a military armored vehicle of any kind, but like I said, I can't even shoot a gauss pistol let alone have the accuracy to launch a warhead based off my sight alone.

"The eye will be really cool. A self-guided targeting system for the warheads will make it so I don't even have to aim so long as I can remember what I want it to find! Also, it will sync up with the arms, telling them how to aim at whoever I am shooting at with any form of weapon so I will be a crack shot with all firearms. When it gets down to the wire and you don't need me in the lab, I want to provide cover fire for you on your assaults. I will be able to hit anything from a mile or more away provided the right sniper rifle. I'll be good cover, I swear!

"Also, as I am sure you noticed as I flung you across the room, these arms are much stronger than my old ones. Sure, they aren't as pretty. The skin is more of a dust cover than anything, but I was working on a tight schedule, remember? Side note, doll face! This lab is amazing! Anyways, as I was saying, they are much stronger both in durability and in force. So even if I am dealing with someone at close range, I should be able to hold my own. That plasma katana you gave me won't be useless to me anymore! So...you like?"

Max was out of breath from speaking so fast. He was like an excited little child showing his mother what he made her in kindergarten. His face looked awful as he smiled. It was hard to imagine he had done it to himself.

"Max... I knew you were smart. But, this? This is amazing. You are more than what I was hoping for. A soldier, a doctor, and a scientist. I knew I needed you for a reason. Next time, try to clean up your excess body parts before I get home, however. I don't want another one of these little tiffs."

Crimson had walked over to him by the time she was done speaking and wrapped her arms around his body. His new arms were cold to the touch as they rested on hers made of flesh and blood. She looked into his one good eye, and as much as she saw excitement, she still saw sadness.

It was more than some random spark of genius creativity that had caused him to disfigure his face like this and she knew it. It may have even been the same thing that drove him to severely modify his body to please her. She had to know what it was.

"Max, why did you hurt yourself?"

"The arms? They didn't hurt much at all. I used anesthetic."

"Yeah, I saw you made a mess of the cabinet as well. You are like a destructive little puppy. I don't mean the arms; I mean your face. Why did you do that?"

Crimson was having a hard time seeing Max's expression under the dried blood, bruises, and gashes on his face. He was contouring his mouth, though, to a frown, and she could tell he was hesitating to tell her something. Finally, he spoke, looking unsure of himself.

"When I got into college, I became an addict to serenity boosts. They ruled my life. I couldn't get by without them. I needed them to sleep and I was severely addicted. Finally, I broke the habit..." He began to trail off as if he wasn't going to finish, but her eyes pierced a void into his heart and he began to tear up. "I relapsed the other day. I was so nervous and worked up after I met you in the office, I couldn't calm down and I used one again. It was the first time in three years and my cells have been screaming for more ever since. It's going to take awhile to break, but that isn't the hard part. I felt like I had failed. I don't like failure, never have. Failure makes me loathe myself, and when I loathe myself, I punish myself. I always have, ever since I was young. I would smash my head into walls, punch myself, even cut myself on my legs or somewhere that wasn't visible. It's an addiction, too, but much harder to break than the boosts."

There was a long silence as they stood there holding each other. The tears that were in Max's eyes had now turned into streams running down his face. The last little bit he had said sounded shaky, as if he were going to burst into hysterical crying at any time.

His body shook with the emotion of it all and Crimson held him tight. She could tell his mind was racing a mile a minute as she thought of how she wanted to put this. She wasn't any good at being delicate, and in this moment, that was what he needed.

"Max," she said, sounding firm but soft.

"Yes?"

"Don't hate anyone from here on out except our enemies. I need that rage you feel for yourself, for your failures, redirected. Can you do that for me, please? I promise, we will succeed. You won't face failure."

"I think I can do that."

"Good, then clean up. I'm starving. The date was a ploy of espionage. I completed my mission, had a few drinks free of charge, and now I am really hungry. I can't remember if I even took a bite."

Max was shocked. She didn't run screaming. But what had he expected? She was like nothing he'd ever known. He was happy to be her ally and to fight for her cause. "Okay, sounds good," he said with a sigh, squeezing her tightly, careful not to hurt her with his newfound strength.

Nine

We Would Like You to Come With Us

He had only walked about nine blocks from Max's office when two hover cars came whizzing up alongside him, pulling off of the street and hovering on the sidewalk. The cars were blue with black tint and identical other than their identification tags. When they came up on him, one had strategically pulled in front, the other behind.

One of the cars had nearly struck a bystander that was walking closely behind Zarfa, but he had managed to move out of the way. Zarfa was standing there, still pondering the things he had heard in Max's office. He had yet to decide what he was going to do. The only thing he knew for sure was that he wanted to get back home to Ilyeion, home to his legion.

He had only come to Alexarien to get the Psyker Scream nanobots. He had them now. He had no other reason to be here anymore, but now this. Another annoyance; these cars weren't coincidence and he knew it.

Before he could even blink, five men piled out of each car and encircled him—all of them armed to the teeth, all of them fit, soldiers. One of them stepped forward into the circle that they had formed around him.

"Our boss, Badger—you met him the other night, remember?—would like for you to take a ride with us. He has some things he would like to discuss with you."

This asshole doesn't know how much I hate condescending rhetorical questioning. Let's see, there are ten of them. If I take him down quickly and start firing off rounds from his pistol, I should be able to kill most of them before they even know what's going on.

Zarfa's body tensed and he got ready to execute his plan before a disembodied voice stopped him.

"I wouldn't if I were you."

"What the hell?" Zarfa asked.

"That's right, I can hear your thoughts and can even send you messages. You are a new recruit, only had one treatment, right? It's enough for me to speak to you, and if you are really talented and have a lot of focus, you could intentionally send a message. Anyway, we are all mere underlings here, but I assure you, we are more than capable of killing you or taking you by force."

"I don't want to join you, but if I understand right, I have no choice once I've injected the final treatment of bots. So why are you guys hassling me?" Zarfa was carefully trying to stifle any thoughts he might be having outside of the conversation. He didn't want this guy getting any more information out of him than he could help.

"We would like you to come with us, Zarfa, the easy way, please?"

Zarfa felt defeated. He relaxed his body and dropped his guard. For now, the right move was to do nothing. How could he fight ten men, especially when, from what he could tell, they could all read his mind? He was broadcasting already, and he didn't like it.

"Okay, fine, I'll come with you and hear Badger out."

Five men piled back into the car straight ahead of Zarfa; two got back into the car immediately behind him. Two of the men directed Zarfa into the back seat and asked him to sit in the middle. He complied—he didn't want this to end badly for himself. After he had made himself comfortable, the other two got into the back with him and one stayed on the sidewalk—there was no room for him.

Hotdog, canary, goldfish, butterfly. One, two, three, four, five, six, pepper, eight, nine, ten.

Zarfa started thinking of anything he could to keep anything vital from slipping. Even if he did formulate an escape plan, he was hoping to do so while thinking strongly about something else, so as to muddle his message and make it unclear to them what he was planning on doing.

The whole ride to the warehouse that he had been at the night before was awkward and silent. While he tried to keep the goons Badger had sent out of his mind, they tried breaking in. When they did, all they got was his garbled ramblings or him counting loudly in his head. He was smarter than they had given him credit for.

I hope there isn't two thousand or more of them in there like last night.

Zarfa's concentration slipped and he broke his pattern of useless thoughts. He was upset at himself already. He didn't need the voice of the guy sitting next to him saying, *"There isn't,"* inside of his head. But it was, and it was annoying overkill. He had already caught himself mess up. At least he could relax a little bit now knowing he wouldn't have to fight through a sea to get away if it came to that.

"Very clever making psychic soldiers under the ruse of a band," he stated as they directed him to get out of the back seat.

As he got out of the car, the nine men surrounded him again and directed him to go inside the warehouse. They had him outnumbered and circled to be sure he didn't try anything funny. This certainly wouldn't be an easy situation to get out of.

A large, roll-up cargo door opened as they approached. They directed him to go in through this instead of the small side door he and Max had used the night before. As the door rolled up, it revealed from the feet up a man large and daunting that he recognized as Badger.

"Zarfa, so nice of you to join us without a battle. Their direction was that if you were too much trouble, they could go ahead and kill you," Badger said with a smile.

He was tall, hairy, and intimidating. Even worse, he wore darkly-tinted glasses so that Zarfa couldn't see his eyes. As if he didn't already have every disadvantage working against him.

This is just great! Seventy-eight, forty-five, sixty-nine.

"What is great?" Badger's voice invaded his head.

"I can't even read your eyes with those douchebag-looking glasses of yours, asshole. Like you don't already have the upper hand on me, you had to push it that far? Seriously?"

"I see your point. Come in and have a seat," he said. He

mocked as if he was going to take the shades off, but in the end, left them on.

They directed Zarfa to sit on a bare wooden chair in the center of the room. The chair was facing another three that looked exactly the same. To the right, he saw Zax; to the left, Surge, and he was certain Badger would fill the middle seat.

He sat as he had been asked, and waited attentively and respectfully for the conversation to begin. He assumed there would be one of some sort. If they wanted him dead, they wouldn't have gone to all of the theatrics.His heart and his observations about how they approached him told him that everything Crimson said about them was true. He could see this organization was large, powerful, and probably didn't have people's welfare in mind. He knew they were dangerous and most likely the evil she said they were, but he had to keep these feelings and thoughts out of his mind.

Badger took what felt like a lifetime to Zarfa to take his position at the middle seat. When he did, he just sat there facing Zarfa. He couldn't even tell if his eyes were open or not; he refused to take the shades off of his face.

"Let's talk," Badger said, finally.

"Then talk," Zarfa said with a shrug.

"I can tell you are quickly becoming adept at keeping us confused, keeping us from reading your thoughts, so I am going to be required to accept what you say as the truth. If Zax here can pick up that you are lying to me, the conversation is over, and that is when Surge does his job. You don't want to see him do his job, not to you anyways. We have an understanding here?"

"Yes."

"Good, now I'm going to ask you plainly what Crimson told you."

Zarfa spoke, hoping that nothing he said would sentence Crimson to death. "She tried to recruit me. She said a war was coming. She said that Synaptix was already using mind control technology to build an army, the Psyker Scream army. She said that the other side of this war was going to be Polyhelix. She told me they, too, are building an army and the Faraza are part of that. She plans to somehow stop them both. She is also under the impression that both sides are seeking dominance of not only the Alexarien government but those of the entire world. Oh, she also said your two corporations are both too greedy to form an alliance together to avoid this whole thing."

"Interesting. Well, let me tell you something about this little *Crimson* girl. She has been a disillusioned freedom fighter since the day she got her freedom when she was seventeen. You see, she was a house slave, a concubine, if you will, for a rich man named Chester Williams. Chester enjoyed taking the innocent schoolgirl fantasy a little too far, but as you know, if you own someone as a slave, you can use them however you see fit. He adopted her at six; the sexual abuse began by seven. He had a penchant for the young ones. I am not saying he isn't sick, but it was his right. He did own her, after all.

"Anyway, his fantasy involved more than a simple young slave. He sent her to school as a little girl every day, sending her off with her packed lunch and a kiss on the forehead, only to greet her as a cruel, tortuous devil when she returned home. She was told that if she ever tried to escape, he would murder her family in cold blood. I never did understand why she cared—they sold her to him. They knew what he was looking for. Anyway, I am getting sidetracked. She dealt with this torture and abuse until she was seventeen. Two more years and he would let her go to live her life however she could manage to. He hated it when they started looking like women; it disgusted her owner.

"Finally, one day, she got wise. She managed to make some Paraoxon in chemistry class. Before going home, she coated the outside of her vinyl gloves with the poison. She was a smart kid, she was. When she arrived home, she acted normal. The typical 'Oh Daddy, how I missed you; is there anything I can do for you?' routine that he loved so much, followed by her touching him in the most depraved, unspeakable manners. Well, she was sure this time to touch any part of his skin she could. When he requested she take her gloves off, she asked 'if he could do it for her because she had been having trouble on her own.' She was a helpless little girl, after all. Five minutes later, ol' Chester was dead, and Crimson was a free woman with a large inheritance. Something she doesn't tell many people, I am sure. You see, Chester didn't have any family, no children, no wife. He had his living will state that whoever his current slave was would be the recipient of his vast wealth. Crimson didn't know that, it was just an added reward to her first assassination, one that is speculated but could never be proved. A discreet poison that Paraoxon is; it absorbs through the skin, kills in minutes. There is no solid antidote and it is untraceable in autopsies. Like I said, she was intelligent, cunning—still is.

"She lived through those awful days, but came out damaged, like anyone would. She got an education and built an empire, but the whole time she brewed with hatred. Hatred for the government for making it legal for him to do what he did to her. Hatred at society for voting in the laws. It is what still drives her to her very core. Hatred. Pure and simple, nothing more. We offered for her to join us; she has proven she is a capable assassin by killing many elite assassins on the roster. She has wealth, brains, and ability, all that would further our cause, yet she fails to see reason. She wants control, but she doesn't want to rob the populace of the ability to decide for themselves. This is where we don't see eye to eye with her cause, why she isn't one of us, and why we aren't allies. We want the same thing, to change the world, but she doesn't agree to our terms. She is right, a war is coming shortly and Polyhelix cannot be dealt with reasonably. They want to turn us all into mutants!

"Until now, we thought Crimson was some daydreaming radical that could never pose a threat. We are beginning to think otherwise. She came to you because of the fact that you run Legion Nine, am I right?"

Zarfa was wondering how long Badger would drone on for. "Yes, she did," he replied.

"We don't know what she is planning, but it has to be big. I suspect that if she thought she could reason with us, she would have solicited us for her purposes as well. From here on out, she is our enemy. We won't declare an all-out war on her until we know who her army is, but if an assassination attempt avails itself, then we shall strike. We can't have that damaged idealist out in the wild."

"Okay, well, thanks for the morbid tale and all, but I don't see why you brought me here unless you want me to kill her."

"No, we have our own wet crew. We don't need you for that. We brought you here for the same reason that she pulled you aside. We want Legion Nine to join us. You've already declared war on Faraza, which makes you an enemy of Polyhelix.

"As you know, if you follow through with your injections, you will be able to hear the wasps and where they come from, where they go back to and hide. You will be able to go on the offensive and get what you desire. What our little friend Crimson also made you aware of was that if you go through with the injections, at any time we can flip a switch and, regardless of you agreeing to our terms, you are our soldier. What we offer you is this—an agreement. You keep your free will, add your army as a separate independent army to the Psyker Scream revolution. Join us and fight for us, and when the war is over, you will have a seat at our table of power. Sound good?"

"What about my men? If I understand right, after crushing Polyhelix, you plan to implement a technology that will control the masses around the world. Very few will have free will. What about my loyal soldiers? What will be their reward?"

"Their reward is they will get to see the day their dream comes true and Faraza is destroyed. When we do control the world...well, let's face it, they can't all have free will. That is reserved for the elite; however, they won't know the difference."

"And if I refuse this offer, what then?"

"Simple, you follow through on the treatments. You will have free will until the day we determine you don't need it. You don't follow through on the treatments and we will still let you live until our common enemy is defeated, or until you work up the nerve to try and fight us. No matter your answer, you walk out of here alive today. No sense in killing someone who is an ally, even if he is an inadvertent ally. I really encourage you to take our *best* offer."

"I see. How can I be sure that if I follow through on the injections and take your best offer, as you put it, that I won't be subjected to mind control? How can I be sure you aren't lying to me?"

"Simple, say yes to us now and you stop the treatments. We give you a reversal nanobot that destroys the others. Then we implant you with a chip that will make you immune to the frequency that we are going to use to spark the mass controlling of the populace.

"The frequency is only a first step. All it will do really is make people want a new product we are going to release. The product will be cheap enough for everyone to afford and when the two combine, they will be under our control. By the way, I am telling you this because it is inevitable; you can't stop it. Not even with Legion Nine. So I am sure you see where I'm coming from. We are truly trying to be generous to you, Zarfa. What do you say? Join us?"

Zarfa sat and stared at Badger a good long while. *I wish the prick would take off his damn glasses already. I know he is doing it just to bug me.* He knew Badger could read his thoughts, and he had alluded that Zax was even more skilled at it, but he didn't care. He knew he was being careful to not give them anything.

"I am going to have to respectfully decline. If you make me some mindless subservient after the war, so be it. As for now, I am unwilling to make a decision. I am also unwilling to sell out my men only to save myself. So if our business is over now, can I leave?"

He was cool, calm, controlled. Badger's cheeks were red, and Zarfa knew, if he had his glasses off, he would see an annoyed look in those eyes of his. Zarfa could tell by the disposition of the other two that their plan had not worked the way they hoped. Zarfa, for his part, hoped they weren't lying about allowing him to leave.

"You know we could forcefully implant you with a mind control device, right, and send you on your merry way, don't you?" questioned Badger, trying to remain calm.

"Yeah, I know. You said you wouldn't. You said you would let me leave unhindered. I questioned why that might be when you told me, then I realized something..." Zarfa paused for a long while, making sure to think random things so they couldn't discern what he was going to say.

"And what was that? What did you realize?"

"That you wouldn't have a clue how to contact Legion Nine. Only I know that. They are secretive and hide other than when there are raids from the Faraza. If you controlled me now, my return wouldn't be natural. I wouldn't contact them the way I always do, the way that you don't know. You can't control me. That is what I figured out."

Badger removed his glasses and he stared down Zarfa with a look of befuddlement mixed with rage and aggravation. Even with all of the tricks up his sleeve, he still couldn't best Zarfa, and Zarfa knew that got under his skin.

"How are you doing this?" Badger's voice blared in his mind.

His reaction only confirmed Zarfa's hunch. Zarfa leaned back and smiled a bit in the satisfaction that he had found a way to beat the odds. He always had, and he always would. Folding his hands behind his head, he let out a sigh of mocking boredom. "So, gentlemen, how about a ride back downtown? I need to get my stuff then I'm going home."

Badger sent mental orders and, shortly, Zarfa was being escorted back outside. They got him in a hovercraft and took him back to where they had picked him up as if nothing had happened. Several hours had passed and it was late in the day. Zarfa was hungry and near broke.

He began walking back to his house, relieved he was still alive. He was also happy to have gotten rid of the Psyker Scream freaks; he knew in his gut, though, it wouldn't be the last he saw of them. He replayed Badger's story of Crimson in his mind over and over and wished he had probed more into what exactly Crimson's plan was.

He felt bad for her; he wished she had never gone through what Badger described. But Zarfa didn't feel she was broken, he just felt that she truly saw the world. He wished he had listened to her better, but he still wasn't sure if he would align himself to her cause.

That night, after returning home to get his things, Zarfa boarded an underground rail back to Ilyeion. He had only a backpack full of belongings and he felt it best for him to bring the next four rounds of injections with him. He would be home in a matter of two days. He would be greeted by his men, and he would have to make a decision, one they would be a part of.

I've got to warn her about Badger. I have to tell her what happened. Hopefully, I am out of their range and they won't hear me. I'll be their mortal enemy for sure then.

He looked around and came to the realization he should have thought about it sooner. He didn't have the number for her com-link, neither did he have the number for Max's. He

could look it up on the interface, but there wasn't one anywhere on the train. It would have to wait until he reached
Ilyeion.

"He's coming back home," said Ghast, sounding annoyed
and relieved at the same time.

"Father? Why is he coming back to Ilyeion?" asked Sarah.

"Not your father—Zarfa."

"This is good news. He should be easy to take into captiv-
ity then."

"How do you propose? The plan was to get him at Alexarien when he was by himself. He is on a train headed back
right now. The intelligence came in too late to deploy an in-
terception team. Our only chance will be to pick him up at
the train station. After that, he will be reunited with his trou-
blesome army and we have had little success taking any of
them in any other way than corpses."

"True, they seem to fight like the berserkers of ancient
Norse mythology. They don't care if they die. In fact, they'd
rather die than be taken alive. He seems to fight better than
all of them and, even worse, he is always surrounded by his
elite guard when they face us on the field of battle."

"So, as I said, our only chance is at the train station,
right when he gets off the train. It will be tricky. In fact, we
should call it a massacre and take whoever is in the station,
kill those who put up too much resistance, and try to mini-
mize losses by using...them."

Sarah thought about it for awhile. She stared at Ghast,
trying to figure out if he was serious. "They are ready? I
thought it hadn't been perfected yet."

"It's close—we have some early prototypes that respond
well to commands. They aren't optimal. In all reality, they
are somewhat failed experiments so we need to dispose of
them anyway. Any that we lose will help us with that."

"Are they able to execute a capture command or are they
too unruly still?"

"Ugh... How did I know you were going to ask that? It is
about a twenty-eighty split. Twenty percent of the time they
go insane and do whatever they please. Eighty percent of the

time they execute their commands exactly. The genetic coding needs to be refined a little bit better to make them more subservient. However, they are the best soldiers we currently have. They are strong and fast. Their eyesight is unmatched; the tentacles have progressed nicely on this round of creation, and escaping their grasp would be near impossible. Even for him. Also, they are able to blind with their ink."

"How many do we have to send?"

"We created thirty from this last round of raiding. As I said, almost completely submissive. We still don't know what is causing the twenty percent to enrage and turn on the handlers, or anyone within their field of vision for that matter."

"How many handlers do we currently have available?"

"Handlers aren't an issue. You forget we are preparing for a war that we expect to end quickly. Currently, we have far more handlers than we do these monsters."

Sarah thought long and hard. She envisioned how it might go. She realized that there was a chance he would be killed by a renegade solider. She also came to the conclusion that this was their best opportunity. If she waited for another raid, he might be killed there too.

They had been unsuccessful at capturing him because he never backed down. He never surrendered. Once, when they had him encircled by thirteen men and they thought they had him, he managed to kill six on his own before his reinforcements had arrived.

It was coming to be the final hour. They had to capture him as she wanted or do away with him completely. She regretted not telling him the plan the day they took her. She knew it was a pick-up, that she would go peacefully, but he would never want anything to do with Father's plan.

As far as he knew, Mother and Father were both dead. That was only the half-truth, but still, she knew if he had any inkling of what was really going on, who was behind the Faraza, he would probably fight it with the same or even more viciousness than he currently displayed.

He was a danger to the cause. Even if she did take him alive, the treatments would change him so much that he would no longer be himself. Her selfishness and her desire to have her older protectorate brother back in her life had clouded her vision for many years. Finally, she saw that, and she saw that he had to be dealt with, one way or another.

"Okay then, send all thirty of the chimeras along with thirty handlers. I want one on each one. If we can take him alive, do so. If not, kill him." Her voice was stern and cold.

"So we let him go? Just like that?" asked Zax.

"We really have no other option. We can't make him join us, he doesn't seek for us to be destroyed, and for now, we have a common enemy," Badger replied.

He was annoyed at how the events of their meeting had played out. He didn't like hearing no as an answer. Especially since he had at his every beck and call a large army of psychics, ever loyal and always connected to the network of his mind. They always carried out his orders, never said no, even the ones he had left with a degree of free will.

But he knew, sooner or later, he would have control over Zarfa. The signals he transmitted weren't strong enough yet to be linked to the network, but he had only had one treatment. He knew in a matter of weeks, he would complete the injections from the bots. At that moment, Zarfa would be vulnerable, open to his manipulations, and then he would have what he wanted.

"We will have him in due time, but for now, we should send Surge to keep an eye on him," Badger stated, looking dismissively at Surge.

The escort crew had recently left with Zarfa to take him downtown. He knew that anyone who had honed their psychic abilities as well as the three of them could at least pick up a faint signal at the radius of two miles or so and be able to follow him.

"You got it, boss. Shall I take my axe?" Surge questioned.

"Yeah...we don't know how this will all work out; don't go unprotected. Also, be discreet. As we know, the Faraza have infiltrated Alexarien, but Ilyeion is their base camp. You are going to be deep into enemy territory, so be sure to not draw undue attention to yourself. They would love to get their hands on you."

"Understood. You can trust me. Plus, the three of us know that I am the best fighter in this army. They won't kill or capture me, you can be sure of that."

"Don't get cocky, you idiot," Zax said, annoyed and speaking out of turn.

"It is not your place, Zax!" Badger snapped. "But he is right, don't get cocky. It would be a shame for us to lose our best fighter before the war begins."

Surge smiled and looked at the other two with a glimpse of defiance. "You know how I operate. I'll take my best weapon, but in case I run into a spot where I can't use it, I'll carry a plasma long sword as well as a dagger...perhaps a gauss pistol too just to be on the safe side. Satisfied?"

"Take two of our top ranking soldiers as well. It isn't much, but if the event arises where it is safer to flee than to fight, leave them. Better to lose some subservient than to lose you. You know I left both you and Zax with free will not only because you are my friends, but also because you are generals. In the event of our separation from the psychic network, or in the event of my demise, you both have authority to command the army when the war starts. Let's hope that never happens, but if it does, I trust you equally."

"They will probably slow me down, but if it makes you feel better to be safe, then I'll take them. I wouldn't want you losing any sleep, boss," Surge said with a tone of sarcasm.

At that, Surge stood, bowed his head, and dismissed himself. He knew he would have to act quickly to pick his companions and prepare his weaponry without losing Zarfa's signal.

"Now we have the matter of our little thorn, Crimson. Zax, I shall leave it in your care to crush her and that little doctor she recruited to her side. I want them both dead. I am still uncertain of what she is planning. The fact she was trying to recruit Legion Nine tells me that she has a serious plan and could prove to be a hindrance later. Like a cancer, she should be dealt with before she has time to spread."

"Agreed, she is crafty, dangerous, adept... How would you like this handled?"

"I shall leave that to your discretion. You are quite capable, but understand I don't want failure by any means. Take her out, annihilate her—do it so maliciously that anyone she may already have on her side will fear us so much that they don't dare try to continue her revolution."

"Understood, it will be done."

The train was uncomfortable and bumpy. Zarfa had purchased the cheapest ticket, which only provided a seat barely
large enough for him to sit in. The recliner button on the arm
rest was broken and his legs were in such a cramped position
that it was causing him severe annoyance. He leaned his
head back and tried to sleep, but was unsuccessful.

Two days on this thing like this? Crap.

He unzipped his backpack that was resting on his lap. He
had grabbed some crummy-tasting meals from his home.
The most common type claimed to have some sort of flavor
such as "turkey dinner" or "salmon and potatoes," but they
were really synthesized protein mixed with vitamins and
minerals to keep you alive and healthy. He shook his head in
disbelief. None of these "meals" tasted anything like what
they claimed.

He rummaged around under the bars and found one of
the vials containing another treatment of the Psyker Scream
nanobots. He held it up to the light and looked at them all.
They appeared to be liquid they were so small, rolling around
on top of each other in the jar.

*I wish I had known. I would have found another way. But
now, I'm stuck. I don't want to finish the treatments, but my
men deserve justice as much as I do. As their leader,
shouldn't I sacrifice myself so they can have their day? I
don't know. I'll let them have their say. This is no time to be
selfish.*

Zarfa shoved the vial into the pack and leaned his head
back onto the seat. He was as uncomfortable as ever, but he
folded his arms in his lap and rested them on his backpack.
He closed his eyes and he hummed a little tune he remembered learning as a child.

*Oh well, two days of this. I've suffered worse. I can't wait
to stretch my legs back in Ilyeion.*

"They're grotesque!" Sarah exclaimed as she entered the

room that housed the teuthida chimeras.

Each one was in its own cage with a bed and a toilet. The cages were small, but not too cramped. The beds were adequate, but still, she could tell by the way they paced as she passed by that they weren't happy being in there.

"Obviously, by looking at their heads, they can't speak our language, but can they hear us? Do they understand me?" she questioned.

"Of course they can. How else would they follow orders? They understand but are incapable of complex abstract thoughts. Too much of the canine DNA that we used to provide the submissive quality scrambled their brains too heavily. Not to mention the teuthida DNA. They are barely human any longer. But as you can see, they are still bipedal. The mutations provided a simple ear hole rather than them having an aural appendage," Ghast said.

The chimeras ranged in size, some as short as five foot, four inches up to about six foot, eight inches. They had giant squid-looking eyes and their heads were cone-shaped. Instead of mouths with lips, they had a series of twelve tendrils all about a foot long that could each move independently draping over their chin.

Under the tendrils was a large beak, roughly eight inches in size, most certainly a deadly weapon. Their arms looked like a normal human's, but instead of hands with five fingers, there was a dual tentacle appendage that split in the shape of the letter Y. Each of the tentacles that branched from the wrist was roughly fourteen inches and covered in suction cups.

Each of them looked more muscular than any average human; their skin was an almost translucent off-white. It appeared slimy, as if covered in a thin mucosal membrane. They smelled awful and distinct. Their torsos looked the same as any human, but the skin was that same translucent off-white. They stood upright on two legs and moved almost identical to humans.

"They look awful, they smell gross, and they appear to be incredibly slimy. Couldn't we bring out a little more of that canine DNA and cover them in hair?" she questioned.

"If we were to do that, we would lose the suction cups. We are working within tight parameters with the DNA as it is. We really only isolated one strand of the canine genus that we call the 'loyalty' gene. It is what causes those creatures to be so companion driven in nature. Thus the old adage for centuries of 'man's best friend.' You can kick a dog and treat it awful, yet for some reason, it always goes back to its master when called. Though they may get apprehensive, it was always a rare day that the more docile breeds such as Labradors would turn on their master or owner. It is only this gene that we used. Otherwise, they would lose their suction cups and the ability to shoot ink."

"They shoot ink? Really, and where from? I mean, real squids shoot it from the bottom of themselves. I don't see that being an advantage seeing as they are bipedal."

"We made modifications to how DNA would form the cells and cause the mutations within the human genome. Through careful manipulation, we were able to cause the ink sacs and the orifice to develop directly under the eyes. Look carefully and you can see them."

"Very clever. How is their strength?"

"Roughly twice that of the average human. The mutations did provide a slight increase in muscle mass, as well as density of tissue. However, their bones are no longer rigid and hard as ours are; they are now more cartilaginous. This provides both an advantage and a disadvantage. If struck hard, but not hard enough, they will prove to be quite resilient. However, if hit with the proper force, they will crumple like rags. As I said, they have their advantages as well as disadvantages. Over all, they are stronger than average humans and faster due to the fact that cartilage is lighter than osseous tissue. Their eyesight is unmatched; it is so sensitive they are able to see in almost complete darkness, but with the combination of human DNA, their irises are able to adapt to both daylight and total darkness.

"Their unique tentacle hands provide unmatched gripping power. They are able to fight well unarmed, as well as with plasma blades. They, however, cannot grasp guns or ranged weapons of that nature. They are masters of close combat, which should be perfect for taking down your brother.

"Also, the tendrils on their faces—each are able to move independently and grasp objects, drawing in their victims to their large, brutal beaks. The ink glands and orifices being under their eyes allow them to shoot a very thick, oily ink about twenty feet. It doesn't smell good and is capable of blinding their enemy temporarily."

"I see. What of the issue of them going berserk? What is the cause of this?"

"That, we still don't know, but you need to keep in mind we are dealing with a very intricate and delicate system. By manipulating the DNA, we are fortunate that we are even able to do this. If one chromosome matches up wrong, we would wind up either killing the specimen or altering it into something unusable. These monsters have their place in combat, but are by no means the end all. Certainly a good shock troop to cause heavy damage and frighten the enemy, wouldn't you agree?"

Sarah nodded her head. "Hell, I am even scared of them."

Ten

He Who Draws First Blood

"What are you working on?" Crimson asked, sitting next to Max, who was drawing up the schematic for something he would have the assembly line put together.

It was the morning after Max's last "incident" in the lab. Not only had he caused a lot of damage to himself, but he had also damaged some things in the lab. He also used a large amount of valuable resources that Crimson had planned to use for her projects. It would be a few days before they would be replaced, so her projects for Max were on hold. Meanwhile, Max decided he would create some more things for himself.

"My eye...well, it will be anyway, once I'm done with it."

"Your eye?"

"Yep."

"Why are you making eyes?"

"Eye. Singular. You see, this one," he said, pointing to the one he had damaged while bashing his head on the pharmaceutical locker, "it's pretty busted. Not just the damage I did to it—it's weak...flesh."

"Right... Mine are flesh too. Care to enlighten me?"

"You are agile and know how to fight; it's your job...when you aren't amassing an army, that is. I don't know how to fight. I plan to support you on the battlefield. These arms I made are perfect for it—they don't shake; I could crush a tank with them; they have an electro-nervous system that gives me tactile sensation so that I know how hard I am grabbing, squeezing, hitting, you know, etcetera, but they feel no pain. They are amazing, if I do say so myself, so I plan to use them at range as the perfect hands to be holding a sniper rifle to support you at a long range. If someone sneaks up on me or gets near me, I should be able to defend myself by melee or martial arts of some sort. Also, if someone manages to shoot one off or even slice through it with a plasma blade, well, it won't hurt any. There is, however, one vital flaw, one thing that prevents me from supporting you in practice rather than only in theory."

"You don't say?" she questioned, raising an eyebrow playfully.

"My eyes! They suck, I have no targeting skill. At this point, I would be incapable of hitting anything more than five yards out. So... Well, it's really cool, actually. I am making a new biotic prosthetic. I will replace the eye that doesn't have my interface chip installed in it. The busted one,"—he pointed to it again—"that one has got to go. It will be replaced by my Max two point zero eye. It's going to be great—targeting guidance linked from my eye to my arms. I will be able to tell exact distances and velocity of whatever I am looking at. With this information, the auto logic processor will calculate for me precisely where I should aim to hit my mark, as well as move my arms on its own. It is a feature that I will be capable of switching on and off, of course. With this eye, they'll call me 'Deadeye Max.' Sounds cool, huh?"

"Very, did you come up with it yourself...*Deadeye?*"

Max smiled wide like a child, and happily said, "As a matter of fact, I did."

"Yeah, I could tell. It sounds like something out of some corny children's comic book or something. If it is really what you want to be called, fine, but if we get to the battlefield and someone makes fun of you for it, don't let it distract you and miss your mark."

Max made a dismissive *pfsshtt* noise and waved her off. "Comic book, my ass. Besides...what's wrong with comics? They're great!"

"Figures."

"Whatever."

"Hey, I thought of one other thing that would keep you from helping me," she said nonchalantly as she typed away on a tablet computer without looking up.

"What's that?"

"As far as I can tell, you don't know any martial arts. Nor do you know how to swing any weapons properly."

Max looked up from his schematic and stared past her. "Well...no."

"It's okay, I've got something for you. It's in the other room."

Max didn't want to leave his schematic, but before he knew it, Crimson had grabbed him by his wrist and was pulling him out of his seat. She led him down the hallway and into a room past the lab they were in.

The room was vast, white, and the walls were covered in thick, soft padding. The padding on the floor was some kind of foam. It would soften a fall, but not much, and it wasn't so soft that it would hinder movement. The room was empty except for a weapons rack with any form of plasma melee weapon one could imagine. The only other thing in the whole thirty-by-thirty foot room was a four-armed statue of a skeleton holding carbon fiber electroshock tonfas.

The statue was large and menacing. It had eyes that looked as if it could spring to life at any time. The entire frame of this piece of artwork was made of carbon fiber. Its jaw gaped half open, looking like a ventriloquist dummy that was midsentence. It gave Max the creeps.

"This is the sparring room," Crimson started. "I suggest you find a weapon you feel comfortable with. You're going to need it in about a minute."

"I'm not going to fight you. What if I hurt you?"

Crimson stared at him as if he were joking. "First off, you couldn't touch me if you wanted to. Second, you aren't fighting me. You're fighting Luther over there," she said as she pointed to the grotesque statue.

"Right...I'm fighting a statue, how novel."

"Eratus vincu klaas," Crimson said, as if chanting some ancient spell.

The behemoth statue's eyes lit up in a pale, sickly green color. They looked eerie and vile; the contrast of the sleek black of the carbon fiber against the green gave the statue an almost mythical feel. It began walking toward Crimson and Max at an alarming rate. Max grimaced and Crimson stepped forward.

"Long time no see, Luther!" Crimson called out, waving at

the object as if it were a person.

"Indeed, it has been, Crimson," a mechanical voice bellowed ominously.

Max glared at her and said, "How did you program it so intricately?"

"Program? It's not a program. It's an intelligence much like yours and mine. Luther is an old friend of mine."

"An artificial intelligence? I thought those were outlawed, banned! You remember what happened in 2028? The American government foolishly created one to aid in the civil war that had erupted and it turned on them. It dropped nukes and exploded reactors all across their countryside and exterminated them over night! That was the start of the Great Extinction here on earth and the whole reason we can barely grow real food anywhere! The only saving grace is the AI had destroyed its own mainframe inadvertently before it could back itself up, or else who knows what other kind of havoc it would wreak? And you have one?"

Luther began to laugh and Crimson wore an expression that stated, *"You're an idiot, Max."*

"No, Luther was a neurologist studying what made people's personalities. He was developing a type of brain MRI that could copy every detail down to the last and store it as binary data. You could then upload your personality into a shell of some sort, such as the one you see in front of you now. However, before his work could be completed, Luther was assassinated. By none other than the lovely Alexarien government. I have no solid proof, but it is what we believe. After his assassination, I went to his lab and did some snooping. Apparently, Luther was testing his own technology on himself and had made a backup of his persona. However, he hadn't perfected the technology yet. I created for him this shell and loaded in his personality, trying to bring my dead friend back. It did. He is who he was, the way he responds, voice patterns, feeling, the whole lot of it. However, he has lost his spark of brilliance; nothing makes sense to him the way it once did, so he could never assist me as my inventor the way you will.

"Something severe is missing in him, and since I believe that the flaw was in his early scanning technology, there is nothing we can do to restore Luther to his full potential. However, he still offers himself to me willingly. In case some day he goes out of control, because it isn't really for sure if he is an AI or a person, his shell has a failsafe with voice activation. The words I uttered earlier are from a dead language. When I speak them, he activates and wakes up. If I were to speak them again, he would fall asleep. Luther understands the failsafe and doesn't feel the time he is asleep, so he doesn't mind, do you, Luther?"

"Not at all, mistress Crimson," he said, kneeling.

Luther's body stood about six feet, eight inches and he loomed over both Max and Crimson. It appeared to be designed for speed and efficiency of movement. There were no extra fancy parts bogging down the mobility. His four arms would certainly give him an upper hand in combat as well.

"If you don't feel the time you are asleep, Luther, then why did you say it had been a long time?" Max questioned skeptically.

"Because it must have been, what...five years since you've last awakened me from my sleep? Am I close to correct on that, Crimson? I am making the assumption because I remember you looking much younger."

"It's been seven, Luther, so thanks for the compliment. I must not be looking too bad in my old age," she said with a grin.

"You see when I am off, I am off. I have no knowledge of what is going on around me. So it feels as if I saw her yesterday, but I am sure a lot has changed in the last seven years, hasn't it?" Luther asked, still kneeling before Crimson.

"That it has, Luther, my friend. The revolution is about to begin. In just a little while, I shall rally a call for supporters, but even if nobody joins in the uprising, I believe we still stand a good chance of winning. Max here is going to help me with the last two things I need, and I hope he can reach my deadline. I have all of my *minions* planted and, by now, they've accomplished their tasks."

"I see, very good, Crimson, my friend. My only regret is I couldn't have been of more service to you. I am sorry for being what I am."

"It's no problem really. It isn't your fault you got assassinated."

"What are these minions you mentioned, Crimson?" asked Max.

"Oh, those? You know how I went out on that 'date' with Brian Nash from Barometrics last night?"

"Yeah, I recall," said Max.

"Well, he was the final piece of that puzzle. He has direct access to the last four Pilvikone that I need for my plan. You see, I, over the years, have been covertly having different sales reps or engineers plant hacking bugs in the devices that will allow me to command their power with this little computer I wear on my wristband," she said, pausing to point it out to Max. He had never noticed it before. "Anyways, I put a microchip into his head that allows me to give him commands that he will execute exactly within the parameters I type without him ever realizing he is doing it. In fact, that was what I was inputting on my tablet back in the lab. I took a break because I can get to that later today. I want to do a test run with the Pilvikone before using it in battle, however, not too soon before. It would be a shame for them to get wise to what I've done.

"I felt I should introduce you to Luther here. He is going to be your martial arts instructor. He will train you how to fight unarmed and armed. So, go to the rack and find something that suits you close range, and then, let the battle begin!" she shouted playfully.

"You've got to be frickin' kidding me! He is huge! And he has four arms! He is going to kill me!" Max protested.

"I will not. I helped Crimson improve her skill years ago. I fear now she has far surpassed me and I wouldn't provide any challenge to her even if I were out to kill her," stated Luther.

"Besides, Max, you don't have a choice. You said you wanted to be useful in battle, right? Well, here is your chance," she said as she exited the room. "Find a weapon quick, and Luther...if he dilly-dallys, attack him anyways!"

Max didn't care for the sound of this. He made haste to the rack and began searching for the weapon that most suited him.

Surge stayed his distance from Zarfa on the train. When he boarded, he wore a long black cloak with a cowl on it and dragged behind himself a head amp that rolled on wheels. His two guards dressed in casual clothing, nothing that would raise any red flags or give them away. They just looked like a couple of bouncers following an eccentric musician.

He sat five rows from Zarfa and watched him as he contorted his unusually large limbs to try to get comfortable. The whole ride, so far, it had appeared as if Zarfa was unsuccessful at doing so. Surge felt uncomfortable as well, but more because he was going into enemy territory and knew he needed to keep his guard up. Polyhelix would definitely send the Faraza after him if they knew he was coming.

By now, they had been on the train for about twelve hours and even his mental links with Badger and Zax were severed. They were too far out of range to communicate. It was only him and his two nameless guards now. He would make idle chat with them to make it seem as if they were involved with him, but the reality was they were his puppets.

The two guards that accompanied Surge had proven themselves as very skilled fighters. Both of them were fifth-rounders, however, and had completed the Psyker Scream nanobot treatments. They could be released of their mental slavery, but it was unlikely Surge would do so. These two had been under domination for the last year and they would most likely be angry about their situation if unbound.

So as he made idle chatter, he realized he was nothing more than a man rambling to himself on a train. He had never felt alone before, but he had also not left Badger's side like this in five years. He wished Synaptix had made the link stronger so he could still communicate telepathically with his friend.

Surge glanced over to Zarfa, still uncomfortably wriggling in his seat. After determining he wasn't going anywhere any time soon, Surge closed his eyes and breathed deep. He envisioned what may happen when they arrived in Ilyeion and folded his hands in his lap. After telepathically commanding his two guards to keep watch, he fell asleep.

Zax didn't believe in wasting time. Badger had given him an order and he would carry it out. Only a day had elapsed since he had been handed down the commission to take Crimson's life. He was told to be sure to do it in a way that anyone who might be loyal to her cause would have reason for deterrence, and he fully intended to carry that out.

He collected for himself twenty men, all of which were highly trained but still free will soldiers of the army. If they chose to disobey, he could override them at any moment instantly with telepathy, however the extent of free will they were granted allowed them to problem solve without the need of every little direct command. For a group this large, it would get tiresome having to detail their every command.

After stopping by the armory, he called them all to attention. There they stood, looking grisly and stern. These men knew they were going to go as a gang to extinguish the life that thrived inside of Crimson and Max both.

"Through the means of the interface, we have been able to trace where she is. She lives on the top story of the skyrise that she owns. Her residence is a fortress complete with DNA scan barriers. Whoever she hasn't given the command to accept will be fried on the spot. She has to come out at some time. When she does, we will spring an ambush. We will have four snipers located in different buildings around the block. Two here, one here, and the other here."

He pointed at a strategic map that he had laid out earlier for this use as he submitted his communications to the army.

"The rest of us will stay holed up in an apartment across the street. Our benefactors at Synaptix have already secured it for us from a very 'cooperative' tenant. We will have a new watchman on point every two hours to signal us when she leaves the apartment.

"She is crafty. We cannot rely on the snipers alone. The moment the signal is given, make way to the street. If she isn't dead by the time we make it out there, rain a furious assault on her as quickly as possible. We hope to kill her and Max in the same strike, but if we do not, it won't matter. Crimson is the trained fighter, the elite assassin. Max is just some pathetic doctor. He has no ability to defend himself. He is not our priority. She is. Everyone clear on that?"

The room full of men nodded at him simultaneously. After double-checking their weapons, all twenty-one of them departed and re-gathered at their assigned posts. Now all they needed to do was lay in wait and execute their attack.

Luther came in with a fury of blows upon Max, all of which he deflected with his plasma katanas. Max decided to dual wield since weight of the weapons didn't matter. He would never fatigue or feel pain in his arms again. They did, however, draw calories at an alarming rate when being used this intensely.

His design had attached every nerve to give the most reliable control possible. His hands worked the same, if not better, than his hands before. However, something this complex would need a source of power; the electrical signal carried by the nerves was amplified, but the movements themselves relied on energy stores from the body. Though being synthetic prosthesis, they burned glucose.

That very factor had been an issue with early prosthetics. If someone had their legs or arms replaced, the body needed that many less calories, and weight gain often occurred in the patients. What Max forgot to factor in was that with his design and the fact that he would never feel fatigue, he could quickly burn more calories than he had in his body.

He had been sparring with Luther for about an hour, enough to tire out anyone. Luther never felt fatigue of any kind, and was actually going quite easy on Max. He could tell Max was fading from hunger; he did not let up. Luther deactivated the plasma field of his tonfas and launched another furious attack. An uppercut with his lower right, haymaker with lower left, elbow with upper right, and a quick jab with his upper left.

Each blow connected, each one struck Max with tremendous power. He screamed in pain as he fell to the ground. The jab had caught his already battered eye and reopened a wound on the eyebrow, which began to bleed profusely. He writhed on the ground in pain, both from the battle and from his stomach revolting against him due to his now insatiable appetite.

Luther walked over to the far end of the room and pressed a button on the wall. Crimson came in with a can of medifoam and some towels, both wet and dry.

"Looks like you got your ass handed to you, Max. How did he do, Luther?"

"Not bad for a guy getting his cherry popped. I hope I didn't destroy his eye. It looked pretty bad to begin with."

"Don't worry! I was done with it anyhow!" Max shouted as Crimson knelt by his side and began washing his face.

It burned and was tender. Max wriggled, contorted, and writhed while making noises as if she were torturing him intentionally. He finally stopped squirming after she shot him a serious glance. He relaxed, bit his lip, and endured, motionless, still letting out a deep growl on occasion as she scrubbed sensitive areas.

"Okay, training is over for today. Luther, thanks for the help," she stated with a smile.

"No problem, mistress. Whenever I can be of service to you. Thanks for bringing me back from the grave," he said stoically as he took his position on the far side of the room.

She spoke the words and Luther deactivated and went back into his slumber. There he would wait until tomorrow. She finished tending to Max's wounds by spraying his cuts with medifoam. Within hours, the tissue would be healed and he would look good as new.

"Now, you need to finish that eye. I am pretty sure after that blow, this one is really useless for you."

"No... Now, I eat. I am frickin' starving, woman! I forgot to calculate how many calories these arms would burn in a combat scenario. It made the rest of me fatigue. I am going to need to put on some extra weight and watch my diet...or..." He trailed off as he began scheming a new form of boost, one that was ultra-high in calories to keep his mechanical arms running.

"All right, want to go out for food or scavenge here? It is still early."

"Let's stay in today. Last couple of times we have gone anywhere, it got a little too interesting. I do want to finish my eye tonight and perhaps fabricate it."

After raiding the kitchen for every scrap of real food Crimson had, he went about eating four times the amount of meal bars any normal person would eat. They tasted awful, but Max felt the hunger deep and needed the calories as well as the nutrition. Finally, when he was satisfied, he went back to the lab and put the finishing touches on his blueprint for his mechanical eye.

The eye, though being very complex, would be simpler than the arms. Its draw of energy and sustenance would be very little. Though amongst some of the features he added aside from targeting were night vision, zoom, heat tracing, and ultra violet filtering on nearly every spectrum. All of which he could switch between with a mere thought.

This time, he laid down on the belt, but had the moving mechanism shut off. He positioned himself where he wanted and relaxed. He shot up with another anesthetic boost, this time one that would last the entire duration of the operation.

"I'm ready, throw the switch, please," he said to Crimson, ever grateful that she was here to help him and provide moral support.

"Anything for the cause," she replied casually, though Max felt she was showing more than a professional interest in him.

The arms activated and went to work, extracting his old eye and replacing it, connecting every nerve no matter how small, every ligament, every piece of connecting tissue with elegance and flawlessness. Crimson sat by and watched, somewhat nervous despite the fact she trusted Max knew what he was doing.

After the operation was over, Max went to bed. He'd had quite the day and could barely keep his eyes open. The sparring and the operation drained him physically and mentally and he needed some quiet time. Crimson continued to input commands into the data pad she had been working on earlier.

Right now, Brian was planting devices she had him retrieve from a train station locker in each of the Pilvikones that he had access to. He would do so as a faithful minion then when he was finished, would go about his daily life with no recollection of it. What a great device that little microchip was she had planted in his brain.

He was the last domino in her plot against them. All of the other Pilvikone reactors had already been hacked in a similar manner. Brian was one of her many minions—not the first, and certainly wouldn't be the last either. But for now, that stage of her plan was complete.

She would brief Max on his assignment tomorrow. He

was done monkeying around for his own designs. It was time for him to craft what she needed. Crimson wasn't used to having leisure time like this. It was only ten at night. Typically, at this point, she would still be stalking a target for a job, or preparing for the revolution. She now had nothing to do. It felt strange, awkward...but she took advantage of it and went to sleep.

"There appears to be no movement tonight; commence the two hour watch shifts," Zax commanded telepathically.

"Tell me again why we don't just storm her place?" asked one of the soldiers.

"Because I told you that woman has a DNA barrier and we don't know where to begin with disabling it. She programs it with a little computer on her wrist to scan and allow people to pass through into her home. Anyone she doesn't scan when they pass through the barrier...melts, I guess is the correct term for it. It isn't a pretty sight, trust me."

"Maybe we should work on disabling it."

"Shut up, be patient. We wait until they come to the street, no matter how long it takes."

The rest of the evening remained quiet. Nobody questioned Zax and the watchmen did as they were assigned.

Zarfa didn't sleep at all the first night. He kept thinking about things over and over. How he needed to warn Crimson, what he needed to tell the members of Legion Nine. What he needed to decide. There was going to be blood spilled on all sides in the end—who should he join? And whose blood would be spilled first?

The following day was a long and boring trip. He got up and paced around the train about mid-day, almost tripping on the musical equipment that the strange, shrouded man was toting around with him. He didn't care for this character. He gave Zarfa the distinct impression he was being watched, but he didn't want to confront the man without some sort of obvious issue.

Zarfa had finally fallen asleep in a crinkled up position later into the afternoon. He woke right as the train was pulling into Ilyeion. As the train slowed, he stood, slung his backpack over his shoulder, and began stretching. His legs felt tense from sitting in a cramped seat.

The train pulled to a final stop and he took his position at the door. He was first in line, eager to get off. The time was about nine p.m. Ilyeion standard; it would be about six back in Alexarien. The doors slid open and Zarfa glanced around for the closest public interface terminal. He spotted one across the station.

This is it. After this, I will be an enemy of Synaptix for sure. But I've got to tell her. I may not like Polyhelix and the Faraza...but I sure as hell can't stand the thought of mental slavery.

He made his way to the terminal and connected. Quickly, he found the com-link number for Crimson Felicia Rose. He logged it into his memory and disconnected from the interface. Suddenly, he felt a hand on his shoulder. He spun around to meet the person's face.

"Zarfa, it isn't safe here!" Surge said excitedly, pointing to the squid-like monsters swarming down the stairs of the train station toward them.

"I knew I didn't like the look of you! You spying on me or what?"

"Yes, but I have orders not to kill you and to help you if I can. I have never seen this before, but those squid people coming at us have got to be the work of Polyhelix. Get ready to defend yourself. I will do what I can to help!"

Surge flipped on his audio equipment and threw his guitar over his shoulder.

What the hell is this ass thinking? 'Oh I'm so cool, I'm going to play guitar at a time like this.'

"Zarfa, this might sting a little since you've only had one treatment. Get behind me!" Surge sounded scared as he commanded Zarfa. The creatures and their handlers were approaching quickly.

Zarfa got behind him and dialed in a call to Crimson. It was ringing.

Two...three...four... Crap, Crimson, connect already. I need to tell you a secret!

Finally, he heard on the other end, "Hello?"

"Crimson, it's Zarfa! I am in Ilyeion! Synaptix is going to try to assassinate you. I can't explain more. If I live through this, I'll contact you again!"

Zarfa disconnected and took a fighting stance. The odds were not good. Sixty against four, and thirty of these enemies were some sort of squid-like monster that he had never encountered.

It's times like this I question myself for insisting on fighting with my bare hands. I wish I had a gun.

Crimson had awoken early, as she usually did. It was six in the morning. She stretched for fifteen minutes, as she typically did. When your life involved fighting, it was good to stay limber. She went down the hallway to Max's room and opened the door.

He was lying on his bed, sleeping like a baby. She couldn't help but admire the peace and tranquility on his face. She decided he probably needed his rest, so she went into the kitchen area. She started to look around for something to prepare. She thought it would be nice to surprise him with a real breakfast.

As she rummaged, she recalled how he had completely raided her food supplies the night before and that there was nothing left in the way of real food. All she had now were the synthesized meal packs and bars. None of those could provide a nice smell to rouse Max out of bed politely.

She entered back in to Max's room. She was going to try being nice and thoughtful to him this morning, but it just wasn't working out. She sat on the bed, placed her hand on one of his shoulders, and began shaking him gently.

"Max...Max... Wake up, Max," she said as softly as she could.

Max roared and grumbled, rolling on to his side facing away from her. She shook him gently some more as he growled from his throat and pulled the blanket over his head.

"Why are you always waking me, bloody woman?" he exclaimed from under the covers.

"Because there is work to do, lazy," she stated, not at all

angered by his grumpy morning outburst.

"Right, right, I got it. No rest for the worker bee, gah! I hate you in the morning, you know that?"

"You hate everything in the morning."

Max grunted and grumbled as he poked his head out from under the covers. His blond hair was disheveled and his one hazel-colored eye looked tired and worn. His new silver eye gleamed in the sunlight coming in through his window.

Max had done a great job crafting it. The eye looked almost like a real one; the only difference was that his iris was silver and glistened in metallic majesty. He squinted his eyes and stretched his arms out wide.

"True, you're just going to have to get used to me not being a morning person."

"And you may have to get used to me waking you much more violently."

"Touché."

"Look, I was planning on making you a breakfast out of real food, but when I arrived in my kitchen, I realized...*you ate it all yesterday!* So my plan to be nice to you was foiled. What do you want to do?"

"Ugh, don't worry about it. I'm not much of a breakfast person. What is on the agenda? Maybe I'll eat in the afternoon."

"Fine, suit yourself. I still have meal packs and bars. You should have one. Your first task is another sparring session with Luther."

"Again?" Max exclaimed. He was still sore and hurting from his previous day of fighting.

"Again... Hey, I noticed you picked katanas to fight with... Was the wakizashi sword I gave you a bad pick?"

"Nah, it would have been good if I hadn't modified my arms because they are shorter and weigh less. But I don't need to worry about that now so I decided the katana-styled plasma swords would work out better."

"All right, I'm taking it back then... I've had some good times with that blade."

"Oh?"

"Oh...you'd better believe it, but it isn't story time now, is it? It's time for you to get up and go spar."

"Can I have some coffee first?"

Crimson didn't see the harm in allowing him to indulge in a bit of coffee before he went to the doom of having himself beat to a pulp again by Luther. The two of them sat in the kitchen sipping coffee for about an hour. Finally, by seven-thirty, Max had made his way to the sparring room.

He had eaten two meal bars before going in to give himself the calories to endure for longer than he had the last time. He had progressed substantially since the previous day, but as Max improved, Luther pushed further. Max was gaining control and progressing rapidly. Every time he got a bit cocky, Luther was sure to land a blow right to his ribs hard enough to bruise him pretty badly, all for the sake of keeping his ego where it ought to be.

Max managed to keep it up for about two hours today, but finally, he had enough. He had burnt off the calories he'd eaten and then some. He would lose his small amount of extra weight in no time if he kept this routine up. By ten, Max hit the shower and cleaned up. He was sore and hurting, but the hot shower made him feel refreshed and ready to start on whatever project Crimson had for him.

He found her in the lab. There she was inputting more data into her tablet. She glanced up from her work when Max came in and scanned him up and down with her eyes.

"You're trimming down quickly. How'd you do today?"

"Better...though Luther made sure to make it known to me that he was only toying around. That guy could crush me flat in no time. I mean, come on, he has four arms!"

"In a real battle, you may have ten rushing you. My only regret is I don't have four of him to train you with."

"But that would be sixteen arms to defend against."

"That's the next lesson, always expect the unexpected."

"Got it. Well, thanks for training me. I know my whole time won't be spent in the lab. I'm going to need to be in the war zone at some time. I would hate to get killed early on."

"Agreed," Crimson stated slyly, giving Max a small grin.

"You look like a Cheshire cat when you do that."

"Do I now?"

"That's what I said. So, what task do you have for me?"

"I need two more things in order to fight this war. I've already hacked the Pilvikone machines around the world so I can control the weather. But what I need from you to make it truly effective is a nanobot that will allow my body to act as a lightning rod so I can control electrical energies. I need to be able to absorb electricity into my body and discharge it from myself without it harming me. I know, it's a big order because it isn't a technology that has even been fabricated yet. Unlike your arms, you can't just take a pre-existing design and add to it. You have to start new. Think you could do that?"

"It's going to be tough...but I'll see what I can do."

"Good, the other thing I want from you is a Psyker Scream nanobot that can be airborne," she stated as she had a video display project a hologram of the nanobots' schematic over Max's workbench. "I believe you can reverse engineer it, give it a flight mechanism, and make it smaller. Then I need you to re-write the programming. I want this bot to only infect those who already have Psyker Scream nanobots in them.

"The purpose of your design will be to have this bot act the same as the old ones. Stripping the nerves' mylenated sheaths, but instead of re-working the nerves and reconstructing them, I want it to stop there, leaving them dead. Grisly, I know, but Synaptix has a lot of men in their army and they are growing each day. I don't know how many will join our cause. I plan to recruit only weeks before we begin. In fact, my recruitment videos will be considered the first act of war. You'll understand when you see them. We have a month for you to create both of these things. Think you can do it?"

"Well...the anti-Psyker bots will be easy. I don't see an issue there. Give me maybe...three days? But the other invention, as you said...well, it's new tech. Who knows how long it will take."

"I've got faith in you. You're the smartest man in the world who has spent his whole life wasting his brain. It's time that you stop that. You can do it."

"One thing, what about Zarfa? For now, he is neither friend nor enemy. Won't it kill him? He has had a treatment...and very well might finish them."

"If he finishes them, he will be under Synaptix control. At that point, he will be our enemy. As of right now, he chose to play on the fence, which means he is against us. It may be hard for you, but you barely even know the guy. View him as our enemy."

"Okay, but let's say he stops and chooses deafness... Let

us say he even helps us. Can I develop a bot that will protect him if that is the case? If he turns out to be an ally, I don't see it fit to repay him with a knife in the back!"

"If he turns out to be an ally...sure, just don't let it distract from your other tasks. If it will take too long, scrap the project. We will have a delivery of Quarthonium and Kelmantrium in about a week. Seeing as you used all that I had to fabricate your arms and eye, all I expect you to do is come up with blueprints for them in the meantime."

"Very well, you can quote me on this. I will have the anti-Psykers and the antidote to them finished in three days. As for the other task...well, I will see what I can do in such a limited time."

"Okay, sounds good. I am not half the scientist you are, Max. That is why I recruited you. I knew you were wasting your brain being some doctor in the slums. But if there is any way I can assist you, let me know."

"Can't think of any, but I will."

At that, Max got to work, examining the design of the Psyker Scream nanobots and reverse engineering them in his drafting program. He was making good progress and was very involved in his work. The day flew by without him realizing how late it was.

Finally, though his stomach growled louder than he had ever heard before and he realized he was feeling sick from not eating, he looked over at the clock that he had been ignoring all day.

Crap, it's almost seven.

Crimson had left him alone to get his work done. She was busy on the other end of the massive laboratory working on another project when he approached her.

"I got a lot done, but I'm hungry. Can we go get something?" he questioned as he stood behind her.

"Why don't you go ahead and have another one of those bars?"

"I had three more after my sparring session. I am sick of them. Let's go get some real food, please? Not this synthesized crap we are forced to eat. Cursed radiation," he spat out.

"Fine, fine. Let me finish scanning this in before we go. Go get ready to leave, you big baby. I'll meet you in the living room."

Max didn't respond verbally. He gutturally huffed and went out to the living room. He was ready to go and eat; he was starving and sick of the synthesized meals. He felt awful for anyone who could only afford those meals to live off of; real food was so expensive these days because there were very few places it could be grown.

He was beginning to get antsy as he waited on the couch. It had been at least twenty minutes. Suddenly, Crimson burst into the room. She had an intense look on her face. The same look she had back at the warehouse when she shot Badger's ear.

"Max, eat a few of those damn meal bars and get ready. Zarfa called—Synaptix has decided to draw first blood and put an illegal assassination order on my head. With their power and money, however, I doubt that I'd be able to get any legal agency to intervene. I used the scanners built into this building, and there appear to be four men on rooftops in our location—snipers. Additionally, there are seventeen more holed up in a single-bedroom apartment across the street. They've got us a bit outnumbered. Go to the armory, there is an Mk-147 gauss powered burst firing sniper rifle in there. It's time to test out your eye."

"Wait, what? Why haven't they assaulted us? Why haven't they stormed?"

"Because they don't know how to take down my barrier."

"What barrier?"

"Max, now is not the time for questions. Now is the time for you to steel yourself. Get your damn katanas and that sniper rifle and meet me back here. I am going to go wake Luther. He is going to want a part of this."

"Okay. Understood."

I wish just one night could be simple and quiet. I wish for once we could go grab dinner, come back here, and keep working on our projects quietly. Man, I wish life was...simple. Well, I guess I did sign up to wage a war with her... Stupid, Max, stupid.

Max was torn between excitement and regret as he rushed to the kitchen to grab some food. He couldn't be running out of energy in the battle. He made his way quickly to the armory and grabbed the sniper rifle that Crimson told him to get. He also found a combat suit that would be capable of deflecting a few bullets if he were to get tagged, so he suited up in that as well.

After getting all of his weapons, he met back in the living room. There, Crimson was standing with a wakizashi sword sheathed on her back and toting two gauss sub machine guns, one in each hand. They were compact and held fifty rounds each. She was ready to rain down death and destruction on all who opposed her and she looked more excited than concerned.

The black and pink combat suit she wore fit like a glove and appeared to be the same model Max was wearing. It could stop a few bullets and even had a hood and mask attachment she could pull over her head to protect it. She gave him a vicious smile and did just that, zipping it closed over her head so he could no longer see her face.

Luther was standing next to her, towering over both Max and Crimson. He noticed that the four tonfas were tucked away in his mechanical rib cage and secure. He, too, was holding the same SMGS Crimson chose, but he had four of them. Despite being a robot, Max could see his human emotion bleeding through by the way his skeletal face seemed to be trying to grin.

"Crimson Rain and her shadowy reaper Luther... How do you like the sound of that?" Max questioned jokingly. It would be his first fight and he was nervous, not eager the way Crimson and Luther were.

"I like it fine, Deadeye Max, now here is the plan. There is an elevator at the end of that hallway. It will take you up to the roof into a secured shed. Count to twenty when you arrive and then come out. On the building dead ahead of us there are two snipers on the roof—take them out first then take cover. To the east there is a single sniper on another roof top and to the west there is another. You take those out after you kill the first two and take cover. Don't die on me, Max, and go earn your title of 'Deadeye' If you want me to keep calling you that. Got it?"

"Got it."

"Luther, you're with me on the ground. We've got seventeen guys that are going to pile out with guns blazing, I'll bet. I want you to kill without regard for their lives. Gun them down to the last. We aren't interested in survivors or prisoners. This is war."

"Understood, mistress," Luther said, calm and asserted. "I fear no death, for even if my body is crushed into a million pieces, you have the power to make me anew. I fear for you. Allow me to be the first to step out."

"Agreed, Luther. Now break, I want no losses on our side. I don't care if they outnumber us. They've lost the element of surprise thanks to Zarfa."

After Crimson was done speaking, they put their hands over the top of one another's. Even Luther not having a mortal shell appreciated this human touch. This could be the last time they saw one another, but none of them planned for that to be true. They then broke, and took their positions. It was time for war in the streets.

Surge began strumming out a heavy metal riff and his amplifier began glowing with a yellow aura. His guitar pickups began glowing a bright red, and shortly, a soft red glow enveloped his whole guitar. He pointed the neck of his guitar at the sea of enemies swarming at them.

A nearly invisible beam that looked like a heatwave was shot from the headstock toward a teuthida. Zarfa could barely see it, but it made contact. The chimera's skin began to bubble and blister. First, its eyes burst like a balloon that too much air had been blown into, and then its whole body followed suit.

A rain of gunfire descended toward them. The handlers were each equipped with a standard AL-105 semi-automatic gauss rifle. Surge stepped back and strummed out a few minor chords as hard, fast, and as loud as he could. A similar-looking wave emanated out of the speaker.

This time, it wasn't concentrated in a beam, however. It looked almost like a translucent tidal wave crashing toward the Faraza. The bullets streaking toward them were all stopped mid-air and came tumbling to the ground, chiming in a symphony of chaos.

"I'm going to have to keep this up to keep their gunfire at bay, Zarfa. I am controlling these two guards with my psychic powers, but they will assist you. Time to show me what you've got!"

What the hell is that guy's instrument? Is that his weapon? I've never even heard of such a thing. Whatever it is, he has created a barrier to stop the bullets. I guess now isn't the time to question it.

"Oh, one last thing. This barrier is three-hundred-sixty degrees and about forty-five feet in diameter. Don't step outside of it."

"Got it, will you be able to provide offense?"

"Not until they run out of bullets. And it won't harm any of those monsters passing through. Looks like you've got twenty-nine left to slay. Give 'em your best, tiger!"

"Right, and it's more like rhino if you want to be accurate," Zarfa spat out sarcastically.

The first beasts passed through the barrier. Some were running faster than others. There were four that had broken free from the pack and made it inside the barrier before the others. Surge's two bodyguards proceeded firing their pistols with incredible accuracy. Each creature was dropped in a single shot that entered an eye and lodged a bullet in their brain. Blood, cartilage, and brain matter spattered out the other side as they fell flat.

It was dark inside the train station and the four of them were having trouble seeing. The fight had started well, but they had yet to begin. Zarfa had come out of cover and was waiting for his prey to come to him. He noticed one of the monsters that had just been dropped had been wielding a plasma powered saber.

Zarfa sprinted to the corpse as fast as he could. He was trying to reach the weapon before the next group managed to make their way within the barrier. Zarfa was kneeling when seven more entered into the barrier and were within range of attacking him. An assault of attacks from tentacles and plasma weapons rained down upon Zarfa.

He rolled backward, avoiding every attack in his burst of agility. He stood to his feet and took a defensive stance. Two of the mutant beasts assaulted him. One swung a bladed weapon; another flailed a tentacle at him. He sliced the tentacle off in one clean blow. A puff of vaporized tissue filled the air, blowing into the enlarged black eyes of his foe.

The other blow he quickly parried and followed with a

slash toward the demon's chest. The blow sliced through the creature's rib cage, flaying it wide open. Its lungs slipped down out of the wound. The creature screamed in pain, still alive.

Two more mutants sought to join in the battle with Zarfa when, suddenly, he heard shots fired. The two monsters dropped to the ground. He didn't bother to look; he knew it was the support of Surge's henchmen. The chimera missing its tentacle shot ink from under its eyes toward Zarfa's face. He was narrowly able to side-step it, almost tripping on the corpse of a teuthida he didn't see lying near him.

He quickly recovered, but now had a third enemy directly behind him. He pivoted and threw a roundhouse. It caught the enemy in one of its eyes, bursting the globe and sending blood and ocular fluid running down its face as it hit the ground. He quickly spun back to meet the severely injured monster's blade. He deflected it once again then pierced one of its exposed lungs, followed by a deep slash across the top of its head and down its face. The monster dropped to the ground. It wasn't dead yet, but would be soon.

The maimed monster launched an attack again while Zarfa was distracted. The beast was rather agile. With its one good tentacle, it grabbed hold of Zarfa's left arm—the one not wielding the saber. He pulled Zarfa into his body with tremendous force and, before Zarfa could respond, the monster's large beak was rending the flesh on his left shoulder.

In a moment of horrific pain and terror, Zarfa stabbed the saber into the monster's stomach. He then raised the blade upward with all the force he could muster. The plasma vaporized through tissue like a hot knife through butter. He could feel the hot steam blowing out from the wound. He pulled the blade all the way straight through the monster, splitting him down the middle from his belly to the top of his head.

A portion of the squid beak stuck in Zarfa's shoulder as the monster fell to the ground. He was hurting badly and bleeding worse. The monster he had kicked had recovered and was now standing behind him, ready to charge. He had two more chimeras standing right in front of him dual wielding bladed plasma weapons as well.

He heard a shot fire; the bullet passed through the back

of the monster's head and whizzed right by Zarfa's ear. The monster behind him would be of no trouble now. Zarfa rushed in toward the two beasts charging him. They swung high; he dropped to his knees and slid toward them, slashing his blow at their legs. All four were separated just above the knee and they came tumbling to the ground in a heartbeat.

Zarfa sprang atop the mutant on his left and sunk his blade into its head, ending its life. He quickly snatched the plasma blade out of its now limply-wrapped tentacle hand by the hilt. He then launched another assault with both of his blades into the head of the next monster that lay writhing on the ground from the pain of losing its legs.

Before he could celebrate, ten more of these grotesque beasts were upon him. Half of them shot ink; one of them hit its mark, blinding Zarfa. He flipped backward, pivoted, and ran toward where he thought Surge and the guards were standing.

"Duck!" screamed Surge.

Zarfa flung himself down to the ground and slid in the direction of the voice. He felt himself make contact with the legs of someone. He almost struck them hard enough to knock him over, but he fortunately didn't. He heard a volley of shots fired. Too many to count. He could only assume this meant ten more mutants were added to the pile of the dead.

Zarfa let go of his weapons and began rubbing his eyes. The ink was thick and oily. It smelled awful and it burned his eyes. He was tearing profusely and, within a short bit of time, his eyes had flushed the darkness out and he could see again, even if it wasn't well. He took hold of his weapons again and leapt to his feet. He couldn't help but notice the guards had dropped their gauss weapons and were now holding blades.

They must have run out of ammo. I'm losing blood fast. We need to end this fight.

"How long until they're out of ammo?" Zarfa questioned. He hadn't been paying attention to the shots fired because he knew he was safe inside the barrier.

"I know you haven't been paying attention, but they've reloaded three times already. They didn't come to play, Zarfa— they came to kill. Prepare yourself, the last of those mutants are closing in. I know you can't see well. Bear with me."

The two guards charged in to the swarm of eight monsters. They swung their weapons wildly, even managed to kill one. They were quickly overwhelmed, however. The beasts took hold of them and they couldn't break free or defend themselves the way Zarfa had.

Right before his eyes, the two guards were devoured like food. In a matter of about ten seconds, they were chewed to bits by the seven remaining monsters. Zarfa began to tremble; he had no support, no help. Surge had to maintain the barrier. He had just killed seven of them, but he'd had someone watching his back.

Luckily, the guards had bought him a few moments of time for the tears to flush his eyes further. His eyesight was still hindered, but not too badly. He could at least defend himself.

I can't let them reach Surge or else it is all over. Their volley of bullets will tear me to shreds if I let him die.

Zarfa was hurt, enraged, and desperate. He charged forward into the final seven with all of the strength he could muster. Two monsters were standing in front. He quickly dispatched them by running between them and cutting them in half from their waistlines.

He stood in the middle of the remaining five, tentacles and swords flying at him from every direction. He jumped into the air and split-kicked two of them in the head. The blow was enough to send the two monsters stumbling backward and falling onto the ground. As he came down, he felt a tentacle grasp his leg and pull him in for another bite.

Before the monster could take a bite of his flesh, he had severed its tentacle from its body. He landed on his back hard. It knocked the wind out of him, but this was no time to nurse injuries. Stunned and unable to breathe well, Zarfa leapt to his feet. He followed, severing the beast's tentacle with taking its head in a scissor attack aimed at its neck.

As the squid-like head rolled across the ground, Zarfa felt the burn of plasma blade slash across his back. It hurt, but it wasn't deep enough to kill. Zarfa dropped down and spun, performing a side kick to the monster's ankle and dropping it to the ground. He shoved both blades between its eyes into its forehead and pulled apart, severing its head in half and revealing its brain.

Zarfa jumped to his feet and took a few steps away from the remaining three. The two he had kicked had recovered and he could tell they were sizing him up. The flesh on his back still smoldered. The three shot ink in his direction again. He quickly slashed at it with both of his blades, sending it up in a cloud of black vapor.

The three rushed him. He threw one sword at the beast on his right, one at the beast to his left. His swords sank deep in their chests as they ran toward him. They stumbled a few feet then fell dead. The chimera in the middle proceeded to charge, tentacles preparing to grab Zarfa.

He jumped into the air at the last second, plowing both of his knees into the beast's chest. He landed on top of the creature with a loud popping noise. He could feel the cartilage on its ribcage popping and crushing beneath the force of the blow. The monster's lungs and heart were being crushed, but it still flailed with strength and ferocity. The tendrils on its face grabbed hold of Zarfa's chest and it proceeded to sink its beak into his pectoral muscle on his left.

The pain was excruciating and Zarfa couldn't leap back no matter how hard he tried. He was trapped by the tendrils as well as the bifurcated tentacles that the monster used as hands. Zarfa began pummeling the beast's head with both of his fists as furiously as he could. He felt its soft skull caving from the force. In moments, the creature was limp and lifeless beneath his body.

The grip of the nightmare slowly released Zarfa. Injured, bleeding, and in more pain than anyone should ever experience, Zarfa stood triumphantly. All he could hear was Surge's guitar. He was still holding the barrier, but the gunfire had slowed; it was coming to a halt. He stumbled back to where Surge was standing, covered in his own blood, as well as that of the mutants.

"Good job. I guess it is you that is the real monster. Those creatures didn't stand a chance."

"Tell that to my body. I nearly went down the way your guards did."

"Yeah... A grisly sight, wasn't it?"

"Tell me about it."

"So, what now?"

"We wait until they're done firing. We have another thirty

to kill after they run out of ammunition. Don't worry, they appear to be simple humans, not spliced up or anything fancy like that."

"I doubt it. Almost every member of the Faraza is spliced. Even their insignificant raiders. These guys must be important if they were escorting that company of critters."

"Well, you've had more dealings with them than I have so I will take your word on that one. Think you can do your share in taking some of them down with me?"

"Ha, I think you owe me, what? Twenty-nine?"

"Some of those kills were my men, ya know? I think I owe you more like twenty-five," Surge said with a smile.

"We can talk when I see you killing super-charged squid beasts. How 'bout that?"

Surge bellowed laughter. He knew Zarfa was joking on some level. Even at a time like this, Zarfa was still sarcastic and calm. If the element of ice could manifest itself an avatar, Zarfa would be it. When he fought, however, he was a tempest of rage and fire. Surge knew he was a mere man, perhaps one spliced with a rare DNA, but a man nonetheless.

The handlers had run out of ammo and were drawing their melee weapons. They were ready for some combat and were determined to not accept defeat. They began filing down the stairs toward the two of them. Surge changed rhythms again and was once again strumming chords. It sounded like a heavy metal ballad the way he was progressing the chords.

Zarfa could see the beam emanating again. This time, it was flowing out of the pickups and creating what looked like a wire stretched out in front of them. It was faint, hard to see. The wire was about fifteen feet ahead of them, floating in the air. It stretched out in an arch about forty feet long, making a half circle around Zarfa and Surge.

Surge began strumming faster and heavier. The tones were magnificent; if Zarfa weren't in the middle of a battle, he would be inclined to head bang. The mystical wire began moving like a wave, but stayed fixed in its location. The soldiers were closing in on them rapidly. Zarfa once again took a fighting stance with his fists out in front of him.

I wish I would have retrieved those blades. I really could have used them right about now... What the hell is Surge do-

ing? I sure do wish he would explode a couple of them before they got to us!

Zarfa was getting nervous. Before he knew it, twenty-three of them had crossed over the wire. Zarfa assumed they didn't see it. They must not have, or they didn't think it could do anything. All that had run though it blatantly were cut in half and fell apart mid-run. Blood and guts were everywhere in a sea of visceral remains.

Zarfa's morale perked up at this sudden turn of events. The seven that hadn't crossed over yet came to a screeching halt. One threw a sword at Surge. Surge quickly changed to a riff and directed the headstock at the sword. The plasma sword exploded into thousands of pieces. He then directed another beam at the one who had thrown it. He too boiled, bubbled, then burst the same as the monster had.

Surge changed it to a solo—it was fast, wild, and screeching electric. Zarfa wasn't sure if he could hear it because of the Psyker bots he had injected or not. He only knew when he heard Surge change things up, it meant death for who he was directing it at.

The last six began trembling and clutching their heads. Surge stepped toward them, pressing them with a sonic attack. He was now only five feet from the six, seemingly paralyzed by whatever it was they heard. Surge leaned back and strummed out three more chords as hard and as fast as he could. It sounded like the conclusion of an old flamenco song.

Blood trickled out of the mouths of the six standing before him. And in the suffering sound of silence, they all fell on their faces dead before him. Surge turned and faced Zarfa.

"That final one is called 'heart stopper.' I came up with it myself. So, it looks like I was able to handle those... I think you owe me five now."

"*Right,*" huffed Zarfa with his hand on the wound on his chest. He was trying to stop the bleeding. He had lost a great deal of blood in the fight and was beginning to feel weak. He was glad that the combat was over for the time being. There were bodies strewn all over the train station. The wake of destruction was massive and the smell of death was rank in the air.

"One last matter to attend to. Did I hear you call Crimson with warning before the battle?"

Zarfa's heart leapt to his throat. He knew Surge had heard; he knew it constituted him as an enemy of Synaptix now.

Why did he protect me? What is his game? Bastard.

"Don't forget, I can read your thoughts the same as Badger. Also, I informed Zax. It was a valiant attempt, but they will succeed in taking her down. She and that stupid little doctor are severely outnumbered. She is the only one who can fight, y'know."

Yeah, I know. I had to save that little guy from the gang the other night.

"*I guess since you won't speak aloud, I will just have to talk to you this way.*" Surge's voice invaded his head.

"So, what? Are you going to kill me now, or are you chicken? You are reading me for a reason. I assume you only kept me alive because you couldn't deal with ranged and melee at the same time. Now that I've served your purpose, you plan to slaughter me, right?"

"*Precisely!*" The voice screamed so loud in his head it echoed.

Surge began to strum; the wire appeared again. Zarfa charged ahead. At the last second, he leapt over the wire. Nothing happened; he was still intact. He came out of the air, descending like a hawk on its prey. His foot stuck Surge's guitar first.

It was knocked out of his hands and the strap broke. As the guitar clattered on the ground, Surge reached for it as quickly as he could. Zarfa snatched it from his grasp and held it out, kicking the neck hard. It snapped in half; wood and wiring scattered everywhere. It revealed something Zarfa was already aware of. This was no regular electric guitar.

Zarfa dropped the body of the guitar that had been in his right hand and kicked it as it was falling to the ground. The body split in half and went sliding across the floor, stopping on a mound of corpses.

Surge pulled a gauss pistol from his side holster underneath his robe. Zarfa, as quick as lightning, knocked it from his hand with the neck of the guitar. He heard a single shot fire. One that, had he been a second slower, would have surely ripped the life from his weakened mortal shell.

Before Surge could respond, Zarfa had grabbed him by

the wrist with his right hand and pulled him forward, giving Zarfa his back. Zarfa plunged his left elbow into his humerus. The loud snap told Zarfa the blow had done as he had intended. Surge let out a blood-curdling scream. He obviously wasn't used to being hit in battle.

As Surge dropped to his knees in pain, Zarfa broke the neck of the guitar over the back of his head. He dropped what was left and kicked him in the neck. Surge was planted face-first into the ground, barely alive.

"Surge, you really shouldn't have done that. I didn't want it to come to this. I guess this means there is now war between the Legion and Psyker Scream. You can tell all your little Synaptix buddies that right now, correct?"

"No," Surge coughed out, defeated and humiliated.

"No? I thought you alerted Zax about my tipping Crimson off?"

"I was bluffing. Our psychic link isn't that strong. I lost communication about a day ago. I would need to call his com-link and, if you hadn't noticed, I've been a little busy."

"Right, well thanks for coming clean. I guess if I kill you here, we can simply say it was a tragic loss in the face of a Faraza ambush. Badger doesn't need to know about my moving of a pawn piece if you remain silent."

Surge managed to roll over, looking Zarfa in the eyes. He was scared; it was a look that Zarfa hadn't seen until now.

"Please! Can't we can work something out? Be civil!"

"Ha! Civil? You should have thought about that before you attacked me. Funny how when things don't go according to plan, people suddenly want to negotiate. You make me sick."

"But it wasn't my—"

Surge's words were cut short by Zarfa stomping the soft part of his neck. His trachea collapsed like a tent and he was squirming like a worm, trying to breathe. Zarfa picked up the gun he had knocked out of Surge's hand and pressed it to his forehead.

"This is my mercy, that I don't let you suffocate in agony."

He pulled the trigger and blood, brain, and bone splattered into Zarfa's face. Surge didn't even twitch. He instantly stopped moving and lay still on the ground, cold. Zarfa picked up his backpack that he had set next to the speaker.

He proceeded up the stairs out of the train station, covered in blood and holding the pistol in plain sight.

No more letting my guard down. Who knows what might be waiting for me up there. I've got to find Zajifa and gather the Legion.

Eighteen... Nineteen... Twenty. Max took a deep breath and tried to calm himself. If his hands weren't perfect and robotic, only responding to conscious thought, he would be trembling. He burst through the door of the shed the elevator had taken him to. His eye locked onto two targets across the street on the rooftop of the apartment building that Zax and his posse were hiding out in. He fired two bursts of three shots each without even looking down the scope. His hands were perfect and steady. Both bursts hit their targets, eliminating two enemy snipers immediately.

Max sprinted toward cover on the roof, hiding behind a large air conditioning unit. His eastern side was covered and the sniper would have to guess where he was from at that angle. The sniper on the western building could still see him and was no doubt lining up a clear shot.

Max had heard bullets whizzing past him as he ran to take cover. He heard a round crash into the air conditioning unit he was taking cover behind. The bullet hit the large fan and clinked around as the shot echoed in the distance. His eye was drawn to the target, who looked as small as an ant. In the time it took for a single heartbeat, he had raised the rifle to his eye and was looking down the scope. He saw his enemy.

He was ugly, wearing a black leather jacket with chains and spikes decorating it in the gaudiest fashion. He was lying prone, a large cigar smoldering between his teeth. Tough guy biker shades rested askew upon his face and he had a mohawk he must have thought made him look like a real badass.

The sniper was grinning and Max could see his finger slowly squeezing the trigger. It was too late; Max had already fired. Three more rounds came with tumultuous fury. The first round pegged the sniper in the shoulder. The second, in the neck. The third found its spot nestled right between his eyes. He was never even able to fire his shot, one that would have definitely wounded Max.

One more... One more... Stay calm, Max, stay calm.

He had quickly killed three of his four targets with ease, but he was still nervous. Still scared that Crimson and Luther may be on the ground dealing with rounds coming from above while he plotted his next move. Max ran out from his cover and knelt facing the east.

The sun stood behind Max, painting him as a perfect dark silhouette. He quickly spotted his last target, who had also spotted him. Max could see him down his scope, squinting, trying to not be blinded by the sun as he lined up his shot on Max. Max's eye had locked on and he adjusted his arms for another precise shot. Without hesitation, he pulled the trigger, as did his enemy. A bullet whizzed past Max's face, scraping his right cheek and causing a minor cut that would bleed worse than it really was.

Max's burst found its spot dead on. Three rounds straight to the enemy's head. The enemy sniper that had been lying down already went limp immediately. Max's work with these four was done. He rushed over to the north side of the building and looked down. He saw Crimson and Luther exiting the building on one side of the street while the seventeen were spilling out of the building on the other, taking cover behind hovercraft or whatever they could find.

Max looked down his scope at Crimson. She had a wild look on her face, as if she was having fun. She quickly took cover behind a car and started laying down suppressive fire from both of her guns. Luther charged into the center of the street, his four arms aiming in different locations, wildly sweeping bursts of shots toward the enemy.

A hovercraft that several of the Psyker goons were hiding behind erupted in a ball of smoke and fire, killing six of the seventeen. It had taken too many rounds in the fury of their rain of bullets. Two men sprang from behind cover and began firing on Luther. Several rounds hit his body, knocking chunks off of it. He directed his guns toward them and, in a barrage of bullets, tore their bodies to shreds.

There was another cluster of men hiding behind the columns of the entrance to the apartment building. Crimson pulled out a de-ionizing grenade from her belt and pulled the pin. The grenade had been designed to break down and turn to dust organic particles, but would leave objects such as concrete, glass, and steel alone.

The grenade found its mark and the men couldn't scramble out from behind their cover in time. It exploded nearly the moment it had landed and, in a white flash, they were turned to smoke, leaving only a pile of clothing and their weapons behind.

There were only four men left and one of them was Zax. He had no intention of going down without a fight. He commanded the other two soldiers to try and flank Luther while he and his partner tried to get to Crimson's flank. The two who were going after Luther took cover behind a short concrete barricade; they began firing upon him from his side.

Several bullets hit, destroying one of his carbon fiber legs and nearly dropping him to the ground. His frame had been made light for close range combat. She did, after all, only use him to train for close combat. As his large frame struggled to remain upright on one leg, he faced the two who had maimed him.

Another torrential downpour of bullets rent into pieces the concrete barricade they were hiding behind. Dust mixed with blood misted the air where they had once been keeping cover and Luther fell to the ground. His balance mechanisms were having trouble compensating for all the damage he had taken.

Max targeted Zax's partner and let a burst go. He dropped dead, revealing their location. It caught Crimson's attention and she spotted Zax. She took aim and let a bullet fly in his direction; he did the same. Hers hit his gun hand, blowing it off. It had been shredded to strips of confetti by the bullet and Zax dropped to his knees. Crimson stomped over to Zax and kicked him in the chest, planting him backwards to the ground.

He lay there on his back, terror filling his eyes and blood spattering his face. He was trying to break free from Crimson's combat boot pinning him to the hot, uncomfortable concrete. He tried hitting her ankle with his good hand. She laughed maniacally and pressed him into the ground harder.

"You're Zax, Badger's second-in-command, right?" she questioned, pressing down hard enough to force the air out of his lungs.

"Yea... Yeah, I am. Let me go or there will be hell to pay!"

"What kind of hell? Like, he might try to kill me? Oh wait..."

"I can make it worth your time!"

"Oh really, how do you propose?"

Zax was being irrational. People tended to be that way when they were trying to save themselves. He was about to make offers that meant nothing to her, but in his mind, they would be worth considering.

"Money... And I'll get Badger to leave you alone..."

"I don't need money, and what got you here is you taking orders from him, not the other way around. You can communicate with him telepathically, right?"

"Yeah! Yeah! I can!"

"Good, you tell him this. Tell him I am going to let you go, but first, I want him to know that I killed his pathetic little assassination party. Can you do that?"

"Yes!"

Zax was silent for a moment as he communicated with Badger. The look on Zax's face told them that Badger probably wasn't thrilled to hear the news.

"Okay, now that you have his attention, tell him I received a tip from a friend. He'll know what it means."

Zax told Badger; it was apparent what she meant by it.

"Now tell him I lied," she said as she held her submachine gun over his body and unloaded the last of her rounds into him, riddling Zax's body with holes against the pavement.

She had no idea what Badger may be thinking, but she knew he would be able to sense the severing of the psychic bond. She knew there would be wrath and vengeance directed at her, but she didn't care. It was Badger who sought to draw first blood, not her.

Max had made it down to the street too late to hear any of the conversation between her and Zax. When he arrived, he was panting and happy to see that Crimson had lived through the onslaught.

"I'm surprised you didn't shoot more from up there, 'Deadeye,'" she said sarcastically.

"You looked to be enjoying yourself. I didn't want to ruin your fun."

"It's good you didn't. I would have been upset."

"I know."

"Let's get Luther back inside. He will need repairs and an upgrade if we keep taking him outside like this."

"After he's in...can we get some real food to eat? I am really sick of those bars."

"She is going to pay!" Badger screamed at those who were near him.

He went on a rampage, destroying whatever furniture was nearby. He was kicking things and hitting them until bones in his hands broke. He was acting like a five-year-old who hadn't gotten what he wanted. Nobody had a mind to care, though. They were all his subservient drones.

Anything Badger said aloud was for his own good; there was nobody around him anymore who could give him an intelligible response. He and Zax were friends. That was how he was able to convince Synaptix to allow Zax to keep his free will and be a commander of the army. Now, his friend was dead, and his other companion was out of range for him to be able to communicate with.

Badger went into an office at the back of the Psyker warehouse and sat down at a terminal. He linked in and contacted the main powers at Synaptix. There were five with positions of authority above him.

"Zax, the second-in-command, is now dead. Surge is away on an assignment and out of range for me to contact. What are my orders?"

He disconnected from the terminal and waited for a command to come into his head. They had always contacted him via psychic communication. He, however, did not have access to their minds. He knew his place. Shortly, it came in. He sat back at the terminal and sent them a message back.

"Understood, I shall proceed as you command," was all that it said.

"They should be back by now, Ghast," Sarah said.

"You're right, *should be,*" he muttered.

"So why aren't they?"

"I just received word from a scout we had sent. They're all dead."

"All of them? The teuthida too?"

"Yes," Ghast said, tapping his foot behind the table, clearly aggravated.

"Are you sure he was traveling alone?"

"We checked the security cams; he got off alone. Made a brief visit to a terminal, then he and three others killed the whole force. All sixty slain, he killed a good majority of them by himself. Then the man who appeared to be with him turned on him. Your brother crushed him like he was nothing, despite the fact several of the shock troops had managed to wound him pretty badly."

"So where is he?"

"Don't you think if I knew I would be pursuing? He is injured—now is the best chance we would have to be able to take him down and end him!"

Sarah sat staring at Ghast; she was upset. Zarfa had eluded them once again. She was sick of it. She hadn't been on the battlefield in months and it was eating at her. She needed the taste of blood in her mouth.

"You have sat idly by for too long! You withdrew me from raids and attacks and told me to be patient. You told me you would handle getting my brother. Well now it is too late for that. Now it is time that he dies. Our only chance of capturing him is playing on his emotions. It's time he sees me again. I am sick of him being one step ahead every time. The next time we strike, I am joining the battlefield and you, for your part, you are getting out there too. I know you have the skill required to kill or capture him and yet you've hidden down here behind a desk! I am sick of it!"

"I am in charge of Faraza. It is your father's orders that I do not go above!"

"I will deal with Father. You do as I say. The next attack, we are both going to the surface. I will not allow this incompetence to permeate Faraza any longer."

Ghast didn't argue, just stared down his nose at Sarah. He hated having her talk to him this way. He tried with all of his might to keep from turning red hot with rage. He felt that she was belittling him.

"Oh, and one more thing. We are sending a party of raiders to scout. Tonight! We find my brother, we strike. There is no way he will escape, not with him this badly injured. We might even capture him rather than kill him. Then I can have some real fun."

"Very well," Ghast grumbled as he conveyed the command to a raiding party.

He and Sarah got suited up for combat and joined the raiding party. There were eighty in total, including Sarah and Ghast. Each would take thirty-nine members and split up, searching through the city, looking for Zarfa.

The commands were clear—none of the normal business. No pillaging, kidnapping, or murder. They were to be as incognito as possible; their objective was finding Zarfa or flushing him out. Sarah would do things her way, and leave it to Ghast to do things his. She was determined to be in possession of her brother's body by the end of tonight, dead or alive.

Eleven

Commercial Deities

"Did your best friend steal your girl and now they're getting married? That bastard. You hate them both and want revenge, right? But you don't feel like taking up a black contract? Want to ruin that special day where they say 'I do' outside?

"Well now you can! With Barometics Corp. We can rain on their parade. Using the most advanced technologies, our Pilvikone can project the right storm at the right time, making that special day one they won't forget any time soon!

"Remember, Barometics offers any weather, any time, on time, for the right price. All applicants must complete background check prior to purchasing our services, so if you don't have a completely legal past, then don't bother.

"Sun or snow so nice you won't think twice! At the price that is... Remember, folks, Barometrics—'order in a world full of chaos.' That's our motto."

"Is your kid too mentally slow? Having trouble learning in school? You think he might be 'special?' Well, we can fix that. Life doesn't cut any breaks when it comes to genetics. Some of us will always have an edge on others, but Synaptix is here to help.

"At Synaptix Laboratories Inc. we can speed up what has slowed down. Whether it's our most simple multiprocessor interface enhancement or brain-altering nanobots, you can achieve the desired result.

"With the base Synaptix multiprocessor interface, a small

microchip, transmitter, and electrode are simply implanted into the retina and connected right to your child's Hippocampus portion of the brain. With this device, he will be able to search the interface for anything he would like in a matter of seconds.

"What does this mean for him? Increased learning! All those things he wasn't grasping will be immediately imbedded into his brain, leaving him smarter and more intelligent. We can't all be geniuses, but we aren't required to be stupid either... *Are* we? No! Dumb-dumb, so stop thinking that.

"I am sure you are wondering, 'won't the operation hurt?' Of course! But what is a moment of pain for a lifetime of knowledge? Knowledge is power. Synaptix, start doing what you've been thinking about...today!"

"Is your slave not loyal the way you wish she would be? Does she try to escape every time you beat her and you are just fed up with her attitude? 'Why can't she be more loyal like that Labrador Retriever I had growing up?' you find yourself asking. Well, now she can be!

"That's right, with Polyhelix's new gene splicing therapies, you could achieve the desired results. We have isolated the gene in such breeds of domesticated dogs and have discovered how to splice them into your unruly slave's DNA, affecting the way she will think about you.

"Don't worry, we assure you, unlike some of our other gene therapies, this one is totally perfected. She won't be licking your face or peeing on the carpet. Just an unbreakable bond that will keep her coming back to you no matter what it is you do! Doesn't that sound nice? Unquestionable loyalty, that's what we all really want.

"All treatments perfectly legal as long as you rightly own slave property. All regulatory permits required at purchase of service. In no time, you too could have a perfectly obedient slave!

"Polyhelix, always better than a dual."

"Seeking that memorable day in the sun at the park? Getting downright sick of it being hot all the time? Or would you like the weather to match your mood?

"With Barometrics, all things are possible. Orders delivered in as little as ten minutes from the time a credit transfer is verified. You can make the weather last as long as your account can sustain. Remember, Barometrics, order in a world of chaos."

"Still having trouble learning new things or remembering old ones? Remember the days when diseases could deteriorate your brain and make it nothing but a lump of fat sending random signals, confusing you and the ones around you?

"Not anymore—say goodbye to the brain decay brought on by old age. With Synaptix Corp Intelli-Bots. That's right! Intelli-Bots are the finest in nanobot brain enhancement technology.

"The standard IQ boost is nearly ninety points! And say goodbye to those third world diseases of Alzheimer's and Dementia. Why not be useful in your old age? Why not have control over the things you imagine? Why not actually remember the good ol' days?

"Remember, you're never too young or old for Intelli-Bots. Once they are in you, they're there to stay. Synaptix, start doing what you've been thinking about."

"Do you miss your limbs and can't afford those expensive cybernetic appendages that you so desperately desire? Wish you could walk again of your own volition? Wish people would stop looking at you so strangely and treating you like a third-rate citizen?

"Too bad your parents never invested in reptilian gene replacement therapies when you were a child. For as low as twenty-five thousand credits, your parents could have ensured your safety and you would have never had to know a life of pain and heartache. With reptilian DNA therapies, you would be able to regenerate those poor old limbs!

"But it still isn't too late. With the right treatments, you could still get your life back. But we warn you, the process will be slow if you are beyond the years of development. Still, wouldn't you like limbs of flesh and bone, and for cheaper than the cybernetic replacements on the market that often times overload or malfunction?

"Side effects include increased shedding of the dermis, an excessive need for vitamin D intake, lethargy due to cold temperatures, over activity in hot weather, and happiness from a life of never knowing loss!

"Don't forget, folks, Polyhelix, always better than a dual."

"My name is John. The first time I made an order, I had them create weather in the seventies in the early morning followed by brief snow flurries and heavy rain by the evening. I felt like a god. Everything happened exactly as I had told them. It was well worth the price."

"You heard it yourselves. A very satisfied customer. No order is too heavy or obscure. We aim to please and our weather generators are able to respond and adapt quickly. It's never a dull moment when you're the one in control. Our only rules are no 'acts of god' themselves, that is no weather event that would create catastrophic damages. Small pranks, however, or just the perfect occasion, are fine by us.

"Don't forget, Barometrics, order in a world of chaos."

"Do you think we are all work and no play? Most definitely not! Here at Synaptix, we offer nanobots aimed at the musical connoisseur wanting to hear something never before imagined.

"With our patented Psyker Scream bots, you can enter into a new world of audio never before heard by even the most hardcore audiophiles. Once you hear Psyker Scream, you will wonder how you ever listened to those inane digital streams, or normal instruments.

"There are many complications; side effects may include permanent deafness, catastrophic brain degradation, and in some cases, even death. But we assure you, this sounds so good you would be glad to die for it.

"Synaptix, do what you've been thinking about."

"Wish you could turn back time to your youth? Wish you had a second life to do it all over again? Tired of all the aches and pains? What would you pay to have a fresh new body?

"New from Polyhelix! The fountain of youth. Monetary cost can be negotiated; if you can't make the full purchase up front, no problem! Don't forget, you will have another seventy years to pay us back, but what fun is life if you're fully indebted to us? You decide for yourself after you make an appointment with one of our specialists.

"But now, let's talk real cost. What requirements must you face to make this dream of reverse-aging a reality? Well, the process is simple. First, we make a clone of yourself in one of our many laboratories from your own DNA and one of our donor's eggs that would provide to you the best match.

"After a short incubation time, the embryo is aborted and the raw stem cells are given time to replicate. Once the process is complete, you are ready for treatment, friend! All it takes is a quick, painless injection. The results will be seen in mere days as the stem cells rebuild your body from the inside out.

"The only question is, does this bother your conscience? Because it certainly doesn't bother ours. Call now! Due to concern of overpopulation, this is a limited supply run. Only a few thousand treatments are allowed each year.

"Never forget, Polyhelix, always better than a dual."

"These are the gods of these days. These are what people seek out blindly and with fervor so fierce they will stop at nothing to obtain what they want. The laws only require that a company is outright with their product, no hidden dangers.

"Nothing is required to go through multiple phases of testing to be sure it won't harm the masses. If they want it, they can have it. The populace is the new Guinea pig. Alexarien is the central laboratory for this new technological religion.

"Depending on how you look at it, it seems to be spreading as an era of enlightenment. Or a blight causing nothing but death and destruction in its wake. Its new fanatics are the everyday people, and with their bodies completely saturated with technology.

"These are your priests, your crusaders, your Christ, your anti-Christ, your Imam, your cardinal, your fanatic, your zealot. These are your worshipers... Break free. Follow me. I am a partaker, but I shall bring to ruin that which I've partaken.

"Places like Ilyeion have already felt its effects. People consider places like that to be third world and unsophisticated, even barbaric. Why? They have all the same technologies that we do; the only difference is the poverty level is higher there. They have less people buying the crap these companies are selling. They still try to keep alive some of the old ways. Alexarien says get rid of anything older than six months, and we buy it!

"What of the countries whose capitols we are unaware of? What of the less affluent areas of the world? What are they? Less than animals? Animals have value; we have turned our backs on them and, in effect, have said they have none.

"Even in our own land, if you don't have the money to purchase your own life, someone can buy it from you. Whether it be a black contract or slavery, your life can be purchased. I intend to rebuild this country and all the others around it, but I need your help.

"Many will say that you are insane for joining my cause. Many will say I am trying to destroy civilization. Many will say that I am wrong, but let me ask you this. Who is it that is cannibalizing their own to turn a profit or make an advancement?"

This was the first video log broadcast by Crimson Rose. The broadcast ran on 3033 C.E. in the beginning of that summer. Though the time of year was about to matter very little to all involved in the dramatic inauguration of the bloody conflict that was about to ensue. The only solace would come in the climax that would proceed shortly after the birth of war.

—From the tome of Demicles 4001 C.E.

Twelve

Aftermath

The weather was dry and hot. Seasons didn't mean a whole lot ever since the invention of the Pilvikones. One day, the weather could be like this, over a hundred degrees Fahrenheit after sundown. The next, it could be negative twenty. Today, Zarfa would have preferred for there to be some semblance of moisture in the air, regardless of the temperature.

He stumbled down the streets in Ilyeion. Sand storms brought in lots of dust regularly and one had passed by recently. Dust and sand was caking up in his open wounds and creating clots of blood and dirt. It would clump up and fall off as he walked. He was getting woozy from all of the blood loss.

"The Sheik's Tavern," Zarfa muttered under his breath as he clambered in through the door.

He had managed to hobble his way three miles from the train station to here. He felt as if he might die and anything he did tonight would be pointless. As he staggered in through the door to The Sheik's Tavern, he heard loud music. Two old fashioned acoustic sitar players were battling one another.

The crowd was clapping and chanting a traditional song as each of the musicians tried to best the other in a game of wits, skill, and musical prowess. Alcohol permeated the air and tribal belly dancers performed in the dim lighting. For a price, any of these girls would take a person into a back room and give a private show. With all of the commotion, it seemed as if it would be difficult to gain anybody's attention. It would have been, if it weren't for the fact that everyone knew who Zarfa was and loved him.

As Zarfa's presence emanated ahead of him, blood still

dripped down from all of his injuries and splashed on the floor. His injuries made his body move slow and jerky. He smelled as if he had just risen from the grave, and the scent of his blood rose above that of the alcohol itself.

"What the hell happened to you, my brother?" came a concerned shout as the entire place dropped to dead silence.

The sitar battle ended abruptly and nobody would argue who the victor was tonight. The dancers stopped, and even ones who had retreated to the private rooms made their way back to the main hall of the tavern. Five men surrounded Zarfa before he could even respond to the voice.

He couldn't make out who the men were. His vision was getting blurry and he was tired. Before he even realized it, they had lifted him up and taken him to a pillow-top mattress and laid him down. Some of the female performers immediately began washing him off and tending to his wounds.

"Zajifa, they have a new weapon... The Faraza, we need to be on guard. I don't know how many more they have, or if they will attack again soon."

"Calm down, Zarfa... Don't expend too much energy—you can't die on us here." Zajifa sounded shaky, truly worried about the condition of his friend and leader.

"Send a call—" Zarfa paused and held his breath as two of the women sprayed medifoam into his every wound. It stung, but it wasn't worse than what he had already been through. "Send out a call to the Legion. Get all of the soldiers that could qualify to be platoon leaders together, bring them here. We need to develop a plan *now! We need to be more organized than we have ever been!"*

"Zarfa, surely it can wait until the morning. What you need right now is rest!"

"Zajifa, listen to me. We do not have time. There is much I need to fill you in on, but I fear we do not have enough time for that right now. Kick out all who are present that aren't members of the Legion and bring in our upper echelon."

"But my liege—"

"Now!"

Zarfa's breathing had slowed and become less labored. The medifoam was helping him to regenerate already. He would still be injured in the morning, but not nearly as badly as if he hadn't received care. His body no longer hurt; it felt numb and comfortable—it was a pleasant change from how he had been feeling the last several days. One of the women still washing him with hot water and removing his tattered, bloody clothing felt like a centipede crawling on his bare skin.

He could feel the touch, but it didn't seem human, though he was certain that without the medifoam's analgesic effects, he would have been writhing in pain under her careful touch. He stared at her with a steely gaze, one that told her he was appreciative, yet he feared she may wind up in his condition this night.

Nobody in the room had ever seen Zarfa so close to dead. It was a familiar feeling to him, however. He had been worse off the first time he had ever dealt with the Faraza. He was afraid that ones he cared for would be lost tonight. They were afraid that he would be lost and that Zajifa would be left to command Legion Nine on his own, something he was not yet ready for.

Zajifa returned to the room and kneeled next to Zarfa, resting his forehead on Zarfa's bare stomach. Tears were streaming down his eyes onto Zarfa's flesh, but he wasn't audibly crying. He kept taking deep breaths and kneading his head into Zarfa before he finally spoke.

"Zarfa, my brother, my master, my commander, my king! I have done as you asked. All of the squad leaders, platoon leaders, and the other seven commanders are en route. What happened? How did they do this to you? What is this new weapon?"

"A new mutant, powerful, fast...gruesome. Half man, half...squid or some other extinct sea creature. It was terrifying to look at and even worse to feel grasp your body. I could barely break free from their tentacles and they have vicious beaks that caused most of this damage. Also, some assassins came for me several days ago in Alexarien. One of them gave me some cryptic information on his deathbed. He alluded that my sister was giving orders within the Faraza and they seem to be after me... I don't know if I believe him, but it is possible. That is all I can discuss for now. I am so tired. Wake me when they arrive. We need to come up with a plan," he barely was able to say before falling asleep.

Zajifa nodded and rested his head back down on Zarfa. He loved him as dearly as he loved his own family. When he

said, "my brother," it was no mere courteous title or formali-
ty. It was what he actually felt for Zarfa.

Zajifa stayed by Zarfa's side as he slept. The woman who
was attending to Zarfa continued to do so. She had stripped
him earlier to wash him and now was slowly pulling new
clothing over his nude body. The blood flow had stopped
from the treatments and it seemed as if he would pull
through despite the fact the injuries were quite severe.

Zarfa awoke startled, and looked around the room in
confusion. The woman who had dressed him was kneeling by
his head. She stepped back and allowed him his space. Zajifa
awoke and stared at Zarfa.

"What is wrong?" Zajifa asked.

Zarfa stared him in the eyes, not shifting his gaze away
from Zajifa's face. He was conscious and frightened. Nobody
knew Zarfa could even be frightened. But here he was, looking into the eyes of his best friend and close companion—
scared. His voice had a small tremble as he said, "I think I've
doomed us all."

"So, we are at war now, I assume. I don't think that Synaptix is going to take this lightly. I had questions before and
allowed you to give me incomplete answers. I, however,
have joined you and have proven a formidable ally to your
cause. Now I deserve answers," Max said sternly as he
leaned over the table.

He had a serious look in his eyes, one that said, "don't lie
to me." But he wasn't angry, purely determined and looking
for answers. He knew war was coming, but he never realized
it would be so quickly upon him, and now, the small frag-
ments of information Crimson had given him weren't enough.

"You assume correct," Crimson said, sipping on her dry
gin martini. "What would you like to know?"

"First, do we have an army? As far as I can tell, it is you,
Luther, and myself."

"An army? No, but I will be sending out the video feed
tomorrow. That is bound to recruit a few. I don't think we will
need a huge force for what I plan to do and how I plan to do
it."

"That leads me to my second question, what is it you plan to do exactly?"

"Take over the government. You and I both know they don't do anything to help the people anymore. Everything is legal, there is nothing moral or immoral so long as you can afford the license it takes to commit any kind of deed. We also both know that giant corporations that feed the government income can get away with anything they want. We are an open human testing lab and powerless to stop it. The law says that full disclosure is the only law, *let the people decide.* Right? Wrong! Did Synaptix let anyone know they were drawing them to a product that would make them lose free will via their advertising? No! Does Polyhelix let people choose to further advance their bio-engineering? No! They have the Faraza kidnap lab rats for that cause.

"Does Barometrics care if sunshine here causes a flood in some developing country? No! They don't care at all. The government? Doesn't care so long as they're fed and fat. Nobody has a conscience anymore and nobody gives a damn what happens, so what I plan to do is destroy the companies that practically control this globe and, as a finale, take down the fine Alexarien government. After that, Ilyeion will soon follow, and we shall rewrite history. Give people a choice."

"Well, that is all great and everything, but how do you plan to do this without an army?"

"For one, I've got a few aces up my sleeve. For two, when the video feeds start going out, I assume the masses will rise up with us. I know I should have been trickier and developed a small following sooner; there are a lot of things I wish I had done different, but now we are out of time. I hope that people will open their eyes to the deceit and lies that permeate our society. I hope that our cause spreads like an infection, and I hope for it to be immaculately in time.

"You see, right now Polyhelix and Synaptix are both seeking to take the government as their own and expand to global domination. Both have the means to do so, however, neither of them wants to unite. If one goes after the government right now, they get weakened and are vulnerable to an assault from the other. Neither is strong enough to wage war on two fronts. The government will stay neutral so long as it is just a war between companies. They don't care about war and murder in the streets. If something happens that the company hasn't paid for yet, they will retroactively produce a license at a high cost to make things right.

"When all is said and done, there will only be one corporation left standing. When that time comes, they will prepare for war with the government. They might strike immediately or it may take a few years for them to build their ranks back up. Both have had oversight enough to try their experimental technologies right at that moment in an all or nothing play. The government won't stand for that, but their thinking is that it will be too late.

"This is where we come in. If we can gain support and open people's eyes, then we stand a chance. I hope to drop in at the critical moment that decides who the victor will be, Synaptix or Polyhelix, and strike a deathblow to both. After that, I hope to lead our army on to perform a coup d'état on the government. It's risky, we might die, we may never build the army I hope for...but we are going to try."

Max sat there with a bite of food in his mouth as she spoke. He wasn't chewing and he didn't swallow it. He was slightly in shock. Nothing should surprise him any longer, but still, this did. He hadn't blinked once while Crimson spoke.

Finally, he took a deep breath, picked up his water glass, and swallowed his masticated food with a gulp. He set the glass back down on the table abruptly and Crimson still couldn't tell if he was angry or not. He had a look on his face that was hard to read.

"Well, we all gotta die some time, right? So, I say, let's give it all we have. First thing tomorrow, I will get to work on your other tasks for me. I know you gave me a month time frame, but after today, I assume the deadlines just got moved up. I think Zarfa has proven himself. For now, I am counting him an ally. I am going to make the anti-bot that will spare him if we use the airborne bots.

"Other than that, I've got no idea if I'll be able to fill all of your orders, but I will try. Don't think I'll slack off or do anything... I was going to say stupid, but I already demonstrated that I may do that. By the way, keep serenity boosts out of the building. I'm already craving one. You don't want me down that path while I am trying to help you, and I figure I would give you fair warning right now.

"And finally, I want you to know...I am pretty sure I am in love with you. I want to follow you to the ends of the earth. Maybe it's only my obsessive nature, but really... No time for romance in war, but after..." Max trailed off, not finishing his thought or giving any indication he was going to continue.

"Right, Max, so let's go cause a revolution, right? Let's go be the trouble we want to see in this world. Let's go liberate all the slaves."

"Right."

"This carnage...all him? I know he is in bad condition after this, but still, the very fact he even lived is impressive," Sarah said out loud to herself. She shook her head as she stood in a puddle of blood. The train station still had corpses lying about in it. The blood of the chimeras had a particular odor that was quite unpleasant. She wasn't at all disturbed by the carnage, but she got chills looking at all that her brother had done.

The way he fought was an art. Every move so precise even against such innumerable odds. There was no way any normal human could do what he did. Even the average splicer was no match for his skill and precision. She had seen the security video, but watching it was like watching some campy movie made by an action director who liked to shock his audience with unrealistic images.

Seeing the carnage, the aftermath, right at ground zero, made it real. It put more vivid imagery into her mind than even the videos. She could smell it, see it, feel it, and it brought her a feeling of rapturous ecstasy. She couldn't help but let her mind linger on the thought of meeting her brother in battle. Even if he was wounded, she would derive great pleasure from breaking him however she could.

She closed her eyes and breathed deep. She took in every subtle note of the fragrances in the air and let them stay in her nose. She devoted them to memory and then, in a blink, snapped back to reality.

"We need to move. I think I know where he is," she commanded, giving her squad of raiders a hand signal that meant for them to move out.

"What do you mean you doomed us all?"

"Synaptix, they sent a guard with me from their Psyker Scream division. He helped me fight those monsters and the other Faraza. When the fighting was over...well...I killed him. There has got to be security cameras at the station, ones that Synaptix has access to.

"I came back to discuss with you guys if we would join them and their cause or go to war with them. I'm sorry, but my actions decided for us. We are going to war on two fronts—Synaptix and Faraza. I think I may have doomed us all."

"I think we should call the other eight. I didn't include them with the others."

That was all that Zajifa said back to Zarfa. He was concerned, but not the slightest bit upset. He understood that Zarfa had to do what he had to do. He knew his leader wasn't reckless, looking to cause as much destruction as possible. Zarfa had created Legion Nine by accident, by means of his purpose to destroy the Faraza.

Zajifa went into a room adjacent from the one he had gone to sleep in with Zarfa and made a call on a communicator. He was gone for about five minutes before he came back. Zarfa was breathing a bit heavier than usual. The medifoam was helping him to regenerate quickly, but the analgesic had worn off and some of his injuries had gone deep and were still aching.

"How'd he sound?" Zarfa questioned.

"Who?"

"You know who; don't be all coy."

"How does he usually sound?"

"Angry, mad at the world, completely perturbed, like he is going to kick my teeth in even though the rest of you call me boss... Should I continue?"

"Yeah, he sounded like that...but worse."

"Yeah, that sounds like Sofronio to me," Zarfa said with a chuckle.

"Well, I promise he will arrive first, the rest to follow. You are injured, and I don't stand a chance in a fight with him, so let's just hope he is barking like a mad dog the way he always does and never acts on any of his threats, okay?"

"Let's hope, but if he ever does try to take my spot as commander and chief, then tonight will be it."

They both chuckled and sat with each other. The Legion was something that myths were made of; many had seen them in action. There were always casualties, but there were always more on the side of Faraza. It was rare that all ten of the commanders would meet together to discuss organizational direction.

The way it typically worked was there was a raid by the Faraza. A rally call would then be sent out. Everyone would meet in one location, and a defense would be formed. Zarfa and the other nine would always take the lead and knew most of the regulars that showed up by name.

Even though Zarfa formed Legion Nine when he'd brought up the idea of staging an attack of their own on the Faraza, it had been met with skepticism. Some were in favor; others felt that the Legion should only serve to protect Ilyeion from raids, nothing further.

Sofronio was the most opposed to the idea. He had even once made the threat of killing Zarfa and taking the lead, claiming he was a bad leader. The others all felt he did a great job at organizing a group of hoodlums who didn't know when to roll over and accept that the Faraza were going to pillage them no matter how hard they fought back.

Sofronio, however, felt it should be more organized. That there should be a roster, qualifications to join, ranks, rewards. He wanted to make a true military, not only a simple minutemen militia. Zarfa always raised the points that if there were a roster, the Faraza could get a hold of it and hunt everyone down.

In battle, there was no rank, not if your superior was killed and the others were out of sight. That was always Zarfa's take on it anyhow. He felt that each of his soldiers had to be leaders in their own rights. He also didn't want anyone fighting for him out of the fear of embarrassment of how humiliating it would be to have to resign in front of others.

Zarfa had started this organization alone. Alone, he would go into the streets and fight. It inspired others to stand up and fight alongside of him. But Zarfa was so determined that if he lost every single supporter, he would still go out and fight. He wanted any and all who joined him to have the same attitude, so he was never in favor of ranks, rewards, or any other system to discern anyone from one another.

The only form of organized leadership he gave was that of the nine. He gave his original nine supporters a chance to vote to decide what actions they should rally for. However, as those other eight died in battle, they were replaced. Zajifa was the only one to remain from the very beginning. Eight never questioned him; they venerated him in such high regard. Sofronio, one of the newest to be invited into the fold, on the other hand, couldn't agree with him on anything, and went so far as to not agree with him even if it was obvious he was right.

Once in the middle of a sand storm, he had argued with Zarfa over whether it was windy or not. Anyone could see the sand was being blown in as thick as fog, but he stood his ground in front of the other eight and argued that Zarfa was a fool and that it wasn't windy outside. He finally conceded when he said, "Well, perhaps a little, but we've seen worse. That's what I meant when I said it wasn't."

As Zajifa had predicted, Sofronio was the first to arrive. As surly as ever and steaming mad.

"What the hell is going on? Why are we rallying so late? There isn't a raid in progress!" he blurted, red-faced, stampeding like a bull.

He was tall and bulky. He stood at least a head over Zarfa. His skin was the color of the sand that surrounded Ilyeion and his eyes were a dark brown. He kept his hair shaved at all times and always wore tattered olive green clothing, the look of a true solider.

"We are at war is why," Zarfa spoke sternly.

"Oh, really? Thanks for letting us give input on this, captain! Anything else you care to inform the dogs about?"

"Take it easy on him, he was going to—"

"Well, he didn't, did he?" Sofronio snapped back.

"That is why I am calling this meeting, to inform the nine of what happened, tell them to tell the others. Tell all who want no part of this to get out now if it's what they want. Maybe even leave Ilyeion for a little while...while they still can."

"Aww, how nice of you. Why didn't you just not get us all

involved in something we couldn't handle in the first place?"

"Are you a total moron? We've been fighting against Faraza this whole time. We were already in over our head; it has escalated as we all knew it would. Look, I'll explain when everyone arrives. If you want out, fine, leave. But I won't tolerate you being disruptive or talking down to me any longer. It's time for war. I've never asked anything of any of you men. Now I am, but you will all still have a choice."

Sofronio stared down at Zarfa, who was still lying down. He was still clearly not in top condition. Both Zarfa and Zajifa were shocked that Sofronio wasn't pursuing the conversation further. It was the first time he'd ever ceased arguing with Zarfa.

Within minutes, the others had trickled in. All in one room in the back of The Sheik's Tavern. Zarfa, out of respect, stood from the bed he was resting on and addressed the nine.

"I went to Alexarien to get the Psyker Scream nanobot alterations. The plan was I would lead us to battle with Faraza because I could hear where the wasps were coming from. I wasn't aware that Synaptix was using these bots to control people's minds and to create a psychic army. I've already had one treatment and have decided to stop. I am going to lose my hearing altogether, the bots will be sure of it. Synaptix tried to recruit me to their cause. They would have left the nine of you alone and allowed you to keep your free will. As for the others, they wouldn't have...so I rejected their offer. They sent one of their commanders and two bodyguards to follow me back here. When I arrived at the train station, we were ambushed by Faraza. After the battle, Surge, one of Synaptix's best, turned on me. I took his life.

"There are security cameras at the train station. If Synaptix doesn't know of my actions yet, they soon will. This act, I can only assume, will mean war to them. I still plan to find where Faraza is hiding and crush them under my heel. However, we have an added threat.

"My message to you, as well as all other members, is that this is the final hour. It is now kill or be killed. Within the next few weeks, I will be deaf, and I am not sure how yet, but we will find a way to locate Faraza. It is then we shall attack their base. In the meantime, expect retaliation from

Synaptix, as well as whatever raids may come about. If you want to leave, leave now. If you want to stay, then trust me, stand by me, and fight to your death. I shall do the same. That is all I can say, other than I'm sorry for bringing this vengeance upon us all."

The nine stood silent, glancing back and forth at each other. Zajifa made eye contact with Sofronio, and Zarfa stared at the floor like a scared little boy asking permission from a parent.

Finally, Sofronio broke the silence by clapping. "Well done, sir, no bull. I'll follow you. Let's destroy those evil spawn," he said calmly and sternly.

Everyone's mouths dropped open and Zarfa looked up. The shock on their faces was almost comical. It was the first time Sofronio had ever called him sir, complimented him, or agreed with him in any way. There was some laughter and clapping from the others, most of which were still too shocked to verbally respond. Finally, the rejoicing settled down and as if in one voice, the other eight all said, "We are at your command, sir."

"So, what are you working on over there?" Crimson asked.

"Well, I am trying to reverse engineer these little bots to do what you wanted them to do. You know, make them fly, make them kill all the Psykers, you know, whatever that simple little task is you asked of me," he responded with a tone of sarcasm.

"Well excuse me for asking."

"Excused. Sorry, I'm just stressing. I heard your feed earlier while I was out getting some groceries. I've known we were in danger from the start, but it donned on me, Synaptix is going to want us dead as well as Polyhelix, and even if we do manage to take them down...the government will want us eliminated. Have we even recruited anyone yet?"

"It's hard to tell... We are raising supporters for an idea to strike without warning. We didn't exactly provide a barracks for them to report to or anything. It is in the hands of the people now. As well as us. All we can really do is hope when we strike that our message was heard and appreciated. I've got another one I plan to send out. We might start seeing a visible presence of the Crimson army after that, but until then...only phantoms loyal to an idea."

"Crimson army? Right, only you could be that narcissistic."

"Oh really? Deadeye Max?"

"I'm going back to work. I think I'm making progress here, almighty leader of all that is good," Max said with a smirk.

He didn't know if he would live or die. He didn't know if they would make a change. He wasn't even sure if they were the good guys in all of this. He knew he wanted to make a change and that Crimson seemed to be someone with a good vision. He knew he didn't want the others to win out, but he wasn't sure if he would want to overthrow the government even if he could.

He just knew he wanted to see this thing through to the end. To hopefully improve some people's lives, help them. He didn't want to be remembered; he hoped he never even made it into history books. All he wanted was for his actions to be remembered.

The door to The Sheik's Tavern exploded into thousands of tiny splinters. Fire and smoke filled the main hall where, hours before, girls were dancing, men were drinking, the bartender was entertaining, and laughter had filled the air—where only hours before, Zarfa had stumbled in almost dead and caught everyone's attention.

When the explosion went off, the women took arms and stormed into the main room to make a defense, along with the bartender and all of the commanders of Legion Nine. Now, smoke and heat from flames filled the room. Faraza were dropping like flies, but they weren't the only ones losing lives.

Sarah had seen a well-known member of Legion Nine step into the tavern. She'd waited for things to die down a little then planned the assault. She had set a detonator on the entrance and commanded all thirty-nine of her men to storm in and take no prisoners the moment the charge blew. They were fulfilling that command. Upon their entry, they managed to kill the bartender and several of the dancers who were fighting back with gauss pistols and minimal cover.

Once-living bodies were falling to the ground in chaos and horror. Even one of the commanders of Legion Nine was reduced to nothing more than a cold, lifeless object after catching a bullet in the head. Zarfa was enraged and found a plasma katana before making his way into the main hall.

His body ached and some of his wounds that weren't quite sealed re-opened—blood poured down his shoulder from the bite he had sustained earlier. By the time he made it into the main hall where all of the gun fighting was going down, most of the smoke had cleared. There were roughly twelve of the Faraza raiders left alive.

His men were firing back or trying to advance for hand-to-hand. None of the other fighters had the strength, dexterity, agility, or grace that Zarfa had. He rushed head-on into gun-fire. Focusing on the streaks of the bullets, he swung with his sword and vaporized them. He made his way to a table that had been upturned with three raiders taking cover behind it.

He leapt over the table and assaulted the three. Before his feet even touched the ground, he had cut them all to shreds. Before one of the unfortunate raider's arms had even hit the ground, he snatched a gauss pistol from it and turned. Taking aim, he shot dead four more raiders. By the time his heroics had ended, his other men managed to clear the other raiders.

From out in the dark, they heard a single pair of hands clap and a woman's voice. "Bravo, bravo, dear brother. You did well," she said. She sounded happy.

"Sarah?" Zarfa screamed with intense rage as he exited onto the street.

He saw her standing in a combat suit in the middle of a deserted street, still clapping, staring at him with a steely gaze. He marched over to her and glared at her.

"Why don't you flee? We killed your men."

"And why do you hesitate to kill me?"

Zarfa punched his little sister in the face so hard it broke her nose and dropped her to the ground. Without hesitation, he placed his boot on her neck and screamed as blood flowed down her face. "I won't if you prefer to go quickly."

Sarah began to laugh as she used to when they were children, when his job had been to protect her, to keep her safe. Back before she had been cruelly snatched away from his life.

"I really would rather keep living. I didn't come here with the intent to die tonight," she said, still giggling a little and squirming under the pressure of Zarfa's boot.

The remaining members of Legion Nine had surrounded the event in a semi-circle. They were watching the event like it was a high school brawl between two rivals.

"Why did you do it? Why did you come for me to kill me? Why aren't you a brainwashed drone like the others? It would make this much easier," Zarfa said as tears filled his eyes. They were streaming down his face and dripping onto Sarah's. His tears were causing the blood from her nose to be washed away. The dust in the air was clinging to Zarfa's face, making it look as if two great rivers flowed from his eyes.

"Because I had to make it look real, because we need to stop Father. That is why. I am sorry about those that died tonight, but I couldn't be found out."

Zarfa stepped back, shocked. He removed his boot from his sister's throat and bent down on one knee to be beside her face. The rest of the members stepped back; some kept their weapon's drawn on Sarah.

"What did you say?" Zarfa asked. He sounded stunned and angered at the same time.

"We have to stop Father. He wasn't taken like we thought; he's in control. He still loves us in his own sick way, which is why he had me taken. You were supposed to be with me, but you were too damn stubborn. They didn't brainwash me or condition me by his command. I pretended to want to be a part of his cause, to be loyal. I did everything right. At times, I even fooled myself, but it was all for one moment. Either the moment you saved me, or I saved you," she said with her eyes full of tears.

She wasn't crying because of having her nose broken. She was crying because she had never seen her brother in this much pain. Not the physical sort, but emotional. The kind of pain that ate at one's very soul and could rend even the strongest man made of iron in two like a wrapper of rice paper. His body was trembling and his eyes went blank at the news of his father still being alive.

"Mother?"

"Killed. Father had gotten what he wanted from her...children, strong children, and he had her put to death. He is sick; he is making an army of mutants. You've seen them. He plans to not stop at Ilyeion. Ilyeion was just an experiment. He has already moved on to Alexarien. Gathering people as raw materials. He is going to go further, push to the ends of the world. He wants to be in control or to watch it all burn.

"I know I have acted as a monster. You've seen me on raids. I came with a squad under the guise tonight of killing you. We haven't spoken in years, but ask yourself, do I sound like I am lying to you, brother? Why wouldn't I flee and save myself after you killed my minions? I sent them in so there would be no witnesses of me changing sides. Take me with you, brother, and I shall lead you to their base."

Zarfa stared at her long and hard. He mulled over the things that she said, the tears that she shed, and how pathetic she looked on her back with her nose broken, staring up at him in the light of the run down streetlamps. He was still crying and trying to sort all of his emotions out. He never dreamed he could save his sister. He always thought he had to kill her to free her.

Is this for real? Is she intact? She isn't crazy, brainwashed?

Zarfa lifted his gauss pistol and aimed it at her head.

"Brother, no! You have to believe me! Brot—"

A shot fired from his pistol and the loud noise ended her sentence. A bullet struck right near her ear, causing a loud ringing and dust and debris to fly into everyone's faces.

"On this day, the Faraza are to think you are dead. Welcome back, sister," Zarfa said as he extended his hand to help her up.

She stood and hugged Zarfa tightly, pushing her face into his good shoulder. The blood from her nose soaked his shirt and the blood from his re-opened injury stained her clothing. They held each other for minutes as the others watched. They cried and laughed together simultaneously. It was the happiest Zarfa had ever felt. But all moments in life have to end at some point, whether good or bad.

"One more thing, brother. Ghast is about tonight. He is

certainly nearby. He wouldn't return without me. He has thirty-nine more raiders with him. Highly trained and seeking your head."

"So I guess the fight hasn't ended yet, has it?"

"Nope."

"Sarah, why did you let me hit you? Why didn't you explain sooner?"

"I had to know you had the resolve to do what needs to be done."

"That is?"

"Kill Father. You knew him better than I did. You were older when we were orphaned. Over the last couple of years, I had the chance to three times. I hate him; he's a monster...but I couldn't do it. I knew you could handle the minions thrown at you, but I could never have killed you either."

"I see, don't worry about it, sis. I'll take care of any monster that goes bump in the night."

"You demonstrated that," she said with a wry smile, bringing her face to meet his.

Her eyes were already forming big dark circles from the broken blood vessels in the bridge of her nose. In the morning, she would look like a raccoon. Zarfa would continue to feel regret for having laid her out on the ground like that. But to Sarah, it was a symbol of the complete trust she had in her brother to do what needed to be done.

"Let's hunt Ghast down," Zarfa said, giving his sister one final hug and a kiss on the cheek.

His body was wracked with pain and it hurt to move. He was feeling woozy once again from the blood loss. But he would not stop until he hunted his final prey of the evening.

"Zajifa, Sofronio, I'm tired, but I want to see this through. Send out a rally cry. Call the entire Legion together. We will show them what being caught off guard feels like. We will not only kill Ghast; we will crush him into dust."

Thirteen

A Call to Arms

"'Give me your tired, your poor, your huddled masses yearning to breathe free...' It is a good ideology and a nice concept. Poor Ms. Lazarus would be turning in her grave. These words of an ancient poem spoken on the shores of an ancient civilization many years ago inspired people from all around to flock to a land of hopes, dreams, and promises.

"The promise of a better life, of better things to come. The promise of new technologies, care, comfort, and a life that many would dream of and envy others for. Only when many landed on the shores of the promised land of freedom, they were sold into slavery.

"Slavery on the docks, on the rails, and if it wasn't that, it was a slavery to things. A slavery to existence, a slavery to living up to the dream that everyone around them wanted for them. The times moved on and industry revolutionized. Automobiles were produced and sent out to rove across the countryside.

"Soon, many of the railways that people lost their lives for to build were dismantled. The hopes and dreams of one generation became something to be destroyed by another. Those hopeful immigrants of every nation went from one form of bondage to another. All of which has been forgotten. It was forgotten a thousand years ago, and never is it brought up now. But if you look hard enough, you can dig up the skeletons of the past anywhere.

"That mighty nation known as the United States of America continued to grow. It expanded and collapsed upon itself several times. Things became better, faster, easier, and deemed simpler by the early two thousands. By this time, almost nobody in America the Great didn't have their hands on the newest technologies.

"Families would go so far as to forego food for big screen monitors to watch decaying, drug-abusing athletes that would soon be dead and forgotten. All without ever having to leave the couch. Indentured servants, the whole nation. Not one of them truly free in the fully ironic, iconic nation dubbed, 'the land of the free.' Yes, slavery has never ended.

"There are always those on top and those being taken advantage of. The trick is to convince the victim that there is no other way and that they deserve this. It worked—they suffered many recessions, depressions, and even a great drop in population due to disease and famine, all brought on by themselves.

"It meant something back then; it meant pain, misery, failure, heartache. All it means now is numbers on a graph and a blip in a history book. Fast forward to about 2021. Here, technology was something one could not live without. The pollution brought on by the generations before had caused the land to be barely habitable.

"People's hearts and minds all controlled by microchips and processors. It wasn't much different than hundreds of years before, except that now, these things were internal—symbiotic with technology, unable to sustain themselves without it. If a power outage were to ever occur, it was sheer pandemonium. Again, it was panic, death, terror, pain and agony then, but only numbers and statistics now.

"Move ahead to the year 2028 when they decided they didn't even need human interaction any longer. They felt they could make an artificial intelligence and use it for every-thing from love dolls to military intelligence. The plan seemed good and they rushed ahead without thinking of any undesired consequences. As we know, in a single night, one rogue AI detonated a nuclear arsenal that had long been talked about being disarmed.

"In one night, all five billion on that continent were dead. The price paid for such great technology was the Great Ex-tinction. The fallout was so massive it killed everything from the Pacific Ocean west. Plants, animals, people, all dead, all just statistics. Technology ceased to progress for a short while, but then again we began to build and research along a different path. The path of biotechnology and nanobots.

"The fallout worldwide crumpled governments and destroyed land masses. The ice caps melted, people drowned, nations were torn asunder, and in the midst of all the destruction and chaos, there was a lesson to learn. *Turn back now, those of you who survive, or face the same doom.*

"And, once again, the lesson was ignored. The death, destruction, and decay of the world around us became only statistics. Just numbers and nameless faces. Technology moves ahead and offers answers, offers hope, and people cling to it even if it is false. The polar ice caps were restored and thus people cried out—peace, security, freedom, balance. In their ignorant eyes, the world was corrected.

"I ask now, who of you are content? Who is happy? Who can look at the last two strongholds of civilization and say that this won't happen to us? We will survive; we will not fail where those before us did?

"Which of you can proudly say, 'I am not a slave to anyone?' Only a handful of people, and it is the same handful that is going to try to remove this broadcast. They will be infuriated by it going on air, but they will be unable to stop it. It is already too late; the code has been embedded into their digital video loops. Shutting me down means shutting themselves off from all that their media has to offer.

"They won't do that—Synaptix won't allow it. As we speak, they are airing ads that will make you want to buy their products, make you want the gifts they have to offer. More slavery! They are using a rudimentary mind control signal to corral the weaker minded in and then sealing it by means of their Psyker Scream nanobots. This is something they've kept from the public, and the government that promised full disclosure allowed it to happen.

"Polyhelix is kidnapping in Ilyeion and Alexarien in order to raise a mutant army. I am your herald, your messenger, your prophet, your voice of doom. Listen to me and be saved! The hour is coming where you will be drawn into the conflict without choice, so act now while you still have one. Join the Crimson Crusade! All I ask of you is to identify yourself with a small red 'C' on your body and wait for the time of chaos to act.

"We shall topple the corporations that are making your life hell. Once this is over, nobody will be without a home. The government will belong to you for real, not this mockery of democracy we have now. You have the power to change the future, to prevent this generation from becoming a statistic that nobody will ever read about.

"Come with me, you tired, you poor, you huddled masses yearning to breathe free. Come with me all of you who are oppressed, loaded down, and toiling for nothing but perhaps your next meal. Come with me all of you who fear that tomorrow you may be purchased for slavery or for death.

"The road that looks like oblivion is salvation, I say! And the road they tell you is salvation is most certainly our oblivion for all eternity. If you want to truly live, join the cause and I promise you change. Change now, change for the future.

"If you are hearing this now and are in favor of toppling these false deities of government and technology, then give a battle cry in the streets. Join the Crimson Crusade and be freed.

"No longer become beguiled by things, by people, by activities, or by empty promises. Give yourself to an idea, an idea that this is larger than you. An idea that the common man can be what changes the course of a world doomed to die from the foolish leaders pushing us ahead. Give yourself to the ideology that we can restore the earth to a time of healing!"

This was the second video feed of Crimson 3033 C.E. This video sparked an idea that nobody could extinguish. It sparked a sort of fervor everyone once thought lost. This would go down in history as the true final crusade.

As she had dubbed it herself, "The Crimson Crusade." Soon it would be clear she had support. Tattoos, most commonly on the hand, would become ever popular. A small red "C" that showed their allegiance. Every supporter blended in to everyday life. They went about their business doing the same mundane tasks they always had done before. The only difference was they were ready to act when the time came.

Nobody from child to old woman knew exactly what it was that would be required of them when the time came. They expected another missive and a direction for the com-

ing battle. When asked if they knew what they were fighting for, they all gave the same answer—"To be free."

It was viral, and though nothing had changed, yet many admitted to being happier already. In their minds and in their hearts, they were already free. They already knew what they would do with themselves when the chaos had ended. When the Crimson Crusade had finished cleaning the earth.

—From the tome of Demicles 4001 C.E.

Fourteen

Tombstone Territory

"I am so glad to have you back," Zarfa said over his shoulder.

Sarah was trailing behind him at a close distance; it wasn't hard because he was moving slowly. He was in a great deal of pain from all the events earlier. He looked forward to finalizing this evening by taking down Ghast.

He had never dreamt it would be so easy. For years, this obscured figure, this name that ran the Faraza, had been an apparition. Nobody could grab hold of him, but now he was within Zarfa's grasp. The feelings of joy overwhelmed him.

"I'm not going to lie," he continued. "I really did plan to kill you... That sounds bad, it's just that I figured you had been brainwashed and tortured. Never did I dream that—"

"You'd have your sister back?" she asked. Her voice was nasally from the swelling in her nostrils.

"I didn't think it possible."

"Well, I am here. Furthermore, I am proud of you. I know Faraza is evil. I know Dad is evil, but I still couldn't..."

"It needs to be done."

"I couldn't agree more, but you have to be the one who does it."

Zarfa didn't say a word more. He just quickened the pace. His body was stiff and didn't want to move faster than he was already going. The faster he moved, the more pain riddled him, but he was determined to reach the ambush location.

Sarah matched her pace to his and trailed him like the younger sister. Zarfa couldn't help but let his mind drift to when they had been children. Not innocent, but pure. They knew pain and loss, but they had never known atrocities like this before.

Now was a time of undisputable chaos. Zarfa, for his part, would have taken all of the pain, horror, tragedy, and sadness from his sister if he could have. He knew even though she was resilient, she was hurting deep down. All those years in the Faraza, she had been forced to do terrible things to innocent people.

It was all for the sake of fitting in. All for the sake of keeping a cover. All for the sake of reuniting with him and hopefully, someday, destroying the evil organization that had taken her life from her. On the outside, she acted as if nothing bothered her, but he knew her deeper than that. Something was amiss inside of her and he didn't know how long it would be until she couldn't carry the weight any longer.

"Well, we're here. From what you told us, he should be passing this way this evening. He and his raiding party. Now we go into the tower and wait," Zarfa said, motioning to a spire that stuck out of the residence.

"I thought you preferred to fight with your hands? What are we going to do up there?"

"I do prefer to, but not after I've been nearly killed multiple times in the same day. We go up there, we wait. I contact Zajifa when he comes into sight, and more than a hundred men will descend upon him. I come down to interrogate after it's all over."

"I see. Well, you always were so smart, big brother," Sarah said with tears welling up in her soft eyes.

"Hey, a warrior never cries in battle. Try to hold yourself together, sis."

The two of them entered the huge residence they were standing outside of. It belonged to a member of Legion Nine and the family had cleared out of it in case the fighting spilled over into the home.

As they reached the top of the spire that loomed twenty-five feet into the sky, Zarfa pulled out a box about the size of a coffin from underneath a shelf. He cracked it open and revealed an MK-341 gauss assault rifle complete with a military grade sniper scope.

"No movement," he commed over to Zajifa.

"Noted," he heard back in his ear.

Ghast was terrified as he realized his men were dropping to the ground dead like poisoned flies around him. Zarfa could see it on his face from his scope. It started so quickly he barely had time to respond. He didn't hear a single shot fired, only the bell that was ringing to signal the attack. All according to plan.

As his men were thinned out by the sniper fire, they tried running and taking cover. Those that made it to the alleyways or behind cover were cut down by the support troops. In less than two minutes, the perfectly executed ambush had killed his entire raiding party of thirty-eight.

Ghast stood by himself with a plasma katana in his hand. He was still taking a defensive stance as members of Legion Nine surrounded him. The bell stopped ringing and there was dead silence in the night's air.

"I'll kill anyone who gets too close!" he shouted, trying to act as if he were in charge of the situation still.

"As if a support sniper couldn't drop one between your eyes at any given moment?" Zajifa asked, stepping out in front of him.

"So then why hasn't it?"

"Don't worry."

The timing was immaculate as the shot rang out. The bullet flew from Zarfa's gun into Ghast's right arm. Ghast dropped the plasma sword and screamed in terrible agony. A second shot fired and hit his left knee. Blood sprayed onto the sand as he fell to the ground crying like newborn.

"Being the victim isn't any fun, is it?" Zajifa questioned as he stood next to the writhing Ghast.

"What do you want? If you're going to kill me, do it already!"

"And spoil the fun?"

"You're sick."

"Understood," Zajifa said, responding not to Ghast but a command that came over his com-link.

Zajifa began kicking Ghast in the ribs with all the strength he could muster. With each kick, Ghast rolled over more and more. Zajifa could hear the ribs cracking and finally, when he had rolled Ghast over one complete revolution, he stepped back.

"Proceed," he said as another shot rang out.

This shot aimed true for Ghast's left arm. It struck exactly where the humerus attached to the radius and ulna and blew his arm apart from the elbow. His forearm and hand lay next to his face and Ghast continued to scream and whimper.

"Understood," Zajifa said as he raised his hand into the air, forming a signal with his index and ring fingers.

A member from the crowd threw Zajifa a can of medifoam and he caught it. Zajifa stepped back over to Ghast, who was screaming every form of obscenity but not saying any real words. Zajifa sprayed the foam into each of the gunshots on Ghast's body then eventually on his severed arm.

He had lost a lot of blood and was beginning to lose consciousness as Zajifa knelt next to his face and greeted him with a big smile. He slowly stroked his hand across Ghast's face in a gentle manner.

"There, there, little guy. You aren't going to die...yet," he said as he drew back his hand and slapped Ghast as hard as he could. "You're going to die later. As for you calling us sick... Think of those experiments you've been helping with and you still dare call us the sick ones?"

"I thought you were brave, fearless defenders? I thought you were above this."

"Oh, we are brave and fearless, and it is our duty to defend, but part of that is making an example. Raising morale, building an army off of a victory... I hope you understand this has a purpose," Zajifa said as he struck Ghast in the jaw with his fist hard enough to knock him out.

When Ghast awoke, it was daybreak. He had been tied to an obelisk that typically served as a grave marker for a prominent member of society. This particular monument had been erected in the middle of the city. He couldn't break free even if he had his full strength. His missing arm saw to it that he couldn't untie his bonds. He didn't say a word as he stared Zarfa in the face.

Zarfa had been waiting for hours for him to rouse—he and

about thirty thousand who came to see him executed in public. The crowd stood behind Zarfa all chanting, "Kill him! Kill the leader of Faraza. Kill the one who took our loved ones."

Zarfa realized that he was nothing more than a puppet in his father's scheme, but that was a secret he could keep between himself and Sarah for the time being. Zarfa approached Ghast and stared at him silently for several minutes until the crowd finally grew silent and still.

"You've caused us a great deal of heartache, you know?" Zarfa asked calmly.

"And? So?"

"So I feel sorry for you."

"You feel sorry for me?" Ghast scoffed.

"Yes, you. I feel sorry for whatever it was that made you the way that you are. I feel sorry that you had no issue leading bands of raiders to rape, pillage, steal, murder, kidnap, and all sorts of other grotesque crimes, all for the sake of making those pathetic mutants that I slaughtered like mere defenseless sheep. I feel sorry that you placed hope in a false one. I feel sorry that you angered me. I feel sorry that you were ever born. I feel sorry...that we never had the opportunity to be friends. You know that I don't enjoy killing at all? I'm just damn good at it. Maybe in the beginning I enjoyed it...but it's getting all too tiresome now. I wish we could all get along. Someday, I hope that is possible, yet over seven thousand years of human history seems to be against us. There are only two strongholds left in human society, and in both of them there lays an organization seeking to conquer what is left of this pathetic planet. I'm going to do my part in destroying them and I hope that something finally changes.

"I hope that the countries that have nothing, no technology to synthesize food or no means to grow it because we raped the earth too hard for it to grow, are healed and given the technology to sustain themselves. I hope that we work together to heal the earth. And I wish that instead of this being your demise, you were there to see it."

"How touching, you weak, idealistic, hypocrite. You talk about how we are so different? We are the same. Why do you think Faraza did what it did? Why do you think we want to conquer what is left of this earth?"

"It really is a valiant attempt in such a bleak circumstance to try to get me to see things your way. To convince me that you too thought you were being noble. Yet I fail to see the nobility in any of it and I assure you that you are wasting your breath in doing so. You know what I pity you the most for, though?"

"I don't care. My only wish is that I could live long enough to see your own father slit your throat, asshole."

"I pity you most for the fact that the ones you afflicted will be your final executioners," Zarfa said as he stepped away and disappeared into the crowd behind him.

The crowd rushed forward the second Zarfa stepped away. Nobody knew how long it took for Ghast to be killed by the ones he had stolen from and caused great pain to. All anybody knew was that his body didn't exist when they were done. They tore him into literal shreds with their bare hands and not a single one felt anything but justified.

Fifteen

Alliance

"Zarfa called again. Seems that he sees things our way now," Crimson said as she sat at a terminal near Max in the lab.

"Oh really?"

"Really," she said, sounding a bit annoyed.

Two weeks had passed since Zarfa had left Alexarien. Two weeks ago, Crimson labeled him as a low priority enemy that she was willing to sacrifice with her plague of nanobots. Max had insisted on figuring out a way to save Zarfa and she easily dismissed him saying that there was no chance Zarfa would see the light. Now, he had.

"So it is probably a good thing that I was working on the development of an antibody bot to prevent Zarfa from being killed along with the rest of the Synaptix Psyker Scream army, huh?" Max questioned smugly.

"Yeah, good thing. Look, do you always have to rub it in when you're right?"

"You'd do the same thing."

Stifled, Crimson let out a sigh. "You know me all too well."

"Well, I will have you know, the good news is that it is easier than we had thought. In another two days, the machines in the lab will begin mass production of the flying anti-Psyker bots. In one day, I will have an ampoule of the antibodies ready. We just need a way to deliver it to Zarfa. I'm not going to mass produce it... There is no need to."

"Good, he also decided to go ahead with the Psyker treatments. He doesn't want to lose his hearing and he believes we should be able to take down Synaptix within the next two months...before they will be able to control him on the frequency."

"What gave him that idea?"

"I did."

Max, shocked, dropped what he was doing and glared up at Crimson. She had to know what he was thinking by now.

"What?" She questioned him like he was a little boy begging his mother for something.

"Two months? Really?"

"Maybe sooner. Look, Max, you've already proven one thing—that you work very fast. You are beyond intelligent; almost nothing is out of your reach. Look at how fast you made these bots for us. All you have left to do is make the bot that will let me be unharmed by massive amounts of electricity. If you can do that, great—if not, we will do our best without it. The government is taking notice of our actions and Synaptix has been stewing about the blow we struck against them. Not to mention the blow Zarfa struck to them. They're angry, and it is only a matter of time before they strike. We need to be the first to move. Three days from now, Zarfa is going to lead what he thinks will be the final assault against Faraza. They are crippled. He killed their main leader, Ghast, and Polyhelix has no immediate backup to send except for Zarfa's father."

"Zarfa's what?" Max exclaimed.

"Yeah, some other news... His sister is back and informed them that their father was the true founder of Faraza. Also, he sits at the head of Polyhelix. He could come and lead Faraza to a potential victory, but it is too risky. It is almost certain that he will remain in Alexarien at the Polyhelix headquarters. To send him to Ilyeion to fight along with the cultish army of theirs would be a poor strategy. Zarfa promised if I lent him a hand, he would march Legion Nine to Alexarien, where we will crush Polyhelix and Synaptix together. I agreed. In three days from now, I will be taking a huge risk with potential collateral damages to Legion Nine. Zarfa understood and agreed he still wanted what I could offer. I will be revealing that I managed to hack the Pilvikones and that I have ultimate control over the weather. I really hope they don't notice because I believe it will help our victory on our home turf. Anyhow, now is zero hour—

things are going to happen fast."

"So we have Legion Nine helping, but they have, what, maybe two thousand soldiers tops? None of whom have really been trained. That won't be much of a help, will it? Look, I like Zarfa and I don't want him dead, but is revealing your ace this early worth the risk for his army?"

"Max, when he killed Ghast, he made it a public execution. He allowed many families that fell victim to Faraza to take part in exacting what they felt was justice. The mob relentlessly tore Ghast to pieces. People felt great and felt that a hope of putting this to an end permanently wasn't a dream anymore. He now has over fifty thousand willing to fight for him and the numbers are growing each day. Not all will come with him here, but a good amount will."

"Okay, I can see where that would be an advantage. How many do you think we have?"

"You've seen it yourself, Max. Just step outside and look around. You can't go anywhere without seeing people with the mark on their hand. We have a lot of support. Like I said, the government has taken notice of us. In fact, they are beginning to arrest people with the 'C' on their hand, but this is only making us more popular. It seems for every arrest, ten more are fueled to join the cause. If even half of these people take arms when we send out the final call, there is no stopping us. So do you think you will be able to finish my final project?"

"Maybe, give me about a week. I have an idea for your little conductor bots. This is all so surreal. How long do you think it will be until the military gets involved?"

"Probably not until we destroy the other competition. As of right now, to them, we are still a small, worthless rebel faction with many obstacles in our way. As soon as they see those fall, they'll mobilize. You can be sure of that."

"So you think they'll plan to crush us as we cheer in victory?"

"Exactly."

They sat in silence for a moment longer, then Crimson began to smirk and giggle like an insidious little school child planning something mischievous.

"What now?" Max asked.

"Oh, the plan that Zarfa had. His whole reason for coming here was to get the ability to hear where the raiders were coming from. They ride giant wasps that come out of the ground and he figured by being able to strike at their heart underground, they'd be at a disadvantage without their air support."

"Why's that so funny?"

"Because I convinced him to make their strike as public as possible and to wait outside, let the Faraza counter their assault and fight out in the open of the desert."

"And lose their advantage? Why?"

"Oh, you'll see. In fact, Legion Nine is strong, but the forces of nature can be stronger. We will virtually be there for the battle on a live feed, seeing it from multiple points of view. I agreed to help, right? It shall be glorious!" Crimson chuckled as she went back to entering data into the terminal she was sitting at. She had nearly as much work to do as Max and she knew the seriousness of it.

"This is Thomas Cudrow, president of Polyhelix. This is the correct communicator number to reach Badger, correct?"

Badger had been sleeping when he heard the jingle for his voice communicator ring in his head. It had awakened him and he felt uneasy. If it was anyone from Synaptix, they would have directly communicated via his dreams or telepathic conversation. He hadn't received a call on his voice communicator for almost ten years.

"Yeah, it's Badger. What the hell do you want?" he grumbled, sounding as grumpy as ever.

"You. I know you are the only remaining commander of the Psyker Scream army. I know that Zax and Surge were both your friends. I also know you want free will, but the powers that be at Synaptix said to forget revenge and focus on destroying Polyhelix, resume the plan as if nothing had changed. Am I right?"

"Yeah, you're right, but why are you talking to me? You know *the powers that be* are listening to you as we speak, right?"

"That I do. It is part of the reason I contacted you. You see, getting this channel was easy for a man in my position.

Your cohorts, however, are a bit more...private, shall I say? Anyhow, I didn't feel like going to great lengths to uncover who is at the top of Synaptix. I figured I would offer them a proposition through you."

"What if they don't like that you chose to use me as a mediator?"

"Well, then this conversation hardly matters. Seeing as you haven't been given a directive to hang up on me, I assume they're interested in what I have to say."

"They're telling me to let you say what you have to say."

"Good. Well, what I have to say is this. Both of us have the same goal. Overthrow the government and establish our own. We both seek total control over the globe, starting with the last two strongholds of humanity, Alexarien and Ilyeion, correct?"

"Correct," Badger responded, much more awake now but sounding even more annoyed.

"We have both suffered great losses in leadership of our armies, however, have we not?"

"Agreed."

"So why not put aside this petty squabbling over power, control, dominance? Let's cut a deal, perhaps? We help each other out in dealing with this rebel faction. For me, my main enemy is my own son Zarfa, leader of Legion Nine. For you, it is this anonymous Crimson Army. We can strike now on our own and probably be victorious, but at a great expense to our own power. Individually, we will both be so weakened that neither of us could recover fast enough to challenge the government's military. Together, however? It should be no trouble destroying both rebel factions then marching on in our coup d'état. So I say we do this. Let us help each other out, no more backbiting, and we set solid boundaries now so there is no arguing when the bloodshed is over."

"What are your conditions? They want to know, not me. I could give a crap."

"Oh, you will care, my friend. The first target is Zarfa, your chance at exacting revenge. Anyhow, I am gracious and reasonable. The terms are this—I take Ilyeion, you take Alexarien. I am giving you the more advanced civilization of the two. As for all of the third world nations that are struggling to get by? It's a fifty-fifty split once the war is over.

Simple as that, no more fighting. Let's be civil, please?"

"They concur. It's a deal, but if you show so much as a sign of double-crossing them, they are not afraid to crush you like an ant. As for me, how are you going to feel about me taking your son's life myself?" Badger questioned, aroused by the prospect of shedding Zarfa's blood.

"I care not. I was going to try to convert him to my way of thinking, but he learned of me before I had intended. He took his stand and so did his rebellious sister. I shall slay them both, just as I did their incompetent mother. She thought she could convince me to stop my plan, but I had to teach her a lesson about that. Anyhow, do what you will. They are already dead in my eyes."

Thomas's voice was cold and emotionless. Badger felt as if he was talking to the devil himself the way he was so ready to execute his own children.

"I see. Well, we are glad that you have come to your senses and decided to side with us. Seeing what a ruthless person you are, we are glad to not be fighting against your cause. May we both succeed, Thomas."

"Oh yes, one last thing. I expect some support to the battle that my son announced is to take place in three days from now. It is outside the city of Ilyeion in the desert wasteland. He discovered where the entrance for the Faraza's underground facility is. Send me ten thousand support troops and we should be able to kill those peasants. Also, I have some intelligence that tells me Crimson and her little accomplice will be distracted that day. It may be a good time to send another assassination attempt? It's your call. I know you guys are brilliant and could possibly figure something out. Anyhow, if we crush Legion Nine, I will immediately mobilize the rest of my army to strike in Alexarien. I look forward to seeing your competence on the battlefield. Until then, ciao."

The communicator went dead and Badger lay there in his bed motionless. He had a gut feeling this was a bad omen, but he wanted his revenge. He was shocked that the leaders of Synaptix were so quick to make a judgment on this alliance proposition. He didn't think or worry about it for too long, though. He just got comfortable again and closed his eyes to sleep.

"Get up. You will be leading the entire Psyker army to Ilyeion. A helicopter is coming to get you now. Be on the roof in twenty minutes."

"The entire Psyker army? He only asked for ten thousand support troops. Isn't the whole army nearly fifty thousand?" Badger questioned back telepathically to the mysterious messenger.

"We know what he asked for. But we still don't trust him. If this is a trap to weaken us after the battle, we want to be prepared. We will be ready to crush him at a moment's notice."

"I see... I had thought you took his word at face value awfully quickly. So what are my orders exactly?"

"Take the army. Assist Polyhelix, but do not let your guard down. If they give the slightest sign of double-crossing, put them down. Also, get out of bed and stop wasting time. The helicopter is arriving in fifteen minutes now."

Sixteen

60

Sixty hours until the battle of Ilyeion

"This...this is fantastic. Yeah, this will work for sure. A tad dusty in here, but other than that...six SCARA-type robotic arms, fully functional console with all of the programs I need. I'm moving some stuff here," Max said as he walked around Crimson's safe house.

"Yeah... You going to tell me what this is all about or what?"

"No," he said as he handed her a piece of paper with a list on it. "Also, I will need everything on this list within twelve hours. If it isn't fulfilled then I don't know of how much assistance I can be to you."

Crimson glanced over the list and her eyes widened. She scowled at Max as he paced around the room investigating all of the equipment.

"Money isn't an issue, but you do realize what you are asking for? This alloy you named is nearly impossible to get, especially on such short notice. It is the strongest alloy known to man. People consider it nearly indestructible, and the amount you want...it is going to cause some red flags with the military."

"Like there isn't already? You and I both know they are only waiting for the fighting to end between us and the corporations before they sweep in and surgically excise us from humanity. We grabbed their attention when we set out to recruit people for the crusade. They're watching. They've always been watching. They just let us believe they are too weak and powerless to stop us."

"Oh, why do you say that, Max? What happened to you being so positive and trusting me?"

"I am positive; I do trust you. I am saying trust me. We need a contingency. I don't care if I die for a good cause, but I sure as hell am not going to die a pointless death. I am going to make it count. I know you have a plan B if anything goes awry. What's wrong with a plan C if that fails to work out how you planned?" he blurted in exasperation.

"There's nothing wrong, Max, but I think you forget who organized this revolution in the first place. I call the shots, not you. I want to know what you need all of this for. And this memory system you put down—what, are you building a supercomputer of some sort? What do you need all of that digital storage for?"

"I am not saying. It is time you let me do my job and trust me. I am here to design things for you. I've completed all but one of your assignments and then some. I'll have the bots you need designed for you in the next day. I had a major breakthrough. I just ask you provide me with what I need. Get me what is on that list. Trust me. Step back. You not doing that will be interference and I won't be able to get done what I need to get done. Unless you have a good reason not to do this and you won't? Well, then I guess I'll have to call it quits. Like I said, I'm not laying down my life to accomplish nothing."

"Who says you're going to die? Who says you're laying down your life? Why can't we all live through this?"

"We aren't going to all live through this. It isn't a fairytale. There will be losses. Do we stand a chance to succeed in overthrowing the governments and destroying these corporations that have been raping the masses? Yes! But there will be a price to pay and nobody is exempt. I'm not an assassin like you. You stand a better chance to live, but even that isn't a guarantee. You might die as well, but we aren't all going to come out of this unscathed. Let me do what I need to do and everything will work out. Besides, what I'm building...I hope I won't need to use, but if the need arises and you're still alive, you will be grateful. Mark my words."

"I will... Fine, I'll see what I can do. Stop planning on dying, Max. I need you still even if we win."

"I don't plan on it, but it is a reality... In my case, it's even a likelihood. It's also a sacrifice I am willing to make if it's needed. So just deal with that. Did you get the antibots to Zarfa, by the way?"

"I sent a rocket drone to deliver it. He should have them in a matter of hours... I'll see what I can do about the three hundred pounds of Kelmantrium you requested...as well as the rest of this crap."

"Supplies. Not crap. Supplies. One last thing... How is Luther? You said you were going to repair him."

"He's fine. He is back to being operational."

"Send him over immediately."

"What? Why?"

"Do it," he said harshly. "Please," he added, realizing Crimson had never seen him like this before.

"Fine, but you better not be planning to betray me."

"Funny you say that. The same stands for you. Trust me, I've got a surprise that I hope never needs revealing."

Crimson looked at him as he stared into her eyes as seriously as she had ever seen him. She wished she understood him and what the gears in his head were churning out. A spark had ignited inside of him that was driving him to either brilliance or madness and she was curious as to what it was.

"Okay, Max, expect a shipment soon. I think I have a few strings I can pull," she said with a sigh as she turned and left.

"Having gotten Sarah back is a huge boon to our cause. With her back, my hearing enhancements are a moot point. She has shown us exactly where the entrances and exits to the Faraza underground are located," Zarfa said, addressing a large group of Legion Nine members.

The Legion had grown so rapidly there was now need to implement a form of organization. Zarfa decided to allow the first two thousand people to arrive to hear a lecture that would discuss the plan of attack against Faraza. He had arranged for these lectures to take place every day for the next fifty hours. It was up to everyone in attendance to get the others up to speed.

Pulling up a map of the area on a huge monitor, Zarfa continued his lecture. "Here are the areas that they will swarm from with the wasp riders. We are going to fight them in the wide open of the wasteland," he stated authoritatively.

The crowd realized they would be at a disadvantage if they were to fight out in the open, so they began to murmur amongst themselves. There was discord growing in the crowd and Zarfa stopped speaking. He knew they wouldn't hear it until it died down.

"It's crazy, right? Us fighting exposed in the open when we could take it to them by ramming it down their throats? Wrong. We have the advantage. I can't explain it, so I am going to need your faith. I am sure you have heard of the woman Crimson. The one who is leading the invisible rebellion of the Crimson Crusade? Well, she is our ally and has promised to help. She has a plan that I am sure will succeed. After the war is over here, we are going to march on Alexarien and help her perform a coup d'état. I felt it was a fair trade.

"Anyhow, we can't let them swarm us out there and hold our ground. Crimson will take care of a lot of it for us. Besides, she pointed out that the Faraza is crippled and this is war. Their base and whatever they have down there is practically useless to Polyhelix at this time. If we blindly march into the catacombs below, what is to prevent them from blowing it up and burying us alive? Nothing!"

The crowd quieted down and was now hanging on what Zarfa had to say. He was right. Most of them had never considered the probability of being buried alive. It would do them no good if they all rushed underground only to be slaughtered by a few well-placed explosives.

They also knew that Thomas Cudrow was in Alexarien. Them marching there to end this after the battle would serve a dual purpose, pay back Crimson for her help, and put an end to this once and for all.

"So what I need from each of you is to come to the battle fully prepared to die, but don't plan on it. I would love to see this end with nobody lying bleeding on the ground except for those ugly mutant bastards. Organize, pick a buddy, make a squad, and watch each other's backs. This is no time for cowardice. When the skies fill with the black of the wasps and the deep, low drone of them flying overhead, do not try to retreat. Show no fear and show no mercy. The more guns we can bring to this, the better. Shoot with a frenzy into the sky and wait for your deliverance. Because in the flash of an eye, you will see it. It is going to take a lot of faith in me, faith in Crimson, but know this. I will be on the front lines risking all with you. I am not some coward who hides behind his army. I do not want to sit in any ivory tower. I do not want worship or praise, I just want you to trust me and follow my orders. In this way, we will succeed.

"Some of you doubt me, some of you fear. Some of you disagree, but remember this. We are only here because of my actions. It wouldn't have been possible without the loyal support of those in the beginning, but they all trusted in me and followed my lead, so I am asking the very same of each of you. Follow my lead! If we live, we shall live as one! If we die, we shall die as one. We are an unstoppable legion. We are Legion Nine. That was our roots, but we have grown too vast to count. We shall roll over our enemies like the waves of the ocean. We shall wipe the slate clean and start anew. Now I ask you all here, are you with me? Will you follow me? Will you do as I ask?"

The crowd roared with cheering and clapping. The feeling of harmony in the air was contagious. Even Sofronio, who was backstage, was clapping. He was in full support of Zarfa. The members of the audience that came to listen had gleaming looks on their faces of vigor, joy, zeal, unity, and fury. Each one felt unstoppable and Zarfa hoped that truly, they would be.

"There are sixty hours left to our deliverance—to our glory, and to a lot of bloodshed. We hope for this to be the last of the heartbreak that any of you have to endure for the rest of your lives. We hope that this war will change the way humans treat one another. We hope for a period of peace to rule across the globe. Legion! You are dismissed. Go, rest, prepare, and come to the battle at your best."

Badger and the Psyker Scream army has been picked up and transported to twenty miles north of Ilyeion and dropped

in the desert. Synaptix had arranged for a camp to be prepared using the most advanced technology in cloaking and
thermal reflection to prevent themselves from being spotted
by the naked eye or by satellite.

Badger was bored out of his mind. He had no one to talk
to. He was surrounded by fifty thousand troops—men, wom-
en, children—yet none of them could talk. None of them had
thoughts or free will anymore. All of them were linked to
Badger's brain.

Each one was a pinprick inside of his mind and he knew
everything about them subconsciously. He knew exactly
where Sally Montross stood in the crowd. He, without ever
having seen her, knew that she was twenty-six. He knew
that she was six foot and one eighth of an inch tall. She
weighed one hundred-sixty-seven pounds, four and three-
quarters ounces.

He knew her average heart rate was eighty-two beats per
minute resting; she respired on average twenty-two breaths
per minute. He knew before her mind was taken over she
had been turned on by muscular black men. Badger knew
every detail of everyone in the army, and he knew their exact placement and status—always.

He also knew that his every thought was their command
and that it would travel to them quicker than the speed of
light. He knew they were a large army with only one thought,
his thoughts. He was so completely bored.

He missed Zax and Surge. They had been his friends before Synaptix recruited them to be part of this experiment.
Badger had always belonged to the corporation, so when this
opportunity arose, he jumped on it. He convinced his friends
that it would be a great idea and that they may die if they
didn't side with Synaptix while they still could.

He had also realized what a valuable asset he was to
Synaptix and that he did have some bargaining power with
the leaders at the top of the corporation. He had convinced
those men to allow them to keep their free will. They had,
and now Badger hated himself for involving them.

He realized that even if Synaptix won and got everything
they ever wanted, he was doomed and he had doomed himself. Doomed to a life of boredom, a life of solitude. His only
friends were dead. There would be very few with free will af-

ter Synaptix had their way.

Badger didn't desire to have a mindless sex slave that obeyed his every thought. He didn't want a posse to stroll with at night. He wanted conversation, and there in the middle of the desert amongst fifty-thousand living, breathing, warm bodies, he could only speak with himself. Or the faceless voice that invaded his mind every so often, and that wouldn't respond to him unless it had business with him.

Thirty-one hours until the battle of Ilyeion

Max had the computer systems back at the main base on cruise control. His automated program had finished running its simulations and analysis, and the bots that Crimson had requested were in the process of being created. It was a brilliant design, a sort of mix between splicing and nanobot technology.

Half gene manipulation mixed with a viral cell and grafted into a nanobot. He had taken and reverse engineered the DNA in the cells of electric eels that allowed their bodies to generate electricity and pass it through their bodies, dispersing it externally without it harming their cells. Other scientists before Max had done most of the work of isolating the gene. He'd hacked their research and stole it for himself, then expanded upon it.

By isolating the gene, cloning the recombinant DNA of the eel and Crimson, then injecting the product on a microscopic level into a harmless viral cell, he formed the first part of what she needed. He then created a nanobot that would flow through the blood and attach to every cell in her body, delivering this change and monitoring her for any adverse effects.

By means of this, she would have the ability to absorb electrical currents, produce her own, allow massive amounts to pass through her body, and also be able to externally discharge and disperse it, all while suffering no ill effects. It had been cooking back at the main base for roughly six hours and would be done in another three. With that task out of his way, he was free to pursue his own task.

He sat down at the console and began engineering his

masterpiece. It was going to truly be a work of art and a complete marvel. He wanted it to be perfect, flawless, genuine, unique, but he had a time limit. He was also still suffering withdrawal side effects, but he managed to stay focused on his new idea and ignore whatever he was suffering.

He measured and mapped out everything in the drafting program to exact specifications. Luther was staring over his shoulder, double-checking his work. Luther could no long help, as he was not able to do what he once could, however he still provided input when he was able.

"So tell me, Luther, how much do you remember of your brain scanning technology?"

"If you are asking so as to rebuild it...enough."

"I have no need to rebuild it. With some of Crimson's connections, I was able to locate your machines. The rumor was they were destroyed. It's funny how after people get what they want from whatever it is, these 'lost objects' typically wind up being a mantelpiece for some rich jerk who likes to brag about how he owns chunks of human history. Nobody can own history and these objects are valueless except for the value of their purpose. There it was, sitting in some old coot's home waiting to be used. He wouldn't sell it, so I hired one of Crimson's friends to steal it for me. It's in the other room.

"Also, she followed through on my list of requests. They were all pretty simple except for the Kelmantrium I needed...and that experimental crystalline hard drive I requested. Everyone knows there were only ten prototypes made and it is too expensive and advanced at this point in time to mass produce. I am really shocked she had it to me in six hours. Guess she does trust me."

"So what is your plan with all of this stuff, Max?" Luther asked, his synthesized voice sounding apprehensive.

"I plan to rebuild you, Luther, to make you whole again. Also, I need a backup plan...a failsafe, in case things go wrong."

"I see. You seem smart enough. Why do you need me here?"

"Because you are a golem, a gargoyle. I expect you to stay here and chase away any evil spirits that might come to wreck my work. Also, I wanted your take on this skeleton I'm building. Correct me where I'm making mistakes, add to my design," Max said, never taking his eyes off of the screen. He hadn't slept in nearly a day and a half and had no intention of doing so any time soon.

Max was stuck on finishing his work of art. He worked well into the night, all the while Luther towered over his shoulder giving advice on what to change, what might make it better. Luther was getting excited as he saw it shape up in front of his eyes.

Hours had passed and most of the preliminary work had finished. Crimson stopped by to see what information she could gather from whatever she might be able to sneak a peek at. Max promptly shrunk the display and hid it from her sight. Luther refused to answer any questions she might have.

"Max, are you going to be back by the main base before the war erupts?" she asked, sounding anxious.

Max tapped his feet, stood, and stretched his legs. He yawned and looked over at the clock. "Crap, I've been at it seven hours and I'm only this far... Twenty-four...twenty-four hours and it starts," he said, running his hand through his messy, frazzled hair. "I'll be back nine hours before it begins. I'll sleep and be ready to support you as a sniper, shock troop, whatever. Oh. When you return, go to the lab and go to the fabricator. Inside will be a vial with roughly seven ounces of what looks to be a lime green serum. Inject it into your brachial vein. They are the bots you wanted. You know, the little electricity ones? *Zap zap!* Anyhow, nine hours 'til show time. I'll be home. Mark my words. I really need to finish this. I can do it. I just need no interruptions. I'm just going to—" Max was cut off by an alarm from the other room. "Oh. It's done!" he exclaimed, running in to retrieve his creation.

He came back into the room holding a Tubex glass syringe with a stainless steel finger control. He was staring at it madly as if it was a child he loved with all of his heart. He was chuckling softly like a mad scientist as he fixed his gaze from the syringe to Crimson's catlike eyes.

"You were an assassin for many years before you became a revolutionary, correct?" he inquired with a wide grin.

"Yes...why?" Crimson asked, sounding a bit nervous.

"I am going to open my mouth. I need you to shove this

titanium eighteen gauge hollow bore needle through the roof of my mouth and into the cerebral aqueduct. Then I need you to carefully inject the contents. Trust me, I'll be fine as long as your aim is good."

Crimson got goose bumps and the memory of what she had done to Brian Nash popped into her head. The sphenoid was a much easier target than the cerebral aqueduct. Why did Max have to be so specific with his instructions?

"You know it's a difficult shot and I might accidentally kill you, right?"

"We all gotta die sometime, love."

"I need you alive to help in this revolution. You're no good strung out and you're no good dead. You've avoided being a junkie so far, but I'm not going to assist in your suicide."

"Look, I trust you...more than I trust Luther; he is a machine, but he doesn't have his full...brain. You've got your full brain and some of the steadiest hands I've seen that weren't...biotic augmentations like mine... Anyhow, if you don't do it, I can give it a shot myself. I only ask you because I trust you can do it."

Max shoved the syringe into Crimson's hand and forced her to close her fingers around it so she wouldn't drop it. She glared at him. She hated his secrecy and his insane ideas, but at the same time, she was intrigued and curious to see what he had planned.

"Fine, Max, but if you die...I told you so, and I am going to be so pissed."

"Yeah, I know," he said, smiling.

Max stood in front of her and opened his mouth wide. He tilted his head back so she could see where she was placing the needle. If she went too far, she would strike his brain stem and kill him immediately. She took her aim and plunged the needle.

Max didn't have any anesthetic in him and it was most certainly one of the most painful things he ever experienced. Tears flowed out of his eyes and down his face. Crimson cringed as she saw his pain. She thought she was in the right area so she drew back on the syringe.

"Okay, I am drawing back cerebral spinal fluid. I am going to push now. You might feel a bit of a sting," she said sarcastically. "If you are unsure of this, move back and don't let me do this."

Max didn't say a word or make a sound. He simply stood there like a crying statue, waiting. The seconds felt like days to him with this needle so close to his brain and blood trickling down his throat. His stillness indicated to Crimson he was sure and she pushed the syringe. Once the contents where emptied, she carefully and swiftly pulled the needle out of his head.

The second Max was safe, he dropped to the ground and started screaming and rolling about like a child who just gotten his first vaccination.

"Damn it! Damn it! Gaarrrragghgh! That hurt like hell!"

He was in pain, but he was okay. He would live. Crimson kicked him once, not too hard, in the ribs. "Get up, you big baby. You knew it was going to hurt and even asked me to do it. I don't know what your crazy brain is up to, but it was worth seeing you regress from a macho man to a cringing adolescent right before me. Where is the chrysalis this big baby most certainly must have emerged from?" she taunted him as he smirked.

"I hate you sometimes," he said as he stood and rubbed his side.

"You love me," she said as she turned toward the door and spanked herself.

His eyes were drawn to her gluteus and he had a quick daydream that it had been his hand that had slapped it. A smile came across his face and he grabbed her by the shoulder and spun her around. He was acting like a wild man the last several days and was about to prove to Crimson he had gone mad.

He grabbed her by her arms and pinned them to her sides. With his new strength, there was no way she could resist. Her breathing deepened and her face looked unsure. Max leaned in and kissed her gently on the lips only at first. They both lingered in the moment and Max slipped his tongue into her mouth. As he moved it rhythmically back and forth, her heart began to race. Her face flushed and her breathing became labored as she passionately kissed him back. He ended it by biting her lower lip gently and pulling back.

"I'll show you much more when this is all over, babe," he said, spinning her back around and slapping her butt.

Crimson was angry at Max and aroused at the same time. She had never had anyone bring out that reaction in her before. She had always used sex as a weapon, the way it was used against her as a child. She never had any interest in being with anyone in that way. But this little moment had awakened a new feeling deep within her. Catching her breath, she managed to huff out, "I look forward to it. That's why you can't die, Max."

Her breathy voice was the most sensual thing Max had ever heard. If he didn't have a drastic time limit and a lot of work to do, he would have taken her right then and there, but his eyes darted back over to the console.

"I know. Now you need to get lost, sweetheart. Big Daddy Max has got some work to do," he said jokingly.

"All right Deadeye, Big Daddy Max," Crimson said, turning to him so he could see her rolling her eyes.

Crimson left and Max sat back at his console, returning to work.

Zarfa had been giving the lectures all day. No two were the exact same. He drew off of the audience. The effect seemed to be the same each time, however. A general sense of unity and loyalty. He felt that the battle would go great and he predicted less than ten percent casualties on his side.

It was late and he was tired. He went back to his home to rest. When he entered, he smelled his favorite dish. Green curry chicken with eggplant. It was nearly impossible to find the ingredients anymore.

Sarah came out of the kitchen holding a clay pot filled with the delicious food and set it on the table in front of him. Her eyes were dull and weary-looking. He could tell she was worried. He would be lying if he said he wasn't.

"I don't know how many more meals either of us will have," she started with tears in her eyes. "It took me all day to track down the ingredients and I spent a small fortune on them. I knew it was your favorite, though, and I felt you deserved it," she said, sitting next to him at the table.

Zarfa smiled and grabbed her hand to reassure her. He gently caressed the top of her hand and forearm. The loving touch soothed her and helped her to relax. He looked into her weary, beaten eyes and showed her with his actions that he appreciated what she had done for him.

"Join me in eating it, will you? It smells delicious and it wouldn't be fair for you to slave over this gift for me only to have me devour it in front of you. Plus, what is good food if it isn't shared with the ones you love?"

Sarah began crying and fell on Zarfa's chest. She sobbed and her tears soaked his shirt. Her hot breath felt heavy on his chest and he gently caressed the back of her neck, trying to relax her. He didn't feel like he was any good at comforting anyone, but he would try.

"Look, everything is going to be okay, Sarah. I will come back from this. You will come back from this. We will both have families and live out the rest of our days in peace, and whatever evils you've seen and done will no longer haunt you. You will be able to rest at night knowing you've atoned for whatever you have done...and then some."

"Thank you," she said as she began to sniffle. "It's like an awful nightmare I can't wake up from."

"I know, Sarah," he said.

Her long hair looked like spun raven feathers and flowed down to between her shoulder blades. She was still the young, beautiful sister he had always remembered, but now she was damaged. She was damaged by a bad conscience and the horrors of war, manipulation, and abuse of power.

She was damaged by having a trusted parent betray her and the haunting thought of having to seek putting him to death in the name of justice. In the years she spent amongst the Faraza, she'd aged an eternity in mind and spirit. As the battle approached, she felt anxiety and feared that her brother, the only anchor in her life, would vanish.

She feared the harsh reality that at any moment, he may be ripped from her life. His soul may be torn from his body on the battlefield. He had brushed with death so many times it seemed as if he had used up all of his luck, and she worried this would be one of his final nights.

She worked hard to push the thoughts from her mind. She managed to stop her tears and her sobbing before the food cooled off. She drew her face back from her brother's chest and dished him up first, then herself. They sat and ate without saying anything more.

When the meal was over, she sat staring at Zarfa, admiring the strong character he held. Admiring his courage, bravery, and precise way of thinking, she smiled. She grabbed Zarfa's hand and said, "I love you, brother. I wish I could be more like you...and... I don't know what tomorrow or the next day holds for us, but I am glad that we have right now."

He squeezed her back and smiled. Looking into her eyes, he said, "Me too." He leaned over the table, threw his arms around her shoulders, and hugged her tight. It was awkward because he didn't bother standing and the table was jamming into his side, but he didn't care. If his life could remain in this awkward, painful hug for eternity, he would take it. He wouldn't let go of it for anything.

Twenty hours until the battle of Ilyeion

Crimson awoke at three a.m. feeling fidgety. She had a gut feeling of what Max was up to, but had no idea at the same time. After she left him at the secondary safe house, she decided to go home and try to rest. It was the calm before the storm.

She had already formulated her third and final missive and was dying to send it out, but she had no idea when Legion Nine would make it to Alexarien. This wasn't like her. She had always been cool, calm, solitary. But now, she was worried, hyperactive, and thinking about someone she couldn't get her mind off of—Max.

She knew she was going to have a hard time in twenty hours from now. She would be supporting a battle from thousands of miles away, viewing it all from cameras in the sky. She may even get blinded and be forced to go by global positioning satellites and maps only. She was nervous. She was banking her plans on a lot of things she had never tested.

She wished that there was a way to do a practice run. To try it out and see how it went. Before she had gone into the business of killing people to make a living, she'd trained and done simulations with willing partners, but now...there was none of that safety. For the first time since she killed her master that had been abusing her for years, she would have to go out on a limb and try something that she was risking everything for.

She would have to trust that the idea she planted in the masses of oppressed would live and perpetuate. She had to believe that when she sent her final missive, they would respond and be the army of misfits she had hoped for. But no such faith came to her, only anxiety.

She had never wanted anyone close to her. Not since the day she had been sold as a slave anyhow, but now she found herself awake. Lying in bed. Thinking of Max...and wishing he was there with her.

"It's only been four hours since I left him...nine more until he's back," she said as she slapped her forehead and remembered something.

Crimson leapt out of bed and sprinted to the lab. She went over to the fabricator and pulled out the vial Max had told her about. She had been so tired when she got back to her place that it had escaped her mind. She promptly injected it into the brachial vein just as Max had told her to.

She felt it course through her veins. It seemed to pulse rhythmically as it invaded her cells. Her whole body tingled. The feeling was odd, but almost pleasurable. Soon, she could feel that her body was generating electricity and that she had full control over it. A couple of hours went by and she began to feel static charges around her. She could absorb them and disperse them even more powerfully by causing the dispersions to form a centrifuge-type force.

The result was an arch of spinning electricity that would pick up ambient static to add to its charge. This arch would continue until it came into contact with something that would cause it to disperse. *Like a person,* she thought to herself.

Max was typing frantically into his terminal. He had finished the structure to house the crystalline hard drive, and the robotic arms were hard at work crafting it. The hard drive worked off of the principle of shining different colors through a prism. Each color would define a type of memory, and since the color spectrum was nearly endless, it was impossible to know how much data could be stored in colors then re-interpreted back through a processor.

The process of recovering the data one wanted was the speed of light. Science still had yet to define exactly how quickly information traveled over the surface of the brain, making it difficult to compare to the drive. In each person, the speed in which the synapse sent and received infor-mation was different. Augments could be purchased to speed these things up, such as the ones Max's parents had installed in him, but it was still hypothesized to be nowhere near the speed of the crystalline hard drive.

Max couldn't be bothered by tasks such as continuing to add the chemical Traxium to the Kelmantrium to allow it to be pliable and worked with. If a person let it cure before he or she was finished shaping the structure, it was all over. It would harden and never become malleable again. For this task, he had Luther.

"Luther, how's the progress coming?" he shouted across the lab.

"It's going fine, Max. Another two hours until it is com-pleted," he said back.

"Okay, great! I hacked into the military database and copied their plans for an exoskeleton. I reworked some of the modeling so that it would fit you. Just follow that blueprint, but use the excess Kelmantrium instead of the titanium that is described in the blueprint. But not now. Wait until I leave. I know you can handle it!" Max shouted in excitement.

"You know, I am feeling more like a slave than a fellow scientist?" Luther questioned.

"I'm sorry, Luther... At times, I think maybe I am more of a robot than...never mind, that would be insensitive too."

"Than me? Ha!" Luther chuckled at the notion.

"Good to see you still have a sense of humor," Max said, still typing away, never deviating from his work, "because I wouldn't want my lab technician to get upset with me."

Luther's metal frame was shimmying and his voice box was making a noise so strange it could only be described as laughter.

"I don't think that when Crimson introduced us, she thought we would make good friends. I like this, Luther. I know you couldn't back up your whole intellect, but I wish you could have. I am sure you were a more brilliant scientist than I could ever dream to be."

"Thanks, Max, it means a lot to me. It is awful being a shell of one's former self, yet still I am happy to be...alive... If you could call it that."

"I would, and maybe you are merely the first in redefining what it means to be a life form."

"Really, Max? We humans have been arguing this philosophical debate for thousands of years. Let's not have another stab at it. How about that?"

Max roared with laughter. "We humans. I like it, Luther, don't lose that spirit. Because really, that is what you still are."

"Besides, Max, you may be the same as me someday. Then what would you call yourself?"

"The same as I do now—your equal."

The room went silent after that except for the clattering of the keys from Max typing. He was growing tired, so to keep going, he pulled out an energy boost and injected it into his right internal jugular vein. It woke him up immediately and he went back to work designing and coding.

Max worked on everything and finished only minutes before when he told Crimson he would be back. He checked and double-checked his work, then when the time came, he told the computer to execute the command.

"Eight days," he muttered aloud.

"Max, you are asking it to do far more than what anyone else has ever done before. I double-checked your science and it will work, but don't be shocked that it is going to take eight days to complete."

"But still! Eight days. Eight bloody days! We can synthesize a ton of food in minutes, literally, but eight days for this?" he questioned, stomping around the room.

"Max...don't forget, you have one last thing to do before you go see Crimson."

It had slipped his mind, but Luther was right. In the other room, the brain scanner lay in wait. Luther assisted him in getting hooked up. It would take a little over an hour for the machine to scan his brain and back it up onto the crystalline hard drive.

The machine was uncomfortable, and as the scanning waves passed through the brain, it hurt. The pain was searing and blinding like a migraine. He had to sit still and endure it. The whole time, he was wondering how Luther had done it.

If Max had made a machine and the moment he sat in it he felt pain like this, he would have thought his design was faulty. Luther must have really had some determination in the name of science to sit there and endure it even though it felt like he was going to die.

Maybe the fact that Luther knew some very bad people were already after him helped him along. Maybe he wasn't heroic but suicidal. Who knows? Not even Luther. He didn't have the storage to back himself up properly. But I do.

The process was half complete when Max's communicator jingled in his ear. He answered and Crimson was on the line.

"Max, where are you? You're needed now!" she exclaimed.

"I'm sorta stuck doing something right now," he grunted out in pain.

"Max...this is serious."

Zarfa was exhausted, but couldn't sleep. He had twenty hours until he was facing the very ones who'd destroyed his life on the battlefield. He was nervous. He had never worried about much more than himself, and now he had a whole army he was leading to either their victory or their doom.

It donned on him that with their announcing of the battle, they could be plotting an ambush. He rose from his bed and called the main commanders of Legion Nine, including Zajifa and Sofronio. Once they were all linked in the same communication, he gave them orders.

"I don't care if you do it yourselves or if you get someone else to do it, but this is what I need. We have twenty hours until the battle. That means I can give a few more speeches tomorrow, retire early to rise early, and march us out into the wastes. Either for the glory of victory or the shame of utter annihilation. We made it this far, but the battle isn't over and, in all reality, this is the start of the war. We still have Synaptix, as well as whoever is remaining from Polyhelix, to hunt down and make pay for what they've done to humanity.

"I should have thought about this sooner. I will admit I made a mistake. I was trying to avoid the responsibility of leading. I know you, Sofronio, would gladly take my role. However, we both know that isn't possible. Not at this point anyway. So here is what I need. I need scouts. We can't walk blindly into the heart of darkness twenty hours from now without knowing if any sort of ambush is being set up. It has been quiet for them to be playing by our rules...too quiet. There is no way they aren't plotting something. I need pairs to go out and scout. I want a fifty mile perimeter swept for any signs of an ambush circularly from the epicenter of our attack. I am humbly asking you, my men, my most trusted men. Can you do this for me?"

They all responded one at a time back to him, each in their own way. Some would assemble teams to do it. Others would lead teams themselves, but they assured him that they understood the importance of the task at hand. Zarfa's mind was now at rest. The prospect of an ambush had been bothering him deeply, even though he wasn't sure what it was that was keeping him from sleeping.

Zarfa lay back down on his bed and closed his eyes. Sleep soon took him and he got several hours of good rest. He was awakened by Sarah in the morning, who had already prepared him some breakfast. When he finished, he went to the city to continue giving rally speeches and to inform as many as he could of the plan of attack.

The rally speeches were going well and the day was winding down. His scouting crews had returned. All except one—Sofronio's. Sofronio was last known to be about fifteen miles north of the battlefield. Zarfa was worried and frantically kept trying to contact him via his communicator. Finally, he got an answer.

"What's wrong, Sofronio? Why aren't you back yet? Why did it take you so long to answer my hail?"

"I'm sorry, I was busy. Sort of in a delicate spot. I found an encampment of Synaptix soldiers. Ten thousand in number."

"Were you and your team spotted?"

"I don't think so. But one can never be sure."

"Good, get back here as fast as you can and get some rest. Tomorrow is going to be serious."

"Yes, commander," Sofronio said back in a tone that Zarfa found suspicious.

Something is up, Zarfa kept thinking. *He isn't acting like himself. Ten thousand... Not good, but we should be able to manage.*

Zarfa quickly connected to Zajifa. "Hey, I need you to fact check something for me. I am going to tell you right now...it's dangerous. I am sorry."

"Go ahead, I would do anything for you. You know I love you as my own brother," Zajifa responded sincerely.

"We have about ten hours until the battle begins. I need you to take the fastest means of transport you have and scout fifteen...twenty miles to the north of the battlefield. Sofronio said that he found an encampment there. Synaptix soldiers. Ten thousand of them. Something is up with him, though. He sounded strange when I talked with him. I don't want it to be true, but...I have this gut feeling he is lying to me."

"Why would he lie to you, brother?" Zajifa asked with total concern.

"I don't know, but if he did...I intend to find out. Make haste, brother, and please be safe."

"I will, brother."

Crimson was checking and double-checking all of her hacks on the Pilvikones. They all looked good and fully operational. If for some reason it didn't work, she still had her failsafe—each of the engineers that she had planted her minion chip in.

Once she was satisfied with the way things were checking out, she began to study the battlefield terrain by global positioning satellites in real time. She checked all of the surrounding areas of the battlefield and didn't spot anything other than the scouting crews that Zarfa had sent out.

She was watching closely as one disappeared from sight, then a few hours later, came back. She didn't think anything of it. She assumed it was a glitch in the system. She had a good idea of where the armies would be gathering and how it was going to go down. She was still confident that her plan of having the Faraza army meet them above ground was a good idea.

It was getting to be close to time for Max to come home and she was excited. She wanted to have one final dinner and conversation with him before the world as they knew it was transformed into a hellish struggle to remain alive and accomplish their goals. The coup would be fast in the grand scheme of things, but very well may last a couple of months, and they would be no picnic.

Right as she was getting ready to close down her visuals, she got a call on her communicator.

"Crimson, it's Zarfa! They have Zajifa! There are more than he could count. He is guessing at least thirty to fifty thousand and they have him!"

"Wait, what? Calm down... Who does? What is going on?"

"Synaptix, they must be allied with Polyhelix now. They sent fifty thousand reinforcements to attack. This isn't good!"

"How do you know it's them?"

"Because Badger is in my head. He is telling me we are all going to die. He is telling me he is going to kill my sister and my friend right in front of my eyes before he puts the final bullet in my head. We have to do something. We can't win fighting on two fronts with only my army. We need backup!"

"Did you take that serum that was sent over a few days ago?" she asked calmly.

"Yes..." He trailed off apprehensively.

"Good, keep Badger out of your head the best you can, but he won't be a problem. Trust me. We planned for this... Well, not this exactly, but remember, Synaptix was originally my beast to slay. I've got something they never planned for."

"What is it?" Zarfa questioned frantically.

"Faith. Exercise it more in me, please. You said yourself Badger is in your head. You think I am going to tell you? Hell no. Have a little faith, Zarfa. We have this handled. Just keep him from killing your friend."

"Okay, Crimson...thanks. I am off to see my betrayer. I am trusting you."

As soon as the com-link went down between them, she contacted Max.

"I'm kind of in the middle of something," he managed to grunt out, sounding like he was in severe pain.

"Max, this is serious. We need your bots. Now!"

"What, why?"

"Because Synaptix sent an ambush for Legion Nine...the Psyker Scream army. We need to get your bots there and now!"

"But how? It's thousands of miles away!" He screamed in what Crimson could only describe as excitement and agony.

"I've got a plan, but I need you to come activate them, asshole!"

"I'll be there in..." She heard him conversing with Luther. "An hour."

"Max! You are already late getting back here! That will leave us with only seven hours before Legion Nine will be out there risking their ass for my plan!"

"It's the best I can do, Crimson... It's the best I can do." Max sounded defeated, like he had failed her entirely.

"Max. Whatever you are doing, it better be worth the lives of those who may die if you are too late."

"I think it is... I really do think that it is. For once I feel like I can make a big change, and if I were to die—"

"You aren't going to! There aren't even troops to attack in Alexarien right now. Both Polyhelix and Synaptix are showing to the grounds of Ilyeion. They must have formed an alliance when they saw the threat. Stop worrying about dying!"

"I'll be there in an hour," he said, and disconnected.

Damn it, Max, we need you here! I need you here. Crimson's thoughts and feelings were raging like a storm within her.

Zajifa was being held in one of the tents on the edge of Badger's camp. He knew that Badger would be by at any time to interrogate him for information. He could tell by the eyes of those guarding him that they had no thoughts of their own.

He wriggled in the chair they had tied him to, trying to reach his hands up his shirt. The drones may have noticed the commotion if they could still think for themselves, but they couldn't, and so they didn't. Finally, Zajifa got his hand to the handle of a small plasma blade that he always kept strapped on to his back.

The chains that bound his hands dug into his wrists and caused him severe pain as he tried to grasp on to the handle of his weapon. After a few minutes of struggling, though, he was able to free it from its sheath and the filament of the plasma dagger was now resting between his hands on the chain that kept him bound.

Zajifa braced himself for the worst as he flipped the switch on. The blade powered up and a loud crackling noise began to emanate from his location as the energy disintegrated the chain that held him. He had hoped for it to cut through quicker than it did. The four drones had turned to see what was going on and he still wasn't through his fetters entirely.

One of the drones stood right in front of him—its eyes were glassy and empty. *Can Badger see me through his drone's eyes?* The crackling noise and the billow of toxic fumes filled the tent. The drone grabbed hold of Zajifa's face and pushed him backwards in the chair.

As the chair tilted back, the blade finished cutting through the chains and his hands were freed. *Lucky I didn't burn myself,* he thought as he toppled backward, rolling to a crouched position.

The dagger was lying on the ground, burning the sand that it rested on, midway between himself and the drone that had just pushed him over. Zajifa sprang into action before the drone could receive a command to respond. He grabbed the blade by its handle and lunged at the drone, driving it into the man's chest.

As the drone fell to the ground limp, dead, the other three sprang into action. *Apparently, that registered with Badger.* The three were swinging plasma katanas at him. He had only his dagger for defense.

Two quick slashes came from different directions toward his chest; he quickly deflected and rolled to the feet of one of the drones that was on the offense. Quickly, he swiped across the man's knees and he came toppling down to the ground. As Zajifa stood, he made another strike at this drone's arm, removing it clean.

Pulling the katana from the severed arm, he swung at the other drone's neck who had just backed its partner in the assault against him. The drone's head rolled from off his neck and Zajifa quickly sheathed his dagger behind his back once more.

The final drone came at him swinging its sword wildly like a berserker. Its blows appeared to be untrained and wild. Zajifa deflected three powerful attacks before countering with a riposte. Zajifa's counter struck the drone in the chest. A large puff of smoke burst forth as he dropped to the ground. If he wasn't dead, he was close. Zajifa quickly picked up that katana and ran out of the tent.

The camp was in chaos as the drones responded to Badger's mental commands. Some were close by and responding quickly to the command to capture Zajifa. Zajifa knew there was no way he could make a stand against the whole camp, though, and ran in the direction of least resistance.

Several shots were fired at him—they all missed. He barreled his way out of the camp, avoiding as much potential conflict as possible. Most of the drones were too slow to even catch up with him. A few managed to get in his way and he quickly cut them down and continued to flee.

Finally, he was out of the camp and back into the unrelenting sands of the desert. He just kept running until he couldn't any more. By the time he stopped to see if he was still being chased, he could barely see the camp. A few drones were still pursuing, but he had created a large gap between them. He breathed deep and continued to run toward Ilyeion.

Zarfa's blood was boiling as he grabbed Sofronio by the thumbs and bent them back until they snapped. He then proceeded to grab him by his right ear and avulse it.

Zarfa had called Sarah on his way over to Sofronio's apartment. He told her that he was okay and everything was fine. He told her he had some business to attend to before he came home.

She sounded worried. He assured her she shouldn't be. Badger probed into Zarfa's mind and told him he should be. Zarfa had to take the second round of Psyker bots to keep from going deaf, but his mental link with Badger was now stronger and they could speak crystal clear.

Zarfa didn't need to worry about being controlled. It wasn't until the third round of treatments that he would be at that level. It was still an annoyance, however, trying to keep his thoughts from Badger. He had to fill his mind with nonsense to block him out and he had to listen to his commentary as events unfolded that Badger was aware of.

"You are so cruel." His probing voice invaded Zarfa's head.

Zarfa snapped Sofronio's right humerus and tossed him to the floor. Blood was pouring down the side of his head as he screamed and looked at Zarfa in fear. Sofronio was much larger than Zarfa, but had never been augmented in any way. Zarfa's strength outmatched his greatly, now that he had fully healed.

"Why do you think I betrayed you and Legion Nine?"

"You don't easily mistake ten thousand for fifty!"

"So that makes me a liar?"

"Of course he's a liar. He had us kill his team when we caught him and planned to betray you to save himself. What I didn't tell him is that Synaptix doesn't take kindly to traitors," Badger's voice raged in Zarfa's head.

"That and Badger confirmed it," Zarfa spat out, grabbing Sofronio by the back of his neck and lifting him back to his feet.

"I wouldn't dare. He's lying!" Sofronio shouted in agony.

"A liar to the end. Do it for me, Zarfa, kill him. He isn't worth my time to hunt him down myself. Plus, he's served his purpose."

"It isn't a risk I am willing to take," Zarfa said, breaking his other arm.

Sofronio screamed and fell to the ground. He had a true look of fear on his face. Zarfa stood over him as he writhed in pain.

"I just want to know why? Jealousy?"

"Zarfa, Badger is lying!"

"Where are your other teammates? You took ten with you, right? Where are they?"

Sofronio was silent.

"Right, underlings without families that nobody would recall missing. I did my homework on the way over. When Badger first told me, I figured he was just trying to cause dissent in the ranks. That is why I gave you the benefit of doubt and dug up from facts before I came here, but they all just confirm what Badger is telling me. I know you betrayed me; this is my justice. Call it what you will. Maybe it's petty vengeance, but your actions may have killed thousands. If it were possible, I would kill you over and over again in the worst ways. But there is neither the means nor the time for that fantasy, so here it is." He grabbed Sofronio by the front of his shirt and lifted him up. His arms dangled by his sides, unable to move. Zarfa spit in his face and said, "At the very least, I give you the honor of dying on your feet facing me, you filthy coward of a backstabber."

Zarfa placed his hands on Sofronio's face and jerked hard. He snapped his neck, fracturing and disjointing the cervical one vertebrae from the cervical two vertebrae. Sofronio fell to the floor like a limp doll.

"Good work, puppet, will you dance if I ask you to?" Badger invaded his mind.

"Shut up, Badger. I'll kill you tomorrow and get my friend back," Zarfa thought powerfully enough for Badger to hear loud and clear.

"About that, he proved to be more trouble than he was worth."

"What do you mean by that?" Zarfa questioned. Even in telepathic communication, he sounded panicked.

"Oh, you'll see," Badger responded, as cryptic as possible.

"Okay, I am heading home, Sarah," Zarfa said over the com-link.

"I will heat your food back up, brother!" she exclaimed over the connection.

"Don't be alarmed, but my clothes have blood on them... It isn't mine."

"Okay, brother, I won't... Whose?"

"A loud-mouthed coward. It's okay. Tell her, Zarfa."

"Shut up."

"It's best I don't tell you," he said coldly to her, and disconnected.

Seven hours until the battle of Ilyeion

Max jumped out of the chair in a hurry. The leads attached to his chest popped off and fell to the floor. His head was aching from the scanner. Luther had tried to explain to Max why it hurt so badly when the waves passed through, but he couldn't really recall all the details of his design with his limited memory.

"You got it from here?" Max asked as he shoved his head through his shirt and pulled it over his chest.

"You can trust me. I remember this part. It is really only a few simple commands with the interface and a waiting period... It won't be ready for...well, three days. Eight for full functionality,"

"Okay, damn," Max said with a sigh, slightly disappointed.

"Three days, Max, for something this marvelous? You really are the sort with little patience, aren't you?"

Max huffed again as he shrugged at Luther, who was staring at him with his cold, robotic eyes. "All right, well, there isn't anything I can do. I've got to get to Crimson fast. It sounded like something was really going on."

"Leave the rest here to me, Max. I promise it will all work out."

At that, Max sprinted out the door and made his way for Crimson's place. By the time he arrived, there would only be seven hours left until the war was to begin in Ilyeion. Max had intended to sleep prior to this in case any of his services were needed. He wanted to be on the top of his game. *It's funny how life never works out how you intend for it to*, he thought to himself.

He dug around in his pocket as he ran toward the main base where Crimson was no doubt eagerly awaiting his return. He felt a few energy boosts in his pocket, pulled one out, and injected it into his neck without breaking pace. The vial shattered behind him as he ran with a new vigor toward his goal.

By the time he reached Crimson's, he was panting and sweating like a junkie going through withdrawals. He crashed through the door so hard and loud Crimson jumped. She was lying on the couch holding her data-pad in her hands.

"It's about time!" she shouted at him as she leapt up.

"I'm sorry," he said sincerely.

"Whatever! Power up your bots!"

"What? Now? But..."

"No talking! Get in there! Power them up! They can fly, right?"

"Yes," he said as he moved swiftly to the lab.

"Good, power them up and let them swarm outside," she said firmly.

"Okay, but where to outside? They're supposed to track people who have the Psyker Scream augmentation. There is no telling where they are right now. We don't want them out free-floating in nowhereville. Then we would have wasted that weapon entirely."

"Don't worry, there aren't any in the city, Max. They're all camped out twenty miles north of the battleground of Ilyeion! Badger must really mean business because he took every last soldier he had with him. The bots won't do any good here."

"What? Shit! All of them are at Ilyeion! I thought he would leave some here. The bots can't fly that far!" Max exclaimed as he entered the protocols to activate the nanobots.

"I figured they couldn't, but I have to show my ace now. Seven hours early shouldn't make too much of a difference. You fly them to this location. All of them, in a swarm, cloud, whatever! Get them here!" she said, tapping a spot on the map two blocks away from where they were. "Fly them up as high as you can, okay, Max?"

"Okay, got it," he said calmly as he entered the commands to do so. "So what's the plan?"

"Gale force winds, time to really test the Pilvikones," she said. "I only hope they can transport quick enough...and precise... It's sort of an experiment. You see, I didn't want to get detected so I haven't tested what all of the machines working together can do, but by my calculations...I can get a wind going about four hundred miles per hour. They should arrive in four hours, fifty-three minutes. How long do the bots take to be fatal?"

"Two hours?" Max asked rhetorically, shrugging his shoulders.

"You designed them, Max!"

"Never tested 'em."

"You...you are..."

"Ready! Let's let down the barriers that are holding them

back." Max pressed the final button to execute the commands he entered and a giant salvariantium container opened up. The bots had been replicating inside of a tank roughly eight hundred gallons in size, and it was filled to capacity. "This swarm may not look like a lot, barely a small cloud in the sky...but considering how small they are, there are more bots in that swarm than you could count in a lifetime," Max stated, in awe of his own work.

"Shouldn't we open the windows or something to let them out?" Crimson questioned nervously.

Max chuckled and let out a little snort. "Ha! No. Why would we do that? They're nano-particles."

"Yeah?" she questioned as she watched an ominous cloud of bots pass through the solid wall into the outside.

"Nano-particles are small enough to pass in between molecules. Solid matter is of no problem to those little guys. In fact, they hunt out people with the Psyker Scream nano-bot augmentation, however, they don't even need to breathe these guys in. One just has to come close to them. The bots will do the rest, drilling through their victim's skin and bone if they have to... Though drilling may not be the best word for it."

"So why did the Psykers have to inject their bots? The serum you made for Zarfa? He had to inject that too."

"Well, you see, those bots we wanted to go directly to the blood to administer to the brain and to pass through the brain-blood barrier. In short, I really didn't want my bots passing through his muscle, just going to his brain as fast as possible. A shot right into one of the ventricles of the brain would have been safer and more effective, however, intravenous should work fine as well.

"As for Synaptix design...well, pure theatrics. Also, if you looked at how they were constructed, the way they were programmed to affect the nervous system, there is no way you would want them coming into contact with peripheral nerves. It would get...ugly. Oh, and muscles, blah. Anyhow, the way they were programmed was to work from the blood to the brain-blood barrier and finally into only the nervous system of the brain. It could have been done simpler— Synaptix did it that way. However, I won't lie, I am a theatrical guy myself. I only wish that you would be there in person to see it."

Crimson had blanked out as Max went about trying to explain to her in *simple* terms the way that the bots worked. She shrugged and asked, "Oh, what kind of theatrics?"

"I added to the bots a gene from plankton that will cause them to be bioluminescent. The rain will be red as they fall and the bots will appear like a fine red dust to the eyes. I figured it would be a fitting weapon for the leader of the *Crimson Crusade.*"

"You are too funny, Max, and it is a shame I won't be able to see them work in person," she said with a grin. "It is going to be cutting it close. Seven minutes before the swarm comes out of the ground is when the Psyker army will begin to feel your bots. I certainly hope this works. It will be too late for Zarfa to retreat. Oh, and Max," Crimson said as she finished commanding the Pilvikones to send forth her storm of destruction.

"Yes?" he said as a strong wind shook the building they were in.

Being at the top of a sky-rise apartment during an un-precedented storm was an awe-striking experience, as he feared that the building would collapse.

"While I assist Zarfa here, directing the weather to turn the tides of his battle, I need you to go to Synaptix head-quarters and purge them of whoever is behind everything. Think you can do that?" she asked in a playfully innocent tone.

"You're crazy," Max said.

Crimson giggled. "I'll send out my third missive in seven hours. It's how long you have to prepare for the assignment. You will hopefully have a large crowd of warriors by your side as you rush the building," she stated, as serious as could be.

"All right, I guess this really is show time. But all of that talk about me not dying, well, it's sounding more like you were building false confidence in me."

"Don't be such a pessimist."

"I'm an optimist. I am quite positive I am going to die."

Zarfa and Sarah were both extremely nervous. They had

decided to try to sleep early when Zarfa had returned home. With the recent incident of betrayal, Zarfa was feeling more and more uneasy about the events that would occur in the near future.

Zarfa's communicator rang in his head. He wasn't sure if it had awakened him because he wasn't sure if he was asleep. He wasn't even sure how long he had been lying on the floor next to his sister, who was also laboriously trying to sleep.

"Zarfa, it's Crimson. Tomorrow you are going to get a bit wet. I can't tell you everything, who knows if Synaptix is listening. But your salvation is coming on the wind. Don't worry about their army, and proceed as planned."

"What time is it?" Zarfa asked.

Before Crimson could respond, there was a crash of knocking on Zarfa's door. It rattled the frame and he leapt to his feet before he had even realized that he responded to it.

"It's about time for you to get up, in fact. Three hours now until the battle. Trust me, everything is going to be okay. In fact, by Synaptix sending their army, Psyker Scream...well...they've only sped up progress. Tomorrow, the same time as the battle of Ilyeion, I am going to broadcast my final missive and command the Crimson Crusade to march on Polyhelix and Synaptix."

Zarfa approached the door as he responded to Crimson. "Then it is only the Alexarien government that we need to topple... Is that right?" he questioned as he opened the door.

"Right, but we can deal with them when you get Legion Nine here."

"Zajifa! Thanks for your support, Crimson, and I really hope that you provide salvation as you promise. Not for my sake or my sister's sake, but for the sake of the people who have put their trust in me," he exclaimed over the com-ink as he hugged Zajifa—who was standing at his doorstep—in joy.

"Um? Zajifa is there? How? I haven't done anything yet," Crimson's voice rang in his ear.

Zarfa took a moment to register her words. He was too happy to see his friend to really notice what she had said at first. "What do you mean you haven't done anything yet? Then how is he right here?"

Zajifa stood there silently with a large grin on his face.

Finally, he spoke. "Guess I'm just better at escaping than you ever gave me credit for."

"Did you hear that, Crimson? He is just as arrogant as ever! Anyhow, if he could escape Badger on his own, I really hope you can crush him on your own the way you say you can."

"I will. I promise. Just do your best fighting out there."

"I will," Zarfa said as his communicator logged off.

He looked down at his sister, feigning sleep. She may have even been on the cusp of it, but he knew she was as worried as he was. He knelt down beside her and stroked her cheek gently with his hand. "It's time to get up, my dear Sarah. You know you don't have to join the battle if you don't want to."

"I know, brother," she said, opening her eyes. "It isn't like I haven't seen battle before. I've seen the atrocities of war... I was forced to do so from the other side. I only hope to have a hand in killing as many of the Faraza as I can. They're sick, twisted, sadistic... I want to destroy them."

"I don't want people to be hurt any longer, sis, and this is the only way I know how to prevent it."

"I can't argue that," she said, pulling herself to her knees and wrapping her arms around Zarfa.

"C'mon, get yourself washed off and have something to eat. We have a long day ahead. Let's hope it truly is over after today."

"I don't see the point in washing off... I mean, we are going to get covered in blood and sand. But I'll have some food," Sarah said in response.

"A good point."

Zajifa stood behind Zarfa watching the brother-sister moment when Sarah's eyes raised to meet his. They looked like beautiful glimmering jewels to him as she smiled and said, "Excuse me for not jumping up and down with excitement. I knew you'd be back, though. Welcome home, Zajifa."

"Excused," he said, shrugging.

From the moment Zarfa informed Crimson about Synaptix sending their army, Crimson activated every minion chip that she had planted. There was one in a member of every Barometrics office that housed a Pilvikone.

Brian stalked down the corridors of the office to the chamber of the Pilvikone. He had come into the twenty-four-hour facility as if it were any other day at work. It wasn't his shift, however, and he had with him a gauss-powered pistol with a silencer hidden under his suit jacket. He also was carrying ten magazines that held eighteen bullets each, all carefully concealed in his clothing.

He came in through the front door, which had two sleepy security guards. They both greeted him with a smile upon seeing his badge. He went back to the security desk where a third was watching the monitors for suspicious activity. A small puff of noise, and a projectile rocketed through the security guard's head, creating a large mess all over the displays.

Brian walked calmly back to the front where the guards were waiting for anyone they deemed a threat to walk through the doors. He calmly, and almost even politely, held his gun to the back of the first one's head, and without a word, pulled the trigger. He quickly aimed for guard two and laid him to the ground with a single shot as well. Before either of them knew there was even a threat, Brian had dispatched them both.

The building had unbelievably low security. They had never had an attack occur before. There were switches under the desks of every employee's cubicle to alert authorities of a threat, but Brian was going in at an off hour where there would be few at work. Even more, every command that Crimson had executed into her data-pad told him to be cautious and to move quietly. In no time, he had slaughtered everyone in the office without raising a single red flag.

Now he moved quietly into the women's bathroom in the hallway leading to the Pilvikone. He stood on the counter with the sink between his feet and opened up a ventilation duct. Inside was a fully automatic gauss projection assault rifle MK-VX2I12. It was military grade and held one-hundred-thirteen rounds. One-hundred-ten in the drum, one in the chamber.

He moved to the room where the Pilvikone was housed and closed the doors behind them. He chained them shut with a Kelmantrium security wire and placed a powerful short-ranged fragmentation explosive on the door.

If anyone managed to get through, the explosive would go off, killing anyone within a twenty-meter radius. Brian was thirty. He sat on top of the Pilvikone with his sights aimed at where anyone might be standing after the blast cleared and they sent a second assault into the room. That was if anyone were to suspect why the weather had suddenly gone haywire.

This was occurring at every facility that housed a Pilvikone simultaneously. Only Brian went by a different name at each place.

Seventeen

The Third Missive

"You have heard all I have to say. Now is my command. Fight! Down with Synaptix, down with Polyhelix, and finally, down with Alexarien and their military dogs!"

-This broadcast played for fifteen hours. From the tome of Demicles 4001 C.E.

Eighteen

Zarfa's Conflict—the Sins of the Father

Badger had awakened several hours before the battle was to begin and commanded his swarm of psychic warriors to travel south to the destination. With Psyker Scream modifications, he could hear the Faraza swarm muddling about in the caverns below their feet. The expanse of caves they dwelled in was vast and stretched for miles under the desert sand.

He could hear the squirming of fresh larvae that had been laid by the queen. He could hear the clattering of chitins rubbing together as they scuttled through the hallways. But most of all, he could hear the high-pitched whirr of their wings as they prepared to take flight.

The Faraza raiders were no doubt mounting their mighty insects and preparing to rain death upon Zarfa and his men. Badger could hear it; they were gathering in large vestibule-type chambers where they could all trickle from exits that would collapse behind them. They were clever with their digging. They only had one true entrance, but thousands of exits.

Badger was about four miles out from the site of the battle when the wind came blowing in furiously as if some greater force had sent it in hot anger. The sand pelted him and hurt his eyes. He quickly put on protection and had the army follow suit so as to not lose their sight.

The wind kept coming with a bite and a sting. It was blowing so hard that the sand was scraping off bits of his skin as it hit him. Blood seeped from his raw skin and soon every bare bit of his body was bloodied and sore.

Suddenly, the wind broke and a loud crash of thunder came. Lightning bounded from cloud to cloud in the sky above him and glistening red drops of rain fell upon him and his soldiers.

It was the eeriest sight he had ever seen. The glowing red tinge in the rain seemed to come up from the ground as a sort of dust and swarm amidst him and his army. A small breath of red haze floated around his face for a few moments and then intruded in through his nostrils.

It looked like a smoke he was inhaling into himself, but he had no idea what it was. His body began to tingle as he marched on. The rain was still pouring torrentially and the lightning and thunder came without letup.

He looked to the sky as if to ask of it an answer to the mystery. None came—only thunder and lightning and more of the crimson rain.

Zarfa stood as the first solider on the battlefield. He knew where the entrance was to the Faraza base and he was ready for them to come swarming forth from it. Sarah was to his left and Zajifa loyally to his right. He was nervous, but no one could tell it from the outside.

"Zarfa," Sarah said, sounding shaken.

"Yes?" he asked as the sun rose behind them and light cast down on the shadows of the battlefield.

"A detail I overlooked the night we discussed this..." She trailed off.

"What?"

"You asked about entrances, you see... This...well, this is the only *entrance*. Brother, don't be mad."

"About what?" he asked as he felt the sand rumble beneath their feet.

"Well, they can exit from almost anywhere in the desert. They have vestibules that hold roughly sixty wasps and when they emerge, it collapses behind them. I...I really don't know why I didn't think of it before now."

"Conditioning. You can't tell me you were down there for three years and they weren't able to imprint something on you, sister," he said as the tremors in the ground grew stronger.

"I'm sorry, brother!" she exclaimed with tears in her eyes.

"It isn't like you tricked us on purpose. We just have to adapt. We can overcome anything," he said, looking at her with comfort.

He stood as if he were a statue waiting in the barren desert for a hapless traveler to stumble about finding a priceless piece of art. There he was at the front of an army that had grown into the hundreds of thousands. Nobody would have ever thought that Legion Nine would become an army this large.

"Zajifa, Sarah...don't die," he said solemnly.

"I will do my best," she said.

"Not unless you do, boss," Zajifa said with a grin.

"Me? Die? I've got nine lives."

"And I recall you using at least eight in the time I've known you," stated Zajifa playfully.

"Right," Zarfa said with a smile that widened out across his whole face, laying bare his teeth.

He readied his rifle as the ground beneath his feet began to shake and tremor more and more. Zajifa and Sarah did the same. Each member of the army had brought their own weapons. Some had none to speak of other than a plasma blade—some had only typical kitchen knives.

It wasn't the most impressive army in skill, but its numbers were quite large. It showed how many had their lives ruined and maimed by the Faraza, and how many were brave enough to seek comfort in bloodshed. Each one in the crowd felt that this was justice for how they had been victimized, and who was there to argue?

Clouds gathered overhead and the ground shook violently. A strong wind swept once across the battlefield and a strong force of static could be felt. It caused the hair on everyone to stand on end. The clouds rumbled and lightning jumped above from cloud to cloud.

Right as it seemed the battle would commence, his communicator rang within his ear. "Yes?" he questioned as he answered.

"See the clouds? Call this your salvation. Look to the north of you. What do you see?"

"I see the Psyker army, Crimson. I thought you were taking care of them?"

"I did—notice something funny?"

Zarfa was silent for a moment as he observed their lines marching toward them.

"Yeah, they're all just...staggering at us."

"They're infected by Max's nanobots. They'll be dead within ten minutes and, by now, their brains are mush. They can't do anything. They're simply following their last command to march toward you. That's all they'll do... Then finally...poof, they'll collapse into the dust."

"You had better be right. Anyhow, I can't wait to see what else you have planned."

At that, the communicator went dead. The movement and the noise below hushed for a moment. It was dead silent except the rumbling of the clouds as they broke forth into rain.

"I'm sure this is good for morale," Zajifa said sarcastically.

"This is our salvation!" Zarfa screamed to inspire confidence of those around him.

There was no response as he had hoped.

"All shall know our salvation hinges on this storm! Be sure that all know!" he commanded.

It took two or three times before anyone understood what he meant. Soon, all of those close to him were shouting and it spread like a ripple in a lake. His army had hope. They didn't know exactly in what, but they could look up and see a symbol of it.

The ground burst forth and swarms of wasp raiders took to the sky. Their black visage mixed with the clouds and they seemed to disappear. Zarfa raised his rifle and began to shoot at them.

The ground exploded behind him where a swarm of raiders sprung from the earth. It suddenly collapsed, taking several of his soldiers to their grave. He turned hastily to face the imminent threat and began firing his rounds as fast as he could. He was killing as quickly as he could and had already shot down thirty to forty wasps along with their raiders.

Swarms were bursting out all over and what formation his army seemed to have was diminishing. Some of the less stalwart souls began to flee in horror as if they could be saved by running back to Ilyeion.

The ones trying to flee were picked off easily by the flying raiders. The swarm was buzzing in full force overhead within minutes and raining down bullets on Zarfa's army. Blood stained the sands red, and more of it was from Zarfa's own army than he had imagined.

Zarfa looked to the sky with tears in his eyes and fired his last few rounds, taking down several more wasps. He was out of ammo and so were those around him, including Sarah and Zajifa.

A wasp came in quickly, aiming right at Zajifa, who didn't see what was coming at him. Without saying a word, Zarfa threw himself between the wasp—which was carrying four riders—and Zajifa. He quickly cut the dive-bombing wasp in half with his plasma sword.

The corpse of the insect split in a cloud of vapors, the two halves narrowly missing Zarfa and Zajifa. Other soldiers were fumbling and tripping out of the way so as not to be struck by the insect's corpse and the riders tumbled off. Zajifa turned in time to see Zarfa quickly making his way back to the line he had been standing in.

The battle seemed to not be going too well and then, as if sent by some sort of divine favor, lightning began springing from the ground. The bolts seemed to be precise, missing the members of Zarfa's army.

A bolt would strike a wasp in flight then scatter outward, leaping from wasp to wasp. The lighting that danced from cloud to cloud would strike down and join with its brother in the sky and continue to bounce.

Soon, the sky was dancing with illuminating electricity. The sun burned behind the clouds. Barely visible but now blinding light filled the sky, charring and burning hundreds of wasps at a time. The falling bodies became the largest threat to Zarfa's army as they all ran around like ants on the ground trying to avoid furious stomps of an angry child that had been stung.

"HA!" Zarfa shouted.

He saw it with his eyes; he felt it in his heart. This was the victory he had hoped for. It was a miracle. In only minutes, the swarm had been thinned out by the electricity. Now there were only a few lingerers circling in the sky.

He had almost forgotten, but he looked to the north. The army that had been stumbling toward him, threatening to crush them as they were distracted, was now collapsing. They fell face first into the dust.

"Who would have thought the same thing that gave them their power would be their undoing? Huh, sis?" Zarfa asked

Sarah.

"Let's hope the same isn't true of us," she said as lightning bounded above and struck several more wasps.

"Mr. Cudrow, my name is Reginald Saunders. I am from Alexarien's thirty-fifth regiment. None can deny that you have attributed to humanity's greatness over the years. It is a shame some don't quite grasp that nor do they appreciate it, your own family included," Reginald said as he stepped from the shadows to greet Thomas.

"Ah, you've prepared quite the speech to take my life," Thomas said indifferently.

"Take your life? By all accounts, no. No! I am not here to take your life at all," he said quite dramatically. "There is rioting in the streets—the *Crimson Crusade* marches toward Polyhelix headquarters where we stand. In fact, some of them are milling about on the lower levels slaughtering employees and wreaking havoc as we speak. But your life to take? No! For that purpose, I did not come."

"Oh? So for what purpose did you come? To act so dramatic?" Thomas questioned sarcastically.

"Your son, well...he destroyed your army and has a great crowd of followers still indeed. He poses a threat to our government and, at this time, our government has several threats to face. My superiors recognize the greatness of a man such as yourself. Right now, actions have been taken to stamp out your son along with his futile attempts to destroy you and overthrow the Alexarien government and eventually Ilyeion's... A great man much like yourself, yet he got greedy and outstretched his hand. I am sure you can relate. Anyhow, I did not come to tell you of your son's small victory, or to take your life. I came to lay out your options. Option one, I do take your life," Reginald said with a pause.

"I thought you weren't here for that," Thomas stated.

"I most certainly am not, however, if it comes to that...I will. I suppose I could have made that your third option, however, it is too late for me to corral already released words. Option two, you come with us and hand over all of your research, even the things you have managed to keep hidden. You continue to work with us for as long as we need you. The higher-ups were impressed with some of your super soldier ideas and would like to provide you with the materials to expand upon your research. If you choose this option, you will be an employee of the government and we shall free you of your service when it is no longer needed.

"We know the true purpose of Faraza and that you planned to make an attempt of a coup d'état toward us after Synaptix was out of the way. We also know that when things got desperate, you chose to align with Synaptix to proceed with your plan. However, that too failed.

"A third option is we take you in to custody and make you comply by any means necessary. I mean, you did commit treason. Nobody will question where you went. However, if you put up too much of a fight, I shall resort to option one— my boss would understand. Synaptix, I can safely say, is no longer a threat. All thanks to my people. Your ally is dead. You are here alone in a room with a man more skilled in the art of killing than yourself, and need I add that I have a whole squad outside of your office? I think not. Anyhow, my point is this. We know all of your transgressions and are willing to overlook them if you join our cause. It is a most generous offer and that is what I came to extend. So, what do you say?"

"The way you said *options* almost led me to believe that I actually had a choice."

"You jest, Mr. Cudrow, but I assure you this is not the time," Reginald said, pointing a gun at Thomas' head.

"Oh, so you did come to kill me," Thomas said, sitting and pouring two shots of tequila.

"No, I already explained. Now I require a decision from you. Either you stand alone, admitting the defeat by your son—at that point I myself put three bullets in your head then set your corpse ablaze. Or you decide to work with us and all of your trespasses are forgiven and you are given a chance to prove you can, at the very least, beat your son. However, Mr. Cudrow, I must inform you that the men that control the strongest nation in the remaining world didn't get there by chance, and you can never best them."

"Sit, please," Thomas said, motioning Reginald to take a seat in front of the desk he was sitting behind. "It is a mere request, not a command. I wish to talk. You seem to enjoy it quite a lot yourself so, please, sit. Have a drink with me?"

Reginald sat in the chair in front of Thomas, eyeing him suspiciously with his hand on his gun. Thomas slid one of the previously poured shots over to Reginald as he downed his own and poured another.

"You had been watching us from the beginning it seems, right?" Thomas questioned smugly.

"Very astute—your point?" Reginald asked, eyeing the drink.

"Don't you find it a bit strange that I would rest all of my dreams of overthrowing the government on my petty guerilla army known as Faraza? An army that I had very little direct supervision over?"

"I see what you're trying to do. Mr. Cudrow, bluffs will not work at this stage."

"It isn't a bluff, only a confession. My goal all along was to grab your attention. Now, where do I sign? With the military's backing, my research shall bring humanity to a level much higher than ever dreamt. We shall all be gods, well...those of us in power anyhow."

"We shall see if that is on the boss' agenda. For now, I take it that you aren't going to put up a fight and I can holster my weapon?"

"You take the matter correctly. Now, have a drink."

Reginald downed his shot and slid the glass back over to Thomas. Thomas refilled it as he downed his second and slid the fresh one over to his new ally.

"I'm glad we drank on this like men," Thomas said. "Now, let's go meet your boss."

Zarfa had not even realized that he answered his communicator when it rang. He wasn't even sure if he had heard it ring. The lightning and thunder were dying down, but still causing a great deal of noise. Most of the fighting had ceased. There were a few straggling raiders left muddling about dismounted, trying to fight for their lives.

The battle lasted less than an hour by the time they were all put down. The storm was coming to an end and now Crimson's voice was in his head again.

"Look, I realize there might be a second wave or some stragglers, but I am withdrawing my support. I need it back here." Her voice sounded frantic.

"No problem, everything is fine here," Zarfa said.

The communicator went dead and Zarfa got a sinking feeling in his stomach. Remnants of fighting continued for awhile longer, but finally, all of the Faraza were dead. Zarfa suffered minimal losses on his side and spirits were still high. Everyone was celebrating the victory and ready to head back to Ilyeion.

Those that were loyal to Zarfa planned to follow him to Alexarien to pay back Crimson for what she had done for them. Those who had only wanted revenge planned to return to Ilyeion and live the rest of their lives peacefully.

Zarfa could see on the horizon those who were getting back within the city limits of Ilyeion before him. He could also see a line of Ilyeion military tanks stretching out for miles. Many were too slow to realize what was going on as the first shots fired into the crowd.

The shells fired would bounce off of the ground and burst into thousands of searing balls of burning shrapnel. The first battery of shots killed several thousand before anyone realized what was going on. Zarfa had imagined a celebration host by the grateful populace of Ilyeion, yet he was greeted with violence from their military. Screams of fear and crippling agony filled the battlefield as bodies dropped lifeless to the ground.

They fought like cowards, seeking to eradicate this militia that had protected them from the Faraza when the government was too weak or cowardly to do so itself. Now, they were the very ones destroying the unlikely rebellion that had brought them salvation from oppression.

"Run! To the caverns underground!" Zarfa exclaimed, checking to be sure Zajifa and Sarah were close by.

"Why are they attacking?" asked Sarah as she followed Zarfa and headed for the entrance to the Faraza base.

"I don't know! Maybe..." He trailed off as his mind wandered to the thought of Crimson double-crossing him.

He quickly dialed the number for her communicator on his wristband and eagerly awaited her answer. There were shouts of terror and agony behind him as he and a scattered crowd ran toward the caverns for salvation. The communicator rang and rang, but there was never an answer.

Nineteen

Max, Bloodshed

Max had somehow managed to get in an hour of sleep before he got ready for his day. Only minutes remained until he would be making his way to Synaptix to end them once and for all. Crimson was directing storms toward Zarfa to act as a weapon of destruction and wouldn't have answered him even if he spoke to her, so he didn't bother with any parting words.

Max was wearing full body armor, some of the best that money could buy. He even donned a helmet that covered his whole face, complete with a rebreather that would negate almost any kind of anti-riot gas he may encounter. His goal was simple—travel sixteen miles west of the apartment to Synaptix Co. Ltd. Headquarters, located in the trade district of west Alexarien. From there, he, along with any members supporting Crimson's cause, would storm the building.

He planned to catch the ones in control of the corporation off guard in their offices and kill them. Following that, he would make his way to the exit, clear the building, and set charges to topple it. After he had destroyed Synaptix, he would start his journey to the Polyhelix headquarters.

Polyhelix was located ten miles northeast of Synaptix in the eastern corporate district of Alexarien. By this point, Max imagined he would have a large crowd following with him, but that military and police would already be on defense with a counter attack. He had no idea how many supporters he would have, or if they would scatter upon meeting opposition, so he made a contingency plan in his mind to travel in the sewers if things got too hot above ground.

He mulled the plan in his mind over and over until he was resolute. He finished gathering anything he thought he might need. Grenades, charges, plasma blades, a gauss pistol as a side arm, plenty of ammo, and his trusty sniper rifle that had served him well in a previous battle.

Max waved at Crimson, engrossed in controlling the storms. She was now reassuring Zarfa over a com-link conversation. He blew her a kiss that he doubted she saw as he turned and left.

When Max made his way to the street, he found a hovercraft that Crimson owned. He got in and started it up. The radio was blasting her message to attack on every station. Max knew that the video feeds were also broadcasting her message. He could see smoke from fires that raged all over town and didn't know if this was a good sign or not.

He drove quickly toward the Synaptix headquarters and everything was going smooth so far. He was roughly six miles from Synaptix when he saw a mob of people rampaging in his same direction.

If you looked closely, most of them had a red "C" tattooed somewhere on their body. They were his allies, yet they were acting in a manner not befitting trained soldiers. They were setting fire to buildings, striking innocents in the streets, even killing them.

Those inspired by Crimson came in every size, shape, color, gender, age, occupation, and creed. They all believed in her ideal of change, but had no one to take the reins and show them how to accomplish their goal. They had a final destination—destruction of Alexarien's government.

Unfortunately, what that government was represented something different to each person in the crusade. Some understood it was a militant government, and that was what they should strike. Others were less educated and saw anyone not on their side directly as their enemy. Quickly, this idea of a cause for change and a rebellion to get the power back into the people's hands had turned into a violent mob.

The mob was like a disease traveling quickly through the city, destroying everything in its wake. Even some groups supposedly fighting for the same purpose would stumble upon each other and, instead of embracing one another as brethren of the same intent, they would open fire on one another.

The whole thing was a disaster. Crimson wanted to generate more than chaos in Alexarien, but unfortunately, that was all she succeeded in doing. Max was driving quickly toward Synaptix when he came to this realization. He also realized he was not branded with the mark, and even if he had been, it probably wouldn't help him.

Those he expected to be his supporters were nothing more than a lot of angry, violent, bloodthirsty cowards. Prone to mob violence and vigilantism. *This is hopeless. We won't take down the government,* Max thought over and over. *But I can destroy these corporations.*

He drove with fervor, zigzagging on the road, not stopping even for traffic lights, until he came to a pile of burning hovercrafts blocking his path. They had been upturned and set ablaze. *Shocking, an entire mob of Crimson's cronies to blame for this*, he thought as he saw the crowd coming toward him.

Max drove his vehicle straight at them and bailed out the driver's door. The craft plowed into the crowd as he rolled to his stop. *Telling them I'm a friend I am sure is useless,* he thought, springing to his feet and throwing a plasma grenade in their direction. The grenade exploded and vaporized the wrecked vehicle and hundreds in the crowd.

They screamed in horror and fear; a few in the mob shot at Max with their weak civilian weaponry. The bullets ricocheted off of Max's armor and the few that felt brave enough to challenge him quickly lost their gall and fled with the rest.

Well, that was easy. Only three miles to go from here. Max took off on foot. He was weighed down by everything he was carrying and it was very laborious for him to get there. He had made it on the other side of the barrier of burning crafts and he could see that there were many more mobs raping, pillaging, murdering, and generally destroying everything in their path.

The police force was mobilizing and trying to put down the riot, but they were overwhelmed. Some of the members were themselves officers of the law. *And these are the people I was trying to save from oppression of the government. They act like dogs or worse. No wonder such a tight leash was put on us.*

He shook the thought from his head and proceeded toward his destination. He was a lone traveler and anyone could see he was heavily armed. For the most part, small groups stayed clear of Max, but the occasional mob would rush at him and he would have to kill a few to make his point. So far, he was doing okay standing on his own.

Max heard the noise of a hovercraft zooming up behind him when he realized he was still on the roadway. He turned and saw it jetting straight at him, clearly someone bent on running him down. His eye locked onto the driver and he raised his rifle. One shot and the bullet blew through the driver's head.

Max sidestepped the craft as it blew past him, eventually coming to a stop. Three others piled out of the car and opened fire on Max with their weak pistols. Max stepped up to the two in front and grabbed them both by their dominant arms. With a quick jolt, he snapped them both. The third had already re-treated from what he deemed to be his early demise.

He stepped over to the driver's seat, pulled the corpse of the driver out, and heaved his body on to the other two men who were just crying, holding their broken arms. Max hopped into the car and sped toward Synaptix. *Two more miles.*

Tears ran from Max's one real eye as he saw the horrors that Crimson's good intent had caused. Piles of corpses were forming in the streets—men, women, children, elderly, it didn't matter. It was absolute chaos with no end in sight. The city would tear itself apart and there would be nothing left even if Zarfa was able to transport his army here over night.

Despair filled his heart and his breathing became heavy. He felt guilty. He'd known his intentions were good when he backed Crimson. He'd known the revolution would be full of bloodshed. He just hadn't expected there to be so many in-nocents. He envisioned this going much differently and was sure that Crimson had too.

His gut wrenched as he saw a girl no older than twelve running from a group of men. She was about three hundred feet from him and leaping over the barrier onto the roadway. He turned his vehicle in her direction. The men were scram-bling over the four-foot barricade that partitioned the road from the sidewalk.

Max slammed the craft into the partition, immediately killing four of them. The girl was behind the wrecked vehicle, standing in the roadway, crying. He leapt from the vehicle and pulled his pistol. His eye locked on to three men rushing him, screaming threats and curses at him.

Rapists masking their intentions by picking up Crimson's noble cause. I should have known these weak and beggarly people would arise from the gutters. I should have known it would turn out like this. Why wouldn't it? With no organization or direction, what was to keep the dregs out? I'll bet we recruited more filthy peddlars, murderers, addicts, and all-around scum than we did anyone with any true sense of nobility.

His thoughts left him as he fired three perfect shots into each man's head. One had made his way behind Max before he realized it and leapt onto Max's back. The man was trying to pry his helmet off to render Max vulnerable.

Quickly, Max grabbed the man by his shoulder with his left arm. In one quick toss, he had launched the man thirty feet. He hit the ground tumbling. Max spotted the red "C" on his neck and sent a bullet flying though it as if it were a target.

"You don't have the right to bear her mark!" he screamed in fury.

The two remaining men turned and ran, fleeing his vengeance. Max ran around the craft and jumped over the barrier, spotting the men trying to run into a building to lose him. His eye locked targets and he put them down with two more precise shots.

The girl was still crying in the street, hugging herself. She was bloodied and had a black eye. She had no doubt already been victimized terribly before she was able to make a break for it. Max felt the guilt of the pains she had suffered.

"The name is Max. Stick with me. I'll keep you safe," he stated firmly as he placed his hand on her shoulder.

She jumped and screamed. Her sobbing got louder as she brushed away his hand.

"What is your name, girl?"

"Xivah."

"Who were those men?"

"One of them was my brother."

Disgusting, wretched cowards.

"They— They—" she stuttered.

Deserved it, cowards.

"You don't have to say. I have an idea. Look, trust no-body. Not even family anymore," Max said, handing her the pistol.

She clutched it in her hand and continued to sob. Max handed her all of the magazines he had packed for it.

"It isn't much—find shelter. Maybe in the sewers. Trust nobody and shoot them if they give you the slightest reason to. I am sorry, I helped cause this. I intend to never stop until I see it set straight," he said, sounding like a champion of righteousness.

"Thank you," she managed to mutter through the tears as she turned and ran into a building.

By the time Max arrived, all of the individual mobs had merged at the doorstep of Synaptix. People were pushing and shoving to get inside. *As if that will accomplish anything.* Synaptix had a security force at the facility that barricaded the entrance and were firing on the crowd, killing as many as they could.

Max, seeing that the frontal approach would be useless, circled a few blocks to a side alleyway that would take him up to the building. The alley had been blocked and few were trying to make their way into the building from this entry point.

He was repulsed by the things he had seen earlier, and now he had a pile of debris and a small crowd of Crimson's rioters between him and a clear side path to the Synaptix building. Without warning, he tossed a couple of plasma grenades into the crowd. Before anyone realized their impending doom, they were vaporized. Max felt nothing for the lives he took.

Some of them could have been good people. Some of them could have been those we were seeking to inspire. But it is true that a little rot can ruin an entire feast. All I have seen today is rot. I expect them to be no different.

He walked mechanically through the mist left behind by those he had just vaporized and right up to the side of the Synaptix building. He could set a charge here powerful enough to topple the building, but something was calling him inside, beckoning him. He could feel it almost as if it were in his thoughts.

Max punched the building as hard as he could. The wall cracked and he punched it again. A few blows and the wall came crashing down. He was inside the building and, by now, the drain that his biotic arms had on him was taking effect. He ate a few meal bars as fast as he could and proceeded down the corridors.

The building was too quiet for his liking. It was on total lockdown with guards at the front firing onto the angry mob of rioters. However, he had yet to see a soul. He made his way to an elevator and promptly got into it.

Looking at the buttons, he couldn't help but notice that there were only six floors. The building, judging by the outside, was at least thirty stories. Max closed his eyes and took a deep breath. He felt that beckoning presence once again. Without thought, he allowed his hand to go toward where he felt he was being guided. Fourth floor.

The elevator was quiet as it took him to the top. He closed his eyes and steadied his breathing, preparing for what may lay in wait. When it stopped, it made a *ding* and Max opened his eyes. The doors opened up and he raised his rifle, ready to fight armed guards. There was nobody there.

He stepped cautiously into the hallway before him. There were a few offices branching off from this main hallway with a large door at the end of it. He didn't bother more than a glance in through the windows of each office as he headed down the hallway. They were all empty.

He reached the door—it was solid, Kelmantrium. Something inside of him that told him the walls had a barrier of this solid material behind them and that a forceful attempt would be futile. He placed his hand on the handle of the door and pressed down. To his surprise, it wasn't locked.

He pushed the heavy door only to have it open up into a grand sight. Before his eyes there was a room that towered at least twelve stories up. There were spiral staircases on either side. Directly in front of him, spanning from wall to wall, was a computer terminal that loomed above to the ceiling like a monolith of titans.

Max stepped toward the terminal and felt that beckoning within himself. Slowly, he realized he had been under the power of suggestion ever since he made it to Synaptix headquarters. He wanted to stop and examine the room more, but his feet were leading him directly in front of the terminal. As he got closer, he saw what must be beckoning him.

In the center of the room attached to the colossus computer was a human brain, four times the regular size, suspended in some strange black liquid. The top of the container was open, and wiring ran from the brain to the computer. Max stopped a few feet in front of it.

"*Congratulations on making it this far, Max Hall.*"

The words invaded his mind, but they were indefinable. It sounded as if a hundred different people were all screaming the same thing at him in absolute synchronicity.

"*It will be hard for you to hear me without the Psyker modifications,*" the voices made out in his mind.

"What do you want?" he shouted in panic.

"*You killed my children. You set back my plans by decades. I want atonement.*"

Max noticed his arms were removing his helmet involuntarily. If he focused with all of his attention, he could counteract it and move by his own volition. If he let his mental guard down, he was controlled by powers of suggestion. He had a feeling it was emanating from this talking brain.

"What children? Who are you?" he asked as his helmet was removed and clattered to the floor.

"*Oh, I guess I can tell a dying man the secret that nobody should know. My name is Kris Asimov. Does that name ring a bell?*"

Max had to think, but it did. "You are one of the hackers that developed the interface!"

"*Ah, so you aren't so dumb.*"

Max was reaching for a plasma blade. He focused and pulled his hands back to his sides. He couldn't get too distracted or else he would die here.

How is he—it?—doing this to me? He could feel that it was clearly happening, but he was perplexed as to how.

"So what is this all about? This big computer, you being a...really huge brain in a jar... I can honestly say I hadn't planned for this."

"*The terminal behind you houses the heart of the interface that billions connect to on a daily basis. I outlived my mortal shell. There was no way for me to continue other than this. I had my friend place me in this state. He was a good man. Then I made him take his own life. I couldn't risk the competition or the secret being leaked.*"

"Every day, anyone who connected to the interface was being subliminally trained to follow my commands. The Psyker Scream army was merely the first stage of my plan. You have managed to set things back a bit. However, with your death, I shall proceed as planned. Because let's face it, Max, I know what you have planned after death. It will only suit my purposes. Do you believe you could make for yourself something like that and it would be out of my reach? Oh, you handed me more than I ever desired. Would you still have pursued this so much if you had known your every invention and idea had been guided by me?"

"That can't be possible, you disgusting monster!"

"It is, Max. Let's face reality here. Yes, you are a genius. Yes, you are talented in your own right. However, you are my child. How many Synaptix modifications did your parents have done to you as a baby? Later in your adolescence? You were crafted from my designs. Everything you have done in life has been to suit my purposes. You've been nothing more than a mere puppet. Alas, free will is more powerful than I could ever imagine. Without taking direct control of you, you managed to disrupt my plans. However, this idea of yours... Well, as I already said, it is more than I could have ever imagined. I know your death won't end you, but it will suit me quite nicely."

"That isn't true! I know I have modifications, but there is no way—"

"Max, really, think about it. The bots you created were one thing, but all of the other advancements you were able to make—your arms, your eye...everything. You think you created that all on your own? The hacking for blueprints and designs that you modified and made better? You think you hacked past governmental firewalls with ease because of your brilliance? You honestly believe I didn't help you in that?"

"Why?" Max questioned, despondent.

"In moments, you will have no use for an answer, so I don't feel like saying. All you need to know is the only reason you are in front of me now is because I desired it. Synaptix will be victorious. I have my hooks into everyone, some deeper than others. Who do you think is really controlling the government? Who do you think is making society progress in the direction it has been? Me, Max. It had always been me, the puppet master pulling the strings behind my iron curtain

of invisibility.

"It really is a shame that you have to die this way, such a brilliant mind. No doubt made more brilliant by my own technologies. I really wish I could convince you to be on my side and allow you to retain your free will. However, as I mentioned, it is too powerful and it is clear you oppose my ideals. Can you just give in to my powers of suggestion already? I would hate for this to get drawn out."

"Sorry, Kris, but I'm not ready to die just yet," Max said as he fought his arms trying to reach up to his own neck to snap it. "Besides, I can still resist you. Sure, I can't quite figure out how you're doing this. I can't fight your will enough to attack you. Looks like we are at a stalemate, so why don't you answer some more questions?"

"Like what?"

"How are you doing this?" he asked with a grin.

"Ah, still a sense of humor even in the face of death. My, how you have grown. Too bad you did not avail yourself and really become one of my children. I would have given you a spot even above Badger."

"How generous of you. Sure it's too late? I always wanted a big, creepy brain as my father."

"You will accomplish nothing with your banter. Max, I need no sleep, my nutrients surround me and are pumped in fresh from the floor below. This whole building exists to sustain my life. You are not leaving alive."

"Your life? Right! I seem to think mine is more worth it."

Kris was responding to Max, but he realized that his own left hand was taking hold of his left cheek. His right was sneaking to the back of his head. Max focused and pulled his right arm back down to his side.

That's how, he thought as he dug the thumb of his left hand into his own left eye. He scooped his thumb back to the root of the optic nerve and pinched it between his thumb and pointer finger. It was his only human eye left, and the one with the multiprocessor interface chip embedded in its optic nerve.

He wrenched in pain as he pulled the eye and nerve from his head. The pain was enough to even scramble visual sensors in his robotic eye. He quickly tossed his left eye across the room, hoping to have removed the chip in the nerve as well. He had done both.

"Where are your strings now, puppet master?" Max said as he moved freely.

"Very clever, but at this moment, I alerted all security staff. It looks as if I will have to kill you ineloquently, Max."

"Nope, sorry," Max said, punching the glass that contained Kris.

The impact of Max's fist did nothing to the glass—not even a chip came out of it. It was clear that it was no ordinary glass. Footsteps clattered down the spiral staircase as Max ran to the base of the giant computer.

He pulled a charge from his pack that he had brought to topple the building. Max kneeled as he set the timer. He knew there was no way out, so he set it for ten seconds. He ran a couple of feet back to the tank.

8...

Max pulled the pins from his last three plasma grenades.

7...

He quickly plopped them all into the tank containing Kris, whatever he was now.

6...

Bodies were swarming from the staircase and blocking the entrance as Max ran for it in a final desperate attempt.

5...

His eye locked to the center of the cluster; they were all firing in his direction now.

4...

Max fired a miniature missile from his right arm—he had three left.

3...

Bodies blew apart in front of the Kelmantrium door as Max continued in his beeline toward it.

2...

The plasma grenades blew the brain and the black goo to vapor as Max fired a missile at each of the spiraling staircases. They collapsed and more bodies tumbled to their deaths. Everyone under the control of Kris just stopped. Max had no way to confirm, but he suspected Kris to be dead...mostly anyhow.

1...

Max managed to stumble over the remains of the people

he had annihilated and get behind the thick Kelmantrium door. He slammed it shut behind himself and heard the explosion.

0...

He let out a sigh of relief, knowing he had slain at least one dragon today. The charge was as powerful as he anticipated and it shook the entire building. The walls cracked and the building began to topple. Max ran for the elevator. The floor fell out from under him.

Max fell into an abyss below, swallowed up by concrete and steel used to craft the structure that would prove his tomb. Like the fingers of death, the inanimate structure wrapped around him and crushed the life from his mortal shell. *Mission accomplished,* he thought as the door known as life was slammed shut on top of him.

Twenty

The Fall of a Phoenix

Crimson looked out of a window that comprised the entire far wall of her living room. Down below, she saw utter chaos. Members of *her cause* creating total anarchy in the streets. The police were trying to put an end to it, and now the Alexarien military had mobilized.

Hover tanks were gliding down streets, alleys, and sidewalks. They had no regard for what stood in their way, just the same as Crimson's army. Everywhere there was conflict and blood filling the streets. Fires raged uncontrollably on every city block.

Helicopters and fighter jets flew overhead, raining down death upon the rioters. Lines of military personnel were canvassing buildings, sweeping every floor, killing all who resisted them. Crimson felt terror like she had never felt before. She saw all of these things from her ivory tower, headed right toward her.

She tried to log onto the interface to find out how much progress Max had made, but it was no use. The interface was down. When she sat at a terminal and tried to log in, she felt a twinge in her eye and then darkness invaded her mind. There was nothing there.

She knew her best bet was to get to her secondary safe house. Nobody knew about it and it had been set up so under the radar that nothing could be linked back to her owning it. Only Max, Luther, and she knew of its existence. She went to the armory and prepared for battle.

She strapped on her battle suit and equipped herself with a helmet much like the one Max had left with. Her strikingly red hair flowed out from beneath the helmet and would certainly be an identifier of who she was. She then selected two gauss pistols, a large two-handed plasma blade, and several grenades.

After grabbing her data-pad and entering new commands, she stood by the window and looked up to the sky. In minutes, the sky darkened and a swirling vortex of clouds, rain, and lightning filled the sky above Alexarien.

The storm was so immense and dark that it blacked out the sun completely. Darkness filled the streets and the few lamps that hadn't been destroyed by the chaos below stood out from her viewpoint as glimmering beacons of hope. The rain fell heavy enough to make one feel as if he or she was going to drown in it. The rain was washing away the blood of those slaughtered in the streets and rivers of red flowed, signaling an ill omen.

Crimson got onto her elevator and hit the ground floor. It took her down to the street quickly and she stepped into the rain. The water soaked her quickly and her hair stranded together in four long, sopping segments. It was so dark that most people couldn't see too clearly, but her cheetah DNA had given her enhanced nocturnal vision.

She ran over to a streetlamp that had been hit by a car in the riot. The light had burned out, but it would still suit her purpose. She grabbed hold of it and waited as she felt the static accumulate around her. A mighty charge of electricity burst forth from the top of the post only to come back down to Crimson as if drawn to her.

She sucked in the electricity then dispersed it around herself and held it there. She now had a force field of one hundred thousand volts. Water hissed and crackled as the raindrops evaporated around her. It was a very powerful barrier encompassing her in what looked like an eight-foot in diameter globe of electricity.

With her defense established, she proceeded toward the safe house. She knew she would be meeting many obstacles along the way.

"It appears that there has been a mighty blow struck to

the military only moments ago, Mr. Cudrow," stated Reginald.

"Oh? And what would that be?"

"It seems as if Kris Asimov has met his demise. This is an unsettling blow to the military. The interface is offline...this will have great consequences. Well, all this means now is that you shall only be reporting to one master from here on out."

"Isn't Asimov the one who created the interface? What did he have to do with the military and the Alexarien government?"

"Oh poor Thomas, nothing is quite as it seems. Synaptix was no mere corporation. It was a branch serving our purposes. Kris was always such a bear to work with. He felt like he had brought a lot more to the table than he really did. What an ego. Nonetheless, he is dead now and this makes your matter of employment much easier. You will only have one superior to report to. This will all be explained at debriefing back at base."

"So Synaptix was part of the government?"

"So to speak."

"Who's this boss you speak of?"

"In due time, but let's just say your recruitment couldn't have come at a better time... Perhaps you can take Asimov's place?"

"I really wish you didn't speak in riddles."

"And I really wish you were a tad bit more intelligent, then I wouldn't have to spoon feed you information," Reginald said with a sigh as he laid back and rested his head.

The hover tank they were in swayed back and forth as it jetted down the streets of Alexarien. Thomas couldn't be more confused by Reginald and the events that had happened. *If Synaptix worked for the government, then why would it offer an alliance with Polyhelix to fight the government?* He kept asking this question over and over to himself.

The rain clattered hard against the metallic frame of the tank and it echoed through the body like a tin can. His mind wandered as lightning and thunder bounded through the city.

"Why the uncanny weather, Reginald? You're top secret military whatever. I am sure you have an answer."

"Our little rebel friend Crimson—well, she seems to have taken control of the Pilvikones. No need to worry, we are dealing with it as we speak."

Three tanks fired at Crimson. The shells were stopped mid-flight right in front of her. The electricity doing as she willed stopped the projectiles headed straight forward. Tendrils of electricity melted them away and she retaliated, striking the tanks with enough voltage to fry anyone inside.

Bullets from a helicopter rained down upon her—all of them were useless. As she used electricity from her barrier, she continued to recharge and keep herself prepared for the onslaught of attacks. She made her way down a roadway where she was met with a line of military.

"Crimson Felicia Rose!" she heard from a bullhorn. "We know that is you. Surrender immediately and you will be taken into custody to face trial!"

She had no intentions of doing any such thing as she stepped toward the brigade. They opened fire—it was useless. She shot a bolt of electricity into the center of them. It arched around and killed everyone, burning them to a crisp.

She proceeded down the roadway for a bit where she came to a crowd of those bearing her mark. They had overheard that the military was looking for her and recognized who she was upon seeing the giant glowing orb of electricity. They fell to their knees and began praising her, shouting, "All hail Crimson, our savior!"

She was touched, but disturbed by what she had seen from the high-rise. Those representing her were not doing as she had hoped. They were not seeking out Polyhelix and Synaptix. They were just blindly rampaging at all in their wake, leaving a trail of senseless destruction.

Crimson felt the urge to eradicate them as she passed by, but decided against it. It was she, after all, who had given them the idea to rebel in the first place. They couldn't be to blame for the fact that she didn't provide them with more guidance. She had been a bad parent and her legacy would be a miscarried idea and these unruly children.

She passed by them as they continued to chant and shout praises at her. There was more commotion ahead as she continued to run into military and police. Occasionally, she would pass a conflict between her followers and another

side. She even passed a few conflicts between her own followers who apparently saw things differently.

She felt pain in her heart—the pain of seeing those whom
she had given an idea to birth it and then raise it up to be a
mutated mess that not even the mother would recognize.
The pain of feeling alone—she had no idea where Max was.
The pain of seeing utter chaos, not the revolution she had
hoped for.

She was getting close to the safe house when she began
to feel her barrier wane. She looked down at her data-pad.
Two Pilvikones had stopped responding. A stealth jet zoomed
overhead. It was traveling fast enough that the sonic boom
nearly knocked her over.

*They've figured it out. They're bombing the Pilvikone ma-
chines.* She felt her stomach sink as she realized what this
meant. Once her powers dropped, she would be defenseless.
She quickly ran into a building and took shelter.

Once inside, she dropped her barrier. It was proving
problematic in a confined space, burning the walls, melting
glass, and destroying anything close to her. She entered
some new commands into her data-pad and hid inside an
apartment on the first floor of the building she had run into.

Soon, hailstones fell upon the city with tremendous fervor
and lightning struck—random and cruel—all over. Wind blew
through the skies hard and fast enough to cause all of the
helicopters to crash. She hoped that the weather would take
down the bombers as well and prevent them from destroying
the Pilvikones.

People were being struck with foot-long hailstones and being killed. Others were being burned up by the electricity and,
soon, everyone that was outside sought shelter indoors. Even
buildings were feeling the effects of the intense weather.

Buildings were cracking as the repeated blows of ice
struck them. Glass shattered as the windows were destroyed
completely. Crimson locked the door of the apartment behind
her. She wasn't sure if it would work, but she knew she
couldn't let this storm pelt the city forever or else everyone
and everything would be destroyed.

She looked to her data-pad and saw one more Pilvikone
had gone offline. She was creating a diversion and destroying
quite a bit, but they were still knocking down her wall. As

each Pilvikone was whittled away, the storm got weaker and weaker. Eventually, the sun shone bright in the sky and the storm had passed.

Crimson, still determined to make it to the safe house, ran back out in to the street. She ran down an alleyway. She was close—only two miles before she made it to the safe house. She rounded a corner only to meet with a squad of military personnel coming out of the building that they had sought refuge in.

"It's her," she heard yelled as a shot fired.

She reached to draw her pistols and the shot struck her left bicep. The combat suit kept the bullet from penetrating, but the shockwave of the projectile fired from a high-powered military rifle shattered her humerus. She fell to the ground gasping in pain as the men surrounded her.

"Careful, boys, she is only wounded, not dead!" the apparent squad leader yelled.

Crimson jumped to her feet and, with her one good arm, opened fire. She managed to gun down two of them before they retaliated. There were six left in the squad and they all began firing at her.

There was still some ambient electricity around her and she could feel it. She absorbed it into herself and began charging her body. She concentrated it into a small aura around herself. It was faint but still visible.

The squad fired at her and she lifted her hand. Lightning arched forth, striking the projectiles and melting them before they could strike her. The bolt continued toward the military squad. They all dodged as quickly as they could, but the bolt swallowed the life of one who hadn't managed to move quickly enough. With her last desperate blow, she could feel that she was depleted and it would take awhile for her to charge again.

She managed to avoid several shots when, finally, a bullet struck her right calf. It knocked her to her knee and another round hit her in the right forearm, disarming her. She knelt on the ground, both of her arms limp by her sides. She was helpless, but she refused to cry for any reason.

"Looks like we got ourselves a live one here, boys," the leader said as he approached her.

He stood in front of her—her on knees—and placed his

hands upon her helmet. He lifted it off and tossed it aside.

"Such a pretty face to match that body of yours," he said, running a hand through her long, still wet hair. "And this hair of yours, darling." He entered a number into his communicator and began speaking. "We have her, alive as ordered. Yes, she's damaged; she put up quite a resistance with me and my boys," he said—to a superior, no doubt.

They went back and forth for a little bit as Crimson stayed on her knees trying to figure out what she could possibly do to find a way out. She felt helpless; she felt nothing. She wanted to scream and fight, but she couldn't. It was the scariest thing she could imagine.

"Okay, will do," said the man as he ended the communication. "Looks like you're coming with us," he said with a smile. He gave a signal to one of his soldiers and the man stepped next to her. The last thing she remembered was the sting of a needle going into her neck, then, blackness.

"So it would seem that they caught the little rebel rioter herself," Reginald said out of the blue.

"How do you know?" Thomas asked.

"I just got word of it."

"Funny, I didn't see you answer your communicator."

"Ah, funny indeed." Reginald went back to resting against the cold, metallic wall of the tank.

"That's it? That is all you say? How did you hear? I was watching you. You didn't receive a call."

Reginald opened his eyes and glanced over to Thomas. "Mr. Cudrow, we would like for you to work with us very much indeed. We would like for you to rule with us, however...you need to stop being so nosy. Also, we are making a slight detour before we go back to base."

"Let's face it, with the damage that's been caused, you need me. So start answering some questions."

"We only need you as much as we needed Asimov. I am sure that we could piece together your research if need be," he responded, then closed his eyes again.

The tank rocked back and forth and whirred as Thomas sat across from Reginald, who looked as if he might already be sleeping. He felt like a child, and questioned if that was the military's motive in sending Reginald.

Crimson awoke tied to a chair in a dark room. There was a single chair sitting adjacent to her with an ominous-looking military man in it. He wore the traditional camouflage military combat uniform and white gloves.

He had a look in his eyes that bordered on madness and he sat in a statuesque manner, staring into her eyes. There was nothing else in the room other than a florescent light overhead that had seen better days. The light flickered and made it seem as if their shadows were unstable and ready to vanish from the wall at any time.

She focused on this, the shadows casting themselves on the wall like great actors in the theatre, then vanishing in the blink of an eye—every moment a new story waiting to be told by the shadows, only to disappear with no warning, only to reappear with just as little warning as the light dimmed then flickered back to brightness again.

"You caused quite a bit of damage, little girl," the man said.

Crimson eyed him and smiled. "Have I then?"

"You have, unless of course you aren't Crimson."

"What if I said you got the wrong gal?"

"I would know you are lying. I assure you, lying is useless to me. In fact, I have about all of the information that I need from you. Indulge me anyhow. My name is Reginald, and I was sent to ask you a few questions."

"Charmed, Reginald, but I doubt I can give you any answers."

"Let us see. Max, where is he?"

"I have no idea and wouldn't tell you if I did."

"That is where you are wrong, however, you are telling the truth with your words on this. Do you have an army we need to worry about?"

"Not unless you call those aimless rioters an army...no," she said with the tone of defeat in her voice.

"Oh? What of Zarfa and Legion Nine then? Weren't they supposed to come and fight with you against us?"

"How do you—"

"Know that? I know all, sweetheart. I told you, lying is wasted on me. Now, tell me, how would I contact him? You see, we don't have his communicator identification number."

"I wouldn't know. When your men roughed me up, they did a number to my memory," she lied.

"Too late, thank you for your help," he said, writing something down on a pad. "Well now, sweetheart, I think I am done with you. I believe I have all I need. My nice friends in the other room will see you to your holding cell until your televised...we'll say, execution? Yes, perhaps that's the right word. We need to make an example out of you, darling. Hope you understand."

At this, Reginald stood and exited through the door. Four men came in to escort Crimson to where she would be held. Even now, in the face of everything, she couldn't cry. Her communicator rang inside of her head and she couldn't answer it. She wondered who it was. Max? Zarfa?

Zarfa had managed to make it underground with more than half of his original army. The Ilyeion military resistance picked off a few in the beginning that were unaware of what was going on, but they didn't bother pursuing them as they fled.

Once underground, they found that there was plenty of room for everyone to take refuge for a while until Zarfa could get some answers. He was pacing back and forth in a small chamber carved out by a wasp with only Sarah and Zajifa with him.

He tried calling Max. The communicator didn't even ring, which meant it read no life signs. He called Crimson and it rang continually without her answering. He paced back and forth angrily. He wasn't sure if he had been betrayed, or if things had gone bad. He needed answers.

"Sarah, how big are these tunnels? Where do they go to?"

"They are vast. They go for miles underground and out in every direction. In the three years I was here, I never ventured far, though. I wasn't allowed to go past the second level of tunnels. I know they grew food down here. We just need to find it. I mean, they housed an entire army, not to mention the wasps." Sarah had hope in her voice and it inspired Zarfa.

"Okay, right. Until we figure out what is going on, let's form expedition parties. One led by you, one by Zajifa, and the other by me. Let's scout out the tunnels and find where the food is grown. These people are going to get unruly if we don't see to it that they are fed."

"Brother, should maybe the three of us stay together? Perhaps assign the other two groups under other generals?" asked Zajifa.

"You are the two closest to me. The only two that I feel I can trust implicitly. Plus, you've both proved yourselves to me. We can let the other generals explore as well, but I feel like this is a task best suited for us. Until we hear something from Crimson or Max, let's just focus on finding the things we need to survive."

"I understand. You are wise, Zarfa," Zajifa said.

"Also, brother, I do not know what else may be down here. Like I said, they never let me travel beyond the second level. We need to remain vigilant and armed. Who knows if Max succeeded in killing Father and what he may be planning if he...failed."

The words hung heavy in the air. Of course, everyone realized that it was a possibility, but nobody wanted to recognize it. Zarfa stared off for a moment.

"I am sure he is fine. Now, let's not worry about these unpleasant things until we need to. Let's only focus on setting up here. We may be here for a long while."

It was noon and the sun burned hot and bright in the sky. Every Pilvikone ever created had been bombed and completely destroyed. Mankind's tampering with the weather patterns had wreaked havoc on the planet's ability to stabilize itself.

Countries that had been dry and desolate wastelands were now getting more rain in a single day than they had in the last ten years. Areas that were typically cool were now scorching hot. A massive shift was in the works, and everywhere that was still inhabited was feeling the effects. Nature was once again trying to stabilize itself, but nobody knew if it would be able to.

The sun beat down on Alexarien hotter than it had since the creation of the Pilvikones. The pavement was hot enough to burn bare skin. It was here that crowds and television crews gathered around to film Crimson on center stage of a platform set up in the wake of her destruction.

The backdrop was her high-rise, home to some of the wealthiest people in the world. Science lab and manufacturing plant of the army she had dreamed of. Home and safety to her.

All around it were buildings still smoldering from fires caused by the riots. Buildings missing all of their windows, cracked and ready to crumble at any moment from the hailstorm she called down upon the city. Piles of corpses on city streets from the rebellion she'd sparked.

Before the stage was a crowd too great to number, all angry at the injustice. Some were even branded with the "C," all seeking a scapegoat and revenge. The angry mob murmured and screamed at the top of their lungs. Every breath they inhaled stung their lungs as the heat evaporated the remaining moisture into steam.

Sweat evaporated from the bodies of the angry crowd, and the smell mixed with the flames and ashes that the breeze carried. The scent wafted into Crimson's nose as she was being held on stage by her two broken arms. Her legs dangled down with her knees barely touching the platform.

Reginald stepped onto the stage and looked dead-on at the camera.

"This is your leader? You hapless cowards and beggarly peasants?" he questioned, with absolute confidence in the force field barrier that had been placed around the stage.

With no fear of the angry swarm before him, he freely spoke. With no fear of an assassin ready to pick him off on a rooftop, he was ready to make callous accusations. With no fear of Crimson—stripped of her power—he was ready to make an example.

"Some of you were resisting the powers that be only yesterday. Yet, here you are today, demanding justice to be exacted on the very one you blindly put your faith! Only yesterday, you felt that the rise of humanity would be the fall of technology. Well, where are your ideals today, you cowards? You villains, you ignorant children?" His words echoed through the city on the loudspeakers that amplified his voice. "Did any of you think that this was the way it would turn out? Did any of you ever dream that this vision was nothing more than a nightmare? This ideal of a better future—actually the fall of humanity? Or did any of you ever think at all?"

The cameras were getting every moment of the speech, every detail, panning between Crimson and Reginald and the angry crowd below.

"You all saw what happened to those who came out of their homes yesterday. Did not one of you learn a lesson? You knew that justice would be exacted and broadcast through the video feeds right into your own home, yet thousands of you decided you needed to be here in person? Why, I ask?

"Is it because you are nothing more than bloodthirsty savages? Perhaps you were hoping that once the barrier was taken down, you could leave with a little souvenir of the event? Or is it that you are all just stupid, vile monsters?" Reginald hurled insults at the crowd.

The crowd screamed and threw things at the stage. The barrier evaporated anything that touched it. Not even bullets could pass the barrier.

"Oh, I will give you monsters what you want," Reginald said, pulling an old world blade made of carbon fiber with a diamond edge from its sheath. It was twenty inches long with a handle six inches in length. The edge was sharpened down to one micron in diameter and made of solid diamond. The blade was light, yet sharp enough to cut through even titanium.

"Let this be a lesson to those who extend their right arm in fury to the authorities, dreaming that you have a better way to run things," he said, taking Crimson's right arm from the man that was holding her up by it.

Reginald ran the blade under her armpit and up circum-ferentially. The slice was clean, and disarticulated her hu-merus from the scapular-clavicular junction. Blood gushed from the wound and bare bone was exposed. Reginald threw her arm into the barrier and it vanished in a cloud of vapor.

Crimson screamed in pain, cursing Reginald. The crowd

roared in excitement. The ratings at home grew by leaps and bounds as word of the carnage being broadcast spread.

Reginald sprayed a can of medifoam into the hole where her arm once was located. It stopped the bleeding and began healing the tissues. His goal was not to kill her, but to make her suffer.

"I ask, why is it that you are all so excited to see this? Is it because she caused your pain and misery?" He paused. He walked to Crimson's left side and held her arm back behind her, forcing her to her knees. The guard that had been holding her stepped back and Reginald continued his speech. "It isn't that for you, is it? No, each of you should know very well that despite her spreading her ideas and her will to overthrow the ones she saw as oppressive, it was you who chose to act on it. Now, let me see by a show of your left hand in the air, how many of you are here because you were victimized by the mob yesterday?"

Many in the crowd raised their hand in protest and triumph. They felt on top of the world, and the feeling of justification swelled within the masses. People at home were turning on their video feeds, salivating at what they called *justice* being exacted on Crimson.

Like so many martyrs before herself, she was hailed a hero of the common people, only to have her death supported by those very people. Nobody could say for sure, but in another thousand years, she would probably move from the ranks of villain back to hero once again.

"Well, here is to you! The *victims,*" Reginald said sarcastically as he brought his blade down upon Crimson's shoulder.

The blade glided through her tissues, disarticulating her arm from her body. He tossed her other arm into the barrier and it vanished. He tended to her wounds once again and knelt in front of her. He lifted her head to meet his and looked her in the face. Her eyes were piercing, full of pain, desire, regret, fear, rage, and remorse.

"What have you to say for your crimes against humanity, oh Crimson savior?"

"I did not intend this! I wanted the best for everyone. I feel that it was my failing to give better direction that caused this to end the way it did. I dreamed that everyone inspired by me would be valiant, fearless, and noble. I envisioned them fighting the powers of corruption, not raiding and ransacking anything in sight. I am sorry to those of you who are innocent in the crowd, yet I am not a fool. Many of you who raised your left hand were the very ones victimizing people in the streets yesterday. My deepest regret is that my dream appealed more to cowards prone to mob violence than to true revolutionaries. Again, I apologize to those who are truly innocent, yet I fear most of the truly innocent are dead. They are the ones I desired to be amongst my ranks, not the dogs and cowards that displayed themselves yesterday."

Her words stung and cut deep into people's hearts. Their reaction was more anger. Yes, people wanted her dead now more than ever—not because she was the one who caused the destruction of a city and of thousands of lives, but because she unveiled truth in her words.

The crowd screamed for a sensational death, one of pain and gore that would make them feel vindicated. People at home who were watching cheered on as they imagined different violent tortures that could be inflicted upon her. The masses were mindless and ready to see senseless violence dished out in the name of justice.

Reginald put his left hand upon Crimson's throat and brought her to her feet. He stood a few inches taller than her with a face of stone. He stared into her eyes almost lustfully.

"You know it is a shame, Crimson. You and I are not very different," he said, his voice still amplified by the microphone. He stepped behind her and put his arm around waist. He drew his hips in close to her and bit her on the ear. He then whispered into it something that everyone could hear. "It is a shame you saw the light too late. The truth, you know? That the common masses are evil. The good of man is very miniature in presence. You give them power and this is what happens," he said, pointing out at the city. "Sure, you caused some of this destruction, but how much did they cause? And for what purpose? Sure, they hid behind your ideals to mask their inner beasts. They point the blame at you, saying that if you had never spoken, this would never have happened...but is that true?

"Just look at history to find out, look at the past. Look at what happens in metropolitan areas where there are blackouts that last longer than a few hours. One day without power in their homes and they revert to savages. Rape, murder, looting, rioting...and that is only scratching the surface. No, your words may have been a catalyst speeding up the process, but you and I both know that this was destined to occur. You and I both know that the common society of man needs to be dominated, to be policed. Which is why after today, with the help of one Thomas Cudrow, the Alexarien government will be requiring all to undergo a single genetic changing inoculation. Yes, in order for mankind to become civil, we must first become more than human! And those of us in power must become gods capable of ensuring change!"

The crowd grew angrier and their rage turned again toward the government. People in their homes began destroying their own possessions in fits of indignation. Many in the crowd tried to rush the stage, only to be vaporized. The masses were angry now at both Crimson and the government.

Many seethed and breathed threats of death toward Reginald. Their focus was constantly led astray and the threat of another riot was on the rise.

"Oh, I bet you wish that you all had a savior now, do you not?" Reginald asked, taking a step back from Crimson.

In one quick swipe, he cut at Crimson's knees. Both of her legs were severed at the knee joint and she came toppling down to the ground. Blood gushed out and Reginald was swift to give medical attention. Crimson screamed and heaved in agony as Reginald rolled her over onto her back.

"And yet, here she is; here she shall sit for the next ten days out in this beating sun to show to all of you that your life could be much worse. Perhaps you have no say in the coming change, but would you desire to have her position? That is your option. As of today, Alexarien is being placed under martial law by the military. Those who resist the inoculation shall become the same as your dear Crimson here," he said, putting his hand into Crimson's mouth.

She bit down on his fingers as hard as she could. Her teeth struck his bone and pierced though it. In her mouth, she held his pointer, middle, and ring fingers. He drew back in pain, blood running down his hand. It caused him to drop his blade on the ground.

The crowd cheered and laughed at this man of power being injured by a defenseless woman. Reginald turned red with anger and stomped over to Crimson, kicking her in the ribs. As his foot connected, she released all of the electricity she had managed to accumulate over the last day. It wasn't enough to kill him, but it caused him a good deal of pain and embarrassment as he jolted the moment his leg connected with her body. After recovering from her final attack, he turned and picked up the blade he had dropped.

He grabbed Crimson by her mandible on the bottom side, careful not to place his hand inside her mouth again. She laughed and spit his fingers out at him as he readied the blade. He placed it inside her mouth and pulled it through her right cheek. He then placed it back inside her mouth and pulled it through the left.

He grabbed her mandible with his hand and tore it away from her. He dropped it on the stage and kicked it into the barrier. He looked out at the crowd and held up his injured hand. She lay on her back with her tongue flopped over to the side. Her breaths were deep and laborious—the suffering that was inflicted was more than anyone should be forced to endure.

"This is not for the injury she bestowed upon me. It is for the lies she spoke that I do this." He then bent down and, grabbing her tongue, cut it from her head.

He sprayed medifoam on his hand to staunch the bleeding before attending to the wounds he inflicted on Crimson. He flipped her over, ran a hook through the skin on her back, and attached it to a chain that was connected to a rafter that spanned across the stage.

He hoisted her up high so that everyone could see. The cameras caught it all. The heat pressed upon the angry crowd. The crowd cheered at the violent punishment. Many began to reason that she was the cause of the government's plan of inoculation.

Others were still angered at the government and now wished for Crimson to be freed and still lead them to their "salvation." Only two things were certain—one was that even those who would support her now were nothing more than backbiting dogs with spirits of cowardice. The other was that this event was the most watched thing being broadcast on the video feeds right now.

"And, in conclusion, I bid thee at home one final warning," Reginald said, bowing toward the crowd.

The stealth jets flew overhead so quickly no one knew what was coming. Incendiary bombs were dropped on the large crowd. Many were killed instantly—others caught fire. Screams of agony and flames spread. Crimson looked out over the crowd with tears running down her face from the unbearable pain she was in, both physically and emotionally.

Black smoke ascended to the sky and the smell of burning hair, bone, skin, and muscle filled the city. Many were trying to scatter to get away from the bombing when a second round of stealth jets came by and dropped their payload. The whole crowd was dead in minutes and Reginald stood on stage. He looked to the sky filling with the black smoke while he was still bowing and muttered, "Are you pleased by my sacrifice, lord?" It was barely audible, but the microphone picked it up.

Once the fires calmed, he stood and began to speak again. "I ask, did none of you learn a thing from the events yesterday? It is much safer in your homes, I assure you. Don't mourn those who died today, for if they had half a brain, they would have left. Change and peace cannot come without great sacrifice. See the smoke ascending? It is the offering of the stupid and weak. Count your blessings that you remained indoors. Take this to heart—do not resist. Unless you don't cherish your life."

At this, Reginald stepped off stage through a small hole he created in the barrier and boarded a helicopter. The helicopter flew into the sky and away to the military base. The cameras remained turned on, staring at the smoldering corpses and at Crimson hanging in the center of the stage. The video feed wouldn't stop until the end of the ten days.

Twenty-One

Requiem

The moment that the rubble crushed Max's skull, it activated the chip that Crimson had placed in his cerebral aqueduct. The chip exploded in a microwave that simultaneously
scanned his brain and liquefied it. The microwave sent a signal with every bit of data or memory that had not been
backed up after he had left the brain scanning machine.

The signal found its way to the mainframe at Crimson's
safe house. There, the signal was picked up by a computer
terminal and the data was downloaded and added to the
brain scan holding Max's personality, thoughts, and memory.
Within minutes after Max's death, all of the information was
being loaded onto the crystalline hard drive.

Three days after Max's death, he had been loaded onto
the drive and his eyes opened. Two mechanical eyes beamed
with the spark of life, only to be stared back at by two more
mechanical eyes.

"Welcome back, Max. I've been waiting," Luther's voice
said.

Max didn't have a full face yet. He was nothing more than
a Kelmantrium skeleton. In the center of the rib cage was a
Kelmantrium box holding the crystalline hard drive. The eyes
embedded in the skull were two exact replicas of the one
Max had implanted in his fleshly body.

"I can't move yet, Luther."

"It has only been three days, Max, just enough time to
finish the frame and load you into the hard drive. How does it
feel? Do you feel like yourself?"

"Exactly...right down to my final memory. I killed Kris

Asimov and destroyed the interface... I didn't even fully understand what I was doing when I did it, Luther!"

"Ah, that you did. Four more days, Max. Your wiring will be completed and this skeletal frame you inhabit will have its...*skin.*"

"So I take it the nanobots are replicating now?"

"Indeed. I would like to see someone try to kill you once you are finished being made," Luther said with a hint of joy in his voice. "However, I bear bad news..."

"What is it?"

Luther turned a video screen toward Max and turned it on. The feed of Crimson dangling helplessly missing her arms, the lower half of her legs, jaw, and tongue was still playing. It took a moment for Max to recognize who she was. He wouldn't have recognized her, except her crimson hair was shining brightly, blowing in the wind.

"What happened?" his mechanical voice screamed.

"She was caught... Her resistance failed. Even more, the government is planning to turn everyone into obedient slaves by the end of the month with the help of...Thomas—"

"Cudrow? The war criminal responsible for Polyhelix?" he exclaimed, pausing for a moment to think. "What then of Zarfa?"

"I don't know, master. I do not have his com-link number, and with the interface being down, I had no way to find it. Perhaps you remember?"

Max thought back and recalled seeing Crimson dial it in.

"I do. One. Four. Seven. Nine. Nine. Eight. Zero. Dial it in my communicator, please."

Luther did as Max asked. "Max?"

"It's ringing, Luther."

"I think you're going to want to see this, commander," Zajifa radioed to Zarfa.

They had been searching the tunnels for days for a source of food. Zajifa's voice had the sound of glee and excitement in it. Zarfa had been resting when he heard the voice echo over his radio. He scrambled quickly to it to respond.

"Yeah? Yeah? What is it?" he questioned in excitement.

"Hydroponics, food—real food. Not replicated crap. It appears the soil this deep is rich in nutrients. There is enough growing here to feed us all! Not to mention the storehouses I found. Everything is going to be fine, brother—food, water, what more could those down here with us want?"

"Ha! I'll let them tell you. It has been nothing but whining and complaining from them. Even threats and murmuring about me and we have only been down here a few days," Zarfa laughed. He got to his feet and motioned for his group to follow him. The caves were vast and impressive. There wasn't a single inch not well lit and reinforced. They had been wandering for three days and still hadn't gone lower than the second level.

Zarfa kept getting an eerie feeling that they may not be the only ones down there still, so he commanded that everyone remain on high alert. Unfortunately, this had resulted in some collateral damage from people with twitchy trigger fingers.

"I can see you on my scanner, Zajifa. Hold your position until my crew arrives. It might be several hours," he said with his voice full of cheer.

"Oh, you don't have to ask me twice, brother," Zajifa said. Zarfa could hear the smile in his voice.

"Brother," the radio piped up. It was Sarah.

"Yes, Sarah?"

"You might want to see this too. We found... Uhhh...well...a hatchery?"

"Wasps?"

"Not quite."

"Well tell me then."

"I don't want to scare anyone who might be listening in. As if being cryptic will really help my cause, but let's just say... Can I hold my position and request reinforcements until you can come and give direct orders, please? Brother... Sir?"

"Request granted, but it might be a couple of days. You said it's a hatchery, right? How do the eggs look?"

"Gross."

"That doesn't really help me now, does it, Sarah?"

"Sorry, brother, but you asked. They look...podlike. I can see the embryos inside and best guess...a week before they hatch?"

"Okay, well, I can make it in about three to four days to your location after I meet up with Zajifa. Until then, tell me how many reinforcements you need—they'll be sent."

"Four hundred...to be safe. Send plasma grenades and anything that can start a fire... You know, in case."

"Granted, sister," Zarfa said as he turned to see the faces of his squad. The talk they overheard inspired less than confidence. They all looked horrified and they weren't even sure of what yet. Zarfa smiled at them and spoke. "Look, if my sister isn't panicking then you guys ought not to worry. I have confidence that, whatever it is, she can handle it."

The men all laughed as they cheered Zarfa on. He had a way about him that inspired good morale and confidence. Very few questioned his leadership and he seemed to be getting better at it as each day passed.

The men that were trembling before looked at him and saw that confidence and integrity filled his face and valor shined though his eyes. The way he walked was with the strut of a lion and many took pride in following him. The air about him could cheer up the most depressed and gloomy of souls and many desired just to bask in his presence.

Zarfa had forgotten that anyone may want to contact him by his communicator over the three days he had been in the caverns. When it rang in his ear, it caught him off guard and, startled, he jumped. He felt the blood drain from his face and the men in his squad who had never seen him show fear, laughed.

Zarfa quickly answered the call. "Yes? Who is this?"

"Zarfa, you may not recognize my voice... It's Max."

Zarfa looked confused and his men wondered who he was speaking with.

"Okay? How? I tried calling you days ago and your communicator didn't ring. That tells me that—"

"I died."

They were both silent for a moment. His men watched in anticipation.

"Have you heard of a brilliant scientist named Luther Dewaldt? He was a leading developmental research scientist in the field of neurosciences over twenty years ago. He discovered how to back up people's personalities in the form of data. He was assassinated and his lab destroyed upon making a great breakthrough. What the Alexarien government—who commanded that this be done—didn't realize was that the machines they destroyed were mocks. He had already sold them to a wealthy man who wanted them as monuments of scientific progress. Luther himself was backed up and restored elsewhere. He lives today. Though the storage mediums they had at the time couldn't fit his whole psyche, he is here next to me in part. Anyhow, with the use of his technology and a new storage medium, I am...resurrected, one might say?" His mechanical voice rang over the communicator.

"Wow, Max... I don't know what to say. Have you—"

"Heard the news?" they questioned simultaneously.

"You first," Max said.

"Crimson saved us. With her storms and whatever it was you provided her with, she wiped out the Faraza and Psyker Scream almost instantly! It was amazing, some even called it a miracle. If she had a presence here, I am sure some would be worshipping at her feet here. The old ways never die, Max. However, after that, she called me panicked-sounding. I haven't heard from her yet. Right now, my army and I are hiding underground in the tunnels dug out by the wasps. The same ones the Faraza inhabited. You see, upon trying to return to Ilyeion...we were declared enemies of the state. Their military opened fire on us unsuspecting. It was awful— thousands died before we realized the need to retreat. Now we are just trying to survive underground, planning our next move. Kind of ironic, we became Faraza...so to speak, hiding in the tunnels, waiting for a moment to strike."

"Very grave news indeed, Zarfa. I am sorry to hear of your losses."

"Thank you, Max, but I guess this is the price of war. The cost of freedom."

"It's a shame, but it is. Now I don't suspect you have access to any video feeds down there, do you?" Max asked.

"Not that we have found. Just today my second-in-command, Zajifa, found us food! And Sarah found us...something."

"Very good then, I will tell you the part you missed. Synaptix is gone, erased. The interface is destroyed. I did that, thank you very much. However, I have bittersweet news. Crimson's army turned into nothing more than an uncon-

trolled riot. Crimson is still alive, but Zarfa...so is your father." Max paused to let Zarfa feel the impact of the news.

"But? How? Wait! Crimson! Why hasn't she answered my
calls?"

"When you're missing your arms, legs, jaw, and tongue...it
puts a damper on communications. I am not sure how, but
they caught her—the military that is. The weather is acting
strange because they destroyed the Pilvikones and the earth
isn't able to cope. I assume that stripping her of her power
was how they brought her down. If you ask me, they should
have known destroying the machines would cause this. Their
greed and their disregard for anyone other than their own
selves caused them to bring destruction to take down one
person. If anyone is weak in my eyes, it's them.

"Anyway, they have Crimson on display in her mutilated
state, roasting in the hot sun. Her skin is beginning to blister
and peel off. She would have died of dehydration days ago
except they connected her to an advanced life support system to prolong the torture, but that isn't even the worst of it,
Zarfa."

Zarfa's eyes welled with tears as he visualized the pain
and suffering Crimson was going through. Sure, she had her
own cause she fought for, but there was no doubt that she
had aided them invaluably in their fight against the Faraza.
"Please, Max, spare me nothing."

"Your father has been contracted by the military to create
an inoculation that will turn the populace into unquestioning
slaves. They plan to put it into effect by the end of the
month. It's dangerous and unethical! What's more, I doubt
their plan will stop there. As of now, the city and the whole
country are under martial law. Anyone on the street after
dark is shot on sight. Anyone who looks suspicious—arrested
and taken for questioning. People can't even sneeze without
being harassed. I have no doubt after they inoculate everyone, they will have an army larger than they ever imagined,
and I believe Ilyeion is next. Ilyeion showed their support to
Alexarien by ousting you and your people. They won't stop
there. After Ilyeion, it will be the rest of the world; anyone
who breathes will be under their control, I am sure of it. That
is why they let us do what we were doing, why they allowed
Crimson, Synaptix, and Polyhelix. They planned this from the

start!

"We always knew Ilyeion and Alexarien were allies, yet both nations stood for a different set of ideals and a different way of life. It is clear now, though, that they both allow their militaries to make their decisions, and the events that are in motion now mean the end of life as any of us know it. I, for one, don't want to be a slave. That is, if they could find a way to do so with me! Even if they could, I don't want to see that happen to Crimson, or you!"

"What makes you think that will happen to Crimson? Max, it sounds like she is going to die soon."

"Trust me, I have a plan. I can stop her death. As for stopping this scheme to control men...I need your help."

"Max, let's face it, my people have things good right now. A self-sustained underground habitat. Plenty of good people to live amongst, and relative safety. I am having them focus on that for now, but it is clear it won't last forever. If they do what you say they are planning, they will hunt us down and make us submit or kill us. I'm with you. Over the next week, I will work on spreading the word that the war is not over yet, and I will seek out anything I can find down here to back the cause. We need you and Crimson here, though, and I fear I cannot help you with that. I certainly hope you can make it here.

"I have an army, strong, true, fierce, powerful. But we need a plan, strategy, tactics. I feel like I am barely keeping them together down here. We need strong leaders. We need you and Crimson. I hope we can restore her to her former self. It sounds like she is in worse condition than one could ever imagine."

"You leave her restoration to me. We will be there in a week. I hope that we can delay your father's production of whatever this inoculation is for awhile. Even the best leaders won't be able to fight an army ranging into the billions in just a matter of months."

"Agreed. If that is all, I would like to end our conversation by saying, Godspeed, Max."

About the Author

Tex was born in a factory in Detroit, MI. Little is known of Tex except he doesn't care to be a part of society or even seen by many. After being exposed to a drug known as TXZ-871 he began to exhibit many abnormal signs of being a "Dreamer."

Sometimes, his mind brings to life creatures and events better left behind; alas they manifest and wreak havoc upon those around. As a Dreamer, he is constantly on the run from "Nightmares." One such Nightmare is Seamus, who constantly seeks to destroy and bring down what he creates.

www.ingramcontent.com/pod-product-compliance
Lightning Source LLC
Chambersburg PA
CBHW021644260626
47154CB00017BA/2249